# QUARTERLIFE

## Praise for *Quarterlife*

'What a blazingly original voice, what a fiercely intelligent engagement with contemporary world politics and culture. Devika Rege is at the forefront of a new generation of authors, from all over the world, who are challenging received notions of what transnational literature can do and remaking global literary culture in the process.'

— VAUHINI VARA

'What begins as a novel of ideas becomes the secret history of a nation. A superb read ... both moving and inspiring.'

— JEET THAYIL

'Dazzling, sophisticated, and wholly achieved in its ambition, *Quarterlife* emerges out of the tradition of the philosophical novel. Devika Rege is a transformative novelist.'

— MAUREEN MCLANE

'For some time now, the need for a contemporary novel that takes on the Indian political landscape head-on has been acutely felt. *Quarterlife*, Devika Rege's debut novel, arrives on the scene with elegance and aplomb ... Carefully steering the narrative away from becoming a crusade to find reason in political pockets ... [Rege] makes the story one that bears witness to an extraordinary moment in history ... *Quarterlife* is an ambitious, exciting debut, and should be read as a testament to the clarity truth can gain from craft.'

– *Scroll*

'You want to admire the way [Rege] uses words to cut and soothe, all at once – to read some of the sentences aloud to yourself and take pleasure in how they sound. What's especially exciting is the freshness in Rege's turn of phrase – the rhythm in her sentences feels new and marks the arrival of a voice we've not heard before in Indian literature in English.'

– *The Hindu*

'[A] landmark novel ... Rege has a vast descriptive repertoire, is willing to take astonishing risks with structure, and is immaculate in her numerous interiority dives. Her hand is so sure it's often impossible to believe that *Quarterlife* is a debut.'

– *The Indian Express*

'*Quarterlife* may be read in terms of an exploration of the relationship of the self with the nation in the fashion of the big novels of Salman Rushdie, Amitav Ghosh ... Rege's biggest achievement is her fidelity to her object of exploration and her refusal to make aesthetic concessions in its representation.'

– *Biblio*

'*Quarterlife* is one of the best character-driven novels out in India this year: this is wholly about how people think, how their perceptions shape their behaviour, and how those perceptions may change ... [It] looks at varied matters: politics, business, religion, casteism, the conceptions (or misconceptions) of history and heritage. Patriarchy, women's rights, corruption. The Bollywood–politics nexus. All, however, are woven so organically into the overall story that it rarely feels forced. This, one feels, is a reflection of reality.'

– *Open Magazine*

'If the novel is, arguably, one of the more democratic art forms, *Quarterlife* demonstrates how this is enabled not only by subject matter but also by technique ... In its refusal to privilege any one (set of) character(s) or standpoint(s), its attempt to elaborate a spectrum of political positions, and its use of language to bolster and simultaneously unravel its characters, *Quarterlife* is an ambitious, demanding, and deeply rewarding novel.'

– *The India Forum*

'Through her young characters (the quarterlifers) Rege teases out and pushes back against the competing narratives at stake: hyper-nationalism, the so-called economic miracle, caste politics ... With such brutality to contend with, it is almost shocking to find such delicacy of attention, such depth of listening, such ability to hold us, simply, directly, with wisdom and grief.'

– *National Herald*

'*Quarterlife* … delves deep into the inner landscapes of individuals on the precipice of crises, both moral and existential ... Rege not only offers readers a literary gem but also a stark mirror reflecting the complex interplay between personal struggles and the shifting tides of politics.'

– *The New Indian Express*

'Ambitious this novel certainly is, but its boldness is backed by Rege's unmistakable commitment to storytelling and her sheer talent for it. A quiet confidence permeates each page ... [O]ne of the exceptional pleasures of reading *Quarterlife* [is] its quiet intimacy. The reader is always in the story, watching what's going on, feeling, thinking and reminiscing. Politics pervades the story, yet it would be a mistake to consider this book merely a political novel. It reminds us that no matter how well or strongly we articulate ourselves, we are all creatures with contradictions.'

– *Moneycontrol*

'This is a brave, astute book ... Rege shows a deep and precise understanding of the fragile complexity of India and the country's intricate web of identities. With Maharashtra as a microcosm of political instinct … she lays it out in all its messiness and all its frailty, pitting one argument against another, propping up a belief only to have it punctured, revealing vulnerabilities, anxieties, contempt, and hypocrisies … The writing, at the prose level, is beautiful. I was astonished by the detail, the veracity … and the openness with which Rege tackles her irreconcilable subject matter.'

– *Hindustan Times*

# QUARTERLIFE

A NOVEL

DEVIKA REGE

FOURTH ESTATE · *New Delhi*

First published in hardback in India by Fourth Estate 2023
An imprint of HarperCollins *Publishers*
4th Floor, Tower A, Building No. 10, DLF Cyber City,
DLF Phase II, Gurugram, Haryana – 122002
www.harpercollins.co.in

This edition published in India by Fourth Estate 2024

2 4 6 8 10 9 7 5 3 1



P-ISBN: 978-93-5699-982-4
E-ISBN: 978-93-5699-087-6



Typeset in 11.5/15.7 Bembo Std at
Manipal Technologies Limited, Manipal

Printed and bound at
Thomson Press (India) Ltd.

MIX
Paper | Supporting responsible forestry
FSC® C010615

This book is produced from independently certified FSC® paper to ensure responsible forest management.

*For my parents, with gratitude*

लाली मेरे लाल की, जित देखूँ तित लाल
लाली देखन मैं गई, मैं भी हो गई लाल

The redness of my beloved is such
wherever I look, I see red
When I went in search of redness
I too became red

KABIR

*Contents*

# ANXIETY

# *Naren*

After eight years in America he finally has a green card, but in the days since it arrived, he has felt neither triumph nor relief. The accompanying brochure is already in the trash, a patronizing guide for new immigrants like they just got off the flight. As for the card, now and then he takes it out of his wallet, this time on the pretext of updating recruiters in Manhattan, and scans the security features, the words 'specimen' and 'void', and the faint hologram of Ms Liberty, only to doubt he is the person the biometrics claim. 'Happy Thanksgiving, Na-wren,' Sally says, the mispronounced name returning him to himself. Beyond his cubicle, the office is already in holiday mode. He returns Sally's greeting. 'Rather early for the coyotes, isn't it?' she asks. He would like to tell her that there are nights he wants to join them in those high, yipping wails; he would like to say, Can you imagine the release? But when he was a boy, he bit his brother once, and his mother (who believed humiliation worked better than violence) shook his arm and said, 'Are you an animal?' 'I'm not an animal,' he said, and she made him repeat it to every relative in the room – uncles, aunts, even his ajoba – *I'm not an animal, I'm not an animal, I'm not an animal, I'm not* … So he looks up from his ergonomic chair, his hair prim, his collar pressed, and he says, 'Surprising, yeah. Must be the darkness.'

Driving to the client site an hour later, Naren strains against the sleep that infects him on cloudy days. Just as well he has a final meeting at three; he hates being home in weather that pulls you constantly to bed. What he needs is coffee, but passing The Bean, he recalls the old man who accosted him twice at the only window table. The first time, he gave up his spot from deference for age, but as he stood, the man muttered, 'Ya think ya own this place?' When it happened again a week later, he remained seated. 'They own the goddam place,' the man barked, gripping the rim of the table for emphasis, and before Naren could react, his espresso was running over his wallet and keys, and the barista was rushing up with a towel, but nothing more vociferous than an 'Excuse me, sir' as the man stormed out. Now if this were Bombay, Naren would have complained to the management, but here in Waverly, who knows, the old loon might own a gun, and driving past the café, he tries not to overthink his recent mention of the incident in office during a light-hearted exchange on local eccentrics, and how everyone went silent like it was his fault for bringing the subject to an uneasy place until Sally with her secretarial efficiency said, 'That's just insane,' and then, just as efficiently, took the conversation elsewhere.

There are no more cafés on the drive. The GPS points to a machine at the souvenir shop in Lincoln Zoo. The coffee tastes like dishwater, but at least it's hot. Since he is early for his meeting, he takes his time walking past the cages. At thirty-one, so embedded in his rationality, it is strange to him there are these sentient beings who don't reflect or reason and simply are. Is that a leopard … no, it is too large. Going closer, every aspect of the beast is incongruent with the other: the black torso is marked by fawn scales, the muscle tone is regal but the face has no mane or stripes, and its kohl-lined amber eyes suggest less of a lion's valour than a sort of treachery. The plaque notes that the 'jaguon' is a hybrid born of the accidental mating of a black jaguar and a lioness. Here on a visit from Ontario, this is one of only two of its kind in the world. That they are of the opposite sex doesn't matter; 'the hybrid is sterile'. And Naren feels empathetic towards the cat's restlessness, the exasperation with which it is pacing a cage barely the size of his kitchen. Should he climb the fence, would the jaguon nuzzle up, expect a ration of beef? Or would it crouch at the smell of his fear, prowl, then leap? What a moment of pure instinct for both! And all the way to the exit, he thinks of how the beast would feel afterwards, its animal brain bewildered by a sudden cellular longing for a non-existent habitat.

Driving down the grey streets, the pumpkins on the doorsteps remind Naren that he has had no invitations to Thanksgiving since he moved to Nebraska. He recalls the last one he attended, the table carved from a single trunk, the candles rising out of an abundance of pears, magnolia, and the pilgrim dolls she had spent the afternoon crafting … *Catherine*. The name never comes to him except as a lament, the vowels stretched into a sigh. He hardly thought of her by her name then, her presence overwhelmed the fixed points of its syllables, but years later, how the name persists; common yet patrician, she could have no other name; ignore it, and he can't fully picture her, but take the name, and it lashes through: the blur of her face, the slope of her breast, her walking down an autumn street in a powder blue Mackintosh … *Stop*. Give him any day an old Midwesterner's surliness over the superficial civility of New York. To comfort himself, he recalls Sally's greeting, her smile so Christian you would think it was from compassion for his all-too-visible loneliness, but the thought of his own awkward reply makes him feel so exposed that on reaching the client site, he takes a moment in the loo to break a Xanax and work his face into a jovial, consultant-like air.

The meeting is prosaic, but it keeps him occupied until he returns home and pauses in the hallway, unsure if this is where he lives. Renting a house with a turret instead of a condo was his final attempt at being any more than an Indian middle-class kid whose first taste of finer things came only in his twenties, but in the three years since he moved in, he has imposed nothing of his will on the home; his books remain in boxes, his MoMA prints remain unframed. Passing headlights illuminate the Morris wallpaper, a repeating pattern of thorns and heavy rose heads, and again he feels that he is losing his grip on who he is, not just his name or face this time, but the fact that he is here at all. Afraid of his mind, he turns on the kitchen lights and refreshes his inbox. A reply from the recruiters. He's got the job. After all this time in exile, Manhattan – but no exclamation follows. His mind turns inwards, a slow scan from the top down in search of a response, but the news simply goes through him like a wave that does not break. What is wrong with him? Whatever it is, he thinks, this can't go on. He pushes his chair, grabs his coat, ignores his boots by the door. The snow hasn't fallen, but an icy wind is blowing and it burns his toes numb. Soon he can't tell the straps of his slippers from his feet, and passing the general hospital, he is certain that if the doctors, often seen by the cafeteria in their pale blue scrubs, were to saw off a toe with one of those small surgical saws, there would be no blood. *This can't go on*. He is less than fifty metres from the bridge when a sharp pain surges through the numbness in his left sole. He slows down, driven by an impulse to savour his discomfort, some notion that this pain is necessary, and it feels good, the pain feels good as he walks over the bridge, ducks into a diner, and orders the salty, tasteless food that, on a warmer night, might have brought him to tears.

When the waitress leaves with her notepad, he takes his feet out of his slippers, first squeezing and then rubbing them. He would never jump, of course not, that is why he is here, the cold from his feet leaching into his palms, the kitchen fans louder than the current foaming past the hedge. Even so, he is aware that a thought that had never entered his mind before, now has, and who would think it could come so innocuously as in the shape of those four simple words, but he has learnt the hard way not to take the first flickers of a new neural pathway lightly. Afraid of his mind again, he turns on his phone and browses his social media feeds through his meatloaf and Coke. The only post that has him pause is a couplet by Mir. *Bekhudi le gayi kahaan humko, der se intezaar hai apna.* For the rest, the East Coast is ranting about the acquittal of a white cop who shot a black teen for leaving a store with candy. Days after the incident, he recalls, he scanned all public places for a glint of metal, but all he feels now is apathy, especially when the outrage comes from educated whites. Back home, campaigns for the national election have taken off, and everyone is raving about the Bharat Party candidate, a Hindu nationalist on a mission to bring India into the twenty-first century. Even Naren's old engineering classmates, those apolitical market-guru acolytes, have turned devotional to the point he envies their ardour. How much he wants to feel, to feel anything, the burning winter on his toes will do if it makes him feel. The job offer changes nothing; his existence in America is like bread gone stale, it elicits neither pleasure nor disgust, only a desire to toss it without much thought into a bin. He scrolls through his newsfeed until the waitress announces the diner is closing. The chairs are on the tables. She is mopping the floor. And he thinks of Mir again, not the poet's meaning so much as his sound, and he knows what will cure him.

# *Amanda*

The turkey gleams, herbed and buttered, its shoulders hunched like its head were tucked below, graciously sparing them all its gaze. But she will not have a bite of it and to strengthen her resolve, she fixes on the split in the bird's rear from where the stuffing spills, while Mom (who thinks everyone's quirks except her own are affectations) lumps the parsnips and bitter greens before her, and Dad refuses to acknowledge anything amiss as he carves the bird's leg, his insistence that this is a joyful occasion indulged by Andrei (laughing as he almost spills Nana's wine), Nana flanked by the same two pies that she and every grandma in Jaffrey has baked for centuries: pumpkin-nut and rhubarb crumble. Then Dad raises the toast, half-registered until she hears the word *Andrei*, how young couples like her and *Andrei* give old fogies like them hope, and that he hopes this is the first of many Thanksgivings with *Andrei.* Nana takes her wine in a shot, Andrei smiles like he's received a medal, and if she were another Amanda, she would call her father out – What was the need for that, Dad? – but she is not another Amanda, so she silently helps herself to the cranberry sauce. 'Everything okay, honey?' Dad asks. She nods, yes.

Later in bed, Andrei repeats the question. It is dark outside the cabin, but she can feel the weight of the old house behind the junipers, the discreet force of her parents' expectation as they put away the silverware that there will always be five forks, five knives – or more, if she and Andrei cooperate. She says, 'There was chicken stock in the parsnips.' Oh. He hugs her. But the point isn't the meat; it isn't about health or cruelty, but depriving herself to toughen something inside that is going soft. 'Your mom doesn't mean it,' Andrei says. 'Not like you need to keep reminding her you've gone veg, but you know how she is, she's an artist' – as if this were not her mom but his, the problem not with him but them, and that Andrei, who has become the glue in their lives, will fix. 'You know what, fuck it,' she snaps, but then he does that thing, the way he scratches the side of his beard in earnest confusion, and it makes her want to cry. She hugs him. Where is the conviction with which she announced that she would move to his shabby studio in town, or even her confused relief when he moved in with her family instead?

The next morning, the snow falls, a comforter under which the house huddles further, the icicles on the window edges inching towards each other like jaws closing in. The heat is on only in the living room and kitchen, which makes everyone press closer still: Mom smudging a sketch by the fire, Dad baking trout, Nana staring, Beau licking his paws, and Andrei editing his report on the river's dying bass. He seemed so singular (sitting on the same couch when she first brought him home) as he explained his flight from Moldova, a country she had never heard of. It didn't matter that the New Hampshire Wildlife Board paid him pennies, or that a PhD in America hadn't neutralized the husky vowels that he compensated for by animating his grey eyes. 'A bit like a monkey,' Mom joked later, and Amanda snapped, 'Gramp was an immigrant too,' and Nana teased, 'Joe was English,' and Dad sighed, 'You two are impossible,' by which he meant Nana and Mom, but he was the last to warm up to Andrei, a true Harris snob on whom the surname Martin felt like a mistake. And here he is now, calling Andrei to help with the oven, his ambition to see his little girl become anything more than a research assistant to her aunt or live further than his old cabin suppressed by the fear he will never articulate: that he needs her and her unborn children to keep him from isolation, irrelevance, death. They are all in love with each other, Andrei with her family, her family with Andrei, a symbiotic banquet at which she is the sacrifice, yet they pretend it is all for her, for her that Nana requests Andrei to play the piano, and for her that Andrei says, 'In a minute, Nan.'

She refocuses on her laptop, her catalogue for Aunt Jess's monograph – *New England's Historic Homes*, beginning with their own – but it is hard to look at the century-old antlers and candle stands without vacillating between their absolute value and utter futility. Online, her friends' updates are an orgy of feasts lit by imitations of such candle stands. The one surprise is a post from an old … would she call him a friend? After a decade in the States, Naren Agashe has booked a one-way ticket to India. Now there is a country she has always felt a connection to, either on account of her British grandfather or Aunt Jess's Hare Krishna years, or Naren himself, with whom she shared a sublet for a semester in UPenn, and who reflected none of the harlequin chaos of the East but only a quiet and perfect decency. Then the piano chords invade her thoughts, and she blots them out to the extent she can without sticking her fingers in her ears, that and all the things that nauseate her: the flat odour of trout baking, the gurgle of boiling roots, and the weight of her wool socks, mitts and layers *in* the house, because Dad looks forward to winter as a time for sweaters and keeps turning down the heat when Mom turns it up. 'Where are you going?' Nana asks. 'Just need some air,' she says. 'Shall I come?' Andrei calls over his sonata, but she is already past the kitchen door.

Virgin snow. Winter grass. The sun's cold light blanched further by the overcast sky. Her footprints are the first beyond the porch. There is a catch in her throat where her breath meets the frosty air, but it is good to be out, her heavy boots steadying her step, the warmth on her chest and ears sweetened by the cold in her face. A red-tailed hawk soars overhead. She walks down the unshovelled path, past the stand that once sold cider, the Ford heaped with snow, the fields long sold. They have been selling bits of the land for years, but they will never sell that house. Lightning fires, an ice storm, the river rising over the marsh: these are the adventures the house has survived, a rosary of tales she eagerly strung as a girl, a chant she now struggles to suppress. She pushes herself to walk faster, to suspend all thought until she is well up the slope. There she presses her hand to a bark and tunes in to the things that lift her out of herself: the spruce rising like a cathedral, the smell of pine cones in the snow, but nothing in the distance glitters. For two hundred years, the Harrises have worked this stony land.

She pulls her scarf to her chin. Just a few feet to the summit, to the clearing from where there is nowhere to go but back down. Already the shadows are rising, the snow blowing in flurries that settle on her lashes, and she can feel the pull of the oppressive magnet that is the house, a force stronger than the will of each of its nine generations of owners, always drawing them back to its museum-like rooms where she too will leave some pointless doodle or talisman that time will make impossible for her children to throw away. A fog is rising over the junipers at the base of the hill, but the house is still visible, the lights already on in its windows. And suddenly it looks so small, so huddled in on itself with its feeble trail of smoke, pathetic in its determination, but admirable too – oh she loves it, it would crush her if they sold the house, and besides, she loves them. They are all such gentle people, well-meaning and proud, and dear Andrei, any day now he will propose, and how can she refuse? Her restlessness is her own beast, the return of a bull-headed force that defined her as a child, when she insisted on straying past the windbreak to befriend the animals. Who can blame them if, however subconsciously, they are desperate to neuter it with the surfeit of their love, their panic at the slightest droop in her smile, and the uncountable reasons they give her for what she feels? *You were always difficult. That's no job for an English major. You won't eat meat so you're always hungry.* And she knows she has no right, no right, yet love will not suppress the question fomented by that toast: Is this all there is to life?

'Right on time,' Dad says, as she latches the storm door. They are taking their seats around the trout. 'I'm okay,' she says from the stairs. No one contests her. Since she can't stand her old bedroom, she goes up to the attic. The door against her back, in the dark her ears lengthen to the window's soft rattle, the wet hush beyond, and every voice or clink from below amplified by its echo, but mostly the sounds are muffled, as if the density of time within these walls is too thick, a pall that dwarfs all lesser motion and makes of any trace of life a symbol of its own immutability: Nana's Singer sewing machine with webs on its needle, the videotapes in the armoire, a mason jar full of marbles – all still; pyjamas on a chair, the iron upright on its board, a tube of ointment by the tap – all still; magazines stuffed over leather spines, a wood and metal chime, the coffee stain on the empire settee, still ... Still are the single crooked balustrade, the metal frame among the gilt, the colour print among the oils, the lighthouse or field or bird in it still; still are the cereals on the kitchen shelf, the dishes stacked around the sink, the soggy boots out by the back, the wreath too ugly for the front, and Beau's empty bowl, and the planters full of snow; still are the plastic tub of rumpled clothes, the water frozen in the pipes, and the nest of odds and ends from which a scoop of infant mice, all blind and hairless, were bludgeoned in the yard, their bones now under layers of dirt and snow and still, all still, all still.

# *Rohit*

It's fine weed plucked off the Himalayas, ironed through a shirt and flown to Bombay in Gyaan's boxers, disgusting, yes, but here they are, talking very slowly or unusually fast, dropping ash before a screen in which comedians dressed as politicians prepare a funeral for the Conclave Party's flag, before a Bharat Brotherhood cadre does a tap dance on the grave. Now Rohit knows every frame, but his friends don't, and their laughter gets him laughing, and soon none of them can control it; within milliseconds of exposure to a slapstick turn, an electric wave cracks over their brains, their heads taking off like balloons until their throats go raw and their livers knot, and finally, finally it subsides though the video is still running, and Ifra takes an exhausted sip of her whisky, and says, 'Satire will be dead if the despot comes to power.' Paws on his paunch, Buddha-like, Gyaan adds, 'We're past ifs. The Hindus are going to beat the Indians.' To speak with as much conviction would sound false from Rohit. He was born in the year the markets liberalized, and any memory of broken mosques and burning trains is too vague to smudge his excitement over the reason for this celebration: Black Box Studio finally has its own address. But to confess to anything other than dread around Gyaan or Ifra is to announce oneself as a moral reprobate, so he listens as they diss the idiot millions all set to vote hate to power.

At the first pause, he asks what everyone thinks of the video. Ifra affirms its relevance. Cyrus confirms that they are finding their voice. Manasi asks when they will make their first showreel. They are being generous, but even generous friends say something good about oneself, and exiting the studio later at night, Rohit tosses his keys high in the February air and catches them with a fielder's grace. The Audi is an extension of his speed and flexibility, the axles passing the motion to its wheels without a sound. To drive home after work feels like proof that adult life is taking off, and was there any other reason to move the Box out of Imperial Heights? His parents never intruded, visitors could take the elevator straight to his floor, and Mukta Bai came up only twice, once with lunch for him and Gyaan, and then at four with tea. Well, there will be no more of that pampering. Life will be hard and brilliant, and it will carry all the validation of paying your own rent in Juhu, home of the stars. He honks thrice for joy as he turns into Bandra West … Oh damn, it's the traffic police.

He pulls over, rolls the glass down to the salt sea breeze. There are two of them, one pot-bellied, one pockmarked: Ganesha and his Mouse. 'Licence,' Ganesha says in the light of a saffron billboard. *Better Days Are Coming. Vote to End Corruption.* Rohit should wait silently as the card is scanned, he should say 'sahib' and apologize, but he can't stand such unctuous fuckery. 'Nice little set-up,' he says. 'Sitting where I won't see the signal because it's in a corner.' Mouse looks indignant. 'Did you break it or not?' 'Arey, Mamu,' Rohit says, 'I was born in Mumbai and I wasn't born yesterday, but you're just doing your job, aren't you?' Ganesha continues to singe the English letters on the licence with his flashlight. He must be the higher in rank since Mouse looks his way uncertainly. Rohit has spoken in Marathi and the presence of one cop must make the other sheepish about hounding a decent fellow man. Though Naren's arrival is still two months away, he says, 'How much is it? I have to receive my brother at the airport. He was in America for ten years and is coming home for good.' 'Isn't the airport that way?' Mouse starts, but it is Ganesha's turn to interrogate him. 'Didn't suit him there?' 'It did,' Rohit says, 'but he wants to work for his soil now.' Ganesha smirks. 'So he too has caught the wind. Good. Who will take the country forward if not its youth? Now go, and watch for the signal next time, or what difference between you and some bhaiya driving a rickshaw?' Rohit takes the licence. Passing headlights flash over a dusty police motorbike. 'Should I give him something for tea?' he asks, pointing his chin at Mouse. 'Do we look like those sorts of cops?' Ganesha roars and slaps the hood. 'I have a boy your age I show my face to every night!'

Rohit salutes them. Poor bastards, inspired by Naren to give up padding their pathetic incomes. Even in absence, Naren has that effect. Does Rohit's urgency to relocate his studio have anything to do with his brother's return? The last time he saw Naren was at his graduation ceremony at Wharton, a totem of such seriousness that Rohit had to control the impulse to clasp his hands behind his back when they spoke. Back then, Baba had wanted him to study engineering too, and he is smart, he is smooth, but he isn't rigorous. After losing a year to the entrance exams, his parents were grateful enough when he got into Wilson College for his Bachelor of Mass Media. At last he was in an institution that his brother hadn't blazed through before him, and it wasn't long before he came into his own. Then the backbenchers he hung out with started a band, and soon, he became their manager and was on the guest list at all the nightclubs, buying girls older than him drinks. Not that Naren has a clue about any of this. An eight-year gap means he has always been loved and given updates, but restricted on social media. Naren must feel their distance too. A week before Christmas, he forwarded Rohit an email from a cute American with an interest in social development. Rohit passed it on to Ifra, whose boss recommended Amanda for the India Impact Fellowship. She is flying in with his brother and will spend a week with their family, yet Naren refers to her as simply a friend. They have never talked girls, and surely, Rohit hopes, that is in the past. Already he sees himself driving Naren and Amanda through town, stopping at pubs and cafés where all the waiters and the occasional someone famous knows his name.

That's right, if his brother had gravity at twenty-four, Rohit has charm. For all he knows, it was for his own charisma that the traffic cops let him off. He looks in the rear-view mirror. As a child he was the Agashe runt, browner than his cousins, brown-eyed, a shabby combination on a six-year-old, but it's what arrests people now, the odd intensity eyes have when they are a shade lighter than the skin, and yet, as eyes are, full of lustre. As if to confirm this, the watchman pulls himself up with a genuine smile. Twelve floors above, the duplex is heavy with sleep. Rohit peels off his T-shirt and flops on his bed, the sheets cool and fresh, the fumigator glowing green, and a glass of iced water by his side just as he realizes he is thirsty. He breathes in the milky scent of his pillow. Soon he will be lost in such wild and variable dreams, it's like a whole kingdom exists between now and the morning, and as he surrenders to it, he is suddenly nervous he may never be as loved and self-satisfied as in this moment.

An hour later, he is still awake, and the thought keeping him up is that it was neither for Naren nor for himself that the cops refused the bribe. They did it in response to something larger. *So he too has caught the wind,* Ganesha said. And what of Rohit? Even a year ago, it was enough simply to have started out. Even an hour ago, an office in Juhu was ample validation. But the world is changing fast, and he worries that the videos he once thought cutting edge are too niche. He wants an epic life, a life of authenticity and relevance. What this will entail, he can't say, but to have articulated what it won't, he decides, is already a step in the right direction. For now, all he must do is stay true to his every impulse until the whole is revealed, and the one instinct he trusts, the one capacity that will see him through, is that he knows bullshit when he sees it. He will take the world for what it is; he will meet it chest out with his potential, which – since he has no claimable talents (but who can say what will surface, what strains might take hold?) – expresses itself in this excess energy, this sense that he is at the cusp of an era and wants to be at the centre when it all comes together, to be at the centre and to be young.

## *Naren*

At Frankfurt airport, the early April light deepens his pleasure in the ambient music – Bach's cello suites under Casals's unsentimental bow – and the thought that, at any moment, he will meet Amanda. He hasn't seen her since his college years, and from what he recalls (she hardly posts online), he can now locate her in a context he was too newly arrived to when they first met. For instance, there is something of the snow and wooded wild in her clear eyes and finger-run hair, and her jaw, which he once thought masculine, reappears as having a cool, assured beauty, the kind that will sit well with pearls. It is girls like Amanda who grow into women like Cathy, and Amanda must be twenty-seven now, the age he was then. But the thought of Cathy is agitating, so he clicks on his iPad to distract himself. In a landmark election, the Bharat Party has won with a bigger majority than any opposition to the Conclave since Independence. Tweet after tweet celebrates the new prime minister's speech, his promise to end corruption and policy paralysis, to invest in jobs, and to clean the holy Ganga – all delivered extempore in Hindi, not English, from the central hall of the parliament. Images show him saluting the 'temple of democracy' that has given a poor man's son its mandate. His government will carry everyone along, he says, but it is dedicated to those Indian youth striving for honour, their aspiration his responsibility, and all he asks is that they give their best to their motherland.

Moved by the strongman's tears, the crowd's rapture, and the thought that he is flying home, *home*, Naren notices Amanda only when she is right in front saying, 'There you are,' her scarf a faded floral blur as he leans in and pulls back before his chin touches her shoulder. 'Look at you,' she says. 'Look at *you*,' he says, though she looks the same, so girlish, as she presses her satchel to her lap, sweeps her hair off her face and sits down all at once. They rehash the serendipity behind this reunion, and that they got the same connecting flight. She thanks him for making her fellowship possible. He tells her to thank his brother. That gets them talking of their kin, and how America is closer to India than Europe in idolizing family, which leads to a chat on city versus small-town life, with both justifying how they landed up in the latter despite their fancy degrees from UPenn. Turns out the move was not as unexpected for Amanda. Philadelphia is the only city she has lived in. And as the conversation proceeds, Naren's shoulders relax and spread outwards, his voice rolls into a drawl, and his global Indian accent comes awake as he opines on both their countries, his insights augmented by business trips to still others (this is just her second time abroad), and quotes from a recent *Economist* – or was it the *Wall Street Journal* – on India's demographic dividend.

'See, in every country's life,' he says, 'there comes a golden generation that will ride its transformation into a modern state. That means they will make wealth in a way neither their fathers could nor their sons will. Ask me what makes my generation the one? India won her political freedom in 1947 and her economic freedom in 1991, but it wasn't until this election that our political and business classes got aligned. And just in time. Two-thirds of our population is under thirty-five. Couple that with a government focused on manufacturing, and we could become the world's biggest labour force and consumer market in one go!'

'Sounds exciting,' Amanda says, and then, as women do when a conversation isn't exciting enough, she gets personal. 'Is that why you're moving back?'

'This winter, I got my green card and an offer from two top Manhattan firms. So it isn't like my labour wasn't bearing fruit … it's just that, for some time, I've had no altar to lay this fruit on.'

Amanda affirms it is a beautiful thought. 'When I was applying for the India Impact Fellowship, I often returned to this Willa Cather quote. If you visit Jaffrey, you'll see it on her tombstone. It says: That is happiness, to be dissolved into something complete and great.'

Naren doubts the inscription is a reference to purpose, but he doesn't point it out. He says it's interesting, and then, from anxiety at her quoting an author he hasn't heard of and irritation at her project in India – the usual white thing, coming for the poverty – he adds, 'To return to your question on what's taking me back, though *back* is the wrong word, the word is *forward* … frankly, it is the numbers. The Indian economy will overtake the US in thirty years. Landsworth, the consultancy I'll be working for, is shifting its management centres this way. Trade flows are shifting too. My point is, Wall Street may recover, but the future isn't in the West, it is in the East.'

'Well, amazing. Good for you,' Amanda says, and it's just a manner of speaking, but Naren senses he has lost the common ground they were closing in on. He tries to correct his course, he was just hitting his stride, but her responses get shorter, and she finally yawns like a child and says, 'I'm so sleepy, Naren. You think I can sleep here?'

Sure, if she is tired. Using her satchel as a pillow, she spreads across the adjacent chairs with enviable unselfconsciousness. What was all that about – the accent, the archaic phrases? Fruit on the altar? Amanda may be paler than Cathy, but he has been out in the world long enough to know the farmhouse in Jaffrey isn't the Tudor in Weston, that her hair is still finger-run, and where the mention of certain publications brings a sparkle to some eyes, to Amanda's it brings a mild panic. He isn't trying to impress her, if only it were that innocent, and given where they are from, his East–West comment was bad form. Over the rim of his iPad, her breathing steadies. Her second time abroad. So, it is not a coincidence they are on the same flight. She has timed her entry with his, her fellowship doesn't begin until later this month, and in promptly accepting a polite invitation to spend a week with his family, she has secured a safe touchpoint in a new world. A survivor, a small-towner with none of Cathy's access or sophistication, still she has grace. Even in sleep, her mouth doesn't open. Her light hair, parted in the middle, catches the sun slanting in through the high glass. Her scarf is printed not with flowers but birds, her high-waist jeans of a well-worn nonchalance that, though retro, seem eternal on her … and though the jacket on her chest is inviolable, and her frame too angular to compare with those reclining women in museums all over the West, she reminds him of their simultaneous frankness and vulnerability, and his own hard-won awareness that the artist's vision was never intended for the likes of him, his opinion uncalled for, his nostalgia surrogate … *Stop*. It is the nature of a weak moment to read too much symbolism into things.

Back on the flight, Naren is relieved they aren't in adjoining seats and that Amanda makes no effort to relocate. By the time they land, both are too bleary for conversation. The terminal is wide awake, the concourse a thoroughfare. Under a welcome sign – *Indian at Heart, Global in Spirit* – the immigration queues are embarrassing. This is the new privatized airport, its arches stupendous, its operations world class, but what can the authorities do when there are so many people? It is past midnight when they reach the exit. The air outside is leathery with heat and engine fumes, but it feels good to stop justifying the airport inconveniences that Amanda is too polite to complain about, and here is Rohit waving over the chaos of heads, placards and barricades, and their hug would be less awkward if Amanda wasn't there, but their faces are luminous. Rohit is wearing a dress shirt on shorts, suede sneakers, and his hair waxed into a hawk. He still looks like a boy, but from the way he introduces himself to Amanda and takes her trolley, from his manner that suggests *I've got this*, his quick smile and quick frown like he is alert yet hovering a bit above the scene, Naren can tell he must be good at business. They reach the parking lot. The Agashes have a driver, but they also have a new Audi, and Rohit has driven down himself for the fun of driving it. Taking off like he was born at this wheel, he chats up Amanda, his questions on the social sector informed, his friends of friends in the space all terrific people with whom he will connect her.

This late, the expressway takes no time. On either side, the city lights rise and fall like piano scales, the slums below lost to darkness, and Naren's chest swells at the sudden expanse of black water, the new Sea Link and the Worli skyline inverted in the sea. Then Rohit swerves into Bandra West, reminding Naren that their family no longer lives in the squat buildings in the East. The shuttered avenues give way to the hush of Pali Hill, and at its peak, a tall wrought-iron gate. Imperial Heights. Five years in, there is still something new about the tower, as if the dust of construction hasn't entirely settled. Once the marble lobby weathers its gleam, Naren thinks, it will actualize its charm. A security guard salutes them, a second gets their bags, a third the elevator. Then they go up, up, up, until the doors open to his parents' faces. How small they suddenly seem, either from age or because he has got accustomed to American physiques. 'You didn't come to the airport after everything I told Amanda about Indian welcomes,' he teases. 'We are getting on, Naren,' Aai says, reaching for a hug, and Baba thumps his back, but neither are teary. It is old Mukta Bai who brims as she clutches his hands and says, 'Aaley Naren Baba.' Stench of coconut oil and sweat. He recoils, embarrassed by her familiarity, she who has massaged his body as an infant, though he regrets saying nothing the moment Aai sends her away.

The duplex is more impressive than its photographs convey: The balcony has a panoramic city view, and the décor a touch of the airport's ambition. The old lampshades have given way to false ceilings with ambient light, the prints of Hindu gods to framed mirrors and metal art, and while the 'global at heart' comes across in the white sofas and French windows, the 'Indian in spirit' is retained by the crimson cushions, a brass Ganesha and tropical palms. When Baba sold their ancestral land, this home was his first acquisition, one floor for each son to inherit after the parents are gone, but to Naren, far away in another continent, the sale of the Bandra East flat felt like a harbour demolished, as if from there on, there was no return to childhood's security and constancy. Such sentiments are astounding now. Either he was so caught up in the American fetish for the Self-Made Man or so confident he would never need his parents' assets, which put together were still rupee rich, not dollar rich, that he never thought of this capital as his, nor was its extent ever more real than now, sunk in the plush upholstery, taking to the new without the slightest mourning for the old. In fact, he is already acting the part of a man who could have no other home. On the way here, he slipped in mentions of the Agashes' land, their staff, even their caste, this last offending his progressiveness enough to commit to shutting up and letting his context speak. When Amanda says an emphatic thank you to the girl serving cold guava juice on a tray, he only asks, as if the girl has always been at hand, 'Coke nahin hai?'

Then he sits back, content to let his mother conduct the preliminaries, her convent-school English complementing this setting so well, one would think the Agashes' past and not their present was the real aberration … until Amanda compliments the woodwork. Aai reports that nothing is ready-made. She has supervised the carpenters herself, 'interior decorators are such bullies', mastering all there is to know about veneers, and she expounds on these choices at length, not that there is any hubris in it, she is simply being generous with her wonder for all the new things she has learned in decorating a home three decades after her first, yet the blood in Naren's cheeks thickens when Amanda turns to him and asks, 'Isn't this the home you grew up in?' Aai confirms that Imperial Heights is five years old. 'Wait, is this the first time you're seeing your new home?' Amanda asks. Naren admits it is, embarrassed at not making it obvious sooner. 'Really? How exciting!' Amanda exclaims. Then Baba offers a tour and they all jump like children delighted at an excursion, looking this way and that as he points out the structural accomplishments, like how a toilet was broken to build the connecting stairwell, and as each door opens, Amanda hesitates before Naren's parents draw her in, looking at the rooms with new eyes themselves, Amanda politely noting a Chinese lamp or silk duvet as Aai hopelessly confesses to the newness of it all.

On the stairs to the upper floor, Naren can feel every muscle in his face. Divided in his desire to play along or not, or to play along not with his parents but with Rohit, who keeps looking his way with a knowing smile as if to affirm they are spectators at a circus, he excuses himself. In the kitchen, the new maid is warming dinner. He doesn't know her name, and she seems unsure of what to do other than to look at his feet, when Aai rushes in. 'Naren, are you okay?' she asks with a child's nervousness. 'Just wanted water,' he replies. Transformed by his helplessness into a mother again, she exclaims, 'But you don't know where anything is!' With the old self-reliance and efficiency of the Bandra East days, she opens one of the endless modular drawers, takes out a crystal tumbler, fills it from a jet connected to the fridge, and holds it up, the shy pride in her gesture making Naren aware that they are at last alone and he may confess his admiration for everything Baba has achieved and she has actualized. 'You've done the place up really well,' he says, and he is sorry, so sorry when she replies, 'I'm happy you like it, Naren. I thought you must have seen much fancier homes in America. Then I told myself he is just jet-lagged, or maybe he is missing the old place.'

## *Rohit*

He is still waking up to the sunny whiff of scrambled eggs and the family's polite chatter when Sita gets the door. 'Kedya, how come? Come in,' Aai says, and Kedar, unlacing his dusty sneakers, replies in Marathi, 'Aai saw online that Naren has reached, and I was in Mumbai so I thought let me drop by.' This is just like their cousin, showing up without so much as a text. 'Kedar,' says Naren, and Kedar says, 'Dada.' Rohit can't remember the last time he called Naren that, though it's hard to tell if Kedar means it ironically, and their distance is confirmed when Naren stands and Kedar steps forward, but both stop short of an embrace. Aai promptly introduces Amanda as 'Naren's college friend' before anything else is assumed. Her attentive hello makes Rohit consider what Kedar looks like to a foreigner. He could pass for an Iranian thanks to Chitra Kaki's pale skin and Ravi Kaka's height, but whatever part of this impression survives his wire-frame glasses and kurta on jeans is destroyed the moment he opens his mouth. 'Heylo,' he says in his thick Marathi accent, with none of the diffidence that accompanied it as a teen. When Baba asks what he will have, Kedar replies, 'Only water, please,' and then, oblivious to Amanda, he says to Naren. 'So, Dada, the party in the West is over?'

'More like the one here is beginning,' Naren says brightly.

'Is it?' Kedar asks.

Spreading mango jam on her toast, Aai says, 'Our Kedya is a journalist now.'

Naren asks, 'For the *Express* right?'

'For *Nayibhumi*,' says Kedar. 'I am also freelancing with others. They are not publications you will find in Bandra. They are for the Hindi–Marathi public.'

Now, Rohit would play a better host if Kedar hadn't annoyed him on his previous visit by saying of his studio, Yaar, amazing, must be easy when Baba is the investor, no – as if a parent's wealth is an original sin you must atone for. This time, Rohit has a good mind to tell his cousin that life isn't about what your lonely efforts deserve, it is about how you leverage what you get, but the spotlight today is on Kedar, who makes no effort to disguise his lack of sophistication (to Naren's distress), and worse, sports whatever is least impressive about him like a badge of honour.

'Are you in Bombay for work?' Baba asks.

'I am getting help to file an FIA appeal.'

'Interesting,' Naren says.

Baba says to Amanda, 'He is talking about our Freedom of Information Act. India wasn't like America where you can ask for a public record and expect a reply. Today, even a sanitation worker can demand a report from a government authority.'

Aai adds, 'Just look at the irony. The Conclave Party passed the act, then the same act was used to expose all their scams. Ha ha. That is how the middle class woke up.'

Amanda asks what motivated the party. Baba says, 'They sat on a high horse saying transparency, transparency, but there was pressure. Lawyers, activists, anti-corruption protests…'

The talk turns to the endless scandals in housing, insurance and fuel, the rot seeping through public relief funds, the exposés on the telecom, defence and mining ministries, and everyone gets louder except for Kedar, who maintains a watchful silence. Aai concludes, 'This is the first time we voted for the Bharat Party. There was no other choice.'

'There was a choice,' Kedar says. 'It was between weak governance and fascism.'

The table goes quiet. Fully awake, Rohit wants to laugh. Who knows when this bland-as-bread cousin acquired such an air of sanctimony, but Naren is unprepared and he looks like he took a sip of dirty water. 'I think *fascism* is overstating it,' he says. 'The Bharat Party played their sectarian games to become a household name, but parties evolve. What got them elected? Not the promise of a Hindu state. People voted for development under a strong leader. The day after the election, the stock market hit an all-time high!'

Kedar purses his lips. 'Mumbai people put their garland on the market like it's Lakshmi and the notes will trickle from her palms to her lotus feet. Don't mind me, but the swamp is rising under those lotuses. For a farmer in the Konkan, development isn't a number, it isn't incremental income. It is about whether to drink pesticide because his field was taken at gunpoint.'

'Sita!' Aai shouts in a tone she never uses with the maids. 'Paani kahaan hai? How long can we wait.' Who knows what upset her, but Sita isn't taking chances. She hurries out with a jug of water and glass tumblers on a tray. Aai says, 'She's new, that's the problem.'

As in the presence of a saint, Kedar's expression goes soft. He leans towards the stunted girl, takes a tumbler, and says with exquisite humility, 'Thank you, Didi.' Sita half-bows her way back to the kitchen. Kedar takes a sip. 'Sorry, Naren. We are embarrassing you.'

'Not at all,' Naren replies, a little too sharply. Baba excuses himself. Aai brings up Amanda's fellowship, but the small talk is strained, and when Kedar rises to leave, no one stops him. In a final courtesy, Aai insists that he leave his empty tumbler on the table, yet he carries it past Sita to the kitchen. He is barely out of the door when Naren says, 'The corruption he's investigating defined the last government. What else can you expect when one family runs a country? Now the nationalists want to dredge the swamp, and they finally have a majority, but these damned reporters are so addicted to their pessimism!'

Rohit doesn't care for Kedar's views, but Naren's intensity is startling. 'He's just Kedar being Kedar,' he says, laying his eggy utensils down. 'He was weird as a kid, and now he's a journalist, and this talk is the only currency he has.'

And whatever Amanda thinks, she adds, 'I just found him really funny. Like he stepped right out of a Wes Anderson film.'

Everyone laughs, including Aai who has never seen a Wes Anderson film but gets the idea, and Rohit likes Amanda for it, he likes people with a talent for keeping things sunny. Even so, Kedar's critical mood drops a shadow over the day. They are done with the usual touristy stuff, like photographing gargoyles in Fort and inspecting botanical drawings at the Prince of Wales Museum, so Rohit drives them to the offbeat alleys of Chor Bazaar. And Amanda is enchanted by the smell of meat and rose water, the antique hawkers wailing, the azan rising from a dozen mosques, but the fury on Naren's face as he kicks a coconut husk off his brogue tells Rohit he has misread everything. Exotic streets and rotting chawls are not the New India that has brought his brother home and that he defends so passionately. But when showing visitors around, there isn't much to see or not enough to prove the new prime minister is all the country needs to take the lid off its simmering potential. The business hubs are still grainy with dust and lined by stinking creeks, the elation of driving over the Sea Link tanks into a jam by the slum at its exit. Only the malls with their bowling alleys and rainbows of gelato are impressive, but strolling past the luxury stores in High Street Phoenix, it is embarrassing to take pride in such crass modernity, to not be the ancient, cultured people Amanda expects.

Driving back, the chimneys of dead cotton mills kaleidoscope into blue glass towers, their western façades fracturing the light. In the tired silence, Rohit feels trapped between what Amanda wants to find and what Naren wants to project. At least in Bombay, New India isn't a vista but a moment: illiterate maids tapping emojis, expats doing non-touristy stuff like buying avocados from carts, the nightlife. He proposes a visit to his studio. By the time they reach Juhu, Gyaan and Cyrus are there to welcome them. Rohit introduces Gyaan as the man behind the camera, Cyrus as the one in front of it, and himself as the man who brings it all together. 'If I can build an ecosystem in which I'm giving people the right energy to create brilliant stuff, I'm on point,' he says. Amanda affirms that's a generous way to be. 'Not that he'll do anything he isn't paid for,' Cyrus winks. Everyone laughs except Naren. Black Box isn't bad for a start-up; they have Macs and Canons, leather beanbags, an espresso machine, but like the city, the studio is still a work in progress. Through a visitor's eyes, it's just a two-man show on the mezzanine of a deadbeat mall, the equipment basic, the software pirated. Which is fine. Keeping lean is a conscious decision. Beyond the right address, a physical space doesn't matter much in a virtual world where teams get pulled together from a pool of roving freelancers, clients are found by word of mouth, pitches made in cafés, and equipment rented on a project basis because you get more range and why buy anything when tools get obsolete every quarter? But Naren is of a generation that still needs brick and mortar to be impressed.

To give them a sense of their work, Gyaan plays their showreel. It's sassy, with new-age brands flying on screen, drone footage of skyscrapers and slums, the haughty faces of brown supermodels, teens grooving in neon light – and Amanda claps and Naren pouts like he is impressed, but when the screen goes dark, he asks if they have plans for anything 'serious'. 'Films, absolutely,' says Gyaan. 'But a film isn't an advertisement. You put your name as an artist behind it, so we better be sure what we are doing. We're still learning our craft…' It is a spiel Rohit usually joins him in, but the vein on his temple is ticking. Gyaan is wearing what he was when they first met at a party, baggy jeans and a tee that reads: *Here for Content*. The summer Rohit graduated, 'content' was the buzzword; it stood for everything that was the opposite of conservative in media; the internet was exploding in India and the pie is still big enough – there are over a thousand set-ups like the Box in Bombay and Rohit doesn't know one that isn't making money – yet he is restless. He would like to make or contribute to a real film, but he is only the dealmaker. Gyaan carries the artist's gravitas, and to mention Bollywood is to say you're pulling up your skirts for money. The day's strain turns to resentment. All this time away, Naren phoned only Aai, and there was nothing to do but accept his ambition and precious time, even as Rohit's only proof that they were ever close are the marks on his forearm where Naren once bit him as they wrestled on their parents' bed. Still he has welcomed his brother home with all the heartbreaking optimism of new beginnings, but Naren is only concerned with his impression on a white girl. Kedar was right. Sorry Naren, he said, *we* are embarrassing you.

As they are leaving, Cyrus reminds him of a party on his boyfriend's terrace to celebrate Ifra getting profiled in India Forum's *30 Under 30*. They reach as the sun is going down on Versova. The sea and sky are the colour of sherbet, there must be about forty guests, two in three look familiar, and the rest might well be. Here is Rohit's scene, and his veins dilate in the breezy excitement of running into people you know in the company of others you know who don't know each other yet, and hanging about the low-lit palms, the clink of crystal in the air, he finally has them both excited: Amanda at being among insiders in the kind of place you won't find in a guidebook, and Naren by the melon martinis and camembert. More unexpected still is Naren's delight in the company – first Manasi, now Cy's boyfriend, Jay – and from his take on subjects like gastronomy and art, Rohit recognizes the global citizen his brother has become, but he no longer feels the impulse to clasp his hands behind his back. Naren is wearing a pink chambray shirt on beige chinos, and such beautiful leather loafers you could cradle them. He insisted on a detour home to dress. Such sartorial care from a man who isn't naturally flamboyant suggests insecurity, same as the shift in register when Naren tries to balance the lilt he uses in America with the singsong accent of home. Not that a puffed-up bumpkin like Kedar is Rohit's idea of authenticity. What is, he is still to find out.

He scans the terrace. Whatever effort these people put into dyeing their hair or getting a tattoo or being among the first global thousand to use a hashtag, they are all imitations of each other. In college, after years of feeling misunderstood by perfectly decent teachers and parents, the thrill of just this similarity united his friends. With few exceptions, their parents got rich too late to send them to international schools or to colleges abroad without scholarships, but they all spoke English better than their mother tongue, and they could sniff each other out. Their clothes were flashy, they drove their own cars, they drunk drove, and even if they had to pre-game, they could afford drinks at Blue Frog every week. What skills he graduated with, Rohit can't say, but he graduated with a network of over two thousand friends across the city's top colleges. Then their decibel amplified, in part because they got into fields like film, TV and PR, and in part because they became a magnet for similar dreamers across the country and the globe, and in a year or two, everyone knew someone famous or seemed en route to fame themselves. All were active online, retweeted, even trolled, which once gave Rohit the sense that they were the voice of a generation, but since their collective shock at the Bharat Party's massive victory, his suspicion has been confirmed: what he once thought of as a generation is really a clique.

Breaking away, Rohit goes to the bar. Across a rattling cocktail shaker, Ifra looks glorious in an olive romper and heels, and Gyaan's genius is heightened by his arm around her waist, but the impression dims when their talk shifts to the national election. They are all outraged that a man with blood on his hands has the nation's mandate, yet they thrive on their exclusivity, and it is not the otherness of dusty poets in prison, but the snobbery of teens who know they are the in-crowd. The bartender is all gums as he serves up a perfect mojito, the lime sharp, the mint fresh, but Rohit's mouth stays dry. What was a passing anxiety has turned chronic. He is overworked and can't see what anything is adding up to, he is over-connected but no longer feels at the centre of things, and hash is not enough to buffer the expectation his peers put on themselves, their parents having slogged nine-to-five so that they might do something more sterling, if not change the world. He wants to knock back his drink and leave, but he has come with guests, and his eyes move from face to glossy face until they rest on Amanda. She is wearing denim shorts with no regard for how nineties that is, a cotton top as soft and faded as a page from an old book, a blue stone from the Atlantic on her sternum. Here she is at the other end of her world, yet he can't imagine her speaking in anything but her own voice.

# *Naren*

As he comes down the stairs, the sight of Aai arranging lilies on the mirror-top console – each stem cut at a precise slant though the ends will be lost to the vase – fills him with regret. How he wants to take her in his arms and kiss her where the hair on her temple is greying, but such familiarity is Rohit's preserve. When his parents talk with his brother, there is none of the awe and mild fatigue that dominates their conversations with him, the trophy son around whom no one can relax. 'Ah, Naren,' Baba says, looking up from the Monday papers on the table. Aai turns, her smile even lovelier for the faint creases on her skin. 'Had a good nap? Did Mukta disturb you with her dusting? I told her…' He says he did. With Rohit at work and Amanda scouting the rental options offered by her fellowship, he finally has his parents to himself. Eager to be useful, he asks Baba about some financial matters that he was to advise them on. The first time he enquired about their corpus, as recently as this winter, he was hesitant, but Baba, warming up to the notion that a family's achievements are cumulative, welcomed his interest. These days, they frequently consult on their portfolio, and that the market is on a high and Naren's instincts are on point holds the scope for a new, adult relationship. 'What's the hurry?' Aai asks, wiping the rim of the vase. 'We can just sit and chat. I'll tell Sita to make tea.' But Naren doesn't trust himself not to wear his parents down. 'Once work kicks off,' he says, 'I won't have a minute.'

They relocate to the 'study', a term his parents must have picked up from the builder's plan because it is furnished like a TV room except for two teak bookshelves dominated by encyclopaedias, dictionaries, translations of the Gita, family albums, and folders full of documents like share certificates and medical reports. Rummaging through them, Baba constantly turns to Aai for help. As a child, Naren took their equation for granted, but having loved and lost, it is incredible to him that two people who barely knew each other before marriage share such an effortless affinity ... Or not so strange, for though Aai is darker, there is something sibling-like about them, an inbred harmony most modern couples lack. And despite the paucity of this library, how far they have come. When they first sold the land, they were still acting their class, treating a windfall like income rather than capital, and spending on expensive cars and stagnant property instead of investments or experiences. But in the years since his father wound up his accounting practice, what was once the dignity of hard work and conscientious living is now a dignity suffused with languor.

'Look at this,' Baba says, handing him a frail certificate. 'It's a satbara, a tract that shows we own rural land. My father got it made when he purchased the Talne plot. He probably thought it would appreciate because Goa was a new state in the eighties and this was on the border. Then nothing happened for years, so everyone forgot.'

'Until you found it in his will. I know.'

'Ravi found it. We were all totally surprised. We called a lawyer and he dug up the deed and said yes, there is this estate. That's when Asha flew in from Brisbane and we three siblings drove to Talne. A beautiful village in the ghats. We thought maybe we could build a resort there, but the land turned out to be a complete mix – part forest, part hill, part farm – meaning, it was too rustic to develop, and what does any Agashe know of farming? So we decided to sell.'

'How did Brahma Mines happen? I don't think I ever asked.'

'One of my clients connected me with Ankush Jain,' Baba says. 'He's a nephew of R.K. Jain of Brahma Industries. Big shots, I know. Ankush has his own company now, but at that time he was working for his uncle and wanted to expand their operations in the Konkan. The government was for it, a Conclave minister's son even has a stake and had figured out the clearances. Then suddenly Ravi said, I won't sell. He had spoken to some villagers and got convinced that mining would spoil the hill. Asha and I couldn't sell until there was an agreement on how to divide the plot. Brahma tripled the price … but you know your Ravi Kaka. I'll be honest, Naren, we weren't on talking terms when our mother died.'

Baba's eyes are bright with a can-you-believe-these-people mirth, but Naren can see that Kedar's visit has pulled at the sutures of an old wound and that the satbara was merely an excuse to bring the conversation to what his father has carried for a long time.

'You never told me,' he says. 'I came home for Aaji's funeral.'

'We thought why drag the children in, and after her, no one was in a mood to fight. Ravi released us, and the minute we sold our plots, half those villagers in Talne did. Today they are living in pukka houses and own trucks to carry the ore. The Goa government recently imposed a mining ban, and the villagers were praying to Ganapati that Talne isn't affected! Still our Ravi has not sold his plot. He's sitting on gold, but because of his tantrum, Asha and I have let him keep the Pune house for nothing. We say never mind, his factory didn't do well. And now his son has the audacity to sit at *my* table and talk about miners snatching land at gunpoint.'

'The land the Pune house is on must be worth a fortune,' Naren says.

His father nods, consoled by this acknowledgement of his generosity. Even so, Naren's cluelessness about the extent of the family feud makes him guilty. All these years abroad, he believed he was the one protecting his family from his disappointments;

when Aai said all was well, he took it at face value. And it was, in a way. The hurt must surely cut deeper for Ravi Kaka, holding on to his bitter pride in Pune while his siblings live it up in Bombay and Brisbane. Flashes of Prabhat House, of summer holidays spent amidst the happy clamour of three generations, Kedar calling him Dada without irony. Not Naren Dada, simply Dada, for they were the only boys among the cousins, at least until Rohit was born, and Naren the older by three years. How had the distance grown? If he remembers right, it had set in before he left for the States. And if the families meet only at weddings and funerals now, he suspects it has less to do with the feud than the gap in their cosmopolitanism. Why else the whole charade of stopping by and trying to impress with all that reverse snobbery? The Pune Agashes have not amounted to enough to stay relevant, and unlike his Brisbane cousins, they have remained vernacular. Naren aches for a time before he categorized people by rank and class, and the lessons that led to this painful knowledge, but there is no going back. This is the world.

When jet lag makes it impossible for him to concentrate, they shut the folders. Amanda has been offered the guest room below, and he the room next to Rohit's, but coming up the stairs, the whole upper floor feels like it already belongs to his brother. There's a lounge with a bar for Rohit's friends, his bedroom, and his 'den', which housed his studio until early this year and has a décor that is utterly distinct: the floor is black, the furniture white, and a stylized city skyline has been painted on the wall by an artist friend. The furthest Naren had ever gone in branding a part of his parents' home was the stickers of wrestlers on his desk as a boy. There is something off-putting about Rohit's confidence, his interrupting their parents and showing off his connections … but no, Rohit is a good boy, he's just trying to make an impression; the real source of Naren's upset is that he can't help think what Amanda will make of his home. Taking off his clothes, he recalls the old bathroom from their Bandra East home, the mosaic tiles, the faded walls stained by rust where the pipes crept out, the pump water that smelled of copper, the exhaust fan letting the sunlight in from between its musty blades, light that exposed motes in the afternoon, and in the mornings, left a great star on the rim of the steel bucket. Not that he is nostalgic … if anything, it agitates him to see remnants of the past clutter the present, like the plastic bucket on the glossy Italian tiles, the ugly steel vessels in the French door fridge, or even old Kedar. Of course his gratification in inviting Amanda was that she stay at Imperial Heights, but now that he thinks of it, what a ludicrous name, just the kind to appeal to upstarts come into money by accident.

He turns on the shower, and the spray from the gilded shower head hits his muscles with exhilarating force. His mouth turns sweet as the water drips down his thighs. His hand goes absently to his crotch but stops at a caress. He doesn't think of Amanda that way, and there is no one else, not even a fantasy that won't seem pathetic when he is done. He shuts his eyes, and within, he sees the dead soy fields of his exile, the barns and silos so lonely for miles, and he thinks, oh America, either you failed me or I failed you. And when he says America, he doesn't mean the lifestyle idealized by movies when he was a teen and all it took to recommend a watch or sweater was to say it was from America, he means the values that made him believe that country could be home. Amanda need not own a townhouse; she is the soil of Cathy's roots, the hark back that Cathy romanticized for all her sophistication, and that he once mistook in her for humility. No, he isn't trying to impress Amanda. He is merely gratifying himself by recreating a dynamic that he was once at the receiving end of, but as her visit has proved, he can't even pull that off. Why else does it bother him when Rohit gets her laughing with such a different style? It isn't envy so much as an affront to something he must protect if he is to remain convinced of his person. He reminds himself of his new pay cheque just in case he is assaulted again by the thought of having invested his twenties in a doomed endeavour and of starting over so late. As for his country, he decides, turning off the shower, it is only a matter of time before this clumsy puberty has passed. The washer and dryer are as much a part of the apartment's fabric as in the West, and the new brands of yogurt and juice suggest that the days of plastic buckets and steel vessels are numbered. Until then, he must take pride in his present, for to suffer it in this way betrays not just your poor stock or choices but that you don't stand by your stock and your choices. He presses his face to the towels, the blue detergent smell he has known all his childhood, and reminds himself: *This is you, this is yours – love it, love it, love it.*

# *Amanda*

At her final dinner in Imperial Heights, she notices afresh all that a week has made familiar: the silk runner, the brass casseroles, and the many little bowls on her plate that Sita, already turning invisible, keeps refilling. The meal is elaborate. There is saag paneer because it is her favourite Indian dish; corn bake, should the curry get too spicy; what she now knows is dal, not soup; yogurt, rotis, pilaf rice and pickle. Her first night here, she asked what order to eat things in, and everyone laughed like it was the most charming thing to say. Tonight, she folds her roti into a roll, one bite for each spoonful of curry, and as the subject of her new rental in Santacruz leads to a discussion on the city's suburbs, she feels reassured that Nana is right, people *are* people; no matter where you go and how confusing or daunting or hilarious they seem, there is always room to be kindred. Then again, enough Americans would find it hard to sit at a table like this without feeling or making others self-conscious, but this isn't the first time strangers are happy to adopt her; who knows why, providence, her blue eyes, her lack of aloofness for a pretty girl, and in this case, a white one too – though this final reflection makes her blush, and she brings her thoughts to focus on the flavours in her mouth: the creamy green of the saag, that hint of cumin familiar from the India Café but with more freshness.

Over the circus on her tongue, the Agashes' hyper-articulate English is still startling, given that only Naren has lived in the West. What did she make of him back then? Frankly, she had barely noticed him, the quiet Indian graduate subletting past the hall, but by the semester end, all that poking boys' ribs, letting them snap your bra and talk of who at eighteen was still a virgin made her connection with him precious: how it had grown from shyness to cordiality, to that evening when they sat on the threadbare carpet playing Scrabble, her amusement (while Naren argued 'faqir' with a q was a word) that a grown man and woman might relate so free of gender consciousness. Now, she is increasingly aware of his … masculinity. He's talking in his professorial way, and she listens more attentively than at the stopover. When he catches her watching, under pressure to speak, she brings the subject back to her gratitude for the Agashes' hospitality. 'I never thought my email to Naren would mean such a generous invitation,' she says. 'But my Aunt Jess told me that Indians are like that, so eager to include you in the family.' Laughter, and through it, Naren says to himself, 'Typical.' The down on her nape rises. Was her comment ignorant or offensive? Or merely dishonest, since it was she who sent him friendly email after email until he invited her?

The conversation moves on, but she remains vexed. 'God, Mom, don't worry. Naren is adorable,' she said, when asked if she was imposing herself on the Agashes, and Aunt Jess replied, 'Careful not to take advantage. Indians have a hard time saying no.' Her cutlery weightless, she doubts this is the case. The home may be new, but her hosts are the type who don't think twice before sending the valet to buy a soda, and sure it's all relative – in her nearly all-white town, everyone owns their house and car – but she was raised doing her share of the dishes. Naren is starting to remind her of her Boston cousins of whom Mom once said that if their manners were perfect, it was not because they found it essential to be kind, but because they did not wish to appear crass. Not that those manners kept them from disregarding your feelings if their fancy ran dry, and she recognizes this isn't the first time she has felt slighted in five days, but that she has been too grateful and too eager to be liked and to account for cultural differences to call him out, even to herself. No one sits around after dessert, and while Naren's parents, who insist on being called Lata Aunty and Raghu Uncle, ask her to visit again, Naren, who will fly out for his corporate orientation before she is up, keeps his courtesies to a goodbye and good luck.

In the guest room, she repacks her suitcases with little thought. Around her Boston cousins, calling out entitlement was a way to protect herself, yet she feels dismayed that Naren must have thought more of her when he made his invitation. When she is done, she changes into denim shorts and a black tee, then changes the tee for a white one, and heads back into the living room with her laptop and camera. Everyone has retired, even Mukta Bai, whom the Agashes refer to as 'part of the family' though she and Sita sleep on the floor in a closet-sized room under the stairs. And here, all this space! But it is too pristine, the light too revealing. The balcony is what she needs, a threshold between the cool interiors and the warm saline night, the artificial light from behind stronger as the skylight recedes. Far below, she can sense a sea of people heaving, innumerable streets, blind corners and signs in garbled tongues. All of this week, the Agashes have been there to lift her out of the chaos and into the kind of swish interiors and company she would be on the fringe of if this were Brooklyn. She allows herself to grieve the loss of this home, the access and safety it promised, an augury that fate was on her side and the roads will unravel as she sets her feet on them.

Footsteps. It's Rohit, his big head detracting from his lean body, two beers in hand. One of those for her? The pint sticks cold against her palm. He drags up a wicker chair, asks to see her camera. Of a photograph of peeling Urdu posters, he says, 'I feel like they've been there my whole life, but I never really noticed them.' Of a narrow alley through brick walls, she says, 'Even laundry on a line looks beautiful here.' He laughs at an image of a lingerie shop staffed by a woman in a burqa, and again at a window grille stuffed with everything from a bicycle to drying boxers, a yellow cat, and roses in rusted paint cans. 'It's like a cabinet of curiosities,' she says. 'Funny,' Rohit says but he doesn't laugh. She recalls the moment in Chor Bazaar when she put her foot in her mouth by lamenting the government's move to bulldoze what Naren thought a 'colonial tourist trap'. This time, anxious to impress Rohit as a culturally aware globetrotter, she restates her view with nuance, 'That bazaar had so many layers: the Victorian buildings, the mosques, the Hindu street names, the shops selling antiques and cell phones side by side. I get that India can't afford to restore it yet. I just wish we could improve the locals' lives without becoming totally generic.'

A sharp beer, fresh and cold in the throat. That was precise, her words spun out like an opinion held all her life rather than one she just sensed the contours of, but when it comes to conversation, Rohit isn't Naren. 'So what do you look for while taking a photograph?'

'For things that surprise me. Some unexpected harmony in colour or line I can isolate from all the visual excess. I love a good juxtaposition. Also … drama. Those human moments even the people in the frame don't see coming. But for that, you need luck.'

'You're talking to a film-maker,' Rohit says with mock seriousness. 'We're all about control.'

'You don't believe in luck?'

'I believe in being prepared, but you must get lucky.'

'Don't know about that,' she smiles. 'I believe in luck because it's beautiful.'

He drops his gaze. She gives his bottle a meaningful clink. 'To beauty.'

'To beauty,' he replies, looking up. They take a sip.

'Are you homesick?' he asks, his redirection less assured this time. 'I'd be homesick so far from home.'

'Honestly, it's a relief to be away,' she says, and when he asks why, she tells him that it isn't so exciting to live within a five-mile radius of where nine generations of your ancestors were born, and how her family didn't make it easier, especially Dad, who suffers a complicated equation with the land, his hands made more for books than tilling, and of his strange brand of pride and insecurity, love and resentment, self-reliance and possessiveness.

'Nine generations in one house. I didn't know that was a thing in America.'

She is ashamed of her bid for sympathy, and that in talking of home, she has eclipsed Andrei. She tells him it is rare, exceedingly so, even in her neck of the country where the pioneers first wrestled back the woods to lay their farms. She slips off her gold ring. 'This is the Harris family crest. That's my nana's family. The ring is a few years old, but the crest goes all the way back to England.'

Rohit studies the ring. His simultaneous naïveté and confidence is as attractive as in a child. She recalls the terrace party. Everyone loved him. Some knew his brother had returned, others didn't know he had one. At some point, she stopped mentioning Naren and said she had come with Rohit.

'Did they come on a ship?' he asks. 'Did they fight the Indians?'

She didn't think there was more to him than business and partying, and at his frank interest in her history, the life she represents multiplies in enigma. Half aware of her father's voice trapped in hers, she recounts the story of the Harrises, from their arrival at Cape Cod in 1643 to their move to Jaffrey a century later, and each generation since: those who tilled the land, those who built the sawmill that became the town of Harrisville, those who fought for the colonies and opened doors to the underground railroad … all the way to Nana, who proved a woman could run a farm even as her siblings sold out and moved to Boston (what with the giant harvests of the West making it cheaper to buy your food than grow it), and that in this, the simple holding of land and passing on of tradition, there was meaning. When she is done, Rohit is quiet but present. She can see his hands, the wrists set wide for a strong vein descending into a fork, its tributaries running along ridges that rise over knuckles into long fingers, flat-nailed and turned slightly up at the tip. Her ring is halfway down his thumb. 'We've sold it,' she says, 'most of the farm and forest.'

'That's sad,' he says. His voice is earnest, and suddenly, she is sad for it too.

Alone in bed that night, the electricity won't leave her limbs. She recalls the flurry of packing, Nana's sour breath as she kissed her, Dad's heartbeat through his overshirt, the dry grip of Mom's hands, and Andrei, his eyes helpless as he said, 'Come back soon,' and she said, 'I'll miss you' – but she felt only release as the plane roared off the tarmac, first the dust blowing off her, then all that was encrusted breaking away, until, at thirty thousand feet above the Atlantic, she was pure and steady as a flame. Since touchdown, however, she is among people again, and they ask: *Where are you from? Why are you here?* Of course, she has had to define herself to new friends before, but the context was always set by her name, her state, her school. This far away, the very basics are called into question; to say home is a white porch, a piano in the hall, a cabin stove, a dirt road to a hayfield, is to make a cubist caricature of the whole. Unlike Naren, who has lived in America long enough to place her, around Rohit, her mystique deepens and her possibilities multiply, each conversation a stage from which to assert who she is, and what traits or events have made her course inevitable. Even so, something always remains unsaid, and she goes on imagining the next encounter, spinning her personal mythology until it sounds like it should.

## *Rohit*

He can't say when he caught on, it wasn't anything she said, but when he looked up from her ring, she held his gaze and the air between them was charged. The next morning, he leaves for the studio before she is up. She is moving out of Imperial Heights, and with Naren at a corporate orientation in Bangalore, Rohit might have filled in, but it feels adequate that Aai has sent the driver with Amanda, and when she texts to ask if she left a book behind, he doesn't reply. Any effort he has made to tease or flatter her, he tells himself, is only to increase his brother's currency. He feels protective of Naren's feelings for her, and indignant that she should have eyes for anyone else. After work, the crew goes over to Gyaan's flat in Wadala where shop talk ends in beer and a game, and half aware of Amanda alone in her new rental, Rohit rakes in the poker chips, blows his smoke, throws his head back and laughs, and turns sheepish when, in a flash of self-scrutiny induced by an especially sweet joint, his new-found benevolence towards his brother reveals its source in his own satisfaction that he too is desirable. When he gets home, it is only eleven p.m., but with Naren and Amanda gone and his parents in bed at their usual hour, the living room is startlingly quiet. Mukta Bai comes out to check if he's had his dinner. Also, she found this while cleaning the guest room: golden grass in deep green leather. Walt Whitman. A name he never located more precisely than from 'the West', and that he now situates in the new template Amanda represents.

Lying on his bed, he takes in the cramped font, the splotches and grain of the faded pages. *I celebrate myself and sing myself.* Nothing, Rohit frowns, could be less characteristic of Naren. What did he make of Amanda when Naren first forwarded her email? A typical white woman who goes out into the world to find herself. But Amanda seems pretty found. Her social media feeds are mostly photography, and while her technique is patchy, from the earliest images of abandoned houses and hay fields to the present crop from Bombay, they share a consistent mood that is nothing like his brash-roving-kitschy impression of America but as quaint and steady as that side of her he has only sensed. There is always silence in her pictures, blurred or dappled light, an eye for the kooky, at least one bright colour for sensuality, and to meet her in person is to meet that mood, and like a mood, she Amandifies everything, from the faded posters to the sky crossed with cables the moment she clicks the shutter. Apart from that, her images betray little about her context. He can't imagine her social life in America – she doesn't give the impression she belongs to either the herd or a clique – and while the source of her individuality remains opaque, it doesn't stop her from echoing a larger world. He recalls Amanda's British grandfather, the family crest, the town of Harrisville, and how her life felt like the culmination of a long history, an emblem of a whole place.

On Friday afternoon, he invites her to a gig at Blue Frog. She takes her time to reply, but by dusk, she is on. Driving over, she is neither quaint nor still, her enthusiasm almost edgy as she shares some insights on poverty from her fellowship orientation, the slum where she will be stationed for three months, how much work there is to be done and how little time for distractions. But the lines of hurt in her posture give her away. Though his eyes are on the road, he can sense that she is curled slightly towards the door and the cruelty in her bored expression when he tries to be funny.

When she is done with her update, he gives her a Hindi swear-word tutorial, and by the time they reach the Frog, she is less stingy with her laughter. The host's recognition is instant. The familiar faces start in the lobby, faces smiling at him even as their eyes rest on Amanda, and he sees her through their gaze: neither a sun-mottled tourist nor a fuchsia-lipped model but a quality girl, her electric blue dress and black mascara brightening her face, her posture gracefully shy, and damn right Rohit Agashe should be by her side, make her laugh at a private joke and lead her into the neon dark, his hand on the small of her back.

Cyrus waves through the smoke and lasers. Ifra was too busy to come, but Manasi has and she asks after Naren. Gyaan whispers something in her ear that earns him a playful punch. Rohit and Amanda squeeze in, their thighs touching. 'This is where we grew up,' he tells her, by which he means he was sixteen when he snorted cocaine in the stalls with Cyrus, but he keeps this detail to himself. Talk of lifestyle, movies, sports, wisecracks and buffoonery: these are his modes, this is how he offers himself for knowing, but it is discomforting to think they are the sum of his person. He points out the people he knows instead. The band performing are old friends, backbenchers who have risen to become stalwarts of the gig scene. If Americans know the latest in electro-house, Amanda is no example, but her sangrias keep pace with his mojitos, and when they get up, it is clear she will dance with no one else, and when they sit back down, they sit as closely though the booth is empty. Her head is a neon blur on his shoulder, her scent fresh through the smoke – is it pine? – as she draws a semicircle above his knee with her fingertip. 'If I cut you, will curry come out?' He doesn't intend to flirt so blatantly, but drunk and in the act of play, he says, 'And if I cut you, I guess I'll find ketchup.' 'That's mean, ketchup is trashy.' 'Ha, I know. You're not one of those Americans.' 'What Americans?' 'You know,' he says, though he isn't sure, no movie or TV series has prepared him for her … not that it matters, what matters is this silliness in an attempt to be accessible, speech superfluous to the high pitch of her voice and the gentleness in his.

Back on the dance floor. Her lips are an inch away but he won't kiss her, and isn't that generous enough? At least it entitles him to hold her close, as if protecting her from the grinding crowd. As the echoes of the reverb fade, she leans in breathlessly, and unlike Manasi or Ifra who disappear into a hug, her body meets his inch for inch. They hold on longer than their acquaintance might condone. He is dimly aware of the words in his head: *What the hell, what the hell, what the hell.* Then, as if to justify the moment given no kiss followed, she leans back and says, 'God, Rohit, I'm so drunk,' and wilts on to his shoulder. She can't recall where she has saved her new address, so he drives her to Bandra. Leaning against the seat, she rolls her head from side to side, says his name. In the elevator, her lips open an inch away from his neck, her breath warm and words lost, and through the glaze of his mojitos, he decides he will tuck her in and get out, even as he kisses her temple and fumbles with the keys – when the door opens from within. 'Naren! Weren't you coming home on Saturday?' Naren checks his watch. It is Saturday. Rohit can see the dial, the large, precise numbers. Amanda looks up from his shoulder sleepily and says, 'Hello you.' Rohit should ask for help, Naren should offer it, but Naren doesn't offer and Rohit doesn't ask.

In the guest room, Rohit unbuckles Amanda's heels. Her feet are cool to touch, the clammy cool of fevers. He turns the air conditioning up, covers her with a duvet. Then he shuts the door softly, goes upstairs to Naren's room, takes a breath, and enters. 'I'm going to say it. Do you like her? Am I being an ass?'

Naren is already in bed with the lights out. He turns slowly, squints. 'You're an ass for drunk driving with her in the car.'

'She's fine. Listen, Naren. She's smart, she's hot, let's not pretend like she isn't, but if you like her…'

'I'm done with flings.'

Rohit registers two thoughts at once: that his brother has been open enough to date Americans, and that he's too conventional to marry them. As if to clear any doubt, Naren says he's thinking seriously now and intends to talk with Aai.

'Wait, the whole arranged marriage scene? Ha, Naren. I always knew you would, still I can't believe you're going to.'

Naren smiles. 'It is not like Baba's family coming to visit Aai, and they ask if she can cook, and she pretends she made the poha her mom made, and they all say wah-wah. Nowadays, you have coffee, you go around; unlike on dating apps, the intention is clear. Many of my Indian American friends met their wives this way.'

Rohit finds his way to the bed. 'In that case, can I fix you a date with Manasi? She grew up in Thane, but she has her own place in Mahim now. We were in the same batch in Wilson, then she did her MBA from IIM. Now she's this sassy corporate chick and Aai just loves her. Don't give me that look! I wouldn't bring it up if she wasn't into you.'

He can tell Naren is impressed at the mention of the institute. 'She said so?'

'She was at the Frog and it isn't her scene. We became friends because I needed her notes in college. Then we stuck. She is no hipster, but she shows up and she doesn't judge. She topped the university. What I'm saying is, she came tonight and she was wearing a dress, and her face got *this* small when I said you weren't coming.'

Naren laughs, but he makes an excuse about finding an apartment first. That he is moving out of Imperial Heights so soon is news. Naren says pre-emptively, 'It's late. I have work tomorrow.'

The shutdown hurts. Rohit should leave, but he can't help himself. 'You remember the last time we met? Your graduation day at Wharton. I always thought that trip was only a beginning, and once you settled down, we would visit more often. Then you disappeared. You didn't come home. When you called, you took all the news from Aai.'

'I was waiting for my green card. It wasn't advisable to leave the country. The process took longer than I thought.'

'You could have invited us there. All my friends would say, bro, when are you going to NYC to party with him?'

Naren is silent. 'Some people keep to themselves when they're down.'

'You were down for six years?'

'Initially, I was just swamped. I was working night and day, and then … things didn't work out.'

'Was it that promotion?'

'I quit before the appraisals.'

'You didn't think you'd get it? The recession…'

'I'd overshot my targets.'

'Then why?'

'It's late, Rohit.'

Naren's face is ghostly in the light from the door. Always the fairer one, but in the line near his mouth and the smudges under his eyes, Rohit can see the old man his brother will become. 'Right,' he says. But walking out, the tiredness in that *late* moves him, and he turns and says to the darkness, 'You'll be all right, Dada. You're home now.'

# *Amanda*

Mud-grey dunes, the furthest a hundred feet high. Bits of glass and scrap flash in the glare; the rest is an amorphous waste glued by shreds of plastic. Slowly, signs of life appear. Raptors circle the colourless sky, dogs and chicken nose their way through fresh heaps, trills of smoke tell of scavengers' fires and hands burnt by chemical waste and blistered by syringes. Up front, the garbage is distinct, the plastic unbleached, and flies buzz over rotting food and a fallen urinal. A century of trash, she thinks, just weltering in the sun. The dull, pervasive stench keeps her breathing shallow until she gets dizzy and tightens her grip on her lens. 'You can photo,' Field Officer Bhagwat says, smiling like a waiter serving up the dish a customer wants. If she was embarrassed to take a picture before, she is now embarrassed not to. Walking back to the main road, Sean has to stop by a tin wall to retch. For the past five days of their orientation, all conducted in the India Impact head office, Sean Walker has been brilliant with his opinions, questions and concerns, and watching him heave, Amanda isn't sure if she feels superior or guilty. Nadiya, the education director at a local NGO, offers Sean water, but he wants his own bottle. It wasn't the smell that got him, he says, but the sight of an urchin squatting for a shit while a hog waited at his ankles. From a shanty above, a woman is shouting.

The Ashray centre is a brick box with two floors and a rolled-up shutter. Bhagwat and Nadiya help Sean to the office upstairs. In the long room below, a young woman in a burqa is writing on a blackboard at one end, and an old woman in a sari is shouting for silence from the other, some thirty children sitting cross-legged in between. The Ashray Foundation's goal, a wall chart reads, is holistic growth. The health department supports pregnant and lactating mothers, while the one for education provides children with day care after school, tuition in core subjects, and outlets for 'creative expression'. But what, other than the free meal, can they achieve in this shack? Then a boy points to her camera and makes a sign that says 'click me'. The teacher smiles. And before Amanda can blink, the children are all over her, their bony faces breaking into grins as they jostle to get in the frame. Oh heart – even if this moment is merely a distraction from difficult lives, the impact is clear.

Or so she thinks, until she notices two girls at a distance, their backs to the wall and hips close in solidarity. They must be ten or twelve, their green uniforms unstitched for length, and while the one with long hair can't resist a laugh, the other, a square face ringed with curls, is watching like she knows exactly what's going on: the camera a weapon, this white woman here to assault them with her empathy, to add to their burden the burden of her response. 'What are your names?' Amanda asks. Long hair says she is Humera, and her friend, Rafia. 'I'd love to take your picture,' Amanda says. 'I'll give you a copy.' Rafia shakes her curls, no. 'Want to click the picture then? I'll teach you.' 'No camra,' Rafia says, her spine resolute, leaning on nothing but on the weight of her fists in her pockets. The other children are watching. 'Learn on mine,' Amanda says. 'Before I leave, I'll try to get the budget to buy one for the centre.' The hope that Rafia isn't holding her cards too long is all over Humera's face as Rafia says, 'Nadiya Ma'am, no.' 'Good God. I'll speak to Nadiya,' Amanda says, and the final spark of Rafia's resistance is doused; she turns to Humera who smiles back in support, and Amanda's chest is a confluence of triumph and shame at winning over this proud heart with such trifles.

Since Sean refuses to recover, Nadiya books them Ubers home at Ashray's expense. Riding back, Amanda thinks of how shocked she was by Chor Bazaar's fleshiness, the stink of meat and faeces, a child's nose stuffed with flies, the fermented taste of coconut water as the vendor's machete hacked a shell so close to his thumb. Here, in Deonar, she has gone blank. Everything is broken, every home a city bird's nest, a chaotic assemblage of broken brick, plastic, wire and tin. Like the landfill, the scene going past is a façade, life-sized but impenetrable, her every emotion underscored by the words: *So this is what it is*. The drive to Santacruz is two hours in traffic. As she takes in the endless swathes of dirty and cramped habitation, the people and animals living on the sidewalk, their honking-braying reality experienced as fragments of sight and sound, as chaos and a blood-thrumming heat, any superiority she felt over Sean ebbs away. When she gets home, the thought of an uncooked dinner makes her fall face down on the bed and cry.

After the tears stop, she unwraps her last granola bar and gets online. Naren is posting statistics about the Indian economy. Now she understands his obsession with change. The thought of herself drunk at the Agashes makes her cringe. So do her photographs of roses in paint cans and colour-saturated laundry. Worse still are the older pictures of antlers on wood, hand-knit sweaters, buttered scones, a blue mandolin – all of it so comforting, rich and whimsical. She has spent a day in the convoluted bowels on which the white homes and glass towers of the world rise, and everything of beauty she knows turns wan, the way a pretty girl's paleness becomes evident when you hear her gut is rotten. She recalls her family's cynicism: Nana's playful remark about Americans always needing a frontier, Dad's support for a trip he saw as normative in young people of her background, Mom's insistence that she was being a perfect Harris Martin in evading the real issue, and Andrei, around whom to say 'India' had become like taking the name of another lover. But where she once felt guilty about cocking her blessings a snook, they now appear not only suffocating but also morally problematic. She starts to delete the photographs. Once her homepage is clear, she turns on her camera. The new pictures are a relief. While her memory of the slum remains abstract, the images affirm her refusal to transcend the moment. Even in this digital age, when filters can make a photograph look like a painting, some connection to the event remains: you can't dream up your subject, you search it out. That is the reason she is here. She uploads a take of the landfill in all its post-apocalyptic despair.

A video call from Andrei. In the morning light, his strong, sleepy face is beautiful. 'Is that a granola bar? I didn't know you get granola in India.' She reminds him that today was her first day on-site. 'Right. I saw your picture.' She tells him about Nadiya, and Sean's pathetic response, which validates her own. Andrei says, 'That's intense, to constantly judge emotions on a scale of usefulness. People feel what they feel.' So it starts, and within minutes they are fighting. 'I can't see why you're defending this person you've never met,' she shouts, and Andrei shouts, 'I can't see why you have to be so negative!' But for the first time, his positivity no longer feels informed, it feels smug. On the other hand, her stomach has taken the landfill. Her pictures are good. 'The old ones were good too,' Andrei says. Calming down, she says, 'Maybe. But when you see people starving, you just feel, I don't know, like art that cares only for form is half-baked…' Andrei listens, then he starts to justify Jaffrey. He knows hardship. He has experienced life in a cold-water flat in Moldova before he immigrated to the States. He was her real until he too became beautiful. Firmly, she says, 'Deonar demands a response. I'm not sure what it is. It is a lot to process, honey, and I can't, not with Nan and Dad and Mom and you panicking about where I am and what I'm doing and if it is taking me away. I need time … on my own … to figure out how I can contribute. What I'm saying is, I need a break.'

She didn't expect the conversation to go this way, yet she realizes that she has come to the table like a good bargainer, ready to walk away from the deal. But when Andrei asks, resigned, if there is any point in waiting, she feels a surge of tenderness. This is her first month in a new world, and she isn't ready to give him up entirely. Of course he must continue to stay at the farm; India is terrific, but it is no framework for a life, and he knows his Mandy, how things always come to her slowly but powerfully. His torso collapsed, Andrei says he understands. When he proposed in the days after Thanksgiving, she didn't say yes but she didn't say no either; she asked for a year, then for the fellowship, now this break, and yet again, Andrei says he will wait. He agrees there is no need to upset Nana or her parents just yet, and as the dichotomy between her desires collapses, the carousel of her thoughts spins faster, secured by a single bolt against the consequences of dizzying speed, and there it is again – the old blankness, less a bull-headed force than a cool magnet pulling her on, her intentions sanctified by honesty. 'Thank you,' she says, and she means it, but when they cut the call, she can't tell if she is feeling relief or despair; the emotion is not as clear as the one on the flight.

A street light comes on. Outside, the buildings are morphing, the saris running down their balconies like flags. She takes a shower and pulls on the printed nightgown she bought off a street cart for a dollar, and a feeling of lightness grows. She surveys the icebox, the vegetables so small and bright as she sets them to boil, pretending to go about it as her landlady would, with a matter-of-factness and familiarity, an unthinkingness in sprinkling spice, a quiet dignity around the gas-stained stove and always-wet toilet. She had the option of living with other fellows rather than alone – or almost alone, since her landlady, who has some deal with the India Impact

Foundation, lives next door – but at the first sight of the studio, she was sold. The building is of middle height, the room has a private entrance, and not a single item beyond the necessities – such a change from all the stuff back home, stuff weighing the attic on their heads and rising from the basement to shackle their feet. Must be an Indian quirk, she thinks, recalling the white walls and tiles of Imperial Heights, its expensive fittings still betraying the same austerity … but the breezy sensuality of her new nightgown gives the room another flavour: an easy slip away from the ascetic, no nest in the light but a burrow shrouded by the city, smelling of a mild, synthetic scent, its dinginess electric.

She touches her breast, imagining a man's hands, deep-veined and colourless until they turn dark, and at the thought of dark hands on pale skin, she shivers. So that early stage where desire is yet undistinguished from curiosity has passed, and it is clear that the moment Rohit approached her at the party on the terrace, his face coming into focus from the crowd, she knew their bodies would be compatible. She can't recall a word they said, yet in the days after, she felt his force field intercepting hers; it was him she hoped to run into when she went back out on her last evening at the Agashes, and she didn't have to turn to know who was in the living room; she could sense his movements with a cock-eared, creature-like intensity. What was she trying to infect him with in all that talk of drama and beauty? She adds salted butter and pasta to the broth. The steam pricks her face. Rohit hasn't texted since that drunken night at Blue Frog. He is playing games, ignoring her, indulging her, inviting her out, and what is the whole deal with Naren? In his company, Rohit changes, treating her with distance or deference, as if it is only his brother's right to be her friend. He is just a boy, a silly boy. Or then, to be a foreigner is to feel like a child, over-stimulated by yet impervious to reality, blunt to dynamics obvious to everyone else, but all these doubts recede the moment her phone lights up.

*Everyone is missing you. / I miss being there.* And now, the kinetics with which their forces are colliding. *Do you do lunch dates? / I'll be at work most weekdays, but maybe come over for a nightcap? / Even better,* Rohit texts, and then there is an awkward pause of better-for-what. How we are reduced in the moment of attraction, but it is corniness that assuages doubt in subtler signs. Roh-hit, Row-heat. She lays his name in her modest continuum of lovers, testing its unfamiliarity, its new familiarity, as she puts the pasta in the fridge and makes a shopping list. With the Agashes chaperoning her everywhere, it feels like an achievement just walking to the end of the street, browsing aisles, counting cash, and lugging home a dozen purchases from salad greens to incense sticks. Already those potential dates have fallen back like dominoes – Rohit is coming over tonight, ostensibly to house-warm the studio with a joint. Neither mentioned Naren. When she gets home, she takes a second shower, rubs cream into dry spots, perfume that will settle into musk. She tries not to make it elaborate. Unlikely anything will happen tonight, it would not be innocent yet, but as the sky deepens, she feels increasingly confident that the sophistication of an affair is not beyond a girl from the small town of Jaffrey. Look at the ease with which she can already compartmentalize her affection for Andrei's Snapchats of furry animals from the blood rush of a text that Rohit's here.

When she opens the door, she can tell from their hug that he is nervous and it feeds her poise. 'Welcome to my mansion,' she says, stepping aside for him to survey the room: the bedcover carpeting the floor, Aunt Jess's sari for a curtain, the white walls softened by a string of lights and Nora Jones's piano. Suddenly, he is laughing. 'Why does the room smell like a temple?' It is the incense! 'Nothing could be further from my intention,' she says.

'Oh no,' he says, 'I didn't think so.' They snuff out the incense, pour the wine he has brought into coffee mugs. Though she didn't plan to, in her new recklessness, or to pay him back for being aloof, she tells him about Andrei, even shows him a picture. 'He's very handsome,' Rohit says, a little too dramatically, before she adds, 'We're on a break,' and explains what it means as if she has explained it a million times because truth has that quality of sounding rehearsed and inevitable. In fact, it is surreal her nerves aren't more on edge, nothing surprising her entirely since she has anticipated surprise; what seemed absurd a week ago, perfectly rational now; her reason, desire and conscience aligned as they settle on the bedcover, and when he is rolling a joint and spills the tobacco, she goes up to salvage the bits of hash before she leans in, still on her knees, pulls him forward by the open ends of his collar, and kisses him, first on the cheek, and then, when he doesn't resist, on the mouth.

# *Rohit*

For the first time since moving to Imperial Heights, Rohit opens Aai's 'Happy Memories' shelf. Here, framed in teak, is his baba's grandfather, who walked from Velneshwar to Ratnagiri; here, Ajoba, who moved the family from the Konkan to Pune; and here, Baba and Aai smiling shyly at their engagement, a year before moving to Bombay. There is also a monochrome of Aai's extended family, most of them estranged since her parents' early deaths and brother's pettiness that once made her sigh she had no home other than Bandra. The rest of the shelf is a mess of plastic albums filled with matte images of birthday parties, summers with cousins, the standard family photo at the Taj … before the world went digital. There are also other accidental remnants of their old life in the study, like a collection of English poetry Aai won at an elocution competition in '81, and Baba's student-day copies of *Gitanjali* and *War and Peace*. That his parents were ever young, reciting poetry, reading Tagore and Tolstoy! He has never asked what they thought of the Emergency or the Soviet Union; when they speak, it is always about the boys, as if their own history began with the birth of their children. He shuts the glass doors on the shelf. There is nothing like Amanda's crest here, no ancestors of distinction, nor any of the things that constitute the sensibility he was warming to when she drew the line between what is hers with that word: *westernized*. She was only teasing, imitating the way he said dude, yet he was offended. He doesn't think of himself as influenced by the West but simply the best-in-class globally, and he has no desire to be anyone but himself, thank you.

Over lunch he asks his parents about the Agashes' origins, and Baba doesn't use the name Chitpavan. He simply says they are Kokanastha, or people from the Konkan coast, and when Rohit tries to confirm that if several of his cousins have light eyes or fair skin it's because they were inbred to retain their ancient Aryan features, Baba laughs and says, 'If you're interested in history, call your Ravi Kaka, the Chitpavan.' Aai laughs too, and Rohit pretends to get the joke. Not that he needs to call anyone. An hour on the internet throws up so many theories, he is surprised. Some claim the Chitpavans were Brahmins who trekked south from the great civilization on the Ganga, others believe they were Egyptian Greeks who sailed east to escape an Arab invasion, one says they were Turkish, and one, Persian, but these get a lot of hate. The only thing all the theorists agree on is that the Chitpavans trace their lineage to Parshurama. There's a blue-blooded Vedic sage, Rohit thinks with satisfaction, and a handsome one, not unlike Christ except that his shoulder bears an axe. According to the myth, Parshurama was exiled to 'the hinterlands' for a vengeful massacre. That's how he came down south, and standing on the hills, he threw his axe into the sea and pulled up the skinny coast called the Konkan. Then he found new disciples by cremating corpses from a shipwreck and resurrecting them to life. Chitpavan derives from the Sanskrit 'chit' for mind, and 'pavan' for purified by fire. When Rohit thinks of Ravi Kaka's character, Baba's joke makes sense.

That evening, he drives to Naren's new apartment, a handsome two-bedroom in Worli with a view of the sea. After Amanda moved out, things with his brother felt strained, and this would be less confusing if Naren actually desired her. Then Naren refused his offer to set him up with Manasi, but the next day, he asked for advice on renting a place, and in helping Naren with his contacts, his hustling with brokers, and talking at the corner tea shop to get a sense of the deal, all concluding in an agreement in less than three weeks, Rohit has gained the recognition he wanted for the adult he has become. Naren opens the door to a snowstorm of foam packaging. The furniture that came with the place is outsized, and the new home theatre he has purchased makes everything appear larger and more expensive still. They get on their knees and extricate the speakers he was struggling with. Then he pours a duty-free Laphroaig into crystal that still smells of cardboard and they toast to his new home and discuss Bombay's real estate, which in turn gets them talking about their old neighbourhood in Bandra East, and on the subject of their parents never speaking of their past, Rohit mentions his plans to visit the Konkan on what Amanda called a 'dig-your-roots tour'. Naren asks if it was her idea. Rohit says, 'I was reading about our community, and Amanda called, and yeah, I guess it was.'

Naren laughs softly. 'For white women dating brown men, it's all about the civilizing project.'

He isn't dating Amanda. They haven't given what they share a name, but his brother rarely talks about his life in America, so he simply says, 'I'll pretend I'm sophisticated enough not to need an explanation.'

Naren laughs again, this time with warmth. 'You know how it was in the Bandra East days. Aai and Baba were all about getting on with life. When I got to NYC, I had a sense of the lifestyle I wanted and it was pretty much the same stuff on a grander scale. A big portfolio, a flashy condo and car, the latest gadgets and suits. But I also wanted finer things, things we think of as cultured or sophisticated, and here I had no map. I thought if I worked hard, the rest would come. Then I met Cathy and she gave me … the particulars.'

So, that is her name. Rohit feels proud at being taken into confidence as Naren recalls a visit to her family summer house in Connecticut. He doesn't say much about Cathy; mostly, he describes the home, which is fair since they have been pushing furniture around, yet the detail is startling given that the visit was years ago and Rohit doesn't recall his brother as having any interest in aesthetics before he left for America. And here, Naren is talking of heirloom roses, a sleigh bed from Cathy's childhood, bookshelves lined with leather spines on quaint subjects like map-making and taxidermy, the private woodland where they went for a stroll and Cathy's father told him the names of the birds. When they came in, her mother baked a pie with strawberries from the garden and served it on blue china that had been in the family for generations. Naren's plate was cracked and there was a charming story about the crack, and another about the recipe, and a third about the antique stove. The conversation was never about anything practical, but according to Naren, to say you liked Van Gogh in company like that was to show up as a brute. And eating the pie off that cracked plate, for the first time, Naren recognized the value of tradition and worthy insiders.

'They say America holds on to these things because their age of domination is over, that they are looking back instead of to the future,' he says. 'Still, it's funny how one goes from a five-thousand-year-old civilization to a three-hundred-year-old country to learn about nostalgia.'

Rohit thinks of Amanda's postcard, the splotched pages in her book, her photographs. Nostalgia. That is what he was responding to. He says, 'The other day Amanda called me westernized. She didn't mean it badly, but I felt like … I don't know…'

Naren's expression turns cynical. 'You better know your abstract art, but there is also this pressure to be more Indian than Western.

By that, I mean Indian as white people want to see Indian. They want access to everything, but everyone else better stick to what is native. And we buy into it and not just for social currency. We were brought up with the same half-baked knowledge of the Bible as the Gita, and in the West, I felt this need to define who I am in terms of where I come from. Amanda is all right. She's cautious of the term *exoticism*, she's self-effacing about growing up in a town that speaks one language, but then she'll judge us for being privileged in a poor country. It doesn't matter that income inequality is a fact of life here and even good people get desensitized.'

Rohit laughs. 'The organic food and pictures with slum kids is exactly the stuff that goes by the label Indie-hipster, but it's cute how unaware she is that it's a type.'

'Which is fine. We're in the age of social media; who isn't cultivating an image? My problem is when you flaunt it like it's some ethical choice. In the end, you can tell a people's privilege from their complacence that they are the good, the aware, the standard-bearers.'

Rohit takes a sip of his Scotch to cover his mouth. He is embarrassed for his brother, the last of the brain-drain generation that truly wanted to be American, and for exposing his own rootlessness to Amanda. His ego asserts itself. He resents the quality that had him charmed. He will be informed, he decides, but he will not be Amandified. That he recognized this feeling when Naren articulated it, or that Naren's saying so might even have created it in him, is irrelevant. For some time, he has felt his life hovering in an endemic superficiality that goes by the labels of 'hip' and 'cool', and if the national election revealed how out of sync he is with his soil, Amanda and Naren have exposed the limits of belonging elsewhere. Tonight, however, he has a better idea of what might constitute authenticity. If he is going to the Konkan coast, he should leave before the rains. Driving home, the Laphroaig unfurling streamers in his brain, he sees the craggy drama of the Western Ghats, Parshurama's axe pulling up the coast from the sea, and the Peshwa armies thundering over it. True, he recalls little more than the scaffolding, the images subliminal, the facts taken in sideways while focused on objects more immediate – as a man of the future, authenticity was the opposite of tradition, and until he met Amanda, it never occurred to him to look for it in the past – but if we are talking of the past, any Indian has plenty. That the family trail goes cold beyond his great-grandfathers hardly matters. Genealogy is trivia when your heritage stretches back five thousand years.

His fingers are jittery on the wheel when Amanda texts him a selfie with slum 'children' who look closer to their teens. *Have fun with them,* he replies, *just not too much.* She responds with a recorded message of her laughter. She is wearing a cotton kurta, a first. So, when a brown boy wears Converse, he is inauthentic, but when a white girl wears a kurta, she is just being herself. *I'm coming over,* he texts and swerves away from Bandra West. The world starts to pixelate. Tantric sky. Ink-blue amphitheatre pinned with neon clouds. Buses bulge through the alleys. Highways clog and release. Santacruz. For two weeks, he has come here every other night to be stripped, licked, bitten, to taste hair, hoist flesh, thrust at each other until they can't tell which thigh is hers, which tongue his. They've confirmed early impressions, asked, when did you know? Fact is, their bodies knew before them. Fact is, they are soft on each other like only strangers can be, too little context for contempt, just enough for endless potential. By the time he reaches her studio, he is properly drunk. Each time, the room feels more personalized than the last. There's a one-eyed teddy on the bed, hazy polaroids on the fridge, her jade Ganesha (a 'lucky charm' her Hare Krishna aunt bought in Rishikesh), and the revulsion he feels for these objects only magnifies his hard-on. Fuck the wine, fuck the pillows – come *here*. Her kurta turns black as she peels it off, her skin gold to green, and … what?

She has her period. She doesn't mind if he doesn't. In fact, it's safe. He can hardly see in the dark, only smell it as she pulls the plug. Iron. Ink. Wine. The room stuffy and metallic as a womb. Go with it before you go soft. A womb, and they are twins, one light, one dark, their bodies matched in size and force. Her fingers grip his hips, part his ass, thrust him in. Fist of a cunt, muscular and wet. Her jaw unexpectedly small. Her neck in his hand. Inside of her upper teeth. Ribs of the pallet. Gaping like a fish. Snapping spit. Air … air, her breasts rise like they are welling out of water, her moans go soundless. He has hit the back of her. She is finite. Taken. But then her sides open, her texture changes. With one arm, she lifts his torso, brings her calf on to his shoulder. A different tightness, a Mobius strip of muscle twisting in. Ink irises turn clear as her head tips forward in a shaft of street light. Stop. Did he, no, did she, no. She has to … okay. He peels himself off. Water splashing in the toilet. The tap turned on to distract from other sounds. He looks at his body, flexes his core. The legs stretching away. Something stupid about the toes. His head is clear but he's gone limp. Oh well. His turn for the loo. Faint smell of Lysol. Water echoing in the pipes. Piss sapphire, agate with her blood. Its baseness excites him, it feels like a repudiation, can't say of what. Back outside. Pale linen folds, her lying long and swollen at the centre. He moves in on the narrow bed, puts a palm on her belly. Red leaves, damp and burning, though he's never seen the fall. Cave of spores, of fern-fingers opening, of slugs, neon centipedes, the primitive life he collected in jars as a kid – a landscape of skin, sweat like dew over a forest, beads, beads shaking. Her mature womb is no longer daunting. He is hard again. This time she mounts him, one palm on his shoulder, the other pulling the band off her tousled bun. Her hair opens like the hood of a cobra, a many-headed snake, her indigo lover in spasms. Tonight, their moves are violent – who is fucking, who is being fucked, how did their bodies get here? She is centrifugal, she sucks in everything, the sheets, the bits of tobacco, the light, until she collapses into herself like a sun, and he backward into the darkness, darkness, and space.

# *Amanda*

The India Impact Fellowship is not an excuse for an exotic adventure. She has no intention of taking leave unless she is sick, yet when Rohit leaves her studio without a morning kiss, she regrets turning down his invitation to his roots tour. She recalls herself at his age, her readiness for the Town Histories, those two mysterious tomes in Dad's library, and her embarrassment at the authors' desperation to prove that Jaffrey was the quintessential New England town, heroically wrested from a clash of civilizations, when in fact its foundation was laid long after the natives, thinned out by disease, had abandoned the land, the furthest encounter with them (pages of mounting suspense to this climax) a night vigil in which a teenaged Scot heard 'something' in the grasses. Still, for years she took a shovel to the past, digging until she was buried under the mud scooped out, and within, only scraps: nothing known of the first Harris before he docked on Cape Cod, or the Martins beyond Grandpa Joe's father, a schoolteacher in rural England, and even less on her mom's side, who goes back four generations to Holland, where she, Amanda, once went looking for ... what? An alley bearing her mother's maiden name and a clutch of graves. Rohit's history, she imagines, has far more to offer, going back, as he claims, five thousand glorious years. Then again, Deonar has stripped any history of enchantment.

She is all set to leave – kurta and scarf, practical shoes, her backpack (with a toilet roll) on her shoulders, her camera on her chest – when she notices a postcard slipped under her door. The front is a Wyeth summer scene of pines though lace curtains; the back, a familiar scribble. She exhales. Just the kind of image to inspire Andrei. *We're out of hay so we've been cleaning out the barn and bailing up the broken bales … two azaleas bloomed in our flower bed … Nana says the unusual spring heat made them mature early* … and he goes on as if these details of their life together are a talisman that will not let him down. He's panicking, she thinks sadly, but she resents him too. In her version of their story, her love is compassion stretched thin, the outcome of an elaborate conspiracy not just between her family and Andrei, but her school, church, society, all of America. In her version, the Amanda in India is consistent with the earnest and rebellious child she was. It is the Amanda in the middle years she can hardly recognize. That Amanda drove home from UPenn in a beat-up Chevy, cleaned out Dad's cabin to Joanna Newsom plucking a harp, stuck poems by Elizabeth Bishop on the fridge, and learned quilting from Nana, a craft Mom rolled her eyes at, but then the idea that young people had to break free was passé; it felt more important to belong. Was it a reaction to not fitting in with the city crowd in college, or something wider, a folk revival in response to soulless modernity, a self-preserving lie that happiness could be found in mindful domesticity if you were lucky enough to have a home through the recession? Whatever the case, that vision had slowly become a cage, and Andrei's relevance so fused with it that to outgrow one was to outgrow both.

Is she a monster for falling out of love with a good man? And is he all that good, and was it ever love? There was *attraction*, there was *the ideal*, but before her feelings had been tested or had time to mature, Andrei had raised the stakes by inviting himself home, ingratiating himself with her people, and demonstrating such affability and care that to call things off is no longer a question of breaking only one heart. Reluctant to stick the postcard on the fridge, she slips it into Dad's copy of *Leaves of Grass*, a parting gift she has almost lost twice, as if trying to forget precisely the way of life he wants her to remember. Nana's words come back, 'Wear all the masks you want, just don't be surprised by your face when it catches you in a mirror.' Locking her studio door, she blushes to recall how she often describes her town and history to Rohit, the very things she is in flight from, as charmed. No wonder he flinched when she teased him about being westernized, though she didn't mean it how he took it. She was merely calling out his bourgeois taste; her own choices, she believes, are inspired by the common people here. From tomorrow, she intends to take the local train to work.

And riding to the eastern fringe of the city in an Uber, she feels an unshakeable pride in that, of the three applicants whom Ashray's founder, the formidable Anu Sehgal, recommended for the fellowship, she is the one they have chosen for the notorious site of Asia's largest slum. These early glimmers of approval have strengthened her conviction that she is not here on account of what she wants to get away from, but what she is moving towards. After all, there were many ways to escape Jaffrey: if she sought out this route, it's because she was born with her mother's instinct for an image, her father's social conscience, Nana's grit, and a final element entirely her own that Deonar will reveal. Where her break with Andrei felt justified by her honesty and his acquiescence, it now feels sanctified by something grander: her *purpose*. Her poetic descriptions of Jaffrey to Rohit were not insincere. She was merely responding to the violent love you feel for an ideal before you abandon it, like the violent love you feel for a person before you leave him. As for Rohit, he is merely a catalyst. The blood is flowing freely in her veins again, and if it was not him, someone or something else would have opened the gates to this freedom, this state essential to becoming the Amanda she can be. But as her Uber goes deeper into Deonar, a new unease takes hold: the old beasts were known and outside herself; here in India, she has only herself to hold accountable for who she is revealed to be and for the consequences as yet unforeseeable.

## *Naren*

The décor is the universal office décor, the smell the ubiquitous office smell, but here in Bombay, he is already an associate partner with a private cabin. Soon the corkboard will be pinned, the whiteboard marked and the shelf studded with trophies. *A partner with art on his walls* – that was his ambition as a young man in NYC where he spent his Sundays browsing the city's art museums with Cathy. She had introduced him to the Abstract Expressionists, and it seemed fair to conclude Degas's dancing girls were not for him who had never seen a ballet, nor Gauguin whose Tahitians caused a vague embarrassment, nor Sargent's pale faces and dark parlours that made him feel like a stranger looking in through a window. But he too had known the vitality trapped in a Pollock, and Rothko's slow dawn, the fragile grace of Calder's bower, the freshness of Twombly's spring; these were paintings that addressed the mute creature in him, the chord unstruck by history. Nevertheless, the prints he intends to order now are not from the MoMA but the NGMA in Delhi. As his final emails go out, he scrolls their webpage. This Gaitonde might project his sensibility: the tantric signs received through an ancient collective past, the ochre and cyan refreshingly contemporary, while the meditative strokes and translucency of light were a reminder that all is maya.

Maya, maya, maya, he thinks as he packs his bag. Is his interest in art less about what he sees in the painting than what he wants to see in the mirror? Art came after he flew West, but what about

Western music – does it matter he came to Bach unschooled; does that count for legitimacy? There was a time his delight in genius had nothing to do with where the artist was from. When and how had that changed? He recalls his model for a partner with art on his walls. Lawrence was a senior partner at KMC whom he had hoped to charm, but when they spoke, he often felt that Lawrence was looking past his shoulder. No doubt, other partners like Persaud saw Naren ace his appraisal but Persaud was thought of as slippery. While it was apparent Persaud was cultivating a coterie of coloured people, it never occurred to Naren that Lawrence's was white. He simply thought that Lawrence was a harder man to impress and was grateful when the popular Weiss took a shine to him. Weiss validated his worth in a way Persaud did not. Naren did not want any credit he hadn't earned; even now, he thinks of himself as 'Naren', sometimes as only 'I', and not in terms of what racial team he is on. For all the Agashes' new money, in this deeply wedged notion of meritocracy, he is still as middle class as they come.

Waiting for the elevator, Naren is returned to the present by LK's gaze. An associate partner in the same vertical, LK has tried ribbing him about being a naïve 'Westerner'. What is the source of LK's cockiness? That an IIM degree is the equivalent of Wharton for fish who never left this pond? Or is LK's swagger like Rohit's, a man who knows every inch of the ground under his feet and how to set it spinning? The doors open to a thick blast of tropical air. Waiting for his Uber, Naren feels annoyed at how his conversations with Rohit keep riling up old wounds and desires. But his mood changes when he scans an email from Cyrus Bulsara's boyfriend, the affluent and charming Jay Malani, with a résumé attached, and another from Ankush Jain, Baba's contact at Brahma Industries and nephew of the billionaire R.K. Jain. Here, then, are the advantages of moving home. Naren envisions calling R.K. Jain a client, and LK's envy, and suddenly affectionate towards his family, he texts Aai that he will be home for dinner. *We won't start without you*, she replies instantly. When he reaches Imperial Heights, Sita is setting the table with the good plates, but now that he has his own apartment, he is less judgemental of his parents' home.

After dinner, once his parents retire, he takes Rohit up for a drink on the balcony, and the talk turns to their schooldays at Saint Stanislaus. 'The climate was so different back then,' Naren recalls. 'The markets had liberalized, but the jobs hadn't kicked in, and if you were the class topper, everyone believed it was your destiny to go West. England, sure, but England was cold and hungover and racist. America was the New World, all of the promise, none of the baggage, or at least baggage that didn't have to do with you. When I got the job at Goldman Sachs, I thought, *this is it*.'

'I remember,' Rohit says, refilling his cognac. 'You were ready for the grind. You called Aai on your first night in New York and said, This is my karmabhoomi.'

'I did,' Naren says, smiling at this youthful grandiosity. 'I was in the right circles. I was working ninety hours a week. At the end of my first year in banking, I was the top-ranking analyst. But by then, I wanted into consulting. Banks pay more at the start, but I had the long view in mind. I wanted to make partner.'

'So, what happened?' Rohit asks. 'You never tell the whole story. Why did you leave New York?'

Naren sips his cognac. Whenever he and Rohit talk of America, the unspeakable in his story takes the form of political views or social commentary. At first he wrote this off as stoicism. Then there was his fear of losing Rohit's adulation, though by now it is clear no rejection will follow. While his parents can't comprehend the seismic shift these past years have meant for him, it is Rohit who, sensing his pain, was kind enough to say, You're home now. And looking past the twilit city, Naren recognizes that shame is the cork in his glottis that won't let the words out, the flint in his heart against which minor insults ricochet and that turns his arguments personal, and this shame stretches beyond him, an ambient shame that has settled in his bones for all the humiliation that he and his ancestors have suffered. 'What happened?' he says. 'Wall Street crashed is what happened. I was three months into my new job at KMC. The consultancies weren't hit as badly as the banks, but the recession touched everyone and insecurities were running high. When I aced my appraisal, there was the usual jealousy, but also surprise. People expect the hard-working, nerdy Indian to nail a spreadsheet, but to ace it at consulting during a downturn?'

Rohit's listening is louder than anything he might say. Naren goes on, 'That was when Cathy noticed me. She was a few years my senior and started taking me on her pitches. The economy was in shambles. Most projects involved restructuring companies and letting people off. It was an emotional time. She made the first move. I was flattered … you understand. In less than a quarter, I was pretty much staying at her apartment, though it was still hush-hush at the office. But things get around, and when they did, there was a recoil. My friend Eric said to my face – and what was stunning was how innocent his exasperation was – he said, I don't get it, you have everyone under this spell. I actually felt sorry for him. We were classmates in Wharton, and I had reached out to him before applying to KMC. He had always been a sport about my grades in school, though maybe there was some assumption that social success was his domain. One time, a senior partner called me *clever little Indian* and it wasn't a compliment. When I learned it was Eric's phrase, I was too proud to confront him. But I started to think, is there something twisted about me?'

'What did Cathy think?' Rohit asks indignantly.

'When we broke up, she never gave me a reason. We were fighting over something silly, and bam, she called things off. When I saw that we were past honest talk, I didn't push it. I threw myself into work thinking I'd let the results speak, but as the fiscal year ended, the thought of the next appraisal wouldn't let me sleep.'

Naren pauses. How to describe the strange psychology that set in at that time? He was afraid that acing his appraisal would reinforce the negative perceptions about him, but he was also afraid that if he didn't, his peers would sit back smiling that the first time was a fluke. Suddenly, it seemed like both success and failure would confirm what he could not bear to admit: that in America, he was expected to come a close second, but not to win. His ambition, which had felt pure until that point, became corrupted. The schadenfreude at his breakup with Cathy and the way she was avoiding him didn't help. He started to act unnaturally. He was aggressive when his pride kicked in and fawning when his insecurity did. If there was any doubt he wasn't what Eric made him out to be, he snuffed it out himself. He was still performing well, but pay cuts had given way to layoffs, and he started growing paranoid. When a client offered him a job at his back office in Waverly, he took it. He quit a week before the appraisals. He told himself that it meant job security and a sponsor until he got his green card and paid off his student loans. Sound logic, though in retrospect, he is quite certain KMC would not have fired him. The move to Waverly was a huge career mistake, but when he made it, he wasn't himself.

Gently, Rohit asks, 'Was it the breakup … or the racism?'

'Was what?'

'The thing that didn't let you sleep. Before the appraisal.'

Naren has never used the term 'racism' in his context despite the Black Lives Matter protests going on when he left America. His wounds are more elusive, yet the word singes them like a hot blade. Rohit's lack of subtlety reveals his innocence, and Naren becomes aware of his need to cauterize his own pain taking on the guise of educating his little brother, whatever the cost. 'How do I explain this?' he says. 'You're in the financial district, no one is going to call you names, but it's not like race doesn't exist. We aren't brown there the way we're brown in the UK where you find an Indian busboy or delivery guy because there's this long history of migration from all classes. Most Indians in America got there in the sixties. They were educated, they had pedigree, they only needed jobs. We're one of the highest-earning ethnic minorities, there's almost a positive bias.'

'But there's also a glass ceiling?'

Naren shrugs. 'We corporate people hate to admit how much of a tribe the office is. You're there for the brand and money, but it's also a community. You have friends and enemies, mentors, protégés, the opposite sex. So when a crisis turns on the heat, tribal loyalties play up. There was no *incident* per se. I could just sense it in the air. The snipes, the exclusion, the doubt I wasn't allocated resources for reasons other than my competency. New York isn't Waverly, but New York hurts more than Waverly. If someone calls you names in the street, you can take it on the chin. But to think you're an equal only to find…'

As he is speaking, Naren is aware that the cognac has loosened his tongue, but he has carried the story for so long, the words come out past his defences. 'The worst part is,' he says to Rohit as much as to himself, 'you want into the club, so you neuter yourself to become this guy who doesn't make things uncomfortable. You never get angry. You sit at a white table and talk about blacks or Mexicans like they're coloured and you're not. Then you get the top rank or dream girl, and the whites are shocked, but they're too polite to articulate even to themselves what they find obnoxious about you. Not like they need to; they're not at the receiving end. Heck, I don't know. Maybe it's the natural progression of any kind of love. You get so carried away at the thought of total acceptance … you think if there's been no limit so far, there is none, so you are freer and freer until it socks you in the face: the point beyond which to be entirely true to yourself is to give up any hope of being loved. It is our excitement at the things we have in common and our faith that we're equal stakeholders which warps our judgement when we go in, and by the time we get out, the unbearable thought that the role of cultural difference is overstated, and that I might be uniquely insufferable.'

In the cab home, Naren reruns his words. More than 'racism', he is agitated by his use of 'love', a feminine word, sentimental, exposing. Whatever Rohit said in reply, his boyish face trying to man up to the moment, it did not have the confidence of *you're home now.* Naren rolls the window down. A drop in pressure is towing in the monsoon clouds. Though he gave Cathy away, the person he still abstracted was his dear friend and colleague, Eric. Eric didn't have Cathy's pedigree though you could hardly tell what he lacked, only that something should account for how closely he cared to project an ideal. He had impeccable teeth, a tennis-court laugh, his belts always matched his wingtips, and for someone that attractive, he was hardly aloof. In fact, he was proactive in befriending Naren, ever hearty and candid. But inwardly, Eric believed he was number one. None of Eric's friends were losers, though few were doing better than him. Those who were had already been that way before they came into his life, and the worst they could say was that Eric often imitated their habits or ticks, though from a man so charming, this was a compliment. But the moment Eric sensed a peer might outdo him, he would start to believe something dubious was up, and abandon the friendship on the pretext of a misunderstanding that was either inconsequential or entirely made up. Then, to justify himself, he would spread vindictive rumours and alienate the ex-friend from his coterie. Neither Eric's superiors nor his beta-men seemed to suspect this side of him. At worst, they thought him a gossip, but he was influential; they bought the talk and aligned with the in-group. And as Naren turns the key to his empty apartment, he wonders in what proportion all these factors – his personality, the interpersonal, society and its institutions – had colluded to land him where they did. He does not have an answer yet, but here where all the faces are the colour of his face, the question feels less relevant. Too exhausted to shower or brush, he lies down in the dark. Past the roar of traffic, he can hear the tide.

## *Rohit*

The Konkan coast has no formal boundaries. In some maps even Bombay is on it, though when Baba says 'amcha Kokan', he means the shadowy strip between the hills and the sea that everyone bypasses on the expressway to Goa. And this is the land that Rohit wants to rediscover when he drives out in the old Civic, the windows rolled down and the monsoon wind in his hair. Online, he has described his #rootstour as a trip to retrace his forefathers' journey from Velneshwar to Ratnagiri to Pune and to visit some historical sites on the way – a template he received from Amanda. Then she declined his invitation to join him, which is *fine*. If this is a trip to understand all the threads that end up in his person, it's fair that he make it in his own company. The first rains are breaking over the great escarpment, its lack of vertical glory made up for by its horizontal expanse, and scanning the land for resonance, every detail feels imperative: trees mirrored in basalt split by dynamite, grass on a thatched roof, new blades of rice, the water-filled fields reflecting the sky … to think this is where he is from, all this wind, rock and water, the stuff of his marrow. 'The Western Ghats,' his GPS announces. Trust the British cartographers to ignore the traditional name in favour of a common word for steps. To his grandparents, this range was always the Sahyadri. He looked up the name and it derives from two Sanskrit words – 'adri' for mountain, and 'sahya' for that which endures – and isn't that perfect? These bizarre ridges go all the way back to Gondwanaland. That valley contains dinosaur fossils older than the Everest. This is the Sahyadri!

Four hours into the afternoon, Rohit arrives at the misty hill from where Parshurama is said to have flung his axe into the sea. There is a temple on the summit, and its architecture looked traditional enough from a glimpse online, but upfront the impression is curious. The white walls are reminiscent of a basilica, the onion dome, a mosque, and there is no Parshurama idol inside, just a black hunk of rock painted with cartwheeling eyes. The only recognizable Hindu motifs are the stone elephants holding the pillars, and this makes sense when the priest tells Rohit that the temple was built by the Portuguese with Siddi money to pacify the locals. 'Agashe, hmm,' the priest says, after pausing to ask his name. 'See, son, our Konkan was overrun by foreigners then. These same Siddis later desecrated the shrine, but our priest escaped to the Peshwa court, and Baji Rao was so enraged that he rode over like a crusader and atomized the barbarians. After that our temple survived on a Peshwa grant until the seculars came to power and the money stopped. We are still fighting it in court, but in these days of caste politics, what chance does a Brahmin have? For seven years, we had no money to light the lamps.' Rohit isn't sure when the expectation crept up that Baji Rao's crusading spirit should inspire him to reach for his wallet. He wants to ask who pays for the air conditioning, but it's easier to give the crook a hundred and leave.

After a night in a nondescript guest house at the base of the hill, Rohit puts the Civic in gear for a new coastal highway that has made the Konkan accessible. Soon the slopes descend and black rock gives way to rust-red soil. Foliage soars; the air no longer smells of rain but a menacing green. The ghosts of Peshwa Baji Rao's men are in these trees, waiting to ambush Mughal armies accustomed to the plains, and Rohit's head is full of the glories of the Maratha

Empire until he arrives in Shrivardhan. Here is the home town of Vishwanath Bhat, ancestor of the legendary Baji Rao, but the road leading to the Peshwa's memorial is so deserted that Rohit doubts the GPS. When he reaches, the high red gateway and bronze statue are as promised online, and if there were no images of the Peshwa's original home, he can now see why. In a grassy square stands a single-storey house with a tiled roof. The porch is covered in tattered saris on which someone is drying rice, and there is nothing in the windows but an empty, cobwebbed hall. In short, it looks like any village house, and its frailness makes the gateway look cheap and new, like someone decided only recently that this was a spot to commemorate. On closer inspection, Vishwanath Bhat's statue bears no Aryan features either, just a stubby nose, stout legs, and a rough dagger at the waist. Rohit uses three filters on his photographs before he decides against posting online altogether.

And driving south, the views do get pretty, like when the highway curves along the lip of a ridge and the rocks run down past thrashing palms, or the sun breaks over a clayey sky and sets ablaze waves heavy with sediment, but any white sand and blue water is Photoshopped. He comes from a wild, brooding place … not that it is undiscovered. Most beaches are busy with horse rides, candyfloss and coconut stands. The tourists are vernacular types who can't afford Goa or Bali and leave their trash on the sand before dusting their saris and heading to a temple built around any rock slim enough to resemble a Shiva linga or wide enough to represent Ganesha. Nevertheless, by dusk, Rohit's heart lifts at the sight of Velneshwar, the ancestral village of the Agashes. The road swerves down a hill that meets two others in a khaki valley, and rising up from the squat trees are tiled roofs and an orange shikhara with bells tolling. He checks into the only decent hotel, a three-star run by the State Tourism Board. His cottage is spare to the point of monastic. In the dining hut, the tables are lit with cane lamps and the coils let the mosquitoes close enough to hear their buzz. A hag with a sari wedged up her bum takes his order. He waits for forty minutes, before walking out to the garden where two drunks are hunched over a table. 'Looks like Aaji's gone to catch the clams,' he says. One of the drunks panics. The other laughs and says, 'Our friend here is the cook.' By the time the food arrives, Rohit's blood sugar is so low, the salty steam is dizzying. The cook wipes his sweat. 'This is how she gets back at me for drinking. Where else would you eat? But by making you wait, I'm in trouble.' Rohit smiles and tips them the price of the meal. After all, those weren't just clams, they were … buttery nuggets of the sea roasted with the finest gifts of the land: coconut, turmeric, chilli hot enough to break a sweat, before the meat, firm yet yielding, releases its briny tide on the palate. Then you soak what's left of the sea juice with sour red rice. The Konkan in one bite!

Turns out, there isn't much to Velneshwar beyond the clams. The Agashes have left no known family or home behind, so the next morning, Rohit takes the first ferry out to Jaigad Fort. And sitting on the outer wall, the rocks rising into its ramparts and nothing in front but the salmon sea and mackerel sky, he lights a cigarette. According to an article Naren sent him, the ancient Hindu kingdoms had ports here, evidenced in bits of Roman pottery and Persian coins, but driving through, he has found little proof that the Konkan had much going for it before Shivaji's rise in the 1600s. The only ruins are the dozens of medieval forts rising out of and crumbling back into the earth: forts of black basalt on the promontories they crown; laterite ones as red as jungle soil in the plains; sea forts on the tips of submerged hills, their walls shingle and lime. But he has seen the forts of Delhi and Rajasthan, and these outposts have none of their grandeur. There are no fountain jets or hooks for chandeliers in Jaigad, only a stone square where the fort's namesake was beheaded in one of many brutal scenes as it changed hands between the Bijapur kings, the Portuguese, the Peshwas, the British, and so many others on this shrouded coast, this womb between the hills and the sea in which all manner of upstarts could gather strength away from imperial eyes.

On the walk back to the jetty, he buys boiled peanuts from a raisin of an old man with eyes so green they make Rohit wonder what it means to identify as a Kokanastha or a man of the Konkan coast. Not a Chitpavan, no. His fascination with the term has ebbed since he found out that Chitpavans are not among the five original Brahmin clans mentioned in the Vedas. The name first appears in the Skanda Purana, a record historians call 'the only living Purana' because it was edited right up to the seventeenth century, often by tribes and foreigners to rewrite their caste. As if to prove the point, the Konkan has countless ethnic groups from Parsis to Bene Israeli Jews; most villages have mosques, churches and synagogues; most forts were held by a roster of chiefs including pirates from Abyssinia. Guess the essence of a coast is just this bastardized mosaic, but since he is searching for his origins, it isn't so exciting. The jetty is crammed with fisherwomen, schoolgirls with babies at their hips, boys scrubbing their foamy backs with water from the river … and their familiar garble nevertheless makes him nostalgic for a time before he lost his mother tongue to English. Then the ferry bellows in with an Indian flag on its mast. And he imagines all the people who have made this crossing, their finite individual lives, their endless collective life. Hell, the gods and kings are dead, and maybe all he wants is to feel less outside this throng.

But halfway to Ratnagiri, he is done. The monsoon has arrived in full force, and the potholes are full of red rain with rocks waiting in them like icebergs. What will happen if he busts a tyre? This far into the interior, the villages are dripping settlements that look like they survive on foraging. Then the place names recall the surnames of posh club-and-theatre types, and what a hoot they come from here! The Peshwa capital, he decides, should have more going for it than where they started out. So he crawls back up the hills, and his mood lifts within minutes of hitting the national highway. He drives six hours north to Pune, where he spends the night in the guilty comfort of an American hotel, but it doesn't matter: he's in the Pearl of the Orient, the Queen of the Deccan, the Oxford of the East. Even sweeter, Gyaan and Ifra have driven down with Amanda for a tour. They meet in the 'historical district'. The ropey alleys are thick with hawkers and dog shit, and though his friends are too polite to say it, it's clear the place looks like a shantytown. As for the museums, most are housed in the brick 'mansions' of the old Peshwa elite, but they look like dollhouses when compared with the Neo-Gothic British behemoths of Bombay. Inside, guards snooze beside dioramas packed with private collections of everyday stuff like ivory dice and foot scrubbers, in short, nothing of the English landscapes, Mughal miniatures or Chinese porcelain at the Prince of Wales Museum, and the only artefacts of value, like the peacock sitars or carved doors, are imported from other states. 'You mean *plundered*,' Gyaan says, pointing to an inventory of Maratha weapons so creative it would give anyone the creeps. 'Spiked mace with extra long spike,' Gyaan reads. 'Two-faced Jamadar dagger. Wagh nakh or tiger claws. They wore those on the knuckles to rip out a man's guts.'

Rohit does not reply. He hopes that Shaniwar Wada palace, which he has saved for last, will redeem him. And the exterior is everything you would expect of Baji Rao's legendary home – giant basalt butt cheeks, a spiked door in the crack tall enough to admit elephants with canopies, a bronze equestrian with a spear raised over a regal face – but when they step inside, Amanda looks at the charred grids and says, 'There's nothing here!' Rohit explains that's how all forts are; centuries later, only the ramparts remain. But Shaniwar Wada isn't some rocky outpost. Rajasthani artisans were hired to design it in a vision of Hindu glory, every stone laid assuming this was the start of a grand era and not its zenith, and he can hear himself getting defensive as he describes the Wada's many luxuries destroyed by the British in a 'mysterious' fire, when Ifra says, 'Please. There was nothing so spectacular about your Maratha Empire. Shivaji is a folk legend that the right wing props up because they love the idea of a Hindu crusader after centuries of Islamic rule. And the Peshwas weren't even kings. They were Shivaji's ministers who took over the show after he died...' Rohit reminds her that the Peshwas almost stuck their flag on Delhi, and that India might never have fallen to the British had Baji Rao's grandson lived. 'Nothing could have been worse,' Gyaan says. 'My ancestral village is south of Delhi. Go there and people will tell you they feared the Peshwas more than the Mughals, but hating Mughals is how the Hindu nationalists make an enemy of all Muslims.'

Rohit wants to shout, This isn't about that, stop making me feel like a right-wing psycho – but Ifra is a Muslim so he shuts up. Now she and Gyaan have gone to buy salted guavas from a vendor near the gate. Amanda is taking photographs of a red-faced macaque scratching its nuts, and Rohit's impatience with her endeavour makes her snap, 'It's not my fault you didn't find what you were looking for.' When she was the one who set him off on this tour! Exhausted, he sits on a basalt stump. There are couples in the bushes and cigarette butts along the path. All the way down the coast, he couldn't get more critical, yet when the criticism came from Gyaan, it felt personal, like he is some barbarian while Gyaan is a lofty Northerner born for sniffing rosebuds. Would it be less frustrating if he didn't suspect that Gyaan is right? His search for a heritage – the lack of which, he believes, saw Naren get so lost trying to claim a world that was never his to own – must begin elsewhere … but where? When he thinks of Bombay, all that comes to mind are the colonial buildings, American brands, and Bollywood stereotypes of India that estranged him from what he hoped to find here.

# TRANSFORMATION

## *Amanda, Towards Purpose*

THE GLARE IS SO BRIGHT, THE SHADOWS FALL abruptly dark, yet the light does not have the same clarity as at home; the air is full of static, the days hazy with dust. How to process this white intensity that blows out every photograph? Standing by the open doors of the Harbour Line, she frames the rays slant off creeks, glint on tracks and metal bridges, and make mercury of the tin roofs on which the city rises. As the sun hits her face, she tries not to blink. Summer in the tropics is like winter in the West, weeks of extreme heat as harsh as extreme cold, her only recourse being to cultivate a mind for it. When she first took the trains, it was what she saw in every face: the face of summer, resolute against the burn. Three weeks in, the train contains a world of expressions as commuters shuffle cards, shell peas, chant rosaries, bargain, text, bitch or stare. Guess the only person as withdrawn into the body was her. Then the train cranks to a stop, and she is belched into a sour-smelling crowd. The station roof flashes silver before the glare is swallowed by a connecting train and sound overwhelms sight: the thudthudthudthudthud of feet hammering on board to the announcer's call and the clapping of bards. Inside again, all is umbra, but there are contrasts to play with – crystals on a burqa sleeve, a dark nose studded with a diamond – until the train exits the station and the windows flood with light. And in all this flitting of shadow and sun, India remains a blur, but the moment she holds up her camera, she begins to see.

THE VIEW IN FRONT IS SHROUDED by a visor and a driver's silhouette dissecting the musty eye of the screen. To either side of the rickshaw, scrap shanties of newer migrants morph into the low brick houses of Ward M, but the gutters remain open and the electric lines chaotic. Which of the faces going past descend from the slum's early inhabitants, the scavengers who have picked the landfill for a century? Which find themselves here since the seventies, when rehabilitation projects to beautify the city were in vogue, or the nineties, when communal riots led to an exodus of Muslims from other slums in the city, or the new millennium through which thousands of India's dispossessed have arrived here to live ghost-like off its refuse? All she can tell is the subject's gender and the universal scars of poverty. With that, she has to create this 'photographic archive' that will revitalize Ashray's media outreach and pitches to donors, this 'deck' layering impressionistic pictures of the slum with portraits of Ashray's people, some of the images titled, others an unmediated confrontation. The rickshaw stops. Was that a raindrop? All over the sky, giant sulphurous clouds are rising, dwarfing these lives that subsist on the world's debris, but at the first word from Tehsin Teacher (or is it Mehrun?) on the centre's steps – 'Hello,' says the scrubbed face from a black burqa, ironed, the rose-printed kerchief also ironed, as she dabs her hairline though there is no sweat – their dignity is evident.

THERE IS NO SHORTAGE OF TRAGEDY IN DEONAR: Slurping her tea on the stairs, Khala's role at the centre is that of a grandmotherly presence who signals trust and decency. She is also a fine raconteur, her expression an alloy of sorrow, resignation, and – not the relish of gossip so much as the bard's salvation in singing of pain – as she relays Deonar's news. Rosy, the secretary, is more clinical when she translates Khala's laments, 'A six-year-old was raped by her brother's friends, they were fourteen … Two sisters fought and the older one swallowed rat poison, the father drank and cut the mother's face with a bottle once in front of the girls … Khala's neighbour went mad for nothing, he got into an argument at the tanker and a man hit his head with a brick … The daughter was fair like you, Amanda, people say she had it going on with some Hindu boy, they found her body and an electric wire in a gutter, the mother has been going to the police for days…' As they speak, they scan her expression, which turns her listening self-conscious, her attention split between their words and fixing her brows in requisite alarm. When will all this talk of tragedy strike home? How will the news arrive, the implications haemorrhage? Could it be one of her students? Rafia, her cynical humour broken, Zaeem, his innocence perplexed as she says, Tell me, you can trust me. The tea is hot and gagging sweet. Can they trust her? Already there are shadows. Mehrun unwraps her scarf and her ear is deformed. Mittu jerks if his arm is touched. She amps the scale of their imagined tragedies … *Awful.* To prepare for the avalanche in this way, not by building ramparts but by this deliberate laying open.

THE WORLD MADE WHOLE: There is Rafia in the street below, waiting for the others. The 'camera class' was her idea. Nadiya, the education director, laughed. A negotiation ensued, Rafia dead serious, hand on her tiny hip. Then Nadiya said okay, and Rafia curved her hands under her chin, jumped like a rabbit and ran off. 'She's a little thug,' Nadiya said, smiling. 'I told her, you kids ask for classes, then you don't show up. I'm not going to chase any kids. You get the group and I'll let Amanda Didi take this class. She has given her word.' And in the weeks since, Rafia has kept it. Her talent for attracting resources makes her the leader, and she is a boy with the five boys, which is its own brand of attention, but being the only girl means getting left out of certain physical spaces, to come too close to becoming an outsider. Humera keeps things balanced. Her hair is long and she covers her mouth when she laughs. She may steal a heart or two, but is too loyal to challenge the leader. Where is she today? 'Hi Didi,' 'Didi hi,' 'Heylo Amanda Di.' Here they come. Bright eyes, bright faces flitting in and out of each other like dots of colour on the sun. Everything she knows is funnelled down a flue of rudimentary words, instructions and analogies until one of them grasps what is intended and they arrive at a translation. Then they take her Nikon in their hands and click pictures of each other while she opens her laptop. What began as an editing class has led to their discovering the internet. The lessons stick because their parents have smartphones on which they can show off. This morning, she googles them a satellite image of the earth made whole, neither hemisphere slipping into darkness. Before they leave, she asks where Humera is and Rafia shrugs like she doesn't care.

A SENSITIVE ISSUE: She has met Ifra as Rohit's friend or then as the Ashray CEO at the head office, so to see her here in a kurta and no make-up is startling. Nadiya says, 'Amanda, come in. You sent a text?' The rain goes silent. She replies, 'Humera isn't coming to class, and I…' 'Her parents won't let her out even for school now,' Ifra sighs. Nadiya whispers, 'Please, Ma'am, this is a sensitive issue.' Ifra waves a hand, 'We could use another head. The thing is, Amanda, our field officers double up as counsellors. Bhagwat was hers, and she's complained of abuse. She told Tehsin, who told Nadiya, who very professionally escalated it to me.' *Humera … Counsellor … Abuse.* Nadiya is saying, 'Can you believe, Amanda? Bhagwat was nine when he came here. His parents were ragpickers. The shops would not give his mother one glass of water. Today, he is an inspiration to the entire community. I said, Bhagwat, you confess? I was sure he would deny.' Ifra taps a sheet of paper on a desk. 'But he has confessed. In writing.' Nadiya pleads, 'No one else would. He even said, I'm telling you it was only a kiss. I'll accept any punishment, but if I write this, I'm in trouble. I told him what Ifra Ma'am said. I said, if there's any chance to settle this, the board needs a written apology. He wrote it because he *trusts* me.' 'He wrote it because he was terrified,' Ifra says, 'and it wasn't sex, but it was more than a kiss. What do you think, Amanda?' She knows that Ifra would not trust a fellow like this if not for their personal connection. She pauses, then says, 'I'd give Humera the benefit of the doubt.' 'Come on, please,' Nadiya exclaims. 'You are here since only one month. Fourteen is not so young in this community.' 'Isn't fourteen legally a child?' 'Yes, but fourteen-year-olds get married in Deonar. Here you will find two types of girls. Some are too innocent for their age and some are too smart. The staff says Humera is like that…' 'That's enough,' Ifra says. 'Bhagwat is popular with the staff. Our board is new, but I'll convince them he has to go.'

NOT THE LAW: 'Imperative' is the word that comes to mind. It is *imperative* to speak. 'Go as in just walk away?' she asks. 'We should report this to the police.' Nadiya's eyes grow wide. 'You don't understand, Amanda. These girls are troubled. They spend time talking, and it gets emotional. Humera was crying, so he took her in his lap. Whatever happened, happened. He knew it was wrong. He stopped first, so she felt rejected. His other students' progress is too good. Fire him if that is his punishment – but police? His wife is young. His son is only…' 'He should have thought of them before,' Ifra says, placing the letter in her bag. Why are girls given male mentors in the first place? 'Boys or girls,' Ifra answers, 'at that age, it makes no difference.' 'The teachers are women,' Nadiya says, 'they work one or two years, then they marry and quit. The older staff like Khala are illiterate, what do they know? Field officers have experience. You think Chagan is a lamb? These things go on, but there is no proof, and even the parents don't care. Their lives at home are worse, so if the girls get something out of it…' 'Please,' Ifra snaps. 'We aren't running a brothel.' Nadiya flinches like she has been slapped. Since Ifra doesn't apologize, she, Amanda, says gently, 'Nadiya … you've given Ashray so much. If news gets around that the management hushed a complaint like this, it could put the whole institution at risk.' Gentler too, Ifra says, 'Think of the work we've done, Nadiya. We've gone from helping a hundred kids to three hundred. You want to throw all that away? Then why are you protecting him?' 'I'm not,' Nadiya cries. 'I came myself with the complaint, but I'm his boss, and I feel *responsible*.' 'I understand how you feel, but we have no choice. We are not the law,' she says, and Ifra nods resolutely. 'Amanda's right. We must file a complaint. Then if the police do nothing, they do nothing.'

AMANDUH / AMANDAH: On the train home, she is as jittery as after a solo performance. To be a protégée is to extract the best from what another has to give, but to be a mentor is to have what you didn't know was in you extracted – patience, equanimity, courage – a result of their insistence that you are a bigger person than you think until, surrounded by those eager little faces, you are. Thunder booms above the train's rattle. Fat drops blot the grille. Often, in a Bandra café, she feels like a ventriloquist's puppet discussing gender, poverty or art. Then she video calls home, and Dad or Nana talk about Beau's asthma like it was breaking news, and listening, the Amanda from Jaffrey grows even more unreal than the one here. Who is the real Amanda? If she is wearing this kurta, tutoring these kids, ironing out the inconsistencies in her narrative and her nature so that they find the model they need, isn't the Amanda they extract as much her as the one left in Jaffrey? Just the way they say her name, slightly off but with such confidence, a gap opens between the *Amanduh* she was and the *Amandah* she is, a space to define this new person. She checks her phone. Rohit hasn't replied to her text on what he will have for dinner. She doesn't mind. Her endless patience with him assures her that the restless thing she was in Jaffrey – lashing out in anger, embracing from guilt – was not despite but because of Andrei. Around Rohit's naïveté, her wisdom condenses, around his recklessness, her poise, around his selfishness, her generosity. Like the children, he is extracting a new Amanda from her, the one she has travelled to this end of the world to meet.

STILL TINGLING FROM MORNING SEX, she traces the sunlight down Rohit's chest. He rolls in, closing the gap across which he is studied. He is planning a second trip to Pune to meet his uncle on the subject of his ancestry, and this time he hasn't invited her along. She places a palm on the back of his neck, feels the pulse at the base of his skull. In seducing him, she was acting on an impulse to break out of her old life, but the six weeks since have proved that he is not merely a catalyst. She has grown accustomed to him getting her drinks and driving her around, introducing her to new people and places, and his Hindi or Marathi slashing prices by half while she pretends to be more helpless than she is so he can have the pleasure of showing her. This balances their age gap, at times too convincingly. For a while, they stay physically entwined, each in their own heads. Last night they finally discussed past lovers. He admitted to two girlfriends, both of whom 'went crazy' with the result he called things off. She senses there have been others, friends with whom he has had sex off and on. When she asked him about dating apps, he said he did not need one. Now he rises, the first to have his fill of their nakedness. She watches him button his shirt, the hair on his head so wild it makes her laugh and reach out to settle it, but he gives his head – her hand – a toss, and goes out for a smoke, and she recognizes that, though she doesn't care for him nearly as much as for Andrei, she must protect her purpose from his beauty.

THE MYTH OF NADIYA: Rosy says that Khala says these are bad times, but neither will explain. Nadiya has stopped replying to texts. Here is where they turn inscrutable, the people she thinks she is getting to know. What drives Nadiya? She claims to work for less pay than she deserves. The staff insists it is her 'passhun'. They worry she works too hard to stop for lunch. Nadiya is plump (which is not a sign of poverty in India, the poor here are all bones), has sensitive eyes and a determined pout. She speaks English with the fellows, Ashray's founder, Anu Sehgal, and Ifra, who is younger than her but her boss. But unlike Ifra, Nadiya's Hindi is fluent too, a language she reserves for the staff, all recruited from the slum. At work then, she has no peers; she is always many levels above or below. She is also unmarried and known to live alone. A previous fellow warned that Nadiya gets too personal, but she, Amanda, doesn't care for such snobbery. Often Nadiya affects her more than the kids. What would it be like to return two hours by train, night after night, to a dingy flat? Nadiya is unnerving in her isolation and lack of self-pity. Is her strength brittle, or will she go on till the end of time? *The end of time*. Words suited to mythological figures. As the people here become distinct, each appears a type, original and ageless. Surviving Deonar must require some degree of self-fashioning, or is this simply her inability to see them in the way she sees herself, as complex and banal, as individual and symbolic, as caught in the sweep of an era as picking a zit on your nose? Her phone buzzes. She taps it, expecting a call from Nadiya, but it's Ifra.

INFRARED: From a sedan windscreen, a wide-angle view of a street. The scene is slipping into a strange perspective, as if she were seeing it all, herself included, from a disembodied eye as urgent and unsteady as a surveillant camera on a mission. Ifra's voice is overheard – 'I didn't ask Nadiya to come. She's too emotionally close to this…' – then the voice breaks into babble and another rises, this one from within: *Rumi says the wound is where the light enters you. My wound is that I am a woman, and this wound is my compass against vulgar relativity. What freedom is freedom until we are all free?* When they step out, the sky is grey and the police station gum pink. Inside, the floors are ribbed by bands of light. A constable at the far end is writing in a ledger. The sub-inspector's mouth opens under a red moustache, his hairy fingers flat on his desk. Ifra's mouth opens on perfect teeth, the diamond on her index fracturing the light. They are talking in Hindi, but she can tell that Ifra's attitude has gone from solicitous to shrill, and though the sub-inspector's tone is unchanged, his authority is increasingly palpable. *Rights,* Ifra says. *Minor … disgusting … apathy.* And the sub-inspector, *Sex-vex … gori mem … bada problem* – before her inner voice returns: *Gori, that's you. He is saying you are trouble. Remember how your marrow darkened as you told Nadiya we have no choice. The time has come to deliver on that course. Deliver, but how, across the gauze of language and … Come on, Amanda, act:* 'Show him the letter!' she almost shouts. Panicking, Ifra replies, 'I should, right? That was my last resort,' and she dips her hand into her leather bag and holds the paper with vindication in the sub-inspector's face. His brow rises. 'Kamble?' he asks. Ifra says, 'Bhagwat Kamble.' She says, 'That's him.'

FRAMES: It's past noon when she returns, but the upstairs office is still empty. Where is everyone? Bhagwat, understandably, isn't in. But neither is Nadiya, Rosy, Chagan, nor any of the teachers from the other centres who gather here for lunch. She opens her box of pasta and eats it alone. Until this week, her curiosity was still to give way to action; it was enough to be acted on. Now, everything is rattling softly against a storm wind. Take a good look at the room, she thinks. Reality when it isn't broken up in frames … but is it possible? Consider just the details under this one tin roof: white corrugations, pipes for rafters, a ceiling fan, its foot-long blades in a manic whirl, the patterned wall tiles that make the office look like a bathroom; and on the floor: three factory tables with four chairs, a metal safe for laptops, a cabinet of mildewed files, glass teacups on a steel plate, a malaria spray; and behind a plastic door: a sky-blue basin with no tap, a toilet with no flush, just a bucket and its bobbing mug; and beside the door: naked wires, a pen holder made from popsicle sticks and heart stickers, a corkboard pinned with a calendar and rag dolls, their jewellery all broken bangles and bottle caps … *Impossible.* The only way to comprehend Deonar is to break it down into an endless archive of shots.

ROHIT IS LATE FOR DINNER, with the result that she is alone with Ifra and Gyaan at the Yogi Café. They are aware of his upcoming Pune trip, and it gets them talking about the previous one. That was when she first learned that Ifra is Muslim, and she blushed to recall Nana spitting the word 'Mozzies', or Dad joking, 'Home is a place where you can be comfortably racist,' and her own surprise that 'Iffy', who wears heels and loves martinis, might be 'one of them'. Now, she blushes again when Ifra says, 'Rohit doesn't get the danger in all this Marathi pride. His family moved here from Pune after the riots.' Gyaan explains that the chief instigator was a local political party called the Marathi Bana. 'They started out as regional nativists,' he says. 'They were a voice for the Marathi-speaking Hindus of Bombay, and their agenda was to keep migrants from other states out. Then they found that religion is more potent than language if you want to create an enemy, so they became a regional ally of the Bharat Party. Today the right hand pretends it doesn't know what the left is doing...' Picking the watermelon seeds from her quinoa, Ifra adds, 'People say so what, Hindus also get killed. Two months after the riots, terrorist bombs went off in the stock exchange. The point is, Amanda, I was born in the bloodiest decade this country has seen since Partition, and that's the decade the Marathi Bana came to power in our state and the Bharat Party started winning national elections...' As a couple, Gyaan and Ifra must discuss this often enough. Like with Khala's laments, she senses that she is being called upon as a witness. Personally, she feels better about Rohit not inviting her to Pune. Unlike him, she cares less about who she is and more about what she is for.

THERE IS TALK, BUT THERE IS ALWAYS TALK. 'We can't apologize for how the police do their job...' 'The letter was for internal use, Bhagwat trusted her...' 'The minute Ifra Ma'am heard the complaint, she didn't care what was right or wrong...' 'They understood from the surname, what else is a Kamble...' 'Who will hire him? Deonar doesn't give second chances...' 'He's Bhagwat, he will fight his way back...' 'First it was about what's right, now it's about the organization...' Then Nadiya comes in, and everyone hushes and returns to work. Her brusque efficiency suggests everything is under control, but by evening, she asks with unusually large eyes, 'Amanda, can we share a rickshaw back?' And as soon as the fuming highway leaves Deonar behind, Nadiya starts to quiver, then cry. The cops have battered Bhagwat. He was dragged to the lock-up and beaten until he coughed blood. His wife has left for her mother's with their baby. Is this the avalanche? So swift, her first response is to smile, her brain too overwhelmed to impel the right gesture. She forgets what blood looks like, wine red, raspberry, its pressure as it spurts or blots; what part of a man must rupture to cough blood? Nadiya is saying, 'The climate is against Bhagwat. It's all the talk of rape in the papers. People are so paranoid they don't see the facts. The CEO is young and wants to show that she can take a stand. God knows the police never respond, but then you have the head of the NGO and a letter, and the sub-inspector is a caste Hindu, and Bhagwat is a Mahar...' 'What's that?' she asks. 'A Dalit,' Nadiya says. 'What's that?' she asks again, and Nadiya's face twists with exasperation. Is Nadiya aware that she was at the police station with Ifra? She wants to be the first to tell her. When Nadiya invites her over for dinner, she says yes. Rohit texts: *Do you have to?* He is calling now, but Nadiya is talking again, so she lets her phone buzz.

## *Rohit, Towards an Identity*

A sloping roof and brick walls much smaller than he recalls them, but what Prabhat House has lost in scale is made up for in resonance. This was the Agashes' first home when they moved from the Konkan to Pune. Here, three generations of his ancestors have dreamed.

Aai asked if Ravi Kaka invited him. He said he invited himself. Doesn't Kedar show up whenever he likes? And now, her shale eyes full of meaning, Chitra Kaki exclaims, 'Don't take off your shoes! No formalities, please. Aaplach ghar ahe re.' This is your own home.

Brass lamps … lace doilies … an old-school sofa, more wood than stuffing. If the flat-screen TV isn't exactly austere, the pretensions to austerity – this pride in hoarding, reupholstering, and heirlooms that have no market price – is homage to the values of a community that got where it did through hard work, thrift, and as Ajoba used to put it: simple living, high thinking.

Before his bum can touch the sofa, Kaki sends him to his grandmother's room to pray. And not one thing has changed since those childhood summers, but with Aaji gone, the quiet walls have the eloquence of a shrine, and the four-poster that was his pirate ship and the Singer sewing machine that was Kedar's, the weight of idols.

In the bathroom, hanging from a spigot, is Aaji's pumice foot scrubber. He runs a thumb over its rough edge, misses the cracked heels he massaged as she told him stories from the epics. *Time*, the stone whispers, *time, time, time.*

Now he gets the value of the everyday stuff in the Peshwa museums. What is the culture of a place or people other than this – how we lived and how we died? What is an identity but an accretion of all those sensations, however fleeting or slight, aroused by every encounter with the world that tells you where and among whom you belong … or do not?

Back in the living room, he studies his paternal kin with new eyes. Ravi Kaka is fully bald now, but he still wears the ironed jeans, collared tee and loafers that all Pune engineers do. Chitra Kaki is in a green, near-transparent sari, her modesty secured by the thicker cotton of the blouse and petticoat, a gold bangle on each wrist and pearls in each ear. Typical, he thinks, but the word comes to mind with relish rather than disdain.

Kaka says, 'Is it really Roheet? Why so long, yaar? Pune is not Mars.' Kaki laughs a little too quickly, a soda bottle in one hand and an aperitif glass in the other, 'Wait till you try this. It's cold and fizzy, but you get such a clear taste of cumin like in jal jeera.' The soda is delicious, but neither will have a sip. They're watching sugar. They bought it just for him.

Guilty at not informing them about his last Pune trip, he talks of the Konkan instead, but his uncle's face starts going stiff. Wait. Was Ajoba's land just south of Velneshwar? Kaki says to Kaka nervously, 'Arey, didn't you make the same tour at his age?' Kaka heaves, 'I didn't know fancy terms like *roots tour*. But yes, I made a trip. In those days, it took a week to reach Velneshwar, but it was worth it, because that is where it first brushed me – that from here my ancestors started. Maybe you've pre-decided I'm going to feel like I belong here. Doesn't matter. If you feel it, you feel it…'

If he hasn't visited Prabhat House in years, it was not because of the family feud, but that he did not care for country cousins. Now, for the first time, he sees his uncle as an individual like himself, someone who still lives in his parents' home and wants to preserve those scraps of history his siblings want to shed. He can also see what Kaka saw in his wife. Kaki's beauty isn't merely typical, it is symbolic. She is the Chitpavan ideal: shale eyes, auburn hair, the hips too wide and legs too sturdy, a nose so sharp that she always appears in profile.

And as the conversation proceeds, he asks his uncle the questions on history for which his father has no patience. Soon, the stiffness leaves Kaka's voice, and here, in his weathered vowels and gestures, in how he relates to the facts rather than the facts themselves, he, Rohit Agashe, senses something of an arrival.

Ravi Kaka says, 'Your friend Gyaan is not the only one who thinks the Peshwas are the bad boys of history. But our story only begins with the Peshwas. Because the Peshwas were the link between medieval and modern India. See, in every medieval society there were two ruling classes, the priests and the aristocracy. But with the Peshwas, the priests entered politics. When most of India was illiterate, our community had this double experience in scholarship and governance, so once the British took over, they made us their Macaulay men. We were exposed to Western ideas, and now we wanted the rights. That is why so many freedom fighters and social reformers and educators were Chitpavan…'

Chitra Kaki says, 'Tilak. Gokhale. Ranade. Chaphekar. Savarkar. Notice the surnames. At the time of Independence, we were the opinion leaders and decision makers in this country…'

Ravi Kaka says, 'Back then, most Indians could not think beyond their sub-caste. They could not think like a nation. That is why a Chitpavan wrote the supreme Hindu ideology to unite us. I agree it has some extreme views, but please remember that he wrote in a British jail. It was a Chitpavan who founded the Bharat Bhratritva Samaj, or what in English we call the Bharat Brotherhood Society. You look surprised. I am surprised you don't know this…'

Ravi Kaka says, 'Hmm. It is true the organization was banned for some years, so it became secretive by nature. People say we got jealous that Gandhi–Nehru took over the freedom struggle. Yes, it was a Chitpavan who shot Gandhi; you can read his memoir and agree or disagree, but frankly, Gandhi was ready to give away the nation to the Muslims. Still, the stigma was used to break our stronghold. For half a century, the so-called seculars brainwashed the people…'

Ravi Kaka says, 'I don't agree with half of what the Brotherhood says, but I can tell you its roots were in Hindu reform movements. Later, they got into politics because you have to be practical to change society. Today, the Bharat Party, call it the Brotherhood's political arm or ally, is the only national party reaching from village grassroots to the parliament. Their student league is the largest youth organization in the world. Our prime minister doesn't give speeches in British bootlicker English. He doesn't have children to inherit the show. So please, be critical, but also give credit…'

Chitra Kaki says, 'I have not read as much as your kaka. But you have to admit that even in Marathi-speaking people, there is *something* about Chitpavans. Be it quality of language, etiquette, the fair skin or light eyes. My father would say it is like a breed of dogs. After generations of mating, you get hunters or retrievers, and you don't have to be ashamed or proud – it is simply a fact. Why your parents find the name funny, I don't know. Of course we have some jokes. Like, there are only two communities in the world. Chitpavans and … others! Hee hee. Everyone else is others…'

Ravi Kaka says, 'Sheh. Don't listen to her. Your parents are right in a way. These days, no one takes the name because we don't want to put our caste in people's faces. Like in America, I believe, where even millionaires say they are middle class. I always tell young people that if you don't think about caste, it means you are upper caste, so please get off your secular high horse…'

Ravi Kaka says, 'Then today at lunch, our Kedar says, why can't we delete our surnames? Because surnames tell you everything about a man in India, be it his mother tongue, or caste or subcaste. I said, fine, do that. Take any position, but a Chitpavan can never be neutral. We have famous reformers on the extreme left and right. My son is his own self, and I am not obsessed with tradition, but I refuse to be Hindu-phobic because it is in vogue…'

Chitra Kaki says, 'But Rohit, deleting your surname ati zhale, na? First it was environmental issues. Then freedom of information. Now he is talking like those anti-nationals. Any mother will worry…'

Ravi Kaka says, 'She is overthinking. I keep telling her, if you are a sensitized human, you will pass through this ideological travel. Everybody is a communist in his young days. Then everybody reads Orwell and becomes a capitalist. See, my father was very Brahmanical, but I went into a student movement led by the

Communist Party. In those days, they still had some relevance in India. Then I realized, left or right, these guys are ultimately politicians and will use us. So I became an engineer and started my factory, but my approach to my workers was very leftist. They should never be exploited. They should get a fair wage. But it is not always reciprocated. That's when I moved into this practical world of business. You decide you are a decent human being, you want to do an honest trade, you don't want to hurt anyone, that is enough. Arey, please have your soda.'

So, the history of the Chitpavans is the history of modern India! Before this imposing legacy, all family feuds seem trivial. The closest anyone comes to voicing wounds is when Kaka says, 'Come again in winter, when our theatre and music festivals are on. Pune is the height of Marathi culture. We don't have much visual art, but our philosophy is famous, our poetry is famous. You youngsters can't read Marathi, that's the problem. There is also this attitude: *the Pune clan*, your father calls us, like we are some primitives. Tell me, what is the point of being cosmopolitan if you can't take responsibility for your environment?' – and Kaki shoots her husband a look that could blow up a small planet.

He is sorry for them. Since nothing is as tender as the mother tongue, he says in the little Marathi he knows, 'Zhale te zhale, Kaka.' What's done is done. He smiles for sweetness. Kaki says 'Raja', and gathers him into the milky smell of her sari. Then he announces that he is hungry with such entitlement that Kaka laughs and slaps his thigh. 'Your Kaki has made steamed modak because it was your favourite when you were this tall.'

They move to the circular table by the window. All the snacks have been prepared by Kaki's 'own hands' except for the tea, boiled by the maid, 'a wizard at tea', which Kaki pours lovingly from a porcelain teapot painted with roses. And eating the modaks, so hot and sweet, to the cool hush of rain, he recalls what Naren said about the value of tradition and worthy insiders. The effort his uncle and aunt have made before knowing how this would go! Chitra Kaki's gestures are a result of ritual, house pride and belonging, all of which *precede* love, and this thought makes his joy in the modak more acute.

He will not do a Kedar on them. Their generation has seen more change than he can imagine, their desire to be progressive is more endearing than their lapses or confusion, and he wants to love them like when he was a child, that is, to not only love but also respect them as valid ways of being. Must be the same the other way around too. No one corrects him when he goes to the garden for a smoke, and Kaki sends the maid over with Ajoba's bronze ashtray.

In the sunny shade of the ashoka hedge, he phones Amanda. She gets talking of some crisis in Deonar, her reason for keeping him out last night. He listens as patiently as he can. In his turn, he tells her about the Chitpavans with pride; how, in four hundred years, a small, shipwrecked people came to influence the fate of a nation. She says, 'Funny, they sound just like New England Puritans.' From her tone, he isn't sure if that's a compliment.

They close the call. He will not be Amandified, but unlike his exes, she has shown no signs of going crazy on him either. They are both too young to give themselves up. Then again, she was all set to marry, yet she won't so much as look in his eyes when they make out. This should reduce the act to commerce, but the result has been the opposite: an erotic power play that needs no props.

The haughty cheerfulness with which she meets his withdrawals, as if to say: Did you think you have the power to upset me?

'Roheeet.' It's Chitra Kaki, who invites him to rest in Kedar's bedroom while lunch is being prepared. Except for a bookshelf, the room is as impersonal as a three-star guest house. There's a *Communist Manifesto* in the bedside drawer, the way some people keep the Gita or the Bible. The front page has Kaka's name scratched out, and Kedar's initials above it. There's a dried wildflower in the sleeve. The Kedarness of Kedar.

Sitting on the bed, he looks Kedar up online. Kedar was in college when Talne sold, which means he grew up on Ravi Kaka's self-righteousness, and now he's going further. His newsfeed has links to Marathi reportage, a Faiz poem, and English posts that read like he had a dictionary open:

Kedar writes, *Dad leaves zero opportunity to emphasize the 'simple living, high thinking' that elevates the Brahmin above those who can't afford time or money to cultivate thinking plus also those with new money who are yet to realize its value is not in gross display. His Chitpavan-ness is in the books he reads, the songs he hums, his interest in history. But to suggest he is subscribing to this brand in earnest is coming uncomfortably close to accusing him of caste snobbery, not that we have much basis left…*

Kedar writes, *We talk lovingly of grandparents who made racist comments because to judge them in the present daylight is a historical imprudence, and we are careful to talk this way only around insiders who feel the same pride and guilt and will not raise eyebrows because this is polite company. So it is all a little joke, this 'self-deprecation' that makes nostalgia for a past of greater inequality edible, merely something to be sentimental about when the modern world is so vulgar. But the joke will never exhaust…*

Kedar writes, *I will not deny there are aspects of this communal self I find attractive: the interest in social responsibility (except when it results from me-the-reformer vanity), history as a source of enlightenment. But what I can't stand is the hypocrisy. We denounce caste, we believe in affirmative action, we think obsessively about our ancestors' atrocities to underline that we have evolved, that we are modern, egalitarian men. But we will not change our surnames.*

When Indians say 'our community' what they mean is 'our caste'. His journey into his roots has been a journey into his caste. Of course he knew this, yet Kedar's post feels like someone threw cold water on his face.

He wants to reconnect. He wants to begin again where their fathers broke off. But his text to his cousin gets no reply. Chitra Kaki says that Kedar will be back on Monday, so he extends his trip in Pune. Then Kedar gets in at five a.m. and leaves by six. Kaki is sorry. She didn't want to disturb anyone's sleep and Kedar's exit was urgent but his reason was vague, as if his bourgeoise cousin isn't worth letting in on some great revolution.

To make up for the snub, Ravi Kaka connects him with a film-maker from a local mandal for Marathi culture, one Ajinkya 'Jinx' Pradhan. He phones Jinx just to make his uncle feel better. His call gets a reply in text. Jinx's status is Busy, but when he asks if he can come over, Jinx replies, 'Any time.'

At first sight, Jinx Studio is a B-grade version of the Box. There's no place to move between the tripods, cables and desks heaped with stuff. Then he notices that the corkboards are thick with gritty location shots, and the walls are pinned with posters of Marathi-language films on fierce themes like court corruption and gender violence, and more than one is marked with laurel leaves!

'I'm here to meet Jinx,' he says to one of the three wiry kids bustling about. There's a zing in the air, like if he doesn't talk fast, he will be in their way. 'I'm a producer from Mumbai with an interest in regional cinema.' 'Oh, why didn't you say so? Please sit,' and they offer him tea and their opinions.

The scriptwriter says, 'We would watch Iranian or Italian films in subtitles, but not our own regional-language films. That was the hypocrisy. But the audience is maturing now. People go to Hollywood for special effects; they go to Bollywood or national cinema for song and dance; and they come to us for content…'

And the cinematographer, 'Take a film like *Zorat*. A Marathi film set in a village. The director is unknown. The actors untrained. Their Marathi is the kind anyone will be ashamed to speak in Pune. But it is going house-full all over the nation. It is going house-full in festivals abroad…'

And a pockmarked actress in a neon vest, 'What is in that film but honesty? I saw it before the hype caught on and it totally shocked me, the honour killing at the end. The point is, we are making films about real people and real issues…'

He hasn't watched *Zorat* but he has heard of the movie and likes the idea: to be rooted yet universal. To be local, regional, national and global at once, and above all, to be relevant.

Jinx enters to a hush. He has a face like a lion and a bass-drum paunch. He shows off some neat trailers, but at any hint of a collaboration, Jinx smiles like sure but not really. When did this happen? Kedar, Jinx, all these kids with sing-song English whom he has always thought of as *vernies* – which wasn't just short for vernacular, but a term for a herd with no personality – suddenly they've arrived, and here he is, Rohit Agashe, anxious that the great Indian coming-of-age is turning on some other speed.

He is smoking in the basement when Jinx's cinematographer bounds down the stairs and catches his breath. 'Me, Omkar Khaire. Not that I was born with the name.' What kind of person changes his name and won't hide it from someone he just met? Omkar continues in Marathi, 'Meaning, the Indian hockey captain in 1991 inspired my ajoba to name my cousin Pargat, and when I followed, you know how it is in the village, they called me Bargat. Then my father died, and I was sent to live in Wai. I'd done a year at school, but I begged my uncle not to tell the principal. Repeating the year meant a fresh start on the documents, and even at seven, I knew Bargat was a chutiya name for a Marathi man, so I filled the form as Omkar. When I got home, I told Aai, from today I am Omkar. She still calls me Bargya, and so does all of Wai, but if anyone calls me that in Pune, I'll think, who just kicked me in the balls?'

Both laugh. The moment earned, Omkar launches into a pitch. Last year, he shot a two-minute film on the Ganeshotsav parades for a mandal competition. The film won. Now he wants to develop it into a short to send to juries. He says in English, 'Whatever you think, this is not that!'

Omkar's face is brown and browy, the kind one has seen innumerable times behind counters or in queues at bus stops, but it has none of their boredom or fatigue. His English is broken, his Marathi would make Kedar and Jinx seem like real sophisticates. What is the source of this confidence?

Omkar hands him the film on a pen drive. He hands Omkar his card. 'Rohit Raghunath Agashe,' Omkar reads aloud. 'You must have been that from the beginning, no?' 'Yes,' he says with a new aristocratic pleasure in what he's always thought of as a pretty regular name.

Over lunch in a café, he watches Omkar's film. A thirty-foot Ganesha statue turns in the light … a dark boy wearing neon horns laughs … faces decorated in shaving foam holler from a truck. He has never seen the parades up close. But unlike the usual footage, Omkar's shots aren't overwhelmed by their scale. Shooting from the crowd, he strips his subject of its inherent chaos, then injects it with a dark personal energy. He has an eye for the bizarre, yet the first thought that comes to mind is: This is life.

Omkar shows up so fast, he might have been waiting right outside. He won't have lunch. He is not in the habit. When his film is praised, his expression is all pride and humility. 'It's a first step,' he says, and auspicious since the subject is Ganesha or 'Bappa'. He shot it on a borrowed Sony with no stabilizer, but he tried to turn his constraints into opportunities. Yes, he agrees, he could do with a sound artist rather than setting it to an aarti. Yes.

Omkar's tone is self-effacing, though people in the café constantly come over to shake his hand. Like a politician, one would think, just as Omkar asks, 'Agashe, tell me one thing. Did you find my film political?' Now, this is the age of Hindu nationalism, and Ganesha is a Hindu god, and Ganeshotsav, a Hindu festival, but watching the film, he thought only of the world's mad beauty, and minutes in, the maker's talent. He asks why. Omkar says, 'Just, the environment has become so hostile to anything Hindu. Jinx won a National Award last year and the film fraternity leans left, so he won't risk backing anything to do with our culture...'

Sure, but what comes after *Bappa*? Omkar says a feature film (exactly what he wants to hear) and when he asks about what, Omkar says his struggle. Not his story. His struggle. The title is *Ek Sangharsh.* Hard to believe the plot is his actual life. What cuts through are the details, the kind you can't make up. Like when Omkar's grandfather beat his widowed mother with a kharata – a broom used in toilets, those stinking needles that kill roaches in a thwack – for letting the milk boil over. When her mouth started to foam, Omkar shoved the old man off, an impudence for which he was sent to live with his mother's relatives in Wai. For six years, he did not share a roof with her or his sister. In the end, however, it is a story of triumph. Omkar's mother inherits a bit of land and moves to Wai. Omkar and his sister finish school. He tops his district and leaves for Pune, the first in his family to go to college.

That a Brotherhood branch in Wai and its student league in Pune made this journey possible is only a mention, but when he, Rohit, hears it, his atoms start buzzing. His friends talk about Hindu nationalists all day, but he has never met one, and Khaire is hardly threatening. If anything, it expands his chest to know that an institution founded by Chitpavans helped this kid who is, as Omkar puts it, 'backward caste, class, everything'.

In Black Box the next morning, Gyaan (laughing so hard, he has to pinch his eyes to hold back tears) says, 'Let me get this. You want to make a film about a Hindu festival with someone linked to the Bharat Brotherhood, then follow it up with a feature that almost translates as *My Struggle*…'

Gyaan (still gaping) says, 'The Brotherhood has milked social media to whitewash its image, but its branches still breed the old violence, sexism and bigotry. I studied history before I studied film, so let me give you a little prognosis. We are cut off from our roots by colonialism, liberalization, modernity, independent India adopting a model more Western than Gandhian, and a dozen other calamities all with the same result – a cultural vacuum the Hindu nationalists fill with some reductive bullshit about our Hindu identity…'

Gyaan (in frank disdain) says, 'It's nothing new, a young man goes in search of his roots and finds his politics. But you landed on the wrong side, and I'm wondering what happened to your famous bullshit meter!'

He wants to say it's right here, but when Gyaan is in rhetorical mode, it's best not to contest him, so he says, 'Just watch the demo, please? It's beautiful.' Gyaan blinks his hooded eyes. 'What makes hegemony so insidious is beauty.' He has no reply to that, so he does an Omkar and leaves the pen drive on Gyaan's desk. The only thing Gyaan cares about more than politics is film … or so he thought because Gyaan watches nothing. He simply phones Ifra, and the answer is no.

When he tries to explain Omkar's circumstances, Gyaan calls him a Nazi apologist. At that, any apology he feels turns to anger and he walks out. Smoking on the curb, he recalls the time he confessed to Ifra that he feels ambivalent about most stuff, and she said, 'You don't have to find something to hate. You only have to find something you care about.' So here's something: he cares about people.

He looks Omkar up online. There is an image of Vivekananda on his newsfeed, but nothing like hate. Most of his posts are film reviews, festive greetings, updates on social causes, and motivational quotes followed by comments thanking him and calling him Dada or Bhai. Yet Gyaan and Ifra don't see him as a person. To them, Omkar is a political type that stands for everything they despise. Well, he has seen where that attitude got Amanda.

## *Amanda, Towards Purpose*

ALL MONTH, THE CLOUDS INTENSIFY IN DARKNESS, smothering trash hovels and turning the air electric. Where the first rains rendered Deonar's contours distinct, with each successive shower, the slum morphs again – shanties huddle under plastic sheets, a scrap heap turns out to be a bicycle repair shop – a new mutation of junk just as she made sense of the old. Meanwhile, being indoors has given Khala's tales time to foment. Even Rosy is more animated in her translations. Humera's parents, they report, have arranged a match for her, and the wedding will take place after Ramzan. Tehsin Teacher met Humera in their village up in Bihar and asked if she had seen the boy. She said no. Tehsin asked, 'What if he turns out to be a loser?' and she replied, 'Why would my parents pick a loser for me?' In other news, Bhagwat, home on bail, was assaulted by a mob near the abattoir. One of the assaulters took a video of the beating – the casteist slurs, the accusations of adultery and corrupting Muslim girls – and it has gone 'viral' across the slum. Rosy says that the 'tension' in Deonar has been worse since March, when a national election ran on hate speeches and the kind of instant messaging the English press doesn't cover. On voting day, the children saw men with knives the length of an arm in the streets. And here, the police sub-inspector is a caste Hindu, the girl a Muslim, the man a Dalit: a face-off along such fault lines could threaten the entire slum.

REACTIONS TO MISFORTUNE I: Nana sighs a single word by way of admonition: 'Prudence.' Mom worries, 'What kind of damn place...?' Dad backs his Mandy's call with utilitarian arguments as opposed to Kantian ones. Andrei, for all his sympathy, resents the experience that is taking her away. There is a new silence between them, an understanding that he will not probe and she will not lie. He knows about Rohit but doesn't. Deonar is Rohit is India to him. She feels gagged though she has been talking until her throat hurts. At expat parties, other fellows top her story with anecdotes more shocking from the non-profits they are stationed at. At Indian parties, the room goes silent as if it is her fault for bringing the conversation to an awkward place. Some deprecate other Indians to absolve themselves, others deprecate themselves and praise her. Both responses nauseate, but Ashray is her most significant experience in this country, and telling the story over and over is a way to make sense of it. Besides, the more she talks about the incident outside, the more it recedes into the hush of rain in Deonar. Nothing has come of the staff's prophesies, or perhaps they have stopped updating her. When she checks in, Nadiya says, 'You don't understand. In Deonar, everything hangs by a string.' Beyond this, Nadiya will not speculate, as if voicing the possibilities might coax them into being, as if the only practical response is to shut the windows and do nothing that might act as a metal rod on a night of lightning.

THE MYTH OF BHAGWAT: When you photograph the adults of Deonar, they do not smile. Unless you catch them off guard, they simply stare at the camera like her great-grandparents in the monochrome on the piano: This is my face, these are the facts of my existence. She repositions a photograph of Bhagwat between Khala drinking tea from a saucer and a light-leaking shot of tin roofs. Like the children, he is smiling for his portrait, and in this act alone he has transcended his class. She checks her notes on the photograph. *The son of manual scavengers, Bhagwat grew up in a home near the landfill. He is industrious and optimistic. In less than a decade, he has made it to the managerial post of field officer. He isn't tall, but shows no signs of malnourishment. In this dust and humidity, he wears fresh floral shirts without a crease. He is Ashray's poster boy.* When she wrote this, she was unaware of the term 'untouchability'. No amount of research makes the psychological details of this ancient trauma real enough. The internet says the practice is illegal, though caste distinctions remain the basis for affirmative action. It is also a source of systemic violence with dynamics that confound even elite Indians, let alone a foreigner. The sub-inspector, for instance, is 'backward caste', a modern legal term for the lowest castes in the old hierarchy, but not outside it, not Dalit. According to Chagan, the backward castes have tasted political power under the Bharat Party and torture Dalits to prove they are supreme Hindus, while the upper castes sit back and laugh. That Bhagwat has converted to Buddhism doesn't seem to matter.

REACTIONS TO MISFORTUNE II: Rohit says, 'Ifra hasn't told me anything, but if I'm convinced the guy is decent and it's an isolated case, I wouldn't go to the police.' She says, 'Nothing happens in isolation. We're an NGO responsible for three hundred kids. Imagine if word got around that we hushed this.' Rohit says, 'Word gets around. But the law here doesn't work like it should. In such a situation, it's obvious things won't end well. If the officer was innocent, I'd stand up for him.' She says, 'He wasn't innocent! The trouble is that the punishment didn't fit the crime. It got … amplified. There was some caste angle we didn't think about. God knows what the cops did to him. He's stopped talking since he came out. Now he's been assaulted, and whom should we complain to? Not the cops, surely.' 'How about the press?' Rohit asks. She shakes her head. 'I don't know. Ashray could get into trouble. *I* could get into trouble…' but instantly she regrets how it sounds. There is no security at the centre other than that Ashray has been working in Deonar for thirty years with the result, as Nadiya says, 'the community holds you up'. Still she feels guilty for prioritizing her safety. 'You make it seem simple when it isn't,' she snaps, turning on Rohit, so confident that he would have done the right thing with partial information and no hindsight. Rohit sets his vodka down and nuzzles her warm, tense neck. He says, 'I only told you what I think. Can we fuck now?'

QURESHI HOUSE, TARDEO. The apartment may be smaller and older than the Agashes', but Ifra's parents own the entire building. There is china in the cabinets and calligraphic art on the walls. As a maid boils tea, Ifra's mother, Amal, points to books that reflect the Qureshis' many talents: she is a painter; her husband, a thespian; and Ifra's younger brother, a student of design in London. Ifra studied art history at Goldsmiths herself, before switching to a master's in social development at SOAS. 'I wanted to come back,' she says. 'The West never felt like home, but since the election, home doesn't feel like home either. The crazy fringe has gone mainstream. The other day Rohit was like, you want Omkar to have your ideas, you give him a library when he's seven. I said that's how fundamentalists operate; there are no schools in a village, so they set up a madrasa. Then he says the Hindu nationalists haven't given people guns with books. They came to power through an election. I mean, so did Hitler.' After Rohit's sanctimony over Bhagwat, she feels validated, still the comparison is extreme. 'Is it that bad? Have you experienced something personally?' she asks. Ifra snaps, 'Do I have to experience something to care?' More patiently, Amal explains that Ifra was only a baby when the nationalists announced that a famous Mughal mosque stood on temple ruins. Before the courts could intervene, hooligans broke the walls and planted saffron flags on the domes. When the news came on TV, Amal heard firecrackers. Ten minutes away, shops were burning. Ifra says, 'Riots. It's become just a word. If you say, wait, can we talk about what exactly they did to people?' – but Amal flinches, so Ifra stops. 'No Indian party is all that secular,' Amal says. 'But now, even the mask is off. I'm telling you, Amanda, in my in-laws' time, so many Hindus rented at Qureshi House. Now it is only Muslims. Our tenants are lawyers, doctors, educated people, but they can't get a home in Hindu societies.'

REACTIONS TO MISFORTUNE III: Only later in the evening, once she and Ifra have said goodbye to Amal and are on their way to a nightclub, does the subject turn to Deonar. Did Ifra know that Bhagwat is Mahar? Yes, and while she is dismayed by the police official's response, she is unapologetic. 'A Dalit man is still a man.' She braces herself in Ifra's clarity, and what her home and family have made obvious: her sophistication. They are riding into the night in a musty Uber, the book Ifra has lent her on her lap: a dog-eared copy of *Camera Lucida*. Ifra is saying, 'I actually quite liked him. Bhagwat isn't Chagan. You never feel him watching you. He has that frank and genuine attitude, the kind that takes a man further than those who are too aware of their position, so long as, from the same confidence, he doesn't blunder…' The mention of Chagan brings to mind his insinuation (though she suspects it is more telling of him than of Ifra) that the CEO's protective instinct towards Humera stems not only from justice or female solidarity, but that both are Muslims in a hostile country.

EASY INTIMACY: The nightclub is in the basement of a five-star hotel. Cyrus comes over from the Box, where he freelances as an actor but is treated like a partner because his mother rents the boys their premises for a steal. He is petite off-screen, deliciously snobbish, and though he is Zoroastrian, Persia makes her think of the Arab world and 'Cy' and 'Iffy' share a racial similarity she can't unsee. Like beautiful twins, both are fair-skinned and sharp-nosed. They get dancing before their drinks arrive. The party, a 'Pride night', is nothing like she expected: women in campy dresses with glitter on their eyes are air-kissing men in wigs and hot pink turbans. The playlist is eighties' pop, and there is freedom in the air – no creeps looking on, no sense of being judged – and since neither Jay nor Rohit are here, she and Cyrus grind into each other with more abandon than lovers. Catching her breath at the bar afterwards, she checks her phone. The fellows are at an expat party down the street, but she doesn't care for the expats' whining about India, especially those who come for corporate jobs, or the fellows' shock and inability to get below the surface. Thanks to Rohit, she has developed an easy intimacy with the city. Why didn't he come with Cyrus? She knows. She wasn't looking to make things emotional by bringing up Bhagwat, but given the magnitude of the event, his shutdown hurt. No, she wasn't up for sex. For three days, she has not called on him for help. Is this their first lovers' tiff? She texts him. He says he is tired but to have a good time. He is still online, chatting with someone else. She knocks back her gin and tonic, decides her mild repugnance for him while Amal spoke was healthy.

A ROUGH WIND IS SLAMMING WINDOWS, clanging pipes and billowing tarp. The centre's shutter is half down, like a bruised eye. Her hungover gaze adjusts to Khala and Tehsin in the darkness. Where are the children? Tehsin looks up with a hard glance that corks the question in her throat. Upstairs, Nadiya is at her desk, and Rosy and Chagan are sitting on the floor, their profiles outlined by the cold light from the barred window. Nadiya says, 'The electricity is gone,' and then, 'Amanda, Bhagwat is gone. Bhagwat is dead. He hanged himself with his wife's sari.' Dead, she thinks, *dead*, as Nadiya goes on, her eyes emptying over pitted cheeks in a guttural sadness for Bhagwat's life, the things he did and meant that no outsider could understand. Over lunch, she knows the staff knows, but no one says anything, as if silence is the only sincere response. And the rain continues, big clopping drops that hit the roof so hard, the teachers have to stop teaching and wait. By the end of the week, though the staff refuses to recover, Nadiya is making an effort at normalcy again, at perfunctory questions and sad laughter, an educated affectation that intensifies from Deonar to South Bombay where Ifra, smiling competently, assures her that the board will love her photographs. Her gratitude for Ifra's praise reaffirms that they are of one kind (to her distress and Ifra's relief). Ifra asks if she has told anyone about the 'unfortunate situation' in Deonar. They wouldn't want it getting to the press. Doesn't Ifra know the video of Bhagwat's beating had gone viral? Then again, the press might not care any more than the police unless it's her or Ifra telling the tale.

BLACK BILE: During her early weeks in Deonar, she switched from colour to monochrome; there was so much going on that seeing things in black and white made it easy to shut off the noise and isolate what to shoot. Then she went back, believing that you can't *really* see the place if you stay away from colour. Now, as she presents her archive to the board, both modes seem nauseatingly reductive, and as the slides roll on, she feels a black bile rising in her. Anu Sehgal may love her image of children in green uniforms running past a darker green mosque, but when face to face with poverty, something always breaks the scheme. There are no unexpected harmonies, no view free of the ugly fluorescence of a plastic sheet or bucket. The only images of real value, she thinks, are the rejects – outtakes overwhelmed by the sun or blurred by dust, cropped edges with chaotic lines and broken faces – for the only honest composition inspired by such rupture is one that fails. As for the journalistic impulse, braver photographers are bearing witness to the world. So long as she is safe, she is here for beauty, a malaise that infects not only these photographs, but in a deeper vein, includes the impulses that led to Bhagwat's death. Entering the police station, she was not driven by justice but something proud and poetic; she did not act from an impulse to do right but her self-conception as a righteous soul. Bleeding Heart, Impact Fellow, Volunteer in the Global South: it is all so paraded by the media (she too is the subject of someone's frame) that she can barely look past herself even as she stares at death – here, at the heart of it, something of a man's death is still unreal to her, as if there's a wall of glass between her and the world, or a second skin fused around her eyes, nostrils and every orifice … and as the Board claps, the bile, dark and viscous, rises past her lungs to her glottis. When they break for tea, she rushes to the restroom and hunkers over a pot, and she heaves and heaves, but nothing comes.

NO WORD GRANDER THAN CARE: She did not know that the body could roil and expunge itself this way. The fellowship doctor maintains that she has ingested food poisoned with faeces. Her gut will be altered for life. What made her think she could change this desperate world and not be morphed herself? Then Rohit texts: *Can't believe Ifra had to tell me ur sick.* An hour later, he struts in with a tiered lunchbox. There is chicken soup, rice congee with green onions, stewed apples for dessert. There are rehydrating salts and probiotics. This is a peace offering. 'Thank my mom and Sita,' he says, his desire to impress couched in nonchalance, as if it's what he would do for any friend, but she can see the self-satisfied puff of his chest. She wants to cry. She has told no one outside Ashray about Bhagwat, and she is determined not to lean on Rohit, but when he offers to get her an appointment with a doctor who is a family friend, she lets him. Finally, he asks how things are going at Deonar, and from his tone, it is clear that he knows. 'Did Ifra tell you what happened?' she asks. 'Gyaan did,' he says softly, and pulls her into a hug. There is neither lust nor showboating in his hold, but his kiss on her forehead is so brotherly, it suggests no word grander than … care. She presses her cheek on his shoulder. It would have to be more than care for her to cry.

THE PRIVATE HOSPITAL IS CLEAN AND ORDERLY, but every corridor is crammed with patients, their hollow faces tipped back or slumped over. Rohit took this appointment; then, as abruptly as he arrived, he disappeared on a trip to Wai. He is a toxic young man who fosters dependency, she thinks. His favours are a way to secure power and to retain the right of refusal … 'They're calling you,' Manasi whispers to her. Behind a pale curtain, the doctor looks down her throat, presses cold metals against her torso, and a warm, hairy hand on her belly. He confirms the fellowship doctor's prognosis and prescribes a newer class of drugs. In the cab home, her fever makes the dusty city dreamlike. Then Manasi takes her hand, and the life in it prickles like a faint supernova. Until now, she thinks guiltily, she hardly noticed Manasi. There was Ifra's professional relevance, Cyrus's casual glamour, and Gyaan, she assumed, was Rohit's closest. Turns out Gyaan and Ifra have known Rohit for only two years. If they share an unresolved and mildly obsessive dynamic, it is because they are the type he aspires to be. By contrast, Cyrus and Manasi know him from his college days. Like cats, both show affection by hanging around, unperturbed by his antics, and they are the ones he calls on for personal errands. When they reach her studio, Manasi changes the sheets with an ease and familiarity that Rohit lacks. And this simple, unpretentious manner is exactly what she needs. She turns over on the bed and lets Manasi's small, deft hands unknot the spasm.

NAREN BRINGS HER YELLOW ROSES. His text was a surprise, and now these flowers. He sets them in an empty wine bottle, and the petals glow brighter as the daylight fades. He looks tidy and fresh, her studio and fever-soaked bed even dingier against his white collar. 'I'm so tired,' she confesses. 'It isn't just the illness. I've been here for two months and the faces still look the same. Dad once said all Asians look alike, and I told him that's racist.' Naren says, 'When I went to America, I wasn't used to the features. All white people looked the same. All black people looked the same. Then you begin to see.' Barely listening, she goes on, 'It's like, you want to be comprehensible so you speak in this other voice, you don't want to stand out so you wear these other clothes, and before you know it, you're this stranger that isn't you or what you wanted to become. When I first got here, India was a big colourful blur, but I was always whole and watching. Then the air and water eat into you, and I tell myself the old me has to break away for the new me to rise out, but I'm *tired*.' 'That's rough,' Naren says. He must know about Bhagwat. Then again, Rohit promised not to tell anyone, and he doesn't bring it up so she doesn't either. And the weight of the unspoken strains the conversation. She talks nervously and yet on autopilot, like when her censure wells beyond herself and she says, 'I get that it isn't easy. People here look through poverty.' Naren's expression goes cold. He says something cynical about Ashray getting its funding from an investment bank his firm audits. When he leaves, she feels like he wanted to be sympathetic but she wore him down, and she is the reason they have not kept in touch since her stay at Imperial Heights.

LIKE A PHOTOGRAPH EDITED TO THE POINT IT LOSES all semblance to the original, the moment is warped beyond recall: a mouth opening, *Bhagwat is gone, Bhagwat is dead*, and then, a scene so vivid, it sends a torque through her plexus: a purple sari, the face tilting from it grey, the chin crimson. She sits up sweating. Andrei has texted again, and she finally returns his calls. When she tells him about her illness, he sounds almost relieved. 'I could have been there with you,' he says. He doesn't add, Assuming we were married and I could leave the States without worry. 'I know,' she says. 'I know.' When he says goodbye, his voice feels remote, yet distance has not made him irrelevant. If anything, her family is more dependent on him and her sense of obligation deeper. Meanwhile, the woman of purpose that India drew out has struggled to hold up. After Bhagwat, she is less sure she isn't the person Andrei imagines her to be and if her place isn't in Jaffrey. She lies back down in the dark. Flashes of home. Those quiet mornings minus the static from Nana's radio or the TV in her parents' bedroom: urgent drumming followed by a newscaster's baritone … and her sense of the world across the pine boards, all that news of crash and collapse in a voice as muffled as the conscience of an ordinary man. Worse still was when the TV was up front, and horrified by a child's shoe soaked in blood, she felt good about feeling bad, felt relevant if not in action then at least in sentiment, so gratifying her subconscious desire for a life as visceral as when she was a child transfixed by the beaver pond, nothing holding her mind from slipping in with the gold-green newts. Feelings, she thinks, the word itself so sly and bloodless, calling to mind fat housecats that lick their paws and each other indulgently. Feelings.

## *Rohit, Towards an Identity*

He has hit the country's sugar bowl. The clouds are pewter grey, and the cane fields are glowing like they've sucked all the light out of the sky. A month ago, he might have driven past thinking, How prosperous. Thanks to Omkar, he is getting the dew out of his eyes. He knows that cane is a colonial crop that drains the state dry and forces farmers further east to drink pesticide; he knows of the nexus between sugar barons, politicians, banks and universities; and that the women hoeing that ditch by the road will have to grease some palms to get their minimum wage.

Cyrus said, 'You're just addicted to his third-worldness.' Sure, but he isn't Amanda; he has no standard-bearer vanity. To get the scent of what's next, and how to tweak and hoist it towards what should be, *that's* what he's about, and he has sensed that it is in heartland writers and English subtitles that his generation will find its tongue.

Besides, he is done waiting on Gyaan. The man has been working on a script for years, and it isn't imagination that's lacking, it's urgency. Gyaan went to a fancy film school that made him so afraid of failing his potential, he's paralysed himself. Omkar, on the other hand, has the guts to grow in the public eye. He doesn't pretend like the market doesn't exist. He didn't make an ego deal about *Bappa*. He calls all the time to share ideas for scripts.

If Gyaan asks why he made this trip, he will say: I wanted to get a sense of the kid. Who is this crazy Hindu nationalist that keeps us up at night? Where's he from, doesn't the election make you ask? Doesn't what happened with Ifra and Amanda in Deonar make you ask? Or something like that anyway.

The windscreen is starting to blot. He has come over the backbone of the Sahyadri, and this is no warm coastal rain, but a desolate drizzle against which even the crops shiver. In the grey, an old woman is holding her head in her palm. Pathos enhances the beauty of the black earth plumped with chemicals, a red hibiscus on a tin roof … ah, everything is in stacks here – plastic cans, cable rollers, dung, wood, tiles, packets of chips hanging from shacks – everything heaped against the rain, everything, even the heart…

If he isn't playing the hero this morning, it's because he's done with Amanda taking his help like she were doing *him* a favour. There he was, dabbing her forehead and draining the damn sink because she won't keep a maid or do the dishes either, when Omkar texted, *Come to Wai sometime, I'll show you the locations for Ek Sangharsh*, and he replied, *Sure, how about this weekend?* Omkar was startled. So was he … But heck, in these days of refusing to even think too much about Amanda – because he isn't playing it cool, he doesn't want to get invested; Andrei is still on the farm and any pleasure in transgression is long gone – Omkar will be positively salubrious.

The hills are picking up again. The farmhouses give way to thatch huts, the plantations to small, waterlogged fields that mirror the sky. Click, upload, #heartland. Gyaan says what makes hegemony so insidious is beauty. What does that even mean? If this land has any beauty, it's in things hard, humble, and true in the way a life lived close to the elements is true. Here in the placid monotony of heavy industries and ploughs, of hard labour, and a grey tiredness and grim resilience: here is our Maharashtra.

For all Omkar's jokes about being a villager, Wai is a small town. It's hills for miles, then the clouds part, a bridge appears, and you're in Wai: a black stone temple to the right, a market to the left, the intersection teeming with guides for tours to the caves in which the Pandavas rested, a Shiva linga from the eighth century, a Ganesha temple from the eleventh, the hill on which Shivaji ripped out Afzal Khan's guts. The Konkan is closed off between the hills and the sea, but on the Deccan plateau, there is no gap between the country's myths and history. The line from ancient to medieval to modern times is unbroken.

The GPS guides him past the temple crowd and the market crowd, and within minutes, he is parking under a banyan tree so vast you'd grow wise just sitting in its shade. Trust Omkar, with his instinct for a scene, to choose Menavali Ghat as a meeting point. Twin sandstone temples … long steps to a river … the trees reflecting darker, the temples paler in the river's green glass. The architecture is so serene it might have stood this way for a thousand years, and his blood hums to what generations of his ancestors have considered *ours*.

There is no trash, no hawking, no cattle, or even people except Omkar, sitting on the steps. When called, Omkar turns like a Bollywood hero, looks over bright blue aviators and laughs. What's so funny? Omkar asks if he recognizes the place. 'No? And our Agashe calls himself a film-maker.' Turns out Wai is Bollywood's favourite village. 'See that bell house? That was in *Omkara*. That banyan tree was in *Swades*. They solidly spruced up the temples for that shoot.' *Ek Sangharsh* opens with a crowd scene in which a starry-eyed kid paid to be an extra gets his first taste of movie magic.

Now that he, Rohit, knows why the temples are so familiar, he feels stupid about his enchantment. They walk along the steps, or 'ghats' as Omkar calls them, for they were built by a Peshwa statesman in the image of those at Varanasi. That's why, besides the hundreds of temples, Wai is called Dakshin Kashi, the Varanasi of the south. That gets Omkar talking about the same wealth that Gyaan spoke of as robbed and broken, but unlike Gyaan, Omkar's colonizers refer to both the British and the Mughals.

Omkar says in Marathi, 'Your Gyaan is a Delhi boy, isn't he? These North Indians think they have culture because they go to Lucknow for Urdu poetry. Such fetishes are colourful, but India's real culture is preserved in the south. Meaning, the cradle of our civilization was invaded and occupied by foreigners for so long, its essence was lost. But the history of India is not the history of Delhi. The Mughals did not have the same control down here; we had Hindu kings ruling us right until the British. That is why we have confidence in ourselves. And the reform movements, like women's rights and anti-caste, took off here, while the north is still feudal and full of brutes. That is also why the Bharat Brotherhood was founded in our Marathi-speaking state and not the Hindi-speaking heartland…'

Omkar says, 'Why not some other southern state? I'll answer in one word: Shivaji. This idea of swaraj, that Hindus must rule themselves, this was our Shivaji Raje's idea. He is the reason why a Marathi man feels no conflict between his regional loyalty and the Hindu national dream. Today, even in Delhi they recognize that, if not for Raje, all Hindus would be converted.'

Omkar says, 'What do you mean, do many people here feel like me? Who doesn't love Shivaji? As to your question on why is he still relevant when we have no Mughals or British to fight … thing is, Shivaji was a great warrior, but he was a great reformer first. Married a low-caste widow. Ate one meal of milk and rice a day. The Peshwas is how our trunk went soft. The Brahmins entered politics, and when the game was up, they became British babus, and now the English are gone, but the English speakers are looting the country. This is the legacy we have to fight…'

Omkar says, 'Don't misunderstand me, Agashe. I am not saying we have to fight the Brahmins, but Brahmanvaad. Not the West, but Western mindset. Not Muslims, but terror of Islam. There are many battles. One prime minister is not enough. You are also in this fight…'

He doesn't care for Omkar's version of history any more than Ravi Kaka's, but unlike with Kedar, he is not disqualified from coming along. Where they're going, they can debate.

Back in the car, trailing Omkar's bike. Every fifty metres, people holler and Omkar waves back. No one blinks at the plastic bag on his head. He says he doesn't care about getting wet, but he's having trouble with dandruff. Under his yellow stole, his T-shirt reads NIRVANA, and his jeans are stiff even in the rain. Clothes one considers casual, Omkar wears with all the care of a chambray shirt. Bet he has no clue that Nirvana is a band.

Raw air of jungle vines, faint tang of Lifebuoy soap. Everything so wet it makes you want to pee. The heart of the town has all its shutters open. Dreamflower talc … doodh dahi colddrink … STD ISD PCO. Nostalgia for the town's mediocrity, for childhood brands that he assumed the whole country left behind when the Agashes did.

Above the cheap shop signs are billboards and posters in three dominant themes: English Classes, Computer Basics, Personality Development. Here is India's new middle class, fruit of its land reforms, hungry spawn of liberalization. And he loves the people as if they were one person, the ebb and flow of their energy, their thoughts leaking into each other.

They park where the road ends and the fields take over. Whatever he expected of Omkar's home, it wasn't this: an unfinished concrete building, iron cables rising from it like candles off a grotesque cake. To diffuse the impact, Omkar says, 'My uncle helped us buy the place. The builder constructed two floors, then ran out of money. Heh.' There's a salon in the basement with a standee of Justin Bieber, his palms pressed over the words *Welcome-Namaste*.

Omkar's uncle (whose home features in *Ek Sangharsh*) has pneumonia, so they are to have lunch with his mother instead. The woman in the doorway looks ancient for her age, but then one remembers the beatings. Through owlish glasses, she croaks, 'All Bargya's friends call me Mai.' From the kitchen, Omkar's sister says, 'Don't call him Bargya around his city friends. This is Mister Omkar Khaire, or is there a new surname too?'

Pink walls stained by oily heads … a cabinet bench with thin cushions … a plywood unit stuffed with a box TV, an empty fish tank, and all manner of junk from old toys to a Personality Development certificate that makes him ache. Has he done to Omkar what Amanda did to Naren by taking up a casual invitation and bungling into a private life? To compensate, he gets Mai and

Girija giggling at his terrible Marathi, and Omkar is compensating too because he keeps telling 'Agashe and me' stories and grabbing his knee like they're old pals.

The ladies insist the men eat first. There is no dining table, so they sit on the floor. Girija sets a plastic runner with two steel plates and tumblers. There is only one dish, a mutton curry with gland and marrow, but it tastes just grand, the meat gamey, the bhakris hot off the stove and buttered. Omkar teases, 'Our Agashe is a real Brahmin, can't handle our spice.' Everyone laughs at his nose going red. Unlike his friends, Omkar refers to his caste without awkwardness, mostly as a joke. He knows Omkar is a backward caste, but not which one.

Omkar's nose is clear. He is slurping like there is nothing tastier than this food he has eaten all his life. Then Mai complains that he eats meat only on special occasions since he got with the Brotherhood. 'If Agashe's visit isn't a special occasion, what is?' Omkar says to divert her, but Mai's complaints run on, like how he works all the time and won't take a wife who will help her after Girija marries, until Girija snaps, 'Zau de na, Aai.'

After lunch, the Khaires offer him their only bedroom for a siesta. Wonder if they cleared the bed just for him, since there's an insane amount of mess around it, just heaps of clothes and newspapers and stuff piled up the walls, as if this were a rat's nest made from bits of trash. He can see why Omkar doesn't want Mai's home in his film. His struggle has an aesthetic, and this is neither a poetic hamlet nor his uncle's house which is impressive in a traditional way.

And here above the curtainless window is Shivaji, a garland on the frame and sandalwood daubs on the glass like on prints of gods. To Gyaan and Ifra, the king is a property of the fanatics who changed Bombay's name to Mumbai. They won't admit that he is a working-class and peasant hero, not a white-collar one, so some of that recoil isn't so progressive. He looks out of the window. That poor farmer on the road in his dirty white shirt and the manure under his nails, that's the man Shivaji gave dignity. How can you squat on the common people's king and expect them to love you?

Around Omkar, he has noticed, he calls Bombay 'Mumbai' because he doesn't care to flaunt his English. Or is it around Girija? She was skimming the fat off the gravy and pouring it on his pieces like an offering, when he became aware of her body in her kurta and her round face that Aai would think ordinary but that brought a sigh up from his navel that went, *So Marathi*. Funny how he came to Wai to suss Omkar out, and what he has discovered is his own regional identity as a son of Maharashtra.

In the window, Omkar is driving down the road in his uncle's Santro. He waves to the farmer, who waves back. When Omkar comes upstairs, Girija says, 'Just see, Agashe's nose will still be red.' And he looks in the cupboard mirror, and heck, it is.

After tea, they set out in the Santro because, according to Omkar, you can drive it anywhere. Parked rickshaws and fallen dividers flank the road. Barely has the trash and debris eating into one village subsided when the next begins. A white SUV overtakes them. On its rear, a Marathi Bana tiger roars. The Bana is a party for the Marathi working-class man, and if anyone is the essence of this man, it's Khaire, but when asked why he isn't a volunteer with them, Omkar frowns. 'The Bana are political opportunists who exploit Shivaji's name. I don't approve of the Bharat Party tying hands with them, but in politics you have to compromise.'

They park beside a dyke. The black loam is smelling sweet. Omkar has plans to build a farmhouse he will rent to film crews on this field, but for now just a rutty bit of earth fenced in wire. There is no tractor or equipment, only a tin shed from which two snotty children and a snot-eyed goat are sizing them up. Omkar says, 'So, what do you think of your farmer friend's estate?' He tries to match Omkar's irony, but his time runs out.

Omkar says, 'Look there, Agashe. All those big cane plantations don't belong to my people, the original people of Shivaji. My people are Kunbis. Kunbi simply means peasant, and all the people here were Kunbis once. Then some of them joined Shivaji's army and announced they are Maratha by caste and started to think of themselves as warriors. No Maratha will marry a Kunbi, and the only time a Maratha calls himself a Kunbi is when he's fighting for the backward caste quotas reserved for my people...'

Omkar says, 'You asked why I'm not with the Marathi Bana. To tell you the truth, I was attracted to them, but if you really go into it, the Bana only cares about the Maratha caste. Even if they don't appease Muslims like the Conclave, they don't care for all Marathi-speaking men, let alone all Hindus. Only the Bharat Party cares for all Hindus. Whether you're Kunbi or Maratha or Brahmin doesn't matter. They are here to give jobs and electricity...'

Omkar says, 'I've lived in the city, so I understand what a manifesto is, but people here still vote like villagers. Meaning, they vote for the Janata Conclave Party. Some Marathi politicians in the Conclave Party broke away and founded the Janata Conclave saying we will do this and that for Maharashtra, but now they're allies and both are as corrupt and play the same caste games. No one here cares about unity. No one cares about the country. That is why, even in this great election, the Bharat Party lost Wai. But let's see. We have a saying in the village: Keep a bhakri on the stove too long without turning it and it will burn…'

Omkar's voice is swelling with emotion. He may have contempt for Brahmins, but for Marathas, his resentment borders on hatred, and for all his talk of voting like a city man, he wants his new friend to affirm that, as castes left out by regional politics, they share something that the Bharat Party is the solution to. Then suddenly, Omkar says, 'But you know all this, right?' like it's incredible that it isn't evident to a fellow son of the soil. Unsure of his reply, he tells Omkar that the field is a good location for *Ek Sangharsh*. Omkar sighs. 'Not everything is about movies, Agashe. Cinema is only my ten-year plan.'

He is about to ask what comes after, when Omkar's sharecropper appears. The man is such a knot of bones, it's a relief when he puts down his water drum. Resting one foot on the other knee, the poor devil tells Omkar about marigold seeds: with Ganeshotsav coming up, the flower will be in demand. 'Wait here until we're back, Agashe,' Omkar says. 'One look at you and the vendor will triple the price.' After they leave, a woman in a thin sari comes out of the hut and starts washing some pots with ash and water from the drum. When he nods hello, she fixes him with a rock-hard stare. Who knows where she stands on this harsh land?

On the drive back to Wai, they stop for roasted cobs by the roadside. The smell of hot corn in the monsoon air reminds him of childhood. Omkar says, 'Unless you're a total villager, this is how you eat it,' and he neatly nibbles off a row of kernels. Not as easy as it looks. Then he says to the corn seller, 'My friend is from Mumbai, but his parents didn't teach him anything.'

Dusk. They park at the edge of a wide, sandy bank. Omkar hums *Shanth wahate Krishna-mai*. He says the lyrics mean that a truly great person is as quiet as the river Krishna. It's the same river at Menavali Ghat, but here she is in full sweep, dark and slow under the clouds. This is where *Ek Sangharsh* ends, with a teenaged Omkar watching the river surge past the Dhom dam and leave the town.

Standing next to Omkar, he feels a new reverence for this water and soil. Then Omkar takes his hand … and it's just a simpler, sweeter kind of friendship, the kind made in school, intense but free of homophobia, so it's nothing if, an hour later, he is resting like this, his head on Omkar's thigh, the mist coming down the hills on all sides. Beneath them, the Krishna is swelling. He has a quart of rum on his chest since it's 'the thing to do on the dam', not that Omkar drinks. Omkar is telling stories of pranks from his schooldays, and the moment feels pure…

… what the–? A thump sets his back spinning. WOOSHMP. Cold silt rushes into his nose and mouth … the water magnifies his lashes … air, sparkle, chill. On the dam, Omkar is laughing. The bastard! He swims up to the rocks and chases Omkar around the lake, wet, laughing. Before he is out of breath, his anger is laughter. Omkar is ten feet away, laughing, dry. Then Omkar climbs the rocks, holds his nose and plunges into the lake. Nothing to do but jump in after.

When they get back to Mai's, they dry off and sleep on the narrow bed like puppies. He wakes up in the morning to five missed calls – two from Aai, one from Gyaan, and two from Amanda – and he is so dazed that Girija and Omkar can't stop giggling. Their wholesomeness! Eager to be like them, he texts Amanda: *How'd it go with the doc?* She is online, but she doesn't reply. In a way, Omkar reminds him of Amanda – both are evocative, like a folk song so simple you can't believe the hold it has on your city-slick heart – but Omkar isn't up in the stratosphere.

After a breakfast of bread with salted butter and tea, they drive to the nearby village of Wadhe. On the edge of a grassy field is a low, whitewashed house, with nothing to announce it as a Brotherhood branch. There is a rustic gym behind, and a flagless pole in front. Omkar unlatches the door. Woven mats … brooms … a metal cupboard … a vinyl Mother India in a saffron sari … framed prints of freedom fighters and Brotherhood founders. The only object that isn't faded is a table covered in white cloth and piled with history books and religious booklets.

Omkar says, 'This was my first library. Most of the books are by interpreters because the minds of Adi Shankara and Vivekananda are too complex for ordinary men. Honestly, I only read the Brotherhood magazine, and the novels. These are our Marathi classics that showed me I am not alone in my struggle, and that the old guard is a rope burnt through; all it needs is a final kick for the ashes to scatter…'

Omkar says, 'When I was growing up, there was no cultural activity in the town, so my cousin brought me here and I liked it. People say all kinds of things about the Brotherhood, but it is nothing like that. Members wear brown shorts, sing patriotic songs, do yoga, or trek to Shivaji's forts. The goal is to turn out cultured young men who are fit and committed to service…'

Sounds like a desi boy scouts. When they step out, a dhotied ghost is resting his cycle on the wall. This is Sathe Sir, the retired maths teacher who started the branch and helped Omkar apply to a polytechnic in Pune. 'To study printing, was it?' Sathe croaks. Both laugh. 'The degree wasn't much,' Sathe confesses, 'but it got our Bargya out of Wai.' They talk of public health … of corruption … of agrarian distress. Omkar says, 'Sathe Sir is the only teacher I respect in Wai.' And Sathe laughs humbly and tells them to come again.

Wet roads banked with mud. Traffic fuming into acid rain. Not even pathos redeems the view, but with Omkar beside him in the car, the gloomy pylons are high totems of progress, the naked pipes hope for cracked fields, and all the things that are broken or unfinished only reaffirm the work to be done. At the bridge, Omkar hugs him with real feeling and says, 'Don't go to the big city and forget your village friend, Agashe.'

Driving out, he looks at the trucker stops with their red chairs and he can taste the over-boiled tea on which Omkar's batteries run. To know Omkar is to know this world, and to know this world is to make sense of the layers and contradictions that make up his friend: from these damp hills, a reminder of Omkar's bitter past and his desire for reform; from Menavali Ghat, his love of the movies and celebrity; from Wai market, the empty promises of globalization; from his field, the caste fault lines that keep a Shivaji lover from joining the Marathi Bana; from Mai's home, that it isn't poverty Omkar wants to escape but small-town hopelessness and mediocrity. Omkar wants it big, and at each step, you get his frustration. The diploma that got no job, the unfinished cement building, the film fraternity that won't back him because of his loyalty to the one association that hasn't let him down.

Well, he has seen what he came here to see, and he can't imagine why they shouldn't make *Bappa* even if he passes on *Ek Sangharsh*. If his friends have reservations, they can talk them through. It isn't Gyaan's dad funding the Box.

# *Naren, Towards Freedom*

There is no visible sun though the light is slowly building. The sea and sky are one, a solid grey all the way to the promenade. The smug pleasure of waking early, of cheating time rather than chasing it, of stretching the vertebrae to unlock the energy of the spine. Pitch day, Naren. And he's up. His cardio and weights take no more than forty minutes. He enjoys the force of his high-rise shower, and pairing an ivory blazer with blue trousers because his boss may wear a suit but his client likes sass. At last, the fog in his head has burned away. It's like a higher Naren were guiding him – a voice, decisive and unhurried, firing his confidence and bringing him in rhythm with his place and his times – as he steps out on this: his first major deal in India. By now, the many-armed sun is spiralling, the

*you must see the outcome*
*as if it is already achieved*

surge in and out of rush hour has begun. Snug in his Uber, he visualizes his brief to the Magnus board. Half a decade ago, Brahma Industries spun off its pipes business to create an entity run by the great R.K. Jain's brother, and while the core of Magnus Inc. is still pipes for Brahma Mines, RK's nephew wants to go further: he wants to get into sanitation, he wants to become a household name. Ah, Ankush Jain, he is a piece of art with no unity of composition but an unremitting energy, on some days in the vanguard for building a twenty-first-century company, on others a traditional Lala grown tall pushing stocks down the gullet of wholesalers, on all days a sentimental Gujju rubbing his hands over the Bharat Party's promise to build a hundred New Cities. When Landsworth reached out to Ankush, it was already on his mind to go public; all he needed to fund his expansion was a financial strategy to present to investors (and his board and his father) from a mouth other than his own. Nevertheless, he, Naren, has done his homework, he only has to keep this confidence going, this not pausing for breath or doubt, this seeing the outcome as if it has already been achieved. Delta Corporate Park, gate one. His boss is in a charcoal suit, chewing on a cigarette. Yohan says, 'D-day, Agashe. If you ask me, the projections for Magnus *are* bullish. Our internal review committee would have shot down your plan if not for Indrani Dey. Personally, my concern isn't our time or money. It's that our brand as a practice is at risk.' He says nothing to Yohan of his team sitting up all night. He says, 'Trust me, I've got this. I'm lunching with Ankush Jain before meeting the board.' Yohan nods. 'So long as we don't fall on our faces.' This is typical Yohan, he thinks as he takes the elevator, he's the kind of boss who'll cover his ass instead of pumping you up before a pitch; that way, if Magnus rejects you, he can say he told you so. The doors open to the bright office mayhem. Sales is sex when the economy is booming. The libido in the air, boys out to charm the men, others the women, some of the women, men, but not enough women charm women. The managers share an intimacy like that of newlyweds in an arranged marriage, that is, not one built over time but the result of a near-identical background. They are the Indian version of his American colleagues: kids from top B-schools whom the firm will drive to aneurysms for their hunger to buy real estate in Goa and frame Bali on their iPhones. But for all this homogeneity, the social matrix here is already revealing the codes it took him so long to decipher in America, the names and accents that, added to talent and drive, separate the faces he must charm from those he may ignore. Here in the pantry is one he must charm: senior partner Indrani Dey; one he may ignore: LK, the voice of Yohan's old guard; and one to keep an eye on, Esha, Dey's herald for the new. He starts the vending machine and stares blankly at

*the instinct of the firm is to go*
*for the win – always*

the cookie jar. He has barely reached their table when Esha says, 'Is the Magnus pitch today? My grapevine tells me McKnight consultants are in with their finance guys and casting doubts on your model.' So the baiting has begun, the presence of a senior partner frothing it up. Counteract Esha. Show who has the client's ear. Say, 'You think they are sharks here? Try Wall Street. McKnight can get as deep as they like in the finance function's pants. Magnus is an Indian family show and I've got the chairman's son in my pocket.' Dey smiles approvingly. LK panics. 'My issue is the whole political situation. The Bharat Party is holding these massive summits where they make a lot of noise about new hubs and corridors, but where is the money? Ankush Jain wants to go public in a bid to provide the new New Cities with drainage. The central budget so far is eight hundred crore. Tell me how many cities you can build with that, Agashe.' He is about to give LK the reply he will give the Magnus board when Indrani Dey comes in, 'Guys these are the large deals Landsworth plays in. Yes, they are complex, but complexity is what we are here to handle.' He feels a gush of warmth towards her salt-and-pepper bob, her Chinese collar and pearl studs. Esha is a frontbencher who wants to show Teacher Dey that she has the answers, but she has given him information. LK is more stupidly hostile. Well, they can have the battle. He will have his team revisit his model in case McKnight is gaming it. On the way out, he notices Dey fixing a second coffee for her desk. He gets one too. As the machine gurgles, Dey says, 'I got in late on the internal review meeting. Will Magnus's core still remain mining pipes? Good. I've heard the new government plans to amend the Mining Act. Licences will be given at auction. It will open the market to a lot of new players, so Magnus has a backup if the New Cities fail.' He thanks her for the tip. Dey drops her decibel, 'Oh and don't mind LK. He didn't make it to our Winners Circle last year, and Yohan backing you on Magnus means he won't again. Let me tell you something, Naren. The Winners Circle isn't about the holiday or bonus. It is a sign the firm is watching its top performers. If you aren't on it, you can't survive.' He doesn't smile like that motivates him. He looks serious. Dey continues, 'Remember, the instinct of the firm is to go for the win – always. Don't underestimate our networks. We can reach the PMO in two calls. If Magnus Pipes tanks, we lose six months of work and a little credibility. But if it soars? We're talking a key account for the firm, money at each stage of the plan's implementation. As you know, most first-generation Indian companies aren't really first generation. They are the children and grandchildren of the big boys. One brother in five gets into the one per cent and the clan rises with him. They invest in each other, they intermarry and share contacts at the wedding. Given your relationship with Ankush Jain, this could mean a toehold in the entire Brahma empire. What I'm saying is, Magnus Pipes has the potential to become your first rocket client. Tell me why we call them that? Because a handful of such clients is your fast track to a partnership.' Now he smiles and says, 'That's nice.' Dey leaves him with an encouraging nod and a raised eyebrow that suggests: you are in the spotlight, don't fuck this up. As a senior partner in another vertical, she has less at stake than Yohan in getting him to risk this deal. Even so, she has signalled more than once that she

*to have ambition, you must make peace with resentment and have faith that power protects*

supports him, and it isn't only her. His effect was evident right from the recruitment interview: the finance head chatting him up as though on an evening at the club, and if the head of HR had any apprehensions that he was too white for India, he shot through them in a month. If there's one thing America has taught him, he reflects as he strides to his cabin, it's the value of narrative in the theatre of success. He was never shy about personal achievements, like his alma maters or the books he read, but now he has added to his story all those factors that, from some rotten ideal of humility, he never consciously leveraged: that he is male, has a surname that spells pedigree, and speaks an Anglophone speech out of a fair face that might not be in vogue today when it's all about cheekbones, but could pass as a Bollywood hero from the fifties. No doubt his peers are waking up to similar ambitions. The rigid hierarchies of the past have been shaken by over two decades of neoliberalism, a ripening middle class, and the prospect of making wealth in one's own country. But what is a new game in India is old news for him, which gives him a subtlety his peers lack. He never mentions his caste but jokes about his intolerance for spice, he introduces himself not as Naren but Agashe, and he wears shirts of a colour that emphasize his pale skin regardless of what *Gentleman's Quarterly* claims is in vogue. As for social connections, he never drops names too early or brags about lunch with a partner; he waits until the partner casually mentions it to LK, who panics, wondering how many such lunches he has kept to himself. Of course, he reflects, plugging in his monitor, there is a final ingredient: a dash of brusqueness.

The dynamic that began around Amanda on his return – his first clumsy steps towards a new authority – has cohered. He is less out of depth in his potential, and with a little flex here or pressure there, people respond, not to his niceness but to his refreshing arrogance. And this time, he decides, he has no intention of charming with the please-all earnestness he saw to its limits in America. To have ambition anywhere is to make peace with resentment and to have faith that power protects. The censure of men like LK is nothing but the impotent hustle of weaklings; the moment he shoots past them, they will not have the courage to act on their resentment because they stand to lose more than gain by messing with him, and for every nonentity turned off, others delight in his new avatar. Already there are bids for his loyalty – senior partners who want him on their team, junior managers who bat their eyes like girls at his advance – and the Magnus deal will cement that perception; it will prove that his arrogance isn't fluff. He sips his bitter coffee and snaps

*expediency is all: in business, you don't have the luxury of interrogating every risk*

into doing mode. He walks over to his team, their faces mesmerized by their screens as if they're staring into a crystal ball (going by their analysis, they might well be). He says, 'Guys, huddle in ten, I want a status check.' Back in his cabin, one half of his brain scans their slides, the other takes stock of their modes. Shivam has a sideways smile that suggests he didn't go to a blue-chip B-school but is smarter than those who did and knows it; he networks with managers one level up; one has to admit he gets the game, and the more freedom given, the better. Janki is the first woman in her family with a master's; she wears kurtas and thinks women in pants are prissy; she is an emotional minefield who works her clients by playing both lion and lamb, but she needs to know her boss has her back. Cyrus's boyfriend, Jay, studied economics at the London School; he isn't sure if he fits in, but this insecurity is undercut by the profound security that he needn't care; this job is merely 'exposure' until he joins his VC dad. Jay gets along with managers many levels up, yet one can't be sure if he's networking or doing it for fun, and they enjoy his candour; the challenge is to keep him harnessed without falling for his charm. If Shivam and Janki remind him of himself in Manhattan, wide-eyed, hungry for sophistication, Jay reminds him of Cathy. Who in this office is Eric … But here they come, his subordinates, filing in across his desk. Up close, they look more tired than wired. He didn't intend for them to be up all night, but Yohan sent an email asking for ten additional points, and covering them was more a matter of handling Yohan than the client, and it is these guys who did the work while he and Yohan slept. He warms them up with a compliment and an easy tip, 'The Magnus chairman is an old Gujju who won't like this blue theme. Go for yellow because it is auspicious.' Then he brings on the real concerns. 'On what basis is this the market potential for consumer pipes?' Janki says, 'Government MOUs on the New Cities, boss.' He says, 'MOUs don't always get deployed. We can't come across as consultants who take such things at face value.' He tells them to look up a similar summit and see how much money actually came through. Janki and Jay glance at each other. They are wilting as he whips them on to justify his projections, and the only way to push them further is to give them a sense of control. He says, 'I just heard McKnight is in with Magnus's finance team and poking holes in our model. I want to know what you would do in this situation.' Janki stares at a paperweight. Jay gives him a smile suggesting solidarity in a tough moment. Shivam says, 'We have one baseline model. Maybe we could work out two or three scenarios.' He says *fantastic* so loudly, Shivam almost jumps. 'Let's have three scenarios: baseline, optimistic, pessimistic. Our proposal is the optimistic one, but I can use the other two to defend it.' Shivam smiles a sardonic smile and Janki a relieved one. Jay frowns. 'I don't think we have time for that kind of analysis. Should we be going for this pitch if we don't have such basic clarity?' Millennial nerve. Millennial naïveté. He says, 'Fair question, Jay. But in business, expediency is all. Even the best consultants don't have the luxury of interrogating every risk. If there's scope to make a difference, we go in, because if we don't, McKnight will, so nothing changes except us losing the pitch and any control we have on doing a better job.' Jay nods pensively. Janki breathes like she is ready. And having given his team freedom, support and moral pep, he does an Indrani Dey and dangles the Winners Circle carrot until they're rubbing their hands in nervous excitement. Then he takes a final look at their calculating, hopeful faces, and he thinks: Lambs. Darlings. Chutiyas.

*the greatest error is to believe that you are a sinner,*
*a wretch deficient in character*

As they file out, he checks his calendar. In a rush of adrenaline, he sends nine emails, vets two spreadsheets, makes five calls, and books an Uber for the Sofitel. Waiting for the cab, he rests his screen-roasted eyes on his cubicle. His boss, peers and subordinates have all warned him that this deal is preposterous. He recalls his visit to Gujarat's New City, its dismal sandy flats, the feeling that nothing there will need Magnus's pipes for decades. And even if it did, a deal this fat is hardly the sort of fish an associate partner sets out to fry. Then again, when he was a boy, he reflects as he packs his laptop, he was neither the class topper nor the charming delinquent, but had an instinct for understanding power structures and worming his way through them to create a detonation from within. While Rohit's rebellions, all quick victories and flops, relied on churn for success, his involved a slower steering of the ship whose sails he'd so gradually bend that it was not until the final year in school when he became head boy that his peers noticed the dark glacier in him that could break mountains. But somewhere along the way, he reflects as he takes the elevator, he lost this edge. What clouded him? Was it the ideals of his parents' generation, a Gandhian clamp on their balls, a Nehruvian clamp on everything else until the markets opened up? Or was it his convent schooling, the teachers always harping on service and discipline until he could barely think straight without an altar? When he caught the flight West, he was already corrupted, his motto being to do his best and leave the rest to god, which is to say, the justice of the markets. Before he knew it, he was both creating and being created by a brand that could only be described as the congenital Hindu – *There's something very Eastern about your brain*, Cathy said – intelligent but humble, ambitious without envy, happy to work as if work itself was the reward. When the dividends kicked in, he was almost as surprised as his peers at his success, and this time, his peers were no schoolboys; they punished him for their failures, and he accepted the punishment since he had come to hate himself. By the time the ninety-nine per cent occupied Wall Street, he was already in Waverly, but knowing the whole show stank didn't stop him from killing years in self-imposed exile at an offsite as lonely as a silo. Well, Vedanta recognizes no sin, only error, and the greatest error, it says, is to believe that you are a sinner, a wretch deficient in character. At last, he reflects as he gets into an Uber, he is returning to the kernel of who he was as a boy and from which everything he will be shall sprout. Not that he is unchanged. Within the spectrum of his person, here he is at his deal-making best, and since he is new here, people assume he has always been this way. Meanwhile, he is learning from everyone but modelling himself on no one, and for all his personal branding, he is occasionally unpredictable so that no one can pin him down and tack his wings with a tag announcing his phylum, that this is how he was born and this is how he will die.

*when people have power, they suck in the best of everything going around*

The Uber swerves on to the Sea Link, eight thousand tonnes of steel, wires that can wrap the earth's circumference, the sea face rising in a hundred concrete phalluses. BKC, the city's new business hub. When he left India, this wetland was a defecation haunt separating the high-rises of Bandra West from the squatter colonies east of the East, a place for sewage pipes, a mangrove swamp iridescent with scum, and further out, stray buildings with cranes on top like giant antennae. Just how they drained the gunk and made the ground firm enough to lay the foundation of what it is now – nineteen hectares of hulking blue glass towers, their front façades spelling the biggest names in the industry, five-star hotels, the diamond bourse – is a reverie that soothes any doubts about the New Cities taking off. This is what the country needs, this *ambition*. That is why a poor man's son becoming prime minister delights him. Meanwhile, his Uber halts at the Sofitel. Lawns buzz with vents and the hush of fountains. His elongated stride sails past the hubcap of a luxury sedan. The guards barely frisk him before the maître d' guides him to the café. They were likely thinking Paris when they named the café The Artisan and hired whatever artsy fuck to paint that Eiffel Tower. But if this is Paris, what's with the paisley wallpaper, and why are the waiters dressed like a cross between a durwan and a pastry chef? He thinks of Rohit's pursuit of authenticity. How to preserve what makes Indians special amid all this change? He may use his new vantage to play the game, but he wants to be the cream on good milk, he wants his countrymen well dressed and well mannered, their heads high, their roots deep in a bedrock of civilizational pride. He refreshes the content on his iPhone. Here is his surname on a byline. Kedar. Something about a farmer's protest against Brahma Mines expanding in the Konkan. He hopes that no one on the Magnus board has read the article. Should Ankush introduce him like he did to his father, that is, as the son of the man who gave Brahma their foothold in the Konkan (making it sound like it was more than one mangy plot) – he hopes they won't ask if Kedar is a relative. He checks his watch. He could review his notes, though data won't take him further; now is the time to get into character, and to play to the things Ankush loves about him, like his choice to return to India and their camaraderie as the modern and ambitious sons of old families (even if there is little comparison between the Agashes' wealth and the Jains running Magnus Pipes, let alone the Jains running Brahma). Ankush walks in, a navy blue blazer on jeans. He is in his forties but acts like a young pioneer at a start-up, stating what he wants without charts or even logic, but through the bright thrust of his hypomania. They shake hands. They recede. Ankush has lunched with the board, so they keep it to coffee. Ankush says they do the cold brew well. Surprising. The menu boasts ten different cuisines. Shouldn't that make one suspicious? Not Ankush. 'Yaar, Agashe,' he says, 'these days everything has everything in it. The tagline for this café is charcuterie, boulangerie, winery, finery, crap. But I was in Nairobi last week, I stayed at the Empire Hotel, and I realized that when people have real wealth, or had it, like the Brits, they suck in the best of everything going around. The coffee here is as good as in Paris, the sushi in Tokyo, the bagels in New York. So why not?' Why not, indeed.

Besides, this is how Ankush operates: he will infuse you with his mood, and his mood today suggests there is no future except the

*more important than your facts are your pronouns, in this case, 'we' and 'us'*

one in which you win. To mirror Ankush, he uncrosses his legs, talks about life abroad, and how he loves the new roasteries in Bandra not just for the coffee but because it's a sign that local entrepreneurs get a developed market's tastes. Ankush says, 'Catering to the aspiration of new India: that could be the title for our business plan.' He reminds Ankush the New Cities are an extension of that aspiration, the deals already under way, the big boys with the war chests going in. 'This plan will catapult us into their league,' he says. 'The government builds a springboard, and a family-run business sees the opportunity and takes the leap,' etc., etc. More important than his facts are his pronouns – in this case, 'we' and 'us' – to suggest they are a team against a world of sceptics, and by the time the coffee comes, they've worked themselves into a positive froth. Ankush says, 'I've gone through your slides. The story is good. But our board is hyper aware this plan could be the basis for an IPO, and they are a traditional bunch. I hope we're *very* sure about our calculations.' Ankush is being a sound CEO by suggesting nothing will fly without a buy-in from his unbiased board, but he can feel Ankush's tentacles reaching towards him, and the force he exudes in turn meeting Ankush in a fervid copulation above the tidy table, its still life of napkins and coffee, and in this vortex, this intersection of their Eulerian circles, this diagram composed of Set Naren (creatures with legs) and Set Ankush (creatures with wings), the anatomy of the proposition opens up: he tells Ankush about Shivam's three scenarios and asks for tips on what he can expect. 'Watch out for Bala,' Ankush says. 'He's an independent director, an ex-investment banker with every bit of a banker's cynicism. He has a tonne of experience, and the board respects him.' He asks after Bala's concerns. Ankush says, 'He'll say we're basing too much on political promises.' He assures Ankush of his financial model's strength, an adjusted capital deployment plan that can sound pretty cautious. Ankush nods like he already said that. 'There's also a new mining bill…' he starts, but Ankush says, 'I want today's focus to be on new product lines.' 'I know, but it won't hurt to mention this. We also have the right relationships. My senior partner can reach the prime minister's office in two calls.' 'Play that up,' Ankush says, then feels the need to add, 'We donated to their campaign effort. Magnus is on their list, the one they submit to the Election Commission.' He frowns at Ankush like he's impressed. 'You brought these guys to power,' he says, 'let's make the most of it.' Ankush nods, pleased, and insists on getting the bill. Then he says, 'Good luck, Agashe,' and blinks and smiles at once, a coquettish gesture doing the rounds in corporate circles.

*at worst, you may lose some credibility,*
*more important is to survive*

Watching Ankush leave, he thinks of everything riding on this afternoon and it turns his stomach weightless. He hasn't found time to get a Xanax prescription; more optimistically, he hasn't felt the need. To fortify his gut, he orders an egg bagel, his first bite today, and his fourth coffee. He tells himself he has lived through the Wall Street crisis. He, if anyone, knows the cost of speculation riding on political bluster, and what happens when demand swoons midway through a dance with wild debt – but India isn't America, the new government's promises aren't riding on a single horse like housing but on the strength of vast natural resources, a young population and political will. And ultimately, he decides, if there is no making real wealth without slavery or war, then there is nothing to do but use corporate indemnity to take a punt. At worst, as Dey said, you may lose some credibility, more important is to survive. At times, he still googles Eric, the ultimate survivor. Eric is working for a bank bailed out by the US government. He always exits when he's on a high for some place better, and he will go right to the top that way, the harami. What separates the chutiya from the harami, he reflects, is that the chutiya is below the clouds, he feels the nature of business personally; the harami is above, he sees the world for what it is, its architecture universal, if less concealed here than in the sanctimonious West. As for himself, he was a chutiya, but in surveying East and West, the relativity of context has shattered every altar. Before you set out, he thinks, you don't know what you know; when you are out there, you know what you don't know; when you return, you know what you know. His eyes have become icicles, he can cleanly isolate what is essential to getting by and what is extraneous, like cream from milk. The bagel is less dense than it should be, but the scrambled eggs and vinaigrette are top-class. No endeavour has any meaning, he decides, if it doesn't support a man's objectives in a material world – never lose sight of the material world, never forget the taste of this balsamic. And licking his lip, he makes effigies of all his gods: culture, markets, science, even country. Not that this is cause for despondency; this is a freedom different from those yielded by all his personal revolutions. Unlike the freedom he felt when he left home for college, and India for America, and America to return to India, this is a freedom aware of what you can't escape; when, having accepted both the system and your nature, you get on with life. His boss is coming through the door. His heart is steady at the sight of Yohan's urgency. He remembers the examination halls at school, the boys cramming notes while he waited calmly; on the day itself, he always felt above the scene, like a hawk stretched to full span and circling the sky for a final survey of the whole basin before it dives for the kill. He takes Yohan back

> *most people deliver once they are on stage,*
> *you only have to feed and burp them first*

out for a smoke and to review their key messages. Then they take the elevator to the top floor. The long room is lined with windows, the colours muted, the light natural. He opens his laptop at the front end of the table as Yohan and Ankush chat and the stragglers settle around the far U. The last to return from his bio break is the chairman, Jain Senior, a grey-haired patriarch who doesn't know the ABC of banking and would have continued in his brother's shadow if not for his son. The introductions done, Ankush sets the context before Yohan comes in with a macro perspective on the economy. Like most people, both deliver once they are on stage; he's only had to feed and burp them first. And he feels both admiration for their style and mild disdain for their enthusiasm as they go for it, saying *impact* for *effect*, *synergize* for *merge*, *leverage* for *manipulate*, saying of the East, *time to open the kimono, low-hanging fruit* and *peel the onion*, and of the West, *cutting edge, bleeding edge* and *burning platform*. Once they are done, he taps the controls to draw the blinds and turns on the projector. He has barely started on the numbers when Natwarlal Desai croaks, 'The font is too small.' He hands Desai and the other oldies printed copies of the presentation. Then he pitches his pitch for the better part of an hour, and when the final yellow slide announces the end, he returns to himself, Naren Agashe, the face of India's potential, looking expectantly at the board. In the pale, urinary glow, the board looks almost senile. He clicks the blinds open to wake them up. A server pokes his head in, and a tea trolley rolls up with its smell of warm thermoses, cumin biscuits and lemon. Everyone orders milk tea with no sugar except for Bala, who asks for green, Ankush, who asks for coffee, and the chairman who wants 'normal chai with sugar and all'. The Q&A starts to heavy slurping. As expected, the two younger directors ask nothing about their boss's pet project. The first to speak is the doddering Natwarlal. He is only a graduate, but married into the Jains and has held posts across their businesses. He sits on the Magnus board less for income than clout, and as Ankush's star rises, he is insecure. He makes some pointless points to credentialize himself, like talking about his successes before he retired. Indulge him. Say Magnus will benefit from his experience as it pivots. Once the old man is satisfied, scan the room and ask with a rhetorical air, 'Is that all?' No one responds. He hopes his presentation has preempted Bala, yet he makes the mistake of glancing over. A tanned, lanky Southerner, Bala looks like he runs corporate marathons. 'A clarification on the numbers. Are we being too bullish?' Unblinking, he presents Bala with Shivam's alternatives. Bala

*this isn't some conspiracy,*
*this is how nations are built*

is unimpressed. 'Everything is still based on the same assumptions. The government has allocated only eight hundred crore for the New Cities so far.' 'Fair point, Sir,' he responds. 'I'd just like to point out that Landsworth Consulting has worked closely with the government on multiple projects. My senior partner has a direct line to the PMO. We are in touch with the New Cities Ministry, so we have insights on what will pick up when, and we can deploy the capital step by step. There is also a new mining bill in the parliament's winter session that will increase the demand for Magnus's core product…' Bala's frown is the equivalent of a shrug. 'There are things outside government control. Whether you want to build cities or dig a mine, the biggest risk is land repossession. Farmers and tribes are protesting all over the country. It is not as easy as get a clearance and things take off.' He could tell Bala about the vast acres where the government has direct control, like railway or forest land, and how the process of relocating people has improved, but the board must know all this, so he tries inspiring them instead. 'If there is political will, it will happen,' he says. 'This entire business hub was conceived by the state. Yes, the land was reclaimed in the seventies and nothing happened for decades, but once the markets opened, nothing could stop these buildings from rising. And this time, we won't have to wait. The Sensex is already at an all-time high!' His hand pans across the blue glass towers in the window, and everyone looks over except Bala, who drawls, 'The long-term trend isn't promising. The nationalists made a bogeyman of corruption, but India isn't Africa and we aren't in the seventies. Corruption today is almost like a tax; it didn't stand in the way of our boom and won't be the reason for our bust. The emerging-market dream run crashed when Wall Street did. Any resilience we showed to the Great Recession was the previous dispensation recklessly pumping money in, and that karma will return to bite us unless we reform banking and find real engines for growth. Election euphoria can mask the taper tantrum only so long…' Yohan laughs the way he does when he is nervous, and says, 'Right, Sir. The service and telecom sectors have taken us as far as possible, and the economy needs new horses to whip. Personally, I sense the new government gets this. They aren't talking only about corruption. They are talking about new roads and cities, skill development, the whole Make in India thing. We are all set for an Indian manufacturing era, and Magnus is perfectly poised…' but Bala is tapping his pencil. Yohan shifts like his chair is uncomfortable. Bala says, 'The new government hasn't proved anything yet. Let me tell you how this can go. If the New Cities don't move as planned, the consumer won't need our pipes. The first person hit is the retailer who was all excited, and he starts to liquidate his inventory. For every retailer who reduces his order by two per cent, every wholesaler takes a hit of twelve. The multiple goes up exponentially at each stage. By the time Magnus gets hit, we may see a thirty or forty per cent drop in demand. Meanwhile, we've taken on all this debt by going public, so it isn't only us and a bank working it out. Investor pressure will bring the management to its knees. We could be talking hundreds of layoffs. We may risk assets that have taken generations to build. I've just come here from a meeting where we shut down a chemical factory near Lalbaug for this same reason. Want my advice? I'd get a loan at this point. I wouldn't go public.' The silence is so loud, Yohan looks at Ankush for help. Ankush finally coughs up what was fed him at The Artisan and what is not a consultant's place to say: 'The fact is, Bala, how much do you need the government to do? Like Agashe said, the new leadership is clearing bottlenecks and creating spaces where private money comes in, and their story is so compelling, banks are *paying* them to be a part of these projects. The New Cities budget is seed money. It's a springboard from which the government expects us to create an economy a hundred x greater. I mean, this isn't some conspiracy. This is how nations are built.'

*when bust follows boom, your projects*
*may alter, but you will go on*

Bala says nothing. The mention of Agashe has given him, Naren, an excuse to come in, so he slowly raises his hand and says, 'Sir, we at Landsworth Consulting understand the risks. I was on Wall Street through the crash. But I want to add one final point to what Ankush Sir said. Some of the top Indian companies we work with, even global businesses, are already gearing capital for the New Cities. Corporate intent will make up where the government falls short – the tailwinds are all there. If I may, I'm reminded of a depression-era quote by FDR. The only thing we have to fear is fear itself.'

Bala's brow rises. A pitch is hardly the place to philosophize, but Bala looks like he might speak again when the chairman clears his throat. Everyone looks his way including Natwarlal, who has been increasingly abstract. Old man Jain has a narrow face on a double chin, like a turtle with wire frames and a grey comb-over. His peacock blue suit and paisley tie are repulsive, yet Yohan looks at him adoringly. Jain pauses, then croaks, 'My only concern is … our culture is what is making us unique, and while we are leaping, we should be preserving that culture.' He is probably reacting to an American president being quoted, but it doesn't matter, everyone except Bala drinks in this platitude like nectar. Ankush looks over and beams as if to say, We've nailed this, Agashe. He beams back at Ankush, then says to the chairman, 'Absolutely, Sir,' as Yohan and the younger directors come in: 'Right, Sir', 'Great point, Jain Sahib'. He is too scared to look at Bala and provoke another debate. As everyone rises to leave, he overhears Bala asking a director, 'Have we seen any major reforms like in FDR's first hundred days?' yet when their eyes meet, Bala says, 'All the best, Naren,' with a smile that's hardly cynical. They are barely out of the elevator when Ankush texts: *Good job / Board is in / Will send the formal letter soon.* He responds: *Fantastic / I'll be in touch.* At the Sofitel exit, Yohan says, 'Well done, Agashe, just remember this will be a tough project,' but one can tell from his breezy gait that he is high. Once he sends Yohan off, he calls for an Uber. That the demand for cabs exceeds the supply makes him smile. Meanwhile, a beggar in a hijab with a drugged baby at her waist is shooed away by a doorman. She leaves in a halo of flies. Where did they relocate the people who lived on this swamp? Deonar, Mankhurd, one of those lawless, godawful places? He tells himself that he is wiser about economic cycles now. When bust follows boom, the nature of his projects may alter, but he will go on advising clients in the bad times just as he did in the good, and in accepting himself as adequate should he respond competently to both, he is closer to the essence of a management consultant than he has ever been. He looks up at the gaudy city sky. He had forgotten how the light refracts against the chemicals in the air. Since the Uber networks are jammed, he starts walking. Managers wired on caffeine and nicotine are barking into their smartphones along the boulevard. On either side, frangipanis brighten, and the buildings glow like aquariums in the darkening. At the curb, he is overtaken

*one way to know if you are happy is to ask yourself if you would rather be living any other life*

by a tiny figure in a blazer, an arm raised to hail the same cab. 'Worli!' he shouts. 'Mahim!' she shouts over him. The cab rushes past and they face each other sheepishly. 'Naren, is that you?' In fact it is, in fact it's her, Manasi. Her forehead looks higher with her hair in a knot, and one eyebrow is more arched than the other, the little sceptic. A second cab appears. Aren't they going in the same direction? 'Not if you're taking the Sea Link.' Of course he isn't. They are in the same cab now, just in time since it has started to rain. She smiles a wide smile that makes her face childlike while making him aware of her mouth. 'You're a consultant at Landsworth, right?' Yes (so he's sitting atop the system and works smart); she is in marketing with Coke (so she gets ground realities and works hard). 'Like your job?' she asks. He says, 'It's a job.' She mimics him, '*It's a job*. What would you rather do?' He shrugs. She says, 'Good. One way to know if you're happy is to ask yourself if you'd rather be living any other life.' Would she? Nope. Loves her job. 'Are you one of those people who has hobbies?' she asks. He shakes his head. 'Me neither,' she says. 'What's with the pressure anyway? Does anyone ask a poet or dancer if they have hobbies?' He laughs. He confesses he has *interests*, that he likes music and art and the odd philosopher.

She confesses she once wrote poetry. Her phone beeps. 'Please, work first,' he says. She agrees. The rain and traffic become audible again. Something of this old-world black-and-yellow cab stokes his nostalgia for Bollywood romances of the nineties. He notices her feet, the toes held in by the leather strap. That they aren't a man's shoes is a relief. That the nails aren't painted is also a relief. He has an odd desire to close his fingers around them. 'Sent,' she says to the phone. 'Mind if I smoke?' He wouldn't mind a smoke himself. He offers her his pack, strikes the match with a raspy flick, curves his hands into a cave so she can take the fire from them, her eyes narrowing as she pulls. The way she holds her cigarette suggests she is a novice. He remembers Rohit's mention that she grew up in Thane; the flat in Mahim is already an upgrade. He doesn't mind. He never again wants to date the kind of girl whose friends he has to sweat to impress. He wants someone who grounds him while he takes on the world. As they smoke, his eyes pass over the rain splattering the tar, the trash along the dividers, the exhaust from rickshaws on either side. 'Such a crazy city,' he says. She says, 'The worst, but I can't imagine living anywhere else.' They agree it is a paradox: the things one hates about Bombay are what make it irresistible, like a bad drug that wires you up, calms you down, and feeds the delicious numbness that is the only response to a world going to pot. At the edge of Bandra East, they see an empty cab, but he offers to drop her home. This isn't the kind of city where a woman needs an escort, though she agrees the times are changing, and yes, he has heard of the rape in the empty mills in Parel. She says she marched in the protests for women's safety, but when it comes to sexism in office, she can't imagine taking it up. 'You only isolate yourself that way,' she says. 'I get that,' he says (so sincerely, she startles) recalling how hard he tried to blend in in America. Passing the creek into Dharavi, they notice the open workshops where the vast public idols for Ganeshotsav are being sculpted from alabaster and clay, and the conversation turns to spirituality.

*there are no signs*
*as you make your way*

He likes that she has faith, and he senses she is impressed that he doesn't. Both their families celebrate the festival at home; neither attends the public parades. That gets them talking about Rohit's new film. The last he heard, Gyaan was against it, but Manasi claims they've reached a compromise: Rohit will manage the shooting because no way Gyaan will assist Omkar, and Gyaan will manage the editing so that he can control the end result. Sounds fair enough. For himself, he is curious about this Omkar Khaire. Manasi is more worried than curious. People have got touchy since the election, and Ifra hasn't taken the news well. He is about to air his political views when the cab halts. A party is blocking the road with its liveried band and a groom on horseback, and as the drumming falls away, the subject shifts to marriage. He agrees that it is a practical affair, an admission of the fallibility of love in that you seek the support of family, society and state to keep you welded, the purpose less a symbolic exaltation than committing to duties that will build into a successful life. She agrees that the benefits include a 'lifelong witness', and the comfort of setting certain drives and impulses in 'a safe space'. As the cab starts, a beggar presses his padded fists to the window, 'Aa baba, jodi salamat rahegi.' 'He thinks we're married!' Manasi laughs. He laughs too, and gives the beggar a hundred because he is feeling magnanimous. Both complain about the traffic again, but their complaints are hollow. As fast as the traffic is slow, their words rush on, opinions giving way to anecdotes to philosophical views to the questions that remain.

Both celebrate the growth of services, the new cricket clubs and cooking shows; both disparage the reactionary press, godmen and the onions rotting in warehouses across the country; both fear the far left and the far right, wax on apples, the monsoon's growing vagaries and what the internet knows, while resting their hope in technocrats, banking regulation and that man's computational abilities grow exponentially year on year. A week later, when she wakes up next to him, she teases him that these were the signs – the idols, the wedding party, the beggar's words – but he doesn't believe they were any more than random occurrences in a window turned on the Bombay streets, or that the day was different from any other in these early months back home (except in the coincidence that they hailed the same cab), as his thoughts on the life ahead inch towards clarity.

## *Amanda, Towards Purpose*

THE SKY IS A SWABBING BUCKET full to the brim, yet the clouds hold, and the pressure builds as if the city were wrapped in a fever rag. Deonar nears. Deonar grows. Then the road turns into Ward M, and a small figure – gelled hair, arms going up – shouts, 'Didiiii.' Zaeem's smile fills what his sunglasses don't of his face as he outruns the rickshaw to the centre. Rafia is standing on the steps with a self-consciousness that highlights her attire – a very un-Rafiaesque dress, the ruffled chest pinned with three drooping roses. In fact, none of the children are in uniform. The boys are in jeans and polyester shirts. Rafia has a fill-in for Humera, one Priya, in a kurta so white it glows in defiance of every muddy inch around her. 'You are looking *so* smart, my dears,' she, Amanda, says, winking at Rafia. Like an overdressed date, Rafia turns bashful. Priya giggles at the word 'dear'. Zaeem repeats, 'My dears, my dears,' and they all giggle. Khala emerges, one hand raised in greeting or blessing, followed by Tehsin, Mehrun and Rosy, all smiles. Inside, the children present her with a paper card: *Get Well Soon. Our Best Didi. Most Beautiful Didi. We Love You Didi. Get Well Soon. Didi.* Where is the judgement, the censure? 'I don't deserve this,' she says with every muscle of her face. Still, she reads the card aloud and compliments it all: Rafia's idea, Javed's text, Priya's henna design in ink. She hugs even the boys, who are startled, then shy, then bolder than before.

NADIYA IS ALONE AT HER DESK. 'Amanda, how is your health? I thought this is her last month, and now she won't come back.' Nadiya's smile is less forced than resigned as she relays Ashray's news (no mention of Bhagwat or Humera) and concludes, 'I haven't told anyone yet. I'm quitting, Amanda.' Wait, what? The place can't run without Nadiya! Pleased, Nadiya says, 'You just got here, so you feel things were always like this, but I am here for only three years myself. They will find someone else.' She asks if it is about Bhagwat. 'It is everything,' Nadiya says. 'The new board wants to make Ashray a women-only organization. The board is saying our tuitions and picnics, how to measure the impact? Women's health will get more donor money. I want to tell the board: thirty years, that is how long Ashray Education is here. You don't throw it in the dustbin to make a change. If the boys stay on the streets, they will get into bad company. The girls will be put in purdah. This is the end of their childhood. But Deonar can't make demands. Deonar must take what is given…' And as they speak, it is clear that Nadiya feels both betrayed and sidelined by Ifra. In response, Ifra has been made the villain in this plot of successive casualties, from Humera's education to Bhagwat's life, and now, the education department. Increasingly, the staff's silence is understandable, as is their fear of authority, aversion to conflict, and the refuge they take in their powerlessness. Whether Bhagwat was a catalyst or a capstone on the decision to shut the centres, or merely a cheap excuse to give the staff, he was a bad omen, and in this, their instinct was on point. What of her own guilt? In Nadiya's new mythology, she has been cast as a naïve and well-meaning accomplice to Ifra's brash agenda. She tries to breathe over the shame rising up her chest at the system glossing over her complicity, the repression that protects Deonar's status quo now working for her.

HER HAND GRAZES – PRIYA HAS BREASTS! They are in the eighth grade but she never imagined that the girls get periods or the boys watch porn. Maybe because of their eagerness or their tiny, wiry bodies, she thinks of them as 'kids'. What was it like to be fourteen? The age her hair changed from blonde to brown, an identity crisis that evoked the most adult social psychologies. By now, even the boys have become distinct. If Rafia is the leader and Priya her foil, Lalit is the male senior who cements Rafia's authority. He is gentle, mature, and still in school though the teachers call him a 'working man.' He understands the value of Rafia's hustling; if he lends her authority, she gives him respect. When he talks, she tells the others to shut up. Rafia's twin Zaeem is the drama queen: his hair is always gelled and his sunglasses so reflective you can see everything in them but his eyes. Chhota is in the fifth grade but allowed to tag along. He is healthy and brightly dressed; his parents must do well. Mittu is the runt. His clothes are shabby and he annoys the others with his stammer, but he is Rafia's pet, the grounds on which she can tell Javed to fuck off as she protects even her rattiest follower. Javed might have been the leader of the boys if he hadn't joined the group later. He is intelligent without Lalit's over-earnestness. On Ashray's Annual Day, he asked her, Amanda, which girl she thought was dancing best. She pointed to a vigorous one in blue frills. When she asked him the same, he said, 'I like all girls who dance.' The other boys accept that he has first dibs on girls – on Humera, now that she thinks of it, but when Humera's sister visited, his fascination was divided. It extends to her as well, his fascination, and it is disturbingly flattering.

SHIFT UP OR BE CAREFUL: Over the weekend, Rohit invites her to a shoot with a film crew from Pune. The infamous Omkar is there, and nothing like she expected. He has wide-set trusting eyes and talks in bursts the way shy people do. More impressive is Jinx, who tells her all about the American directors he loves. When she makes an effort to involve Omkar in the conversation, he gets bolder. He still does not address her directly, but smiles and nods when she speaks. More than once he is right behind her when she turns, and she apologizes for being startled. Then they are in the car, Rohit and Jinx in front bitching out clients who expect them to guess the script in their heads, and she notices that Omkar has spread his legs like he owns the back seat. Their thighs are touching. Swiftly, she moves away. He looks at her like it never occurred to him anything improper was going on. Later, Rohit explains that Omkar is from a small town and doesn't understand the concept of personal space. It's become a touchy issue, what a person's context has to do with what he can get away with, and they end up fighting. In the cab home, she texts Manasi, who has become a friend. Like Rohit, Manasi draws out the woman she wants to be, but here, it is easier to balance being admired with being vulnerable. Soon they are sitting across a window nook at Manasi's place, eating dim sum and sipping leftover wine. 'I'm starting to wonder if it's all in my head,' she says about Omkar. 'I didn't mean to overreact.' But Manasi says, 'If you feel it, it's there.' Manasi meets a lot of small-town men in her sales job. She says it takes nothing for them to think your friendliness is a sign. 'These days I just tell them straight *can you shift up* or *be careful*. Tell them early. They get it.' Her surprise that Manasi gets such attention is embarrassing. Guess her idea of beauty reveals her own parochialism.

FIRST THE WOMEN WHO SAY, 'WE SEE YOU on this train every day,' though they all look the same to her. Then Ifra, driving to the police station, 'I'd recommend a scarf since your hair is blonde. All women are targets, but most men here have seen white women only in porn.' And now, a rickshaw driver with an elongated fingernail tests her by asking which route to take, then wants to know why America loves Pakistan, if she has a boyfriend, if he is Indian, and if she has more than one. Frustrated at not catching on sooner, she stops the ride a block away and walks home past the traffic with her stole over her nose, runs up the stairs, bolts all three locks, flops on her bed, and allows herself a cry. More than specific incidents, what exhausts her is this shuffling between safe places being alert, alert, alert, and her constant sense that, despite her kurtas, the crowd is watching her as singular while she sees it as a crowd. Can you feel so isolated and so exposed at once? Wherever she and Rohit go, people stare. They think what Rohit's family and friends must think, that he is with her because she is exotic. They still refer to what they share as a 'situation' rather than a relationship, but that others see them as incapable of being serious is insulting. In other interactions too, she is a *gori* first and a person later, but when she hints at racism, the Indians have no sympathy. She hates them all! The grocer's fingers grazing hers while returning her change, the men who thwack her shoulder as they pass on a narrow footbridge (she used to apologize, now she knows it is deliberate) – and what to make of her vulnerability and that of women who spend whole lives like this, versus her guilt over Bhagwat's death?

THE BOARD: She stops midway through her final presentation. What is the point of this archive if the education department is shut down? The board assures her the staff will be retained. Nothing changes except the demographic they are serving. The board also has a request. With Nadiya leaving, can Amanda extend her fellowship by another three months? Chagan will handle the administration, but they want someone on the ground in direct touch with the management. By way of a project, she can digitize the files for Ashray's annual report. She says she will think about it, but if she can't, she hopes the transition will be graceful, and the children placed with other non-profits. She quotes Nadiya, 'As caregivers, even if the care is free, we come to fill a need. To pull out suddenly doesn't feel right.' Silence. Then Ifra says, 'Absolutely,' and everyone echoes this, but she knows it isn't how things will go. She hates their smug, made-up faces, and the prestige they get from this (since none need the money), yet when Anu Sehgal invites her and Ifra to tea, the old founder's charisma makes it hard to decline. As they drive to Malabar Hill, Anu Sehgal and Ifra chat in the back seat, and the boardroom dynamics become clear. Ashray has served Deonar for thirty years, but it is only in the past two that it went from one centre to three. This expansion, and Anu Sehgal's cancer diagnosis (she has recovered, thank you), saw the creation of a new post of CEO. The designation was probably needed to lure a millennial of Ifra's pedigree. Ifra's lack of experience doesn't matter; she has given Ashray's public image a facelift. It is also likely that her age and personal loyalty were a way for Anu Sehgal to retain her hold over her organization before the board. When the car stops, three attendants in white livery rush to their doors.

SPECTATOR SPORT: Parquet floors and a view of the Arabian Sea. Anu Sehgal is on a call when Ifra brings up a job offer she has received from the World Bank. 'I've told Anu Aunty about it,' she says, setting down her sherbet. 'At the end of the day, Amanda, NGOs in India are a spectator sport, an excuse for corporates forced to spend on social responsibility. Even the bigger budgets are nothing compared to a single government programme. We curl our noses up at the state, but we suffer from the same lethargy and bureaucracy. The focus is always on input over impact. It's about how much funds were raised rather than deployed. You've seen the management's tendency to talk in stories. Nadiya loves a good narrative, that one field officer who rose from nothing, the one class the girls attend. I think the board's move to women's health is well intended, but these problems are intrinsic to the model. Policy, advocacy, data systems – that's how you really change the system. I wanted to join the World Bank right after college, but Anu Aunty is like a mom to my mom…' She hears Ifra without listening. She feels like she's in the trenches on Deonar's side even if she messed up, unlike Ifra, who sits at the head office, gets profiled in magazines, and bumps into donors at art galleries and book launches. If they can't talk about Bhagwat and Humera, then like the staff, they should remain silent. 'Take the offer then,' she says coldly. 'My parents want me to,' Ifra says, her composure faltering. 'Especially with everything that's going on in the country. Then I think, what about the people who can't leave?'

RAMZAN IN DEONAR is a twilit sky webbed with lights, women in black burqas shopping from gaudy carts, the smell of hot meat and sugar in the air. Rafia and Zaeem's one-room house is dominated by a large double bed on which she and Nadiya are invited to sit. The walls have been freshly plastered in lime green, and the floral bedcover looks new and much too warm for even the monsoon. Rafia's family sits around the bed as her father praises their guests for visiting their humble home. No one insists that she, Amanda, partake of the iftar meal (Nadiya has told them about her gut) but when they pour bottled water into a tumbler, she notices their shame at her hesitation. Rafia's mother holds up a bowl of hot milk pudding – it has been boiled for hours so it is safe – with an expression that suggests this is a test. She takes a cautious sip. The pudding is tastier than at the Agashes, and at her hosts' delight and Nadiya's pride, she wonders what wound deeper than poverty she almost stuck a finger in. As the conversation slips into Hindi again, the decorative arrangement of steel vessels above the stove moves her. What do Bhagwat and Humera's homes look like on festive days? She has engaged with the slum as a site, not a living space. If she could shoot Ashray again, she would put a cheap point-and-shoot camera in her subjects' hands. That way she would not work with only her own assumptions about what these streets inspire. Then again, her trouble with photographs has gone beyond the shame in their production and the limits of the shutter. The event, Barthes says, is always transcended. She is encumbered not only by what she sees but also how she thinks.

THE PEOPLE WHO CAN'T LEAVE: Her thoughts are still on Barthes when her hosts get louder. Rafia's mother starts to cry. Nadiya apologizes, her eyes wet, and the conversation remains strained until they leave. Walking to the bus depot, Nadiya says, 'We were talking about the elections and I said there are good Hindus, my best friend is one. These politicians spread hate to get votes. Rafia's mother said it is not only for votes, sister. These people are sick in the head. There are pictures of camps. I said, Where did you see this, Sainoo? She said WhatsApp. I said, Please take care, but don't believe rumours. Then she told me her story. Her family is from a small town in the north. Years back, a train with Hindu pilgrims was passing through when it caught fire. No one knew how, but right-wing organizations claimed it was a terror attack and called for a strike. Sainoo's brother went out to buy milk and … they tied petrol bombs to his body. Imagine, Amanda. He was Rafia's age. Bharat Party ministers are in jail for this … still the party won the next election. Today they are running the country. Sainoo said, Now tell us what to believe.' She asks if Nadiya is afraid. Nadiya takes a moment. They have only ever talked of her as the education director; her colourful kurtas and bracelets betray nothing of her faith. Nadiya says, 'After the election, I took my money out from the bank. My father said to keep it at home in case … in case we have to go.'

THE MYTH OF SHEELA: On Friday evening, some thirty women crowd the centre's entrance. They would rather have this space for their children than their health. Sainoo holds Nadiya's hands and begs her not to quit. The children promise to study hard. Tehsin Teacher even cries. Then the crowd parts and someone whispers, 'Sheela Bai.' Bhagwat's health and manner made it easy to forget he had risen from Deonar's poorest, and the sight of his widow is startling. Sheela is as tiny as Rafia, and her eyes have the glassy shine of what is left of life when everything extraneous is stripped away. Sainoo tips the sari on her head back to reveal grey hair, and the women gasp. Rosy says, 'She is wanting to leave her son here from next year.' Nadiya speaks inaudibly to Sheela, then addresses the women in a loud, rallying tone. 'I have quit, but yeh centre na mera hai na unka. Yeh centre aapka hai. Morcha banao. Board ko batao Nadiya ne kya kaam kiya hai. I can't do more. You have to take it forward…' She is calling for a protest, but everyone knows this is it. Going back up, Nadiya says, 'Saw her hair, Amanda? She is not even twenty-five. Her family gave Bhagwat's bail, then he did it from her sari. Some days, I feel so angry with him, but Sheela was telling how he only said good things about Ashray; even when the accusations came, he said negativity keeps us down. Bhagwat believed in Ashray. We betrayed him. Now we are betraying his son.' She tries not to read blame into Nadiya's words. An hour later, when she comes downstairs, the centre is empty. The staff and children have left with the women, but Sheela is still on the steps. Does Sheela know who she is? She says, 'I am so, so sorry.' She hugs Sheela, who stays inert, but slowly responds, the strength in her arms surprising, like in tendrils. The odour of a synthetic sari, of coconut oil, and jasmine buds worn in the hair so long, it persists for weeks after not wearing them. Then Sheela's ribs start to shudder against hers and she feels a spreading damp on her shoulder.

THE CALL IS TAKEN, she will extend her fellowship. Andrei asks if they are over. She surprises herself by saying yes. She is so sorry. She tells him about Rohit. He asks if it is love. She says it is intense but it isn't love; it's symptomatic, though she can't say of what. Andrei says, 'Maybe he validates something, and after Bhagwat it got stronger.' They discuss this hypothesis, and though they fail to reach any satisfying conclusions, for the first time in months she is entirely herself with Andrei, and in the heat of her confession and his hunger to receive it, they find an unexpected intimacy. When he offers to remain on the farm until she gets back – Nana has high blood pressure, it would devastate her to know – she agrees. So they remain 'on a break', if with more honesty. She should be grateful to Andrei, yet all she feels when they cut the call is contempt for his persistence. That night, Rohit stays collapsed on her for a long time. He is breathing inaudibly, like he were tasting something sweet and sour for the last time and holding on to the sensation, but when he sees her looking at him with concern, he sticks out his tongue. And when she tells him of her plans to extend her fellowship, he turns restless. If he has allowed himself to get this involved, she thinks, it's because they had a natural endpoint. Her insecurity makes her cruel. She casually mentions that Andrei is still on the farm. Later, she can't recall Rohit's reply, only him pulling on his pants with a self-conscious dignity that seemed to say: I am an adult. During her last camera class at the Ashray centre, she notices a similar expression on her students' faces.

THE BEACH IS EMPTY except for a few workers building a bamboo pavilion for the Ganesha festival next month. In a rented school bus, Nadiya describes the parades enthusiastically, but the children are restless to go to the water. Nadiya says, 'This is an educational tour!' They all know this is a farewell for Nadiya. After her falling out with Ifra, there will be no official goodbye. Then Rafia says she has never seen the sea. Nor has Zaeem, nor Mittu. Nadiya stands. The kids shout, 'Yay!' When was the last time she said *yay* like that? Dad at the wheel, the blue roar at Portsmouth rising as the sea came closer and closer, and the car was parked and she'd run into the salt slap, the gravelly undertow. *Yay*. The sand is so hot, they put their shoes back on until it turns wet. When the water rushes up, it is met with screams and laughter. There's a garland bobbing on the waves, but no plastic or slime. The boys splash the girls they are crushing on and spit water at the other boys. She imagines the sea sparkling in Rafia's head as she sleeps among siblings whose heads are dark. Nadiya says, 'I'm so happy we did this.' At times, Nadiya is like the older sister she always wanted, softer than Mom, kindred in that eagerness to give and in giving, receive, to make and in making, be made. 'I'm sorry, Nadiya,' she says. Nadiya nods. 'I know why you fell sick.' 'I'm sorry,' she says again. Nadiya touches her shoulder. 'Enough.' *Enough*. Nadiya is right, to apologize further would cheapen her repentance; self-hatred is a form of narcissism. Then Nadiya goes past her to the water. Her camera is in her hands, but she doesn't take a picture. She scrolls through her existing images. There are thousands, and unedited, they induce a strange calm. India is a world complete in itself, and has been so for thousands of years, spinning out wildly but never going off its axis. She wraps her camera in her stole and puts it down by her shoes. She looks at the sea, unframed, unbroken in abeyant frames. Then the kids pull her in, their laughter a variation of the sea sound.

The world is reduced to its elements, the scene rising in relief and receding into this one conception, this one whole. And brined and burnt, she is not separate. The noon sun blinds each grain of sand with sustained intensity, the rush and suck of water holds. The city arches in on both ends, but her *I* and the *I* watching the *I* are stuck in one gasp, and she is breathing over it, stunned and patient...

## *Rohit, Towards an Identity*

The scene is typical of a government university: excess land in the heart of Mumbai but not enough cash to give the rotten buildings a paint job. Still, he loves it: the roads covered in the slush of yellow flowers … a hint of hot samosas and weed in the air … and for all Omkar's talk about student politics, there are no posters or graffiti; everyone from the guards to the stray dogs looks sleepy.

Then Omkar texts, *Come to exam office.* From a distance, the crowd looks insignificant against the empty lots, but there are at least two hundred heads. A girl reports that the university has lost their answer sheets. It's too late to reconduct the finals, so each student will be awarded their midterm grade. No one takes the midterms seriously; for some, this means flunking the year. In protest, the Bharat Student League, or BSL as she calls it, has locked up the staff.

Locking up teachers, it sounds almost like a prank … but there is Omkar on the porch, so severe and sky-eyed, he might be leading a revolution. When Omkar sees him, he pulls him over and yanks up his arm, and the next thing he knows, he is shouting for the vice chancellor to resign: Kulpati, ek kaam karo, kursi chhodo, aaram karo!

An egghead in Gandhi glasses steps out to a loud boo. Omkar whispers, 'The registrar.' A rock flies overhead so cleanly you would think missing was the point, but the registrar ducks, and

BAM, it hits the door. The crowd turns on itself. The leaders shout for patience, but the chaos only settles when a mic appears. The egg wipes his head with a folded kerchief. Then he announces that each student will be awarded their average test result over the year and no one will get less than a B. Shouts of victory … hugs … laughter.

The scene brings to mind a vigil he once attended for women's safety. The capital was already tense with activists rallying against corruption; then a student was raped and murdered on a public bus, and suddenly, protest fever was everywhere. The result was a new political party, but Aai said the real winners were the Bharat Party because they swept the election on the back of all that middle-class rage. He didn't care. He was fresh out of college and waving flags in the street felt like a rite of passage. He recalls his first sight of Ifra, her candle-lit fist punching the sky. Everyone went to Otters Club and got into a drunken debate on Feminism after, and by the end of it, damn him, Gyaan had the girl.

Meanwhile, the exam topper, one Hanmant Holar, is hoisted. 'He missed the midterms because of trouble at home…' 'He's brilliant…' 'If not for today, he would have flunked the year…' Omkar adds, 'Our Holar comes from the sort of village where, if your father is a cobbler, they give you a special mug in school so you won't pollute your classmates' drinking water. Then a friend took him to a Brotherhood picnic where everyone from the headman to the sweeper's son emptied his lunchbox into one vessel and ate the mash to show our unity.'

Compared to the vigil, he thinks, this university protest is hardly glamorous. No press, no police, no public bearing witness, no beauties in handloom with witty placards. In a big unfair city, no one cares if a Dalit kid drops out of college in his final year. Or almost no one. There are a dozen hands under Hanmant's legs and back, his head is thrown up and cleft palate laughing at the sun.

As the students leave, they thank him, 'Rohit-ji', like he was one of their leaders. And here is his youth returned: milk tea in a sooty canteen and the euphoria of a collective achievement. Going by the talk, though, student elections have been banned in Maharashtra since a candidate got shot in the nineties. Most left and liberal outfits packed up, but not the BSL. 'That is because we are not about politics,' Omkar says proudly. 'We are about welfare, and the work of student rights is never finished.'

Walking to the gate after, he asks if Omkar came to Mumbai for the protest. Omkar says he came for work. Jinx has put him on some gig in the city, and he will be staying with his relatives in Lalbaug for a month. 'I wanted to tell you in person,' he says excitedly. If the thought of Omkar hovering around the Box makes him nervous, he doesn't show it. He asks if Omkar is still a member of the Bharat Student League. As usual, Omkar doesn't answer yes or no. He tells a story.

Omkar says in Marathi, 'When I came to Pune, I did not know anything about BSL, but this is the fun. Our student hostel, we called it a chicken coop. Meaning. The rice was boiled in soda. The toilets were full of roaches. More stray dogs attended the classes than students. Ha ha. But as a village boy, even the sight of the warden or principal made me tremble. I was a first-rate coward…'

Omkar says, 'One day, I saw some commotion in the quad and one man is shouting that he is calling a student strike until things improve. I was shocked. An ordinary guy can speak to a principal this way, with so much *gooning* – and the principal is listening! This was a revela … a *revolution* to me. I saw that if you develop some aggression, things can change…'

Omkar says, 'I went up to this worthy and he said, You are studying printing so you can help our media cell. That is where my training began. In how to communicate. In how to mobilize. At our Brotherhood branch in Wai, we always talked about service and sacrifice, but the BSL made that goal concrete. You want to fight for the people. You see the volunteers' passion, and your fear goes. I have got so many threats. I say come kill me, someone else will stand in my place…'

Omkar says, 'When I graduated from the polytechnic, there were no jobs on campus, but by then I was making videos for the BSL, and a senior got me a job at the camera rental where I met Jinx. Today I am not a student, but I can go to any campus in the state, and I have a family. I can go to any town and find a home. BSL made me what I am. So whenever they call me, I am here…'

Omkar's reach is enviable. But for all his realness, he is a romantic. What he wants for himself is what he wants for the world, and if only for this, you want him to overcome.

After leaving Khaire at the bus stop, he considers driving to Amanda's. They could watch a comedy, play cards, or do any of the things they do to avoid talking, but he wants to talk tonight. He has so much to share if it didn't feel so fraught. At times he has to remind himself of what attracted him to her. Sexual and cultural curiosity, her maturity and assertiveness – and sure, she isn't as vacuous as his younger exes, but she can be moody, sanctimonious, blunt.

And if that wasn't enough, he thinks (putting the car into gear for Santacruz), her unhealed gut and the mess in Deonar should turn anyone off, but something about her weaknesses excites him as much as her authority. Forget going crazy on him, she might be driving *him* crazy: he has even stooped to stalking Andrei Jardan online, and how manly he looks, with a reddish beard and a 'Dr' before his name.

That night, it isn't long before an argument starts up. 'Guess I was just an invitation for you to shed old skin,' he says, and she retorts, 'And I was an invitation for you to try a new one.' They can't make out without fighting and they can't fight without making out, and why he won't call it off he can't say, but even as he walks out, he knows he will be back, desire like a hook in his mouth, pulling him into a realm where he can't breathe.

In the weeks after, he spends all of his free time on campus. Then one evening, the BSL volunteers invite him to their fifteenth August celebration. That Omkar will be in Wai for a tree-planting ceremony doesn't matter. 'Is he your only friend here?' Hanmant asks.

Independence Day. The show recalls the Polaris Fest at Wilson College, but that line-up boasted jazz bands and fashion ramps. Here, the Indian flag is hoisted in an open theatre, girl students do a martial arts dance in saris, and a physics prof gives a speech on all the science known to ancient Hindus. His dream, the professor says, is for his students to reclaim India's position as the world's guru.

At the tea stall, Hanmant introduces his sister, Sarita. 'Good to meet you, Rohit-ji,' she says in English, her face all eyes. 'Wilson, right? Fancy college.' She wants advice on 'character-building activities', by which she means the internships, sports, clubs, debates and socials he took for granted as a student. Her mission is to bring all these to public universities. 'Our students go into depression because how much can you study?' she says. 'Many come from far away. Their parents never went to college, so they need guidance. We make them feel like they are part of a family.'

Sarita walks him through the 'gallery' she has organized. There is a mural of Shivaji, a chart on Ambedkar, a papier mâché Shaniwar Wada. Of course, there are no Islamic or Christian artefacts, but these kids aren't bloodthirsty bigots either. Here, for instance, is Gavade who made the murals. He is a postdoc in Soil Science and works with the Brotherhood's Peasant Union to tackle farmer suicides. He is also a tribal boy and an atheist, though he says he'd never disrespect an idol. And here is Arin from Assam who choreographed the dance and eats beef, but never in public. Sounds hypocritical, but Arin says a nation is like a family. Differences are saved for private life; in public, you hold up the national culture.

And here by the water stand is Rahim Ali Khan. Besides the BSL, Rahim is part of a platform called the Bharat Muslim Forum. He says in Hindi, 'You look surprised. Let me tell you one thing, Rohit-ji. I call myself a Hindu–Muslim or a Muslim by religion and a Hindu by culture. You will ask: why not Indian Muslim? Because Indian acknowledges my country and Muslim acknowledges my religion, but what about my five-thousand-year-old culture? My DNA goes back on this land to Vedic times. Some centuries ago, my family converted to Islam, and yes, I like my mutton, but I have more in common with Hindus than Arabs or Turks.'

Who knows what Ifra would make of that, but he is reminded of something Naren once said: *parties evolve*. The Bharat Party has to widen its umbrella if it wants to stay in power. Later that day, he heads to Gyaan's flat for the FIFA World Cup, and Gyaan is in a fine mood, wearing a printed jersey and cheating on his diet with chicken wings, but on hearing of the BSL's good work at the university, Gyaan gets increasingly shrill.

Gyaan says (waving his hand), 'The BSL was active on my campus in Delhi, and by *active* I mean that they are hooligans who buy political cred by burning books and trolling journalists. You don't know better because you went to a private college where corporates have more presence than student unions…'

Gyaan says (holding his head like it hurts), 'I know the BSL has three million members, and not all of them want the minority dead. I also know that Omkar won't tell you what he wants. He gets what's at stake here. As for your request not to politicize everything and just focus on making a film, I'm sorry, bud, but that's a luxury some people can't afford…'

By that, Gyaan means himself as a Hindu man in love with a Muslim woman. If he said he is insecure there's another creative guy on board, one could understand, but Gyaan won't. He's never been honest about his insecurity around Iffy either. He always talks about her being Muslim, never that her parents are wealthier than his or the cultured type he adores.

Behind Gyaan is a bookshelf stacked with names like Guha and Chomsky, the Arendt that Ifra gifted him, and for all their criticism of Indira Gandhi, one side is taped with a Cartier-Bresson print of her and Nehru in a rose garden. The first time that he, Rohit, saw those titles swimming in the smoke, he thought, Heck, I'm shallow – but tonight he believes he can be a reasonable person without reading any of them.

Driving home, he thinks of how Omkar has his canon too, but his knowledge is drawn from the heart of life and has a scent as fresh as the first rain on black earth. Omkar uses language like a blacksmith uses a hammer; even when it's a concept, it's to get the point across rather than charm with the word. Gyaan will take the name of a philosopher like he's biting a peach, but it's never more than talk, and ironically, this is what first attracted him to Gyaan. After his institution-worshipping family and apolitical friends, he loved Gyaan's take on the world, but these days, Gyaan doesn't seem so irreverent. He only has a different set of gods.

The next day, Omkar tells him that the BSL secretary for Maharashtra has heard about *Bappa* and invited them to their state headquarters. He isn't sure what to expect, but a meeting never hurts and he can't deny that he is flattered. Of course there is no question of asking Gyaan, nor any need, since he wants to come in only on the editing.

A building of average Dadar height with shops along the base … smell of grain, of soap, of wet wooden crates … stairs up the back to a heap of shoes by an unmarked door. 'Where is everyone?' Omkar asks, and a boy in brown shorts and a ratty vest replies, 'At the media jobs conference. They will be here any minute. Please sit. We've heard a lot about your film.'

If the branch in Wai was humble, the state HQ of the world's largest student union is worse. The walls are bare except for a bank calendar. The terrazzo floor is dull and the tube lights are duller. The office is furnished like a living room with hard, maroon sofas and a silent TV turned on Zee News, and something of the smell, either of phenyl or citronella, makes him homesick for a time when the Agashes were solidly middle class themselves.

Footfalls … voices … faces fresh from an afternoon of shepherding crowds and talking from podiums. One looks like Naren would with a rakish fringe and narrow eyes, and though he's wearing a simple cotton shirt and trousers, he has an aura. Omkar says in Hindi, not Marathi, 'This is Vikram Singh-ji, our secretary. He has kindly invited us.'

Vikram thanks them for supporting the BSL's activities and offers help on filming *Bappa* through his access to students' homes, adding 'Omkar may film whatever, but for us, festivals are only a way to visit volunteers' families as well-wishers. Because you can't help a student in India without involving the family. What I am saying, Rohit-ji, is that our purpose isn't religious or political…' 'It's welfare, I've heard.' 'Our purpose,' Vikram clarifies, 'is man-making.'

A hush of approval. Smiling, Vikram introduces him to everyone present. 'You are Rohit Agashe,' he says. 'You grew up in Mumbai. You studied at Wilson College. You are making a short film…' Then he introduces the volunteers with similar biographies starting with 'aap', the details as much a show of respect for them as of leadership for Vikram. Finally, he introduces himself. Like Omkar, his story sounds rehearsed yet intimate:

Vikram says in Hindi, 'My grandparents were Hindus from Pakistan. After Partition, they had hours to pack up their lives. My great-uncle couldn't make it to the train the family was on, so he caught the next, and that train was fully butchered. Half my village was on it. Since then, we are living in Alwar. My father runs a sari shop. He visits his local Brotherhood branch, but until I went to college I did not know anything about the BSL…'

Vikram says, 'In Jaipur University, student elections are a big deal, but I was not attracted to politics. I am what you call an *academic*. I loved debates, and the debates at the BSL were in Hindi, not English. They spoke about the nation in a way I could relate to. I was raised with swastikas in the house. My grandmother would tell me stories from our epics. This was the India I recognized. The big foreign words left liberals used was not…'

Vikram says (as the boy in shorts serves metal-tasting Coke in metal tumblers), 'Now you will say the BSL is all about rejecting Western culture, so why we are drinking Coke? My answer: this is *superfacial*. Person who is wearing jeans but having one car and respecting nature, he is more Hindu than the person wearing dhoti who is having four cars like the Western consumerist. The essential thing, Rohit-ji, is this: what are you values?'

Vikram's words take him back to his childhood in Bandra East, when being progressive and Hindu weren't antithetical, Aai's swastikas and his faded Levi's both signifying home. Beside him, Omkar is silent but beaming. Caste, dowry and all the regressive crap one associates with the Hindu right are just the things he is at war against. Maybe because of how his mother was treated, Omkar's hatred of the old guard is real … but he hasn't thrown the baby out.

Around the volunteers, the great Hindu values seem no different than Ajoba's: patriotism, hard work, honesty, self-respect, simple living and high thinking. Not a bad set for people whose whole lives are a struggle, and the struggle can never mean to him, Rohit, what it does to them, but the Brotherhood doesn't expect everyone to be an activist. Running a studio is fine if your values are in place. That's why their alumni span all walks of life. Even

Vikram, who made his reputation strategizing student elections, calls himself an academic or a social worker, and says 'politics' like it's a dirty word.

Before leaving, Vikram promises to introduce them to the bigger Ganeshotsav mandals in the city. Omkar whispers, 'You impressed him, Agashe.' And he replies, 'Vikram impressed me.'

That night, he goes over to Cyrus's. The quaint, leafy lanes of the Parsi colony recall their college days when nothing was further from his mind than politics. Mostly, they smoked weed, and depending on how stoned you were and what mood Cy's dad was in, there were three ways to enter the vast and shabby Bulsara flat. He takes the spiral staircase to the fire escape where Cy is already rolling a joint. His old friend has no love for the Hindu nationalists either, what with their history of burning posters of films like *BomGay*, but unlike Gyaan, Cy hears him out, and suggests getting Iffy and Omkar to meet casually. Like for dinner? 'Why not?' Cyrus says. 'Call the rest of us too. It might make him more human.'

He likes the idea. But there is no time to think with the recces for *Bappa* taking off. Initially, he offers to bring his car, but Vikram insists the BSL only travels by train, 'seniors, juniors, all'. When was the last time he took one? And rattling past the sooty backs of buildings, he can't get enough of the worn station signs and the piss-smelling wind in their faces.

Talk of the country … of education … of cricket. A love for India that he hasn't felt since school. When international soccer clubs play, you are crazy about excellence and personality, but cricket is different; there is that sudden raw investment when the boys in blue take the field, especially if they are playing England or Pakistan.

Then you exit the station and the night is radiant. A man is hammering bamboo poles with satin … shops are stacked with sweets and marigolds … maroon and golden banners reflect in the puddles. Omkar is on a high, going backstage to film the idols and taking notes. He, Rohit, is on a high too, but it has less to do with *Bappa* than a feeling of expansiveness. Wherever the volunteers go, the BSL knows families, businesses, local committees and mandals, and they are welcomed with smiles, asked for advice, told complaints and offered gratitude.

And the backdrop to it all is Ganeshotsav. Every year, the Agashes install an idol at home, but he has never visited a public one. It was the activity of another class … but is it? A headline says fifty thousand public idols have already gone up. Days from now, counting the private ones in every high-rise, mid-rise and slum, two hundred thousand idols will be unveiled. Some will be visited by over a million devotees for each of the ten days before they are immersed in the sea. Multiply that by the times each will be photographed and posted and reposted online…

This is the audience he can reach through Khaire. That said, unlike Naren, he doesn't define success in terms of money. He wants to tell his grandchildren that he lived at the heart of his time and that it was a grand adventure. Maybe that's why he is sick of the *I* in his head. When Vikram talks, it is always *we, we, we*. Even when he says *I*, you can hear the *we* in his *I*.

As the train lurches forward, he recalls his roots tour. Funny how he went looking for himself like it was a matter of driving another mile before running into the authentic Rohit Agashe. To be honest, there has been no one artefact or hero he wants to claim, yet he feels a new centre of gravity in which he is Chitpavan, Marathi, Hindu and Indian at once, and that encompasses all of the ancient Hindu civilization, the Maratha and Mughal empires, the British and the freedom fighters, the old values and the new dream.

What was Amanda's line? *Happiness is to be dissolved into something great.* Bringing her along on these recces would make the boys self-conscious. Then again, she has agreed to dinner with his friends and Omkar despite that incident in the car. Just when he thinks he has her figured out, that she is finite ... her sides open, her texture changes. He has been grateful for the excuse the recces give him to stay away, but tonight he feels ready to take her on. When he gets home, he showers and spends a long time setting his hair perfectly wild. Then he looks in the mirror, presses his palms together, tips his head forward, and gives himself a namaste.

# STALEMATE

A priest blows a conch in three resounding bellows as Naren installs the idol in the prayer room. Chants are chanted, incense burnt, and diyas lit to welcome Ganesha. Aai says lovingly, 'His expression.' Baba smiles in reply. Omkar's camera gives the rituals a staginess, still Naren thinks: This is family life, this is community life; to refuse to participate is to be narrower on account of your rationality. On the priest's direction, he 'bathes' the idol in milk, curd, honey, sugar and ghee, rinses it in rose water, and lays on its accessories: a silver crown, a silk shawl, marigolds, a clutch of grass and a modak – and when he looks up, Manasi smiles adoringly:

The aarti begins to Rohit ringing a brass bell. Ganeshotsav has been the perfect excuse to unite his crew: Omkar is here to film *Bappa*, his friends are here for the festival, and any awkwardness between them has been buffered by his family. Still, he can hardly focus. Do the rituals meet Omkar's standards? Does Ifra see his efforts to involve Gyaan? How adorable are Naren and Manasi, as serious as an arranged match from the get-go. And can Amanda please recognize that he is busy? It's like they're all inside his head, their thoughts louder than his own:

Manasi sings the aarti with perfect intonation. Imperial Heights has been transformed by the thought that this could be her home and family. The tension between her friends fades in priority; for all his faults, Rohit has never felt dearer, he who tried to set her up with his brother and gave her such a hug when he found out. Of course, Naren's parents don't know yet, but when they hear of it, she wants them to recall how well she played the part tonight: no college girl in jeans but a young woman in an auspicious yellow kurta, her voice in harmony with theirs, while the others clap along:

At the main door, Kedar surrenders his damp jacket to Mukta Bai, who smiles with the sweetness she reserves for him. Sita rushes to get him a glass of iced water. Unlacing his sneakers, he is surprised by the number of people exiting the prayer room, giddy-calm and smelling of camphor. He did not expect such a show from the Bandra Agashes: a priest since none of them know the rituals, guests in traditional clothes … just as well he has come at the end. To please Lata Kaki, he makes a cursory bow before the idol. He is an atheist, but the least he can do for his mother is to stop snubbing Rohit's attempts to reconcile their families:

Amanda tries to relate to the absurdity of an elephant-headed god welcomed as if it were a human guest. Lata Aunty is offering Ganesha 'his' meal, a morsel of each of the dinner items on a silver plate, a betel leaf to aid digestion, and a betel nut to ensure satiety. Then dinner for the mortals is served buffet style, and as she ladles the pilaf, she can't help noticing that Ifra is ignoring her as if she is on team Rohit and Omkar. Determined to show that she isn't, she takes a seat at the opposite end of the room:

Ifra usually loves an Agashe dinner – so humble, except for the umami of ghee – but the food has turned tasteless. She is here because she doesn't want to be the person around whom her friends can't be themselves, but are her friends themselves? She has celebrated Hindu festivals at Imperial Heights before, the focus more on the food than the gods, unlike tonight when everything feels insincere and ominous: the priest leaving with a wad of cash, Manasi flaunting her competence at the rituals, Rohit's parents' hospitality extended to Omkar, who is hardly impoverished, his neck thick, his bracelet sharp:

After the senior Agashes retire and the party moves upstairs, Cyrus saunters in. The awkward silence convinces him it's best he didn't come sooner. Gyaan is on the divan, Amanda and Ifra in the wingback chairs, Naren and Manasi on the couch, Kedar a foot above on a barstool, Rohit a foot below on the carpet, and there on the Turkish pouf by Rohit's feet is the infamous Omkar, his hair oiled and spine erect. Cyrus sits in a yogi pose by Rohit's head. 'To make up for being late,' he says, tossing his friend a pouch of weed:

Gyaan suspects each guest is waiting for the lesser friend or the courtesy invite to leave, but the only one rising is Manasi, who goes to the terrace to take a work call. Gyaan fixes his drink last to emphasize his familiarity with this home, and as the conversation warms up, he stays reticent to make clear that he is doing this film for Rohit and not because he endorses Omkar. He tells himself this is his way of protecting Iffy, but half a glass down, it starts to annoy him that the puritan is sipping water while they all slug wine, and the showman in him itches to provoke Omkar into betraying the extent of his darkness:

A corruption of the festival's spirit, Omkar thinks of the stinking intoxicants, but he says nothing. He has avoided Rohit's home from the anxiety that he will not fit in, but now he is twice surprised: the place is grander than expected and Rohit's family more hospitable. And he has been too flattered to be natural and is ashamed of this (since he doesn't care for ostentation), this smiling extra wide, saying only a profuse yes or no-no, and even less since coming upstairs, though he is sitting as attentively as a cat, suggesting with his eyes that he is following every word and is a moment away from saying something wise or witty:

The talk finally converges on a subject Gyaan is certain the puritan has a take on: Bollywood. Speaking as if to the universe (but it is clear for whom the words are intended), Gyaan says, 'Has anyone noticed all the recent films trying to establish some pre-British, non-Mughal, Hindu glory? First they made *Mohenjo-Daro*, now they're shooting for *Shivaji*, then blasted *Bajirao.* They can't handle that a Muslim empire was the acme of our civilization. Now there's this hypocrisy. I see it with my uncle. Talks all the time about the Hindu state, then when he's driving, he will listen to ghazals. At weddings, he will wear a sherwani...'

Omkar takes the bait. 'Gyaan-ji,' he says, 'it can be that, in his heart, your uncle is still in the colonial mindset. If you read Sawant, you will see that in Mughal courts even Hindus were speaking Persian and making portraits smelling the roses. Today also we are thinking in X and Y ways because in West they are doing that.'

'Can you even call the Mughals colonizers?' Gyaan asks. 'They settled here. They built their Taj in India. Two civilizations came together and all the stuff we tout as Indian culture today is the result of that synthesis. The name Hindu itself was first used by Muslims to refer to people south of the Indus. Your kurta, Omkar, your kurta was brought to India by the Mughals. Before that, we didn't wear anything – just loincloths.'

Laughter, and through it, Rohit says, 'You and your Muslim fetish, bro. For those who don't know Gyaan Mahajan, he'll hyperventilate at celebrating Eid on Mohammad Ali Road. Then on Diwali, he'll tell his mom he doesn't care for rituals.'

So Rohit has announced his side! The phrase *Muslim fetish* makes Gyaan turn nervously to Iffy. With eloquent civility – and how he loves her for it – she returns the debate to an objective place: 'The Mughals weren't just Muslims. They were defined by a system of government, an aesthetic, a way of life…'

'If I may be talking on this subject of names,' the puritan says past her, his voice bolder now that Rohit has his back. 'In our Vedas, the Aryans are already having a name for our land of seven rivers. The part ruled by King Bharata was Bharat, and our religion was Sanatana Dharma. Then Muslims are invading, and they are calling our Sindhu river Hindu, so now we are Hindus and our country is Hindustan. Then British are calling Sindhu as Indus so we are India and Indian…'

'You mean the Greeks,' Gyaan says flatly. 'The Greeks called it Indus. The Persians called it Al-Hind.'

'I am meaning anyone can give us any which name, Hindu identity is existing from five thousand years.'

'Five or five thousand,' Iffy says impatiently. 'Why must one religion define our national culture? Aur koi way nahin ho sakta, Omkar?'

Insistent on his terrible English, the hypocrite replies, 'First, please tell me this. Why you are telling Hindu is a religion? Religion is only one aspect of Hindu culture.'

'Hindu culture, Hinduism, it is all fucking wordplay,' drawls Gyaan. 'It is how the right slips the scalpel under the skin, and this is the irony: there is nothing Hindu about their ideology at all. It is a fundamentalist credo that takes its tropes from Western fascists. Hinduism is about non-violence; it is about tolerance.'

Omkar starts, 'Let me be clarifying. We are not wanting orthodoxy…'

'Who is *we*?' Kedar asks from his perch by the bar.

'Our friend is a BSL volunteer,' Gyaan replies, this in itself validating him.

Defensively, Omkar says, 'People hear *nationalist* and they think *fundamentals*. Please, we are not the Taliban. We believe in reform, because how you can have unity if all castes and ranks are fighting? But reform is not meaning total rejection of our culture. Like a person, a national identity is having one foundation that is fixed and other parts that are changing with the new experiences. Freedom struggle, democracy: all this is not Aryan, still we are including it in our national culture.'

'It is a political masterstroke,' Naren says. 'By separating Hindu culture and Hinduism, the Bharat Brotherhood brings eighty per cent of the country under one ideological umbrella.'

'And the rest can go fuck themselves,' Cyrus mumbles over a rolling paper.

Gyaan lifts his brow. Is that who Naren is then? He braces himself for a longer battle. Looks like more than one person will be exposed tonight:

Ifra feels her chest and face thicken into a wall as Omkar, buoyed by the Agashes, says in an increasingly strident voice, 'If I may be saying one thing. As per Supreme Court, Hindu culture is including four religions: Buddhism, Jainism, Sikhism and Hinduism. All are arising south of the Himalayas, all are responses to the Vedas, so this is our way of life. Christianity and Islam are Western concepts; the basics are different. We are not saying don't live here, but if you live here, respect our sentiments. If I am in Dubai, I will respect their sentiments. If I am in Rome, I will respect the Christians…'

Ifra doesn't respond to his use of 'their' for Muslims. She knows a parrot when she sees one, but her boyfriend, intrigued by Omkar's coherence, however warped, has started testing the waters for a genuine engagement. Gyaan is saying, 'To return to Ifra's point, four religions or one, Italian culture has nothing to do with Christianity.'

It must be a debate they have in their rotten branches because the parrot pertly replies, 'Italy is a small country where all are speaking Italian. In India, go from one village to another village: language changes, skin changes, dress changes. Diversity is good, but you need only one pinch of salt or sugar in your food. We are always saying *unity in diversity*. If you are asking me from where unity will come, I will say: eighty per cent of the country is practising Hindu culture. If I am asking you from where unity will come, you are having no answer. Or it is some hyper concept for the extraordinary people.'

Kedar says to Omkar, 'Deshache samvidhan, ha pun ek paryaya aahe…'

'Doubt he's read the constitution,' Ifra says. 'Listen, Omkar, where do you think our unity came from before your Brotherhood? At the time of Independence, no one thought a nation as diverse as ours could survive. But it has, and what's incredible about the Indian experiment is that we have no precedent. Intellectual after intellectual has written about this.'

'What if they are wrong?' Naren interjects. 'What if the only thing that's held us together is the Hindu way of life? Independence was no secular utopia; there was Partition, there were language riots. Women and castes got rights, but the change was at the level of reform. The constitution still discourages cow slaughter – this is a Hindu nation from the start. To be sure, I'm an atheist. If I was clapping in the prayer room, it's not because I worship cows but I appreciate my culture has value in bringing people together.'

The fraud, Ifra thinks. He assumes he is superior to Omkar because he can understand that religion is a route to power. He wants the Hindu identity even if he doesn't believe in Rama. 'Know what, Naren? People like you create the atmosphere in which despots can get away with…'

'Iffy, sweetheart, relax,' Rohit says with the confidence of that age when you discover the pleasure of opinion, and surprised to find adults listening, you fall in love with your voice. 'They are only saying we need to accept that a huge number of Indians *feel* this identity. You can't always define something in terms of a negative. You can't be neti neti all the time. You have to say what you are and make it simple enough to understand. If the nationalists are effective, it is because your secular spiel means nothing to the man on the street.'

Ifra says, 'The nationalists are effective because it is easier to sell hate than love.'

'Have you read Harari?' Naren asks. 'As a species, our ability to cooperate in large numbers is the basis of our dominance, and what makes this cooperation possible is shared myths. That's why the hotbed of war and terror isn't where nation states are strong, it is where they are failing. You don't like the current myths, give people your own.'

'Even if they rewrite history to show every Mughal was a villain?' Ifra asks. 'And little Hindu kings won battles they lost?'

'History will always be curated,' Naren replies in a voice so cool, it undermines her heat. 'Countries like India want their golden age before they are as secure in their psychology as the West. Once we get rich, people won't be so touchy.'

'This is the hypocrisy of the right,' Kedar says over his rum. 'You sing capitalism with one tongue and Hindu culture with the other. Keep opening your markets and see how long your Hindu culture survives.'

'Both you cousins presume progress will lead to progressiveness,' says Gyaan, squinting past a smoke ring. 'If it did, why is India seeing unprecedented income growth at the same time as religious revival? The answer: modernization. People feel cut off from their roots. Everything is changing so fast, people need some values and beliefs that hold, and the Hindu nationalists exploit this.'

Ifra's breath quickens. Insufferable, these men, their objectivity, and for all that, their incredible talent for missing the obvious. She would like to give Gyaan another, less sympathetic answer, that the dream of economic and cultural supremacy is united by the same bedrock: male ego. She looks to the terrace where Manasi is still on a call, and to Amanda, staring solemnly into her wine. She isn't them, but she must hold back until the emotion leaves her voice:

Cyrus sets his rolling paper down. When he told Rohit that getting the gang to meet Omkar might help, this isn't the occasion he had in mind. And while he doesn't care for state-of-the-nation debates, he is done with everyone offering Omkar the stage to show who the bigger liberal is. Meanwhile Omkar, whom they wouldn't give a second look if he didn't have the dangerous aura of a nationalist, carps on, 'If I may be clarifying one point on this culture–economy debate. We are wanting to modernize with new technologies and capital, but this is not meaning westernize. Seed of capitalism is good, but we have to grow it here as per our soil. Jaise, big companies from America are exploiting our resources, but Hindu culture is very much respecting nature. We are praying to plants, and we have to go forward taking that.'

'Isn't this brilliant?' Cyrus says, sniffing his crusher. 'The people bankrolling your government are the country's biggest miners.'

Omkar startles like he didn't expect Cyrus to address him.

'I have a question for you, Omkar,' Cyrus goes on. 'If I ask you, are you a nationalist who is a capitalist or a socialist, what is your answer?'

Omkar stares at the carpet as Cyrus refills his crusher. Slowly, Omkar says, 'Dekhiye. My interest is in history and culture. Not so much economics. I have not studied that. Because, how much I am understanding, India is not about class, it is about caste.'

Gyaan starts laughing, 'The poor idiot. His Brotherhood is an old upper-caste tyranny that talks caste only on election day, and his prime minister wears a luxury shawl gifted by the country's biggest businessmen. But our man can't see the links. Our man is too blinded by the cultural bullshit to see what's keeping his class oppressed.'

Suddenly fervent, Omkar says, 'Our honourable prime minister is backward caste. He is wearing a shawl, okay. He is deserving it. He is not buying it from his father's money.'

And that propels another round of debate –

*It is just tokenism. For every stooge they prop up, they keep a million down…*

*More backward castes and Dalits voted for the Bharat Party than any other…*

*Which is less than a fourth of all backward castes and Dalits…*

– but Cyrus says no more. For one, he has made his point. For another, he feels like he doesn't know enough to participate. He looks at Rohit and recalls the rainbows on his cheeks as they walked through the streets when the country recriminalized homosexuality. That the Conclave Party was in power hardly mattered. They were marching against the establishment and whom it constituted was beside the point. Neither he nor Rohit voted in the March election. If he has played pacifist between his friends so far, it's because he believes they are more than their politics. For the rest, this is an after-dinner party and not the parliament, so he holds his smoke in deep until the weed takes off:

Amanda may not understand the nuances of Indian politics, but Deonar has made her aware of the hypocrisy of boozy debates in the city's finest real estate, and how smug Gyaan sounds when he says, 'The Bharat Party is very clever in how they target each level of society. You can't feed a poor man culture, so they will rename the Conclave Party subsidies and take the credit. Next comes the blue-collar class where you have this small-town youth who just got a phone and a bike and has this inflated sense of his potential, and now he needs to know he's better than the liberal elite who kept him down. It is the revenge of the plebs. And the minorities are collateral damage…'

'Maybe the *plebs* don't have your education,' says Amanda.

Gyaan stiffens. 'Hey, I took the public bus to school and bought my books second-hand off the pavement, so if some kid with a college diploma hasn't taken the responsibility to get informed, I have a problem…'

Cyrus wipes his crusher with a white muslin square. 'The problem with liberals is that we can't have a discussion without being judgy among ourselves.'

And Gyaan, with comical sobriety, replies, 'To understand the chaos on the fringe, you have to understand the contradictions at the centre.'

To Amanda's surprise, it is Kedar who gets her point. 'I can see what your pleb gets out of being a supreme Hindu,' he says to Gyaan. 'The people who have no excuse are the aspirational class. Upper-caste white collars, NRIs. The West is in recession and the whites are getting hostile, so the NRI comes back looking for India. This is what the Hindu nationalists have given him: a chest-thumping Indian dream that nicely justifies all the money he will make.'

'You kids,' Naren comes in, his voice like a cleaver. 'You go to your arts colleges where you develop this disdain for business. Step outside, the first thing people tell you about themselves is that I work for this BPO or bank, and they say it with *pride*. India today is like America in the fifties. Everyone is working all day, every day. All those flyovers and malls and young people buying starter homes, it isn't megalomania or revenge. It is how nations are brought out of backwardness, and the more we have of that energy, the sooner we will get to the other side of the Kuznets curve…'

If anyone asked Amanda now, she would hardly think of Kedar as a character in a Wes Anderson film; it is Naren who seems unreal, but no one is as unreal as Gyaan, saying over a cascade of smoke, 'You can't model the Indian dream on the American one. America doesn't have our historical baggage. It's hard to fly with a heavy ass.'

At the mention of America, everyone looks at Amanda. Under pressure to speak, she says, 'I hate to agree with Omkar, but if one billion Indians lived like the average American, there'd be no tomorrow. The question is how to get people off the street without burning up the planet. I guess my hope for India is to right the wrongs in the development story of the West. India has an amazing spiritual tradition in which non-materialism and eco-friendliness–'

'Indian spiritualism!' Ifra snaps. 'How exotic.'

Ifra's rage is tinted with an anguish that clamps Amanda's tongue. Gyaan says prophetically, 'If you ask me, the so-called alternative modernities of the East are far worse than those of the West. They are all for capitalism without the democratic ideals of the French or American revolution, but some other feudal and regressive crap marketed as our traditional values. It is a poison cocktail, really.'

Almost to himself, Omkar says, 'Bhai aap kya kehte ho kuch samajh mein nahin aata.'

And everyone erupts in laughter except Amanda, who is confused, and Ifra, who looks away:

When Cyrus baited him, Omkar blanked out like when his schoolmaster asked questions to expose what he didn't know rather than what he did, but now his unintended joke revives his confidence, and he pushes the Marathi in his heart through the Hindi in his head out the English on his tongue: 'We are talking, talking, talking. But go to any village, you will see that, left-right-liberal, no one is knowing these terms. They are only knowing party symbols and vote as per their caste. Maybe with a leader like our prime minister, that is changing. For me, I am thinking: what am I doing for my community and who will be supporting me? Aap batao, Gyaan-ji. Forget all this opinions. You told that you are having issues with some films on history. Okay. Write to our ministry of broadcasting.'

Gyaan shuts his eyes. 'The ministry is full of arseholes. I won't take names.'

'Please be taking names. Who is the secretary?'

'Doesn't matter. You can see the state the institution is in.'

'Issue is not that. Issue is that you are not knowing. The secretary is one Ghosh. She is good. BSL is working with her on programmes for women's safety. So don't talk about the institutions, talk about the persons. That is how to make a change. Duniya Twitter pe nahin chalti.'

'If you're asking how I engage,' says Gyaan, turning aggressive, 'I get informed, I vote, I speak up and I protest. I don't want to get into politics. I just want to be a good citizen, and no, I don't need to go to some fucking village to know the state of the nation.

There is something called data. There are intellectuals I trust. So please, Omkar-*ji*, you want to play the village card, tell us about your problems in the village instead of … *What*? He's a fucking hick all puffed up since he learned some fancy words at WhatsApp university. He thinks fundamentals and fundamentalist are the same thing!'

Cyrus snorts a laugh into the silence. Gyaan heaves with something like regret. Past them, Omkar is aware of the low hum of the air conditioner, the distant roar of traffic, a sense of all the miles between here and Wai, and the miles and miles between Wai and his birthplace.

'Wow, it's quiet here,' says Manasi, back from her phone call, and as the talk revives and Omkar's chance for a retort fades, he recognizes that his humiliation is complete. He sits straight and listens with the strain that such English demands, but the words start coming apart:

The American is saying, 'Honestly, people fighting for two meals a day don't care about half this stuff we're debating. They worry about disease, malnutrition, illiteracy.'

And the one called Cy, 'Darling, we get that tweeting doesn't sound heroic when kids are starving. But there's a reason despots target free speech and institutions and identity, and once they are in power, your man who wants three meals a day will feel the burn.'

And the one called Iffy, 'I agree on development and institutions, but identity … as a Muslim woman, it is easy to make politics about nothing else. My grandfather lived through Partition. He always said, identitarianism dries the leaves; majoritarianism drops the match. I mean, are these the only categories we have to define ourselves? Isn't it possible to elevate the agenda, to unite and mobilize people in some other way?'

And Naren, 'Like what? This isn't America where abortion or gun control can become a polarizing issue. No one wants to immigrate here. No one cares about the climate. As for the economy, let's be honest, we're all some degree of capitalist and democrat. If we engage in such debates, it's because they're fun and not that we have any new ideas on how to save the world.'

And finally, the disembodied words run on in Omkar's head –

*Yes, yes, the end of history; a convenient cynicism there…*

*But how do we challenge the fundamentals?*

*A revolution, that's always the dream…*

*The point is, what will you do the morning after?*

– until Gyaan, reviving, says, 'No one is asking for a revolution, but if the right has gone so far right, we must shift left to keep the balance.'

'That's exactly how you lose balance,' Naren says. 'To be a moderate isn't fence-sitting. It is to accept complexity, to understand there are no easy solutions. If right-wing authoritarianism takes hold tomorrow, it won't be because of the failure of the left but the lost opportunity at the centre.'

Naren is speaking, Omkar thinks, because he finds this fun, and Rohit's insincerity is no less evident in the relish with which he adds, 'Look at you, Gyaan. You want to sound like Kedar even if your heart finds any extreme uncomfortable, but then Kedar is the kind of vernacular radical you liberals worship because they counter the charge your views are elitist. The real problem isn't your privilege. It is that you think you're better than the common people who are stupid, bigoted and sexist.'

Cyrus's eyes dart sideways to indicate he is speaking of Omkar. 'They are.'

Omkar pretends not to notice as Rohit sighs, 'This debate would be more interesting if we had a real opposition.'

'All right, if you want me to play the liberal,' Gyaan says, 'what's so unreal about the Conclave Party? They handled the global recession well. Sadly, they are dynasts so they can't risk giving their economists credit. It's a propaganda failure, and I can understand if some uneducated idiot can't see that, but you…'

'I'm not talking of one election,' Rohit says. 'They had decades to fix this country. Like Amanda said, when people are fighting for three meals, it's their lives versus the lives Hindu nationalism will cost us if it gets out of hand. Sure, riots are a more *visible* tragedy, but it's still a freak event. Five thousand farmers commit suicide every year because no one gives a shit about reform. Now you'll say you can't reduce human beings to numbers. Frankly, it's a pretty democratic thing to do…'

Cyrus asks Manasi if she is as tired as he is. Manasi says, 'Actually, I was listening.'

'And I'm done listening,' Iffy says, her voice stiff with tears and eyes shining as she walks past their knees.

'Hey, Iffy,' Rohit says. 'I didn't mean it that way, Iffy–'

She is already halfway down the stairs. Gyaan goes after her. Rohit follows and Gyaan makes a face like he should go back, but Rohit persists. Omkar can hear the locks turning, and Iffy, 'What did you mean then? These aren't some abstractions, Rohit. When you talk about the lives lost to nationalism, you're talking about *my* life, you're talking about *me*.'

The door slams. Omkar had not realized that the beautiful woman with a strange name and inappropriate red lipstick was Muslim; he had only placed her as an English-speaking, Westernized elite. Shame sparks into anger and spreads like hot oil through his veins. Here he is, a Marathi Hindu man, a second-class citizen in his state and country while the invaders fly high, and all these worthies sit drooling, their minds still enslaved:

Manasi scratches the carpet with her big toe as Rohit comes up the stairs. Cyrus makes an awkward apology about heading to Jay's. He will reach the parking lot before Gyaan and Ifra drive out, and Manasi could follow him, but she doesn't. When debates like this come up in office, her instinct is to go quiet. In the run-up to the national election, everyone's thoughts about what this country stood for had splintered; the old assumptions no longer held, the new ones were unclear. Six months since, there is a sense of coherence again; if anything, people seem more acutely aware of who they are that you are not, as if it were impossible to arrive at one without defining the other.

'Anyone want a second drink?' Rohit asks. 'I know I do.' He walks to the bar and cracks an ice tray. 'Sorry. I don't know how we got here. I was simply trying to tell Gyaan that you can't float above the common man and expect him to listen to you. Leaders like Gandhi found a way to talk about secularism in the people's language.'

Sitting across the bar, Kedar says, 'Perhaps you should read Ambedkar on Gandhi. He was a casteist.'

'Does it matter what he really was or said?' Naren says over his Scotch. 'The man has become a myth. Don't use that to your advantage, and someone else will. By calling Gandhi a casteist, you make people like my father shut their ears.'

They are speaking in a gentle, strained way, Manasi thinks, as if to reiterate they can have a civilized discussion, unlike those who walked out. But Kedar, watchful all evening, has a new aggressive spark. He says, 'And some Dalit student finally feels heard. That is why writers like Roy are loved. Yes, she makes upper castes like your Baba uncomfortable. It's good they are uncomfortable.'

At the mention of Roy, Naren sets his Scotch down. 'Forget it, Rohit. We must be the last liberals alive.'

'Hah,' Kedar says. 'You mean the worst conservatives. I'll give it to Omkar, left-right, these are just terms. There has never been a real Indian left. We simply adopted Western models. We never thought of caste. That is why even self-proclaimed socialists like my father are totally conservative now. It is because they always were.'

Manasi's toe stops moving. In all these years of friendship with Rohit, that she is half-Mahar has never been a subject of conversation. They were the two Marathi speakers in the group, and any jibes from friends were aimed at this wider identity. If Lata Aunty or Raghu Uncle can place her surname, they have never brought it up even obliquely. Is their silence, if it is deliberate, what Naren means by 'liberals' or Kedar by 'conservatives'? She isn't sure, but this isn't the moment to ask for a clarification. To keep her eyes and hands busy, she lights a cigarette. The other person who has gone silent is Omkar. Where do the Khaires come from? What long journey has landed one of them here, like herself, in Imperial Heights? He is less seasoned at playing the chameleon, but Ifra's exit has frightened him enough to take no further chances while the Agashes fight it out.

Rohit is saying, 'Ravi Kaka is a sweetheart. Understand where he's coming from.'

Kedar replies, 'Your friend Ifra has left, so I can tell you he said the other day that all Muslims should be sent to Pakistan.'

'We're not saying he's right,' Amanda says. 'We're asking how to change people.'

'By telling them they're wrong!'

Manasi says, 'They're not listening. So what now?'

Kedar turns like he didn't expect her to speak. Neither did she. The words came from some deeper, defensive place. But what is she defending?

Kedar says, 'I'll say it again and again until I'm dead that this is wrong. There's a poem by Dushyant Kumar, a sixties revolutionary. He says, *Mere seene mein nahin toh tere seene mein sahi, ho kahin bhi aag lekin aag jalni chahiye.*'

Manasi says nothing further. The poet is right: it doesn't matter in whose heart the fire burns, as long as the flame is kept alive. In Kedar's presence, however, you would think you had no fire. If the subject of caste has not come up with her friends, she is also to blame. She has never found the words to talk about her MBA professor who mocked students who couldn't solve a maths problem by asking if they had come through the quota, or how hard she worked for the gold medal, unsure of whether employers looking at her CV would write her off for her surname, or if it was possible to style herself Manasi B without betraying her father – and Kedar is puncturing holes in that silence now, his anger like a cold fist pushed out of him, unlike hers, which is slowly turning in at herself:

Naren wants to tell Kedar to fuck poetry and get down to data. Take any metric – genocide, rape, slavery, child marriage, nuclear testing – each has seen a massive drop across industrial nations since the blasted sixties, and it is obvious which way India should go, but he suspects a mind like Kedar's works better with anecdotes than facts, so he says, 'Oh, this nostalgia for the socialist era. Why don't you ask your father what it was like setting up his factory in those days? The austerity, the red tape, the strikes. That's why my parents raised me dreaming about America. Because that's where you could breathe. That's where you could innovate…'

'Please,' Kedar says. 'India was never really socialist, only state owned and corrupt. And don't tell me you went to the West to innovate. You went to get rich and now you're back because it is easier here, and you talk like you have come to build your country. How much should I bet that the day the Indian Dream breaks down, you'll leave again? Look, there are many issues with the welfare state. Still, let us say it is here to stay, and some of my comrades will disagree, but my only request is: be a citizen. Make one land your fate, then you will see.'

'Why should I?' Naren says. 'If the country doesn't hold up its end of the contract–'

'No point having this discussion,' Kedar says. 'You, my parents, all of you. The business class only acts in their own interest.'

Naren stops laughing when he realizes that no one else intends to respond. 'What class doesn't, Kedar? You think your peasants and tribals give a shit about your values? The minute the poor become working class, they wrap their arms around their privilege to keep others out. But what's almost touching is when you lefties buy into your philosophy so much, you start resenting what your decent middle-class parents slogged to earn. You're all so young, barely past your quarterlife. You have all this time and energy, but unlike every previous generation at your age, you have nothing and no one to be responsible for, so you go chasing utopias. Wait till you marry, wait till you get real jobs and have kids. You won't be able to stand your contradictions.'

'If India can stand her contradictions, so can we,' says Kedar. 'And if you're what it's like to be grown-up, I don't want to grow up.'

'You of all people won't. A commie never ages, he only gets shriller. We won't mention you still live off your parents…'

'I chose to become a journalist because some things are more important than money. If I had your job–'

'Landsworth won't hire you,' Naren says, enjoying Kedar's rising heat. 'Think it is easy to get into IIT or Wharton? Ninety-nine per cent of people don't have the chops, and I won't apologize. If there's one thing life has taught me, there are no rules at the bottom and the top of the pyramid. Morality is for the middle class. Morality is the middle class's consolation prize. What else do you have to justify your mediocrity? It soothes you to think all the successful people bribed their way up. I can see it in your eyes, Kedar. This isn't political, it is personal. This is about your father holed up in our grandfather's house while his siblings live it up in Bandra and Brisbane.'

'This wasn't personal but you are making it personal,' says Kedar, holding a hand forward. 'Yes, my father is bourgeois. He has a factory with some fifty workers. I am proud to admit it. Because power is no longer in the hands of small manufacturers. It's with MNCs like your employer and the mining company your father sold our ancestral land to. Don't ask how an environmental clearance is made for a forest with a river, but the mischief was done, and that is how my father is where he is while his brother lives on twelve storeys of blood money!'

Naren's pulse quickens yet he remains seated, his superiority in his self-restraint. 'A Conclave Party minister's son has a stake in Brahma Mines, and if he did something to get a clearance, that's not our problem. If you are so convinced what my father did is illegal, file a case. This isn't Afghanistan where we stone people on suspicion.'

'What minister's son?'

Naren is surprised Kedar doesn't know this. 'Ask your father. The next time you call someone a criminal, check your facts first.'

Almost to himself, Kedar says, 'Even if it was legal, it was unethical.'

'Growing into Ravi Kaka, aren't you?' Naren says. 'Tell me. Do you know why the Supreme Court dropped the mining ban in Goa? Because the public works you lefties love are affected. The country plans to invest five hundred billion in infrastructure and where will the steel come from? Miners, truckers, boatmen, three million construction workers, will you give them jobs? Villagers in the Konkan are praying to Ganesha for the mines to stay open. What you activists hate to admit is that the people you are fighting for are against you.'

Kedar is silent, as if all he cares for is the company of his own thoughts. Naren raises his hands to suggest he is done and heads to the restroom. He doesn't care what anyone thinks of him except for Manasi, to whom he has bragged about his family's connection to Brahma Mines and Ankush's offer to introduce him to his famous uncle – and here Kedar makes them sound like criminals. The idiot, he thinks, unzipping himself. The self-righteous idiot:

Kedar would have left after one drink if the incident with Ifra hadn't set the rum in him on fire. He looks at Omkar, sitting silently and almost pitiable. Like this election, his presence has forced a facetious, smug and apolitical class to reveal what they stand for, and the people Kedar can't stand are not the nationalists, but his cousins, these privileged windbags flashing their concern for society like it was the latest accessory.

'This is the problem with growing up in Mumbai,' he says, aware that Naren can hear him. 'You are clueless about what capitalism does to people's psychology. Take Talne itself. Beautiful hill. The villagers grow cashews to sell the nuts and liquor, and grain and some vegetables for food. The forests and river are their gods, so when Brahma Mines shows up, they protest. But the miners are very smart. They find a weak link like my uncle, and they get hold of their first plot, and they bring in heavy machinery and start blasting. They dump silt in the surrounding plots. The conveyor belts screech so loudly, no one can sleep at night. Explosions send rocks so high, they break walls and even kill people. The villager close to the plot is getting desperate, so when the miners show him a suitcase of money, he takes it and builds a house some way off and buys a truck to carry their ore. Then other villagers want the same thing. That's how the miners break the protest – by buying out one person at a time, slowly, like a river wears a stone. No, please, Rohit, let me finish. Today, even children in Talne want to serve tea at the mine for ten rupees rather than go to school. The next generation has zero skills, so of course they pray to keep the mine open. But the story doesn't end there. Brahma gives its trucking deals to bigger companies in Goa and gets cheaper migrant labour from the poor northern states where mines have shut. So Talne has no jobs and the villagers are protesting again.'

'Kedar,' Rohit says, taking up for Naren, 'aren't we past the debate that we have to mine? Look at China. They did what they had to do to get their people out of poverty. Now that they have the money, they're going green…'

'You love Gandhi, don't you?' Kedar says. 'Then read him. For Gandhi, peace was built into the process. You didn't compromise people today so you can save them tomorrow. Equality or non-violence wasn't just the goal. It was the means.'

'I'll give it to you commies,' Naren says, returning to his seat. 'You're experts at criticism, but you suck at thinking where the ball will drop if what you say is done. Instead of working with the government, you will pick a lost cause to gratify your conscience and hold a glamorous rally. Look at your language. It is so *romantic.* Do I believe in equality? No. Men have never been equal. Do I believe in upliftment? Yes. Is it because I'm an angel or want to keep the poor from my throat? Doesn't matter. I pay thirty per cent of my income towards it, and that's more than anyone in this room.'

'Is thirty per cent enough?' Amanda asks, speaking for the first time since Ifra left.

Kedar barely hears her. The sight of his cousins' clipped English, their expensive clothes and the indignant white girlfriend makes him touch his forehead like he was checking his temperature. Yes, he thinks, pay your guilt money and vote to keep the system that keeps others so poor they're below the tax bracket. 'Want to know where the ball has dropped?' he asks Naren. 'They are blasting the wetlands of Odisha and Jharkhand's forests and the hills in Karnataka. Our rivers are flowing backward, our seas are slick with oil. Millions of skill-less, landless zombies are migrating from state to state to work like slaves. Those who pick up guns are branded terrorists and shot by our army. Our country is like a body starting to eat itself. We have become cancerous...'

And he has gone too far, because Manasi, the quiet one, says, 'You make it sound like the apocalypse.'

Naren puts an arm around her. 'Let him talk, baby. The only people obsessed with the apocalypse are the world's dictators and activists. Our annihilation has the same poetry in a Marxist's head as our origins in a Hindu nationalist.'

Kedar sets his rum and Coke down so hard, Manasi presses deeper into Naren. Her instinctive need for protection from his fury brings a sudden, immeasurable fatigue over him. He exhales and hoists his tired backpack:

Rohit has gulped his gin and tonic at every opening, as if a full mouth was all that scuttled his retort before the talk moved on, and as his cousin stands to leave, he feels the need to prolong the conversation to a point where he has the final word. In a tone as casual as he can affect, he says, 'Kedya, hold on. Sit down. What's the hurry? Did you know that I recently drove down the coast? I didn't get as far as Talne, but I saw enough of your little off-the-map settlements. You romanticize village life. Well, I went looking for the Konkan in her villages and all I got was drunks crapping where they catch their dinner.'

Kedar smiles as if at a child who has ventured into adult conversation. 'Best you didn't see Talne. For a tourist, there is nothing to see. And it is not safe. The mine is expanding and the last resisters are selling their land at gunpoint. Still, no one will file a complaint. Everyone knows what is going on: the contractors in Mumbai, the multinationals, the politicians, the court, the mining mafia. Only Rohit Agashe refuses to join the dots.'

And Rohit is scouring his cranium for an answer when Amanda piles on, 'Kedar is right. Many of our families in Deonar are migrants whose lands were taken by force. That's how they wash up in Mumbai. No one likes the sight of them, so they are moved to the city fringe where politicians carve them into vote banks and set them at each other's throats. Sometimes I don't know where to start. We talked so much about your history, Rohit, and you never mentioned these mines.'

Taken aback, Rohit says, 'It was a random plot bought and sold as an investment. What does it have to do with my heritage?'

'I have colonial ancestors too, but at least I feel *guilty*.'

The least she can do is recognize this is not her fight, but now that he is on the receiving end, she must convince everyone that she is better than the person she is fucking. His anger shifts to her, and it is full of the force of the answer he would like to give Kedar, his shame at Ifra's exit, and his frustration with Amanda's superiority. 'Give me a break,' he snaps. 'By slumming it out here for some months, you think you've earned the right to tell me what my country needs? Want something to feel guilty about? How about that your photos can be locally commissioned for half your pay, but your salary comes from an American foundation so why would the NGO refuse, and the foundation's mission is only to sensitize *you,* another white chick with no skills to teach or medicate or build but whose ultimate high is being a busybody.'

'Done? Thank you,' Amanda retorts in her breezy, ironic way. 'We all start somewhere, so why don't you actually visit Deonar or Talne? Pleasure, your own at least, feels stupid and trivial the more time you spend there. I may do what I do to assuage my guilt, but that's not the same as getting a high.'

'Listen,' Rohit says. 'Listen. If there's one thing I have, it's a solid meter for bullshit. A man is *dead* because of your meddling.'

'Rohit!' Manasi says.

'You understand dead? I don't. I have no idea what dead is. I have no idea what real is. Is this real? You, me, this relationship? Is this a relationship? Or some weird power play in which I'll take crap from a girl because she's an expert at parading her morality.'

'Yaar,' Omkar says.

And Rohit can't stop staring at Amanda's proud jaw and the dark roots of her light hair as he steps towards her. 'We're half-baked, how we operate, what we believe. At least I admit that. I won't pretend I know hunger because you can't know hunger by sitting next to it. But the stench of unprocessed trash – how refreshing. It's like the head rush of a slap. Want a slap? Here, let's try. Slap me and I'll slap you. It will be fun, I promise. It will feel real.'

Naren says, 'Rohit!'

Amanda's jaw is trembling as she stands, but the gin is opening secret furies in Rohit's brain to the point he can hardly recognize himself beyond his mounting decibel. 'Never slapped anyone, have you? The furthest I've gone is wrestling Naren on our parents' bed. So come on. Your slummers do it all the time. It will feel good, better than a fuck for the novelty...' and he pats Amanda's cheek with no force.

A loud snap. His neck twists. He stumbles and has to hold the couch to steady himself. The sting runs from his mouth through his jaw to his skull. He touches his cheek. Looks at his fingers, expecting blood. There is none. He starts laughing as Amanda's breathing steadies and the lightning leaves her eyes.

# *Ifra*

'I just shut down,' she says, her eyes fixed on the tail lights blinking through the rain. 'I don't know which is worse: sitting quiet from the pressure to show that being a Muslim doesn't get in the way of friendship, or being frank and feeling like everyone is waiting for you to leave so they can speak their mind. You know me, baby, as a person…'

Gyaan lets go of the gearshift and cups her knee. His palm is large and damp, his hold gentle. 'I'll talk to Rohit.'

'About what? He makes one new friend and he thinks he's a fucking champion of the working class. Everyone wants development and condemns the sectarian part, but by voting you give bigots the power to do what you condemn, so how does it work?'

A pothole full of rain flares in the headlights. Ifra straps her seat belt and talks on, 'Omkar is just a brainwashed clone. I simply screen out people like that. But then Rohit and Naren back him with all their fucking facts…'

'I get it,' Gyaan says with the same caution with which he drove over the pothole. 'They talk like it's a choice between the economy and the minority. It isn't political thought that's dead, it's political imagination.'

Ifra shakes her head in disbelief. 'It's a scene from *Rhinoceros*. Suddenly the people you recognize as decent, educated types grow horns and hooves and start talking in a language you can't understand and you're *terrified*.'

'I'll talk to them,' Gyaan says, this time in his control-the-situation voice. 'Naren reminds me of my corporate clients. They read every big book in vogue, but they don't read for the truth. They read for whatever justifies their choices…'

For Gyaan, this is a disagreement he can referee. For her, this is a crisis. She breathes over her frustration that her partner of two years can't comprehend the source or depth of her despair as he convinces himself that he is a better man than Naren. But the conversation at the Agashes has betrayed their limits as a couple; it has brought her to the irrevocable knowledge that their frames of reference differ in fundamental ways. For a moment, she feels a cold, pure hatred for Gyaan. It soothes him to set her down safe when she is angry, to play caretaker and pacifist. Well, she will not give him that satisfaction. 'Drop me at the gallery, please? Cy's cousin has a show tonight.'

The gallery means fifteen minutes less in the car. 'Cyrus isn't going himself.'

'The assistant curator is a family friend. I told him I'll stop by.'

'You mean Bobby?'

Ifra nods. They drive the rest of the way in silence. The streets have started flooding, and everything reeks of decay. Gyaan must think she is hysterical. He is probably waiting for her to cool down to work through this. Turning into Delta Corporate Park, he says, 'If you're going to be quick, I can wait in the coffee shop and take you home.'

She says she will call an Uber, and then, to prick him, that Bobby can drop her home. Gyaan doesn't protest. Her anger clefts into frustration and pity. More than condescension or dismissing her feelings, fear has kept him quiet. It isn't easy for him to choose between her and Rohit. She steadies her voice. 'You know what is happening in this country is wrong. You know making that film with Omkar is wrong. I won't ask you to quit because I don't want you to do it for me or us. If you do it, do it because you're you … or who I thought you were.'

Gyaan nods at his hands on the wheel. She gathers her tote, slams the car door, and strides into the lobby. As the elevator shuts, the car is still waiting in the rain.

Three floors up, the gallery is happily thronged. Bobby has pulled it off: the olive and navy walls, the white text, the metal mounts, the bearers going about with wine and cheese on oval trays. This is the world she was raised in. She has come here from a survival instinct, and is still hugging her tote when Cyrus's mother advances, pearls on mint green. 'Dahling,' Meher Bulsara says, '*Love* the drop-shoulder shirt.' Her silver bob and withered pucker lean in. 'Lovely sari, Aunty.' Meher touches her collarbone to acknowledge the compliment. 'My son is not with you. Still at Rohit's?' 'I don't know,' Ifra says, but her expression says they both know he is with Jay. Meher scans her face for a second before looking sideways at the paintings. 'I know it's Homi's show and all, but honestly, what do you think?' she whispers. Ifra looks from frame to frame. 'Ambivalent?' Meher asks. 'Yes and no,' Ifra says. Meher laughs. 'I see what he's trying to do. There's so much conceptual rubbish going around, he wants to be lyrical. But you can't hide your ignorance of detail in abstraction. You have to really know the subject to distil it. You have to immerse yourself…' 'Well put, my girl,' says Tariq Abbas, his white halo bowing slightly over his wine. 'Ram Kumar knew every inch of Varanasi.' They exchange notes on the modernists, Meher panning the new crop, though her condescension is so well informed one can't help but love her snobbery, and even among the crucified, Tariq finds someone to admire, and when he does, he mists over, proof that fame has compromised neither his humility nor his eye. 'Any word on the Husain?' Meher asks. 'The Husain?'

Ifra asks. 'At the Marriott,' Meher says, alarmed at her cluelessness. Tariq explains the pressure on an upcoming retrospective of Indian modernists to take down the master's work for depicting baby Ganesha with a nude. 'The god's *mother*,' he says. 'But a guest at the hotel insists on seeing her as a *naked woman*.' Meher sighs. 'Offence-taking is a major industry today. Want to lay claim to a community? Take offence! I hear the curators are worried about vandalism.'

Ifra excuses herself. She is overcome by Meher's translucent hands and Tariq's wispy hair. They are vanishing before her, these Bombayites, her Bombayites. It was easy to scorn them as elite, but few of them had inherited more than an education and a mouldy bit of property. Wealth is Natasha in Gucci there, introducing her industrialist father to everyone as 'Daddy' because, as the gallery's patron, he needs no introduction. Tariq started in a rental smaller than Gyaan's and lost his early paintings to rats, but the narrow alleys did not narrow his soul. He was a cosmopolite long before he was welcome in Paris. Like her grandparents, he rejected Pakistan when all sense indicated otherwise; they stayed on through Partition, those lovers of Bombay. Personally, she didn't know she was one until she went to London and experienced real racism. Here in Bombay, despite her parents stories of the riots, as a college student in hot shorts, she thought it a compliment if someone said she didn't look like a Muslim. People had stereotypes for every community and anyone would be proud not to appear as typical or orthodox among their kind. When did all of them jell into one monstrous fist with its index finger pointed at the only group left out? How long before that finger curled around a trigger? Was the violence always latent, even in this room of polite laughter? For all their progressiveness, she can't tell Meher Bulsara where her son really is. Not that she has any sympathy for Cyrus tonight. The Hindu nationalists see the Parsis as 'guests', a way to showboat their tolerance by making an example of a numerically insignificant minority. And the Parsis play along; like good guests, they don't intervene when their hosts squabble. A model minority that prospered under the Mughals and the British, they will continue to do so under the present overlords. If Cyrus has a politics, it stops at being queer. For the rest, he will never go beyond his two questions to Omkar. He is as sweet as the trace of sugar in milk his Parsi ancestors promised the kings of Gujarat they would be.

Her thoughts are interrupted by thick lips booming over a silk cravat: 'I love to paint a woman's back. I'm a very visual person, and all the time you are with a woman, you look at her eyes, her front. So there is something about when you get behind: this is what her arse, her back and her hair look like.' Ifra moves away, but each conversation is more enervating than the last: 'Drugs and sex, that's all D'Agata photographs. Tits for breakfast, cunt for lunch. If he were here, he'd have taken a hundred pictures of you…' 'Stop harassing her…' 'This is our Ifra. Amal Qureshi's daughter, yes. India Forum profiled her for their thirty under…' 'Love, can I get you something? You look positively ill.' It's Bobby. Ifra says, 'I'm fine. Sorry. I've been meaning to ask if you need help.' Bobby tilts his head to the door, 'All I need is company.' They take the elevator to the top floor. 'Always love the view,' Bobby says, looking at the back wall of a building a few feet from the ledge. 'Bombay is full of great views.' He sets his smartphone on his notebook. Then he opens a pouch, drops a knob of coke on the phone's screen, and gets cutting with his credit card. The notebook, a Moleskine, is printed with the words: 'i DREAM about the day when HUMANITY will get FREE of dogma and WE ALL will be CONNECTED to our SACRED SEXUAL CREATIVE POWER.' When he is done, he offers her twin lines and a rolled up Post-it. 'It's good for health.' 'Not for mine,' she says, raising her wine. He bends over, tips his head this way, then that, before resting against the wall with his eyes shut. Then he starts talking, art talk, shit talk, inane, endearing talk that soothes her in the way browsing Netflix would. Finally he says, 'You're sad.' 'I'm not, Bobby, really.' 'I can see it,' he says and gives her a hug. 'I love you, but I'm not going to kiss you,' she says. 'I know,' he says. 'The hug's for free.'

She promises to attend the after-party though they both know she won't. Alone, at last, she undoes the button at her throat. A hot blast is rising up the air-conditioning chute. There was a time her mother thought that she and Bobby would make a good match, both children of old Bombay families. Nani said anyone was fine as long as it wasn't a Hindu. The conservative card … it's a good excuse when she needs one, but on days like this, her grandmother seems right; the gulf is overwhelming. She recalls her fight last week with Gyaan, how he refused to understand why, if he has convinced his parents to accept her, she can't tell her wealthier, more cosmopolitan ones about him. How to explain that her parents have given her so much freedom, more than any woman in the family, that to marry outside is too much of a stretch, too close to betrayal? Granted, her parents are not her grandparents, and if she fought for Gyaan, they might accept him. But she loves him only enough to persist without resistance – and this is the part of her that she keeps hidden, that makes him insecure, and that conversations like the one at the Agashes stick a finger into and rip open along the seams of their relationship.

Between the terraces, the moon is so thin, she can see the sky through it. Thrice as bright is the cross-section of a green billboard advertising the Muslim Unity Party. This is the first time the outfit has spilled out of Hyderabad to contest elections in Bombay. Tariq recently told her father that Indian Muslims were done with trusting their Hindu leaders, but he said it sadly, and she didn't have to ask to know that he would continue to vote for the Conclave Party in the hope it will see reform. Those less optimistic were leaving. More than one cousin has gone West, and not for better careers. *We'll get out before they kick us out … Good your daughter is abroad. Keep her there … If your parents are made refugees, they will have a place you have made home.* Of course nothing in her immediate environment screams pogrom; in gentrified Bandra or Tardeo, the nationalists merely want her sidelined with no representation and no voice. Or is she being naïve? She rereads the World Bank's email asking her to join a team assessing primary education in Dubai. *What about the people who can't leave?* She wants to tell Amanda that she needed therapy to get over Bhagwat. Anu Aunty's advice not to go to the press made her sick, but Amanda has no clue how hard it is to raise money since Deonar came under the radar of the Anti-Terrorism Squad. And it isn't the only locality. Zaeem and Rafia's parents are day labourers; on learning that the education centres would shut, they sent the children to live in Nagpada where their grandma is always at home. Rafia's grades got her into a public school, but Zaeem has enrolled in a madrasa that Tehsin Teacher says is up to no good. Ah, no one understands the costs better than Ifra, but what impact can she have where she is walking on eggshells herself?

She googles the impersonal desert city. If she moves to Dubai, she will have her aunt in Sharjah for support, though Khala is more conservative than Mom, and for all that Ifra's cousins drink like fish, it is one thing hiding it from your parents and another hiding it from the state. Besides, the way Khala raised them, home was never a country so much as a religion. Her cousin Zehra's newsfeed isn't defined by India or the UAE, but by issues faced by Muslims worldwide. Yet when Zehra visited, did anyone here see Ifra as different? Sitting at the Yogi Café with hijabi relatives, she could feel that imperceptible shift in perception from the waiters and even the guests. And on the off chance something drastic *did* happen, the Hindus will want her blood, but the Muslims, retreating into their own, won't protect a progressive either. There may be allies in the family, but where does she fit in this new world? The only identity she has ever felt at home in is that of a Bombayite, a lover of printed tiles and creaking balustrades and monsteras by rattan chairs in which you spend an afternoon reading Manto. Does she have her grandparents' courage? There is no difference in serving children in any other country; the reason she came back, the reason she works *here*, is love. Love was what held her grandparents here through Partition, but the city she loves – a Bombay starting at Flora Fountain in town and ending at Haji Ali's white dome before coming up twice for air, once in Bandra and then in Juhu – is as translucent today as Meher's hands, as wispy as Tariq's hair, as wasted as Bobby. It has been almost two decades since the Marathi Bana changed the city's name to Mumbai, and if Bombay doesn't exist, the Bombayite is living on borrowed time. She sighs for the sepia city to which no passport can carry her. Twin tears fall past the ledge and turn to air before they reach the ground. She is already in exile.

# *Cyrus*

The scent of crushed mahogany flowers has set him wheezing since childhood. To his parents, however, there was never any question of a son being allergic to their beloved colony, to these stone benches and wide, curving balconies, and the pride they take in that, unlike the usual Parsi bagh, this bastion has neither a gate nor walls that keep your thoughts insular or your English from picking up a Hindi or Marathi phrase. Cyrus sneezes as he shuts the car door. A stray cat his mother feeds looks up from the porch, and curls back to sleep. He looks up at his squat building, its walls the colour of bone by night. On the top floor, beyond a grille softened by leaves and a window by lace, a lamp is on in the living room. Is it in fact the pollen shortening his breath, or moments like the one at Jay's, when Pappa calls him after dinner and he lies about his location and is asked to give Rohit the phone? In the frantic minutes after, he rehearsed his response with Jay, but the long drive home has shrunk his confidence and every other emotion: his guilt towards Ifra, his anger at Rohit's carelessness in telling his parents his whereabouts, even his frustration with Mamma, whose car is not by the curb because it's safer to come home and comfort both men separately afterwards. Going up the stairs, he clears his nose, but the sneeze won't leave his chest.

The brass lamp above the Bulsara name is so dim as to amplify the darkness. Inside, his father is where he expected him: on the lion-paw settee, his sadra and pyjamas glowing like dirty moonlight.

'Where were you?' he asks, and before Cyrus can reply, 'You think I am an idiot? My only nephew has his first solo art show. Everyone is asking Cyrus kau chhe, where is Cyroo? Bobby is there. Ifra is there. What are we supposed to tell them?'

'Tell them anything,' Cyrus says. 'I'm twenty-four, Pappa. I could be anywhere.'

'Twenty-four,' he says, his lips bruised by the free wine. 'Tu twenty-four, che ne? Motto manas thai gayo ne? Big man, haan. Then please, get your own place and do all this nonsense. At your age, I had a proper job. I had responsibilities. Bheja ma kai jaich ke? I will not have weakness under my roof.'

This is typical of Pappa, this flipping into a rage out of all proportion and context with its trigger. Whether he is upset about the show or something a guest or relative said, in the hours since, that upset has snowballed into everything he can't stand about his son, himself and the world. Cyrus's eyes are on the speckled floor, but something in his chest is pushing upwards. He is done with being a bystander among friends, an onlooker around family, and zoning out when he can't play the pacifist. A voice that is half Jay's and half his own comes up his throat. 'This is not your roof. This is Mamma's flat.'

His father rises. The shadow beyond the lamp grows larger than the man. 'How dare you. This house belongs to the Parsi Punchayet. That is why your mother can live her fancy life in the centre of the city for nothing. That is why she can rent your friends the shop in Juhu for half the rate. And our Parsi trusts are for respectable...'

'Mamma is the tenant. If anything happens, you have no claim. This is my inheritance.'

'Don't provoke me, now. You are provoking me. No one has said anything about that. So don't make me open my mouth. Mohnu na khulao – you understand?'

Cyrus stammers, 'If she writes me out of her will, you lose the place too.'

Paws close around his collar. His father shakes him like he could shake it out of him; thrice his wings are crushed against the wall. Then his collar loosens, his breath comes up his chest. As if his father were angry at his lack of resistance or his own oppressive civility that won't let him bring out a belt, he punches the wall an inch from Cyrus's face. 'Don't you lecture me about the law, you dirty little criminal.'

Cyrus has never heard his father use the word. He is saying it out of weakness. He is saying it to remind Cyrus of what he thinks is his weakness. He is doing what a bully does when cornered, he is lashing out where he knows it will hurt. Cyrus draws his collar in, his thumb and fingers moving mechanically. He wants to say: Do it then, call the police. To do so would be the only thing more disreputable than having an openly gay son – but Cyrus has tested his limits enough tonight. His father makes a sound between a scoff and a snort, and his shadow shrinks as he retreats down the corridor. When the door to the master bedroom slams, the crystal vases and frames on the piano tremor, but none falls. Cyrus does what he has done so many times because his mother will not: he sets the frames that the cleaning maid has disturbed at their proper angles. Here he is on his graduation day at Wilson, his parents on either side. He studies their smiles for strain. There is none. Mamma is wearing a fresh rose in her hair, a happy, defiant gesture. This was a month after he came out to them, the talk surprisingly undramatic, their only request to not tell the extended family. How promptly he had agreed. He wanted to accept them like they had accepted him. He knew that coming out was not a one-time chat, but would involve multiple scenes and subtle reconfigurations until love prevailed. How had things gotten worse instead? Was it since the verdict last September, when he went for his first Pride march and refused to give a damn if his cousins saw the pictures online? Or since he met Jay, the first boy he has wanted to bring home, nudging his parents out of the don't-ask-don't-tell complacency that shrouded his previous relationships? He doesn't have a clear answer, but he can't stand another moment under this roof where he is both supported and suppressed.

Back in the car, he calls Jay and tells him what went down except for Pappa's last word. With everything they have woken up to in this past year, it is a wound he will not inflict on his lover. 'You stood up for yourself,' Jay says proudly. He would love to see him but can't get out again for more than an hour. It's a long drive back to Versova, especially if Cyrus isn't crashing at Rohit's after. Still, he puts the car in gear. The scent of mahogany flowers is in the air, its winged fruit blurring patches of the street, but he doesn't sneeze. When he reaches Jay's building, he walks past the watchman without meeting his gaze, and takes the elevator to the floor above the one where Jay's family lives. Jay is at their usual spot, a pale landing without cameras and a red door that hides the stairway from the building's marble lobbies and elevators. They sit hunched on a step, their sides touching, and talk of Cyrus's parents. 'I grew up thinking of them as progressive,' he says. 'I don't know what changed. Is it a reaction to having a gay son? Getting older? Whatever other shit is up in the country? The other day, my mom was talking with her Hindu friend who was like, *You can understand, Meher-ji, Muslims threw you out of your country, so you came here. Where is your civilization today? That is our fear.*'

Jay says, 'Ha, try a Maadu joint family. This is our dinner table every day.'

Cyrus bites his fingernails. 'I should have stood up for Ifra. I caught her in the lobby and said I'm sorry, but before she could ask if I'd come to the gallery, I gave the same excuse I gave Rohit; I said I have to be here and made off. The thing is, how do you negotiate a choice that doesn't involve you? She keeps saying Rohit has changed, and sure, he has all these opinions and he's kind of preoccupied.'

'So preoccupied, he forgot where things are with your parents and told your mom you're with me?'

'That's not connected. I might have made the same mistake telling a friend's parents about a girlfriend. Rohit doesn't get that the repercussions are worse for us. It's just a dumb, straight-boy slip of tongue.'

Jay nods. 'Sure. Nationalism isn't making Rohit who he is. It's who he is that draws him to this sort of thing. He will do whatever it takes to stay centre stage, even if it means throwing his friends under the bus.'

Cyrus's frustration grows. 'He hasn't thrown me under the bus. Or Ifra. I mean, this is just talk. No one's life is at stake here. Even if the city went mad and riots broke out, Rohit would be the first person to help keep her safe. His stupid political connections might even help.'

'And that's attractive?'

'What is?'

Jay smiles. 'This popular dude-bro who doesn't flinch at throwing an arm around you. And now, he's got even sexier. An organization full of men. All that structure and discipline. There's an allure, isn't there? Who said it? Every woman adores a fascist.'

Cyrus laughs. 'You're being thoroughly over the top. As usual.'

'Am I? His brother is my boss. Naren is blazing his way up Landsworth. Rationally, I hate his politics, his guts, his arrogance. I shouldn't want this guy's attention, but I can't help how good it feels when I see him making an effort to charm me because he likes my irreverence and wants me on his coattails.'

For a moment, Cyrus hates Jay's guts. Then he realizes that his anger is a result of knowing this is not who he wants to be and exactly who he is, and yet, Jay is calling him out without judging him but by implicating himself. He has a sudden desire for Jay's skin on his skin, to release the tension in his nerves, to not know where he ends and this man who sees him more clearly than he sees himself begins. The mouth of the trash chute is stinking, and it feels desperate to make out here, but he feels desperate. He reaches under Jay's kurta. Gently, Jay stops his hand and brings his head on to his shoulder. Cyrus closes his eyes. He understands that Jay can't spend another night out, that his parents are getting suspicious and a hotel for just an hour is a luxury that no junior associate, even one at Landsworth, can afford in this city. But it simply isn't enough, the hard comfort of bone when what you want is the tenderness of flesh. Sullenly, he says that he has to go. Jay doesn't protest, but he walks him to his car. He has parked in the back alley that leads to the beach. They are still too close to Jay's building to feel free, but the alley is walled and its far end is dark, and he is unlocking the door when Jay touches his elbow.

The rain has stopped and the city smells as if it's on fire. They are kissing to the crash of the waves when a loud thudding shakes the hood. Not tonight, not tonight of all nights, Cyrus thinks, squinting at the flashlight on his face. When they step out, Jay does the talking since his Hindi is more fluent. There is no point in asking whether the watchman or a neighbour tipped off the cops, or resisting the hands on their shoulders as they are led into a navy blue van. At the police station, they pay a fine for 'obscene behaviour in public' without a word. But when they are asked to call their parents and tell them where they are, they refuse. Half an hour later, they are waiting behind bars when a constable tells them that 'Sir' has come. Both stand up, but Cyrus is asked to sit back down while Jay is escorted to a cabin. Through the open door, Cyrus can hear the scrape of a plastic chair on tile. Either the inspector is not your usual Marathi cop or he is going by the surname on Jay's ID because he addresses him in Hindi. He wants to know what Jay does, where he studied, and whether he picked up these ideas in the West and knows that he can go to jail for them here. 'This is not London,' he says, 'this is India.' Jay says he only thought of his studies in London, that he came back to work for his country, that he works hard, just like the police, and would like to show them his appreciation. The sum must be generous; when the inspector speaks again, his tone is warm, even avuncular. 'Look, son,' he says. 'You seem like a good boy from a cultured family. Why are you wasting time with people like him? Muslims, Parsis, foreigners … this sort of company will spoil your habits. Now go home. He can go too, but mind my advice.'

# *Gyaan*

Three years into life on this island city, the coastal monsoon still undoes him. His joints are heavy, his curls frizzed, and he feels stale, like he has slept too much or not at all, but if he's pulling out of *Bappa*, there is no waiting until Monday. Always the first to arrive, he unlocks the studio door. In the rainy-morning light, the tripods and mics stand as eloquent as antiques. He recalls the night barely six months ago when the crew gathered here to celebrate their new address. A studio in Juhu meant they were living the film-maker's life, that they had made a commitment, and like every gig down this strip, they spent their days paying rent and evenings writing scripts in cafés where you were never far from a chat that saw you rush to the loo to save an idea on your phone. Still, they believed that they were special. They would stay free of Bollywood's nepotism and greed; they would make honest art but would not be insignificant; they would cross over, the avant-garde that reshapes the mainstream and is studied in schools like his alma mater. *Oh potential*, he thinks, opening the back windows. Past a narrow parking lot are the rehabilitation chawls that house the maids and watchmen who service the office buildings along the road, their corridors hung with laundry, their human and animal dramas on display. He recalls his first night here with Iffy, how they made love on this couch, the blinds up, the lights out, and she looked past the darkness and said, 'It's a scene right out of *A Streetcar Named Desire.*'

*Oh desire*. Gyaan loads the espresso machine. Last night, an hour after their fight in the car, Iffy sent him a long text about leaving India. She did not say where they stood and has not replied to his reply; his only notifications are pending bills. The thought of his mother's flat, its smell of ink and porridge and the constant racket of tuition students, tightens his gut. He will never return to Delhi, though freelancing again will mean chasing clients and arguing with rentals and that whole side of business Rohit takes care of so effortlessly. He could get a job at another studio but he won't have a stake; his deal with Rohit has been sweet and serendipitous. It was easy to mesmerize the boy until he met Omkar … and there is Omkar's pen drive on a stack of books about film. *Bappa* makes no mention that the festival was made a public affair to build Indian solidarity in fighting the British, and how, now that the British are gone, the drumming gets louder whenever the revellers pass a mosque. That said, the footage is enviably bold in its love of salt-of-the-earth faces, its eye for the absurd, its unintended juxtaposition of the sacred and the profane. And scanning the book titles under the pen drive, Gyaan worries he will amount to nothing more than a consummate consumer, his best insights lavished on living-room talk, social-media rants, and corporate brands signalling virtue to keep a woke generation hooked. Six months in Juhu's ecosystem have opened doors that will come in handy when he has a script, but the funnel is overwhelmed, the flue too narrow to capture everything he knows and knows he doesn't. Had artists of the past less change to process, less self-consciousness, lower costs? How did Bertolucci do it at twenty-four? Or is it Gyaan's lack of – the word catches in his chest, the hope, the shame – *genius*?

'Hey,' Cyrus says, returning Gyaan to the room.

'Was the door open? I'm making coffee.'

Cyrus sits on the window ledge, his T-shirt a deeper pink than the bougainvillea on the grille. Gyaan's breath relaxes at the thought that it won't be just him and Rohit working this out. He is handing Cyrus a mug when the door slams and Rohit walks in, raindrops like dew on his big hair, his eyes shot and cheek bruised. 'What happened to your face?' Cyrus gasps.

Rohit looks at Cyrus, then Gyaan, then Cyrus again. Sitting heavily like a drunk on the couch, he says, 'Amanda and I broke up.'

'Why?' Cyrus gasps again.

Typical Rohit. From the moment he enters a room, it is all about him. Cyrus is saying, 'Christian sanctimony meets New World idealism, it would drive anyone nuts. And now she has competition, your new toy from the sticks…'

Rohit looks at the ceiling. 'I do *not* like Omkar's arse. I like his *work*. It is raw. It is real. It is not the regurgitated commercial bullshit we've made all year.' He holds a palm up to the montage of their advertisements on the exposed brick wall.

Gyaan's cheeks turn hot. It may be Agashe money in the Box but it isn't Agashe sweat; it is *his* sweat in those ads, *his* vision in this décor, two years of *his* mid-twenties burnt up. 'You want it real, bro?' he says. 'Here's some real news. Black Box is a passion project for you, but for me, it's bread and butter. Maybe your dad helped us with bootstrapping, but I'm tired of your bullying. Last night, I was drunk enough to think I could expose Omkar. You can catch the undercurrent of chauvinism in everything he says, but that's the thing with his type, they're experts at cloaking bigotry in ideological terms, and the person finally exposed was *you*.'

'Sorry,' Rohit says, but his brow suggests Gyaan is overreacting. 'I shouldn't have said all that around Iffy … but the way you guys put Omkar down. Our friendship isn't charity. I *like* him. Where's your love of the people if you shut them out the moment they are fucked up enough to think right wing?'

Gyaan wants to tell Rohit about his allergies made worse by the pigeon shit in the air conditioner his landlord won't replace, his rage at his father for failing to hold a job, the shame of his married sister sending money home because he doesn't earn enough … and a dozen other wounds and obstacles as he keeps going at an art form no one in his family respects, but to talk of his struggle is to defeat the point. He says, 'Look, it's very Mary Shelley, this even-a-monster-is-a-wounded-heart thing, but not every angry young man joins the Brotherhood. Your Omkar is all pumped up because the new prime minister is backward caste. He doesn't realize he will never be anything but a foot soldier for their stinking ideology.'

Clearly, Rohit hasn't read their ideology. There was a time his blankness would manifest as a blush under his tan, a hand through his hair to reassure himself of his charm, a change of topic. Now he says smugly, 'Doubt Omkar cares. It's already a dream how far the Brotherhood has got him.'

'Until he wants more,' Gyaan says. 'He thinks he's special because he got out of his village. He's bought the dream, he wants to be you, everyone does. Don't smile. One day he will find out you want to be no one but yourself, and he will see you as a symbol of everything wrong with this world. Because hate is a way for people to protect themselves. A puritan always rejects before he is rejected. My point is, I don't care where your Omkar comes from, I judge people by their actions, and that includes me.'

Rohit starts laughing. 'Action? You and me talking about action? Talk is all we do. We're brilliant. We're better than everyone. This city is a huge mango tree and we're so ripe we're quivering, but the mango never falls. Omkar isn't waiting to break even or find a voice. He's out there focusing his lens. Call his politics crap, but he's on the ground, working.'

'It's all fun and games now because we're shooting. But tell me how we'll promote this film? Can you imagine that lunatic at a film festival? Can you see us on a panel?'

'At least we're talking about our careers now. No more moralizing bullshit about saving the country.'

'Rohit, bro,' Cyrus says in the way only he can, a man who finds arguments vulgar and has mastered the art of lightly bringing everyone back to base, 'let's talk careers then, because backing this dude is suicide.'

'For a certain kind of film-maker.'

'So you want to be one of them,' says Gyaan. 'One of those Bollywood nationalists peddling films in which all the Muslims are terrorists and the cops are Hindu. You want your debut to be a jingoistic war flick between India and Pakistan that gets televised on Republic Day while you pose for selfies with a despot. Don't make that face. Because that's the kind of film-maker Omkar will be if he gets his break.'

Rohit presses his bruise. Yes, Gyaan thinks, Omkar and you too; this is the new world, and you, Rohit, will align your mediocre talent with the zeitgeist to go further than me, who will set my talent against it. 'I said I'm sorry,' Rohit says. 'We're not going to dump a film three days before shooting because my partner is insecure about his girlfriend.'

Gyaan feels each vertebra pulling the next up. Rohit has never recovered from the shock that Ifra did not go for him; he had never met a girl who found brains a bigger aphrodisiac than a boyish face in a fancy car. But Gyaan isn't so sure of his own powers any more, and he would rather not give Rohit the satisfaction he felt on hearing of Amanda's slap, so he stops short of telling him that Ifra wants to leave. 'You, my friend,' he says, 'are a party boy whose charm is nothing but a wool coat with squat inside. That's why you need all this identity bullshit, and *I'm* the insecure one?'

Trying to calm things down, Cyrus says to Rohit, 'Dude, you're restless, we get it. We'll get there, promise. You haven't invested anything yet. You can cancel the rentals.'

Rohit says to the floor, 'You're not on this assignment. This isn't your business.'

Cyrus sighs, 'I'm just here for Iffy.'

'Are you? Or is this about what happened with your parents last night? I told you I'm sorry. They called out of the blue and asked where you are and I thought Meher Aunty is okay with you and Jay. Sometimes she is and sometimes she's on your dad's side, and honestly, it's hard to keep track. The point is, we're *not* cancelling…'

As Rohit is shouting, Gyaan recognizes that his own talk until this morning has been an indulgence, his politics about other lives that he pities and must fight for from a position of privilege as an upper caste, English-educated male. Yet what has he given up? He's simply trying to get by, and with luck, critically hailed. He knows from his father's life how misstep can lead to misstep, and while he can't say precisely what those missteps might entail for him, he feels a nameless dread at their undertow. And yet, *do it because you're you*.

'We? Or did you mean you?' he asks, surprised by the steel in his voice. 'You want to fund *Bappa*, fund it, but let us be clear, it is not the Box. Because if it is, I'm out. It's either Omkar or me.'

A stubborn silence. Before the steel pulls out, Gyaan says, 'Right. Guess I'm quitting.'

Rohit looks out the window. 'Guess you should.'

'Guess we will,' says Cyrus.

Gyaan senses Rohit's anger turn brittle with hurt. To Gyaan, Cyrus is like an in-law, neither snobbish nor over-friendly, his loyalty always contingent on the links, but to Rohit, he's a best friend, his main man since college. Without expression, Rohit says, 'Go on.'

Cyrus sets his unfinished coffee down. 'Good luck with your bigot.'

Following the building's exit signs, Gyaan feels the slabs on which he's built his life coming apart. He focuses on his feet, the sunny sidewalk and the smell of wet cement, until the scented interior of Cyrus's sedan gathers him in. 'What happened with your parents?' Gyaan asks. Cyrus shakes his head like he would rather not speak. 'Sorry, bud,' Gyaan says, and then, 'What did you think of Iffy's text? Did you talk to her?' 'She isn't taking my calls either.' Both are silent. Then Cyrus asks, 'You think they'll go that far? Like genocide?' He is comforting Gyaan in the only way Gyaan will accept comfort. Or perhaps the question is genuine. Iffy used the word in her text, and walking out on Rohit is the first time Gyaan has seen Cyrus take a stand. 'We're only six months in,' Gyaan says. 'The public isn't ready for hate. The people who get hurt now are those who fall through the cracks or stand in the way of the juggernaut. But if growth tanks, the Brotherhood will need a scapegoat. That's how fascists operate: they are men of hope until they are men of hate. I don't know what shape it will take, but Iffy isn't waiting to find out.'

Cyrus nods again. His mother's driver, patiently looking past the wheel, asks where to. Cyrus proposes the Monkey Bar. It's nine a.m.! Cyrus offers to get drinks. Gyaan gives him a wry, grateful smile. He misses what Iffy would say to what he said. He hopes his quitting the Box will change her mind, that their fight was within the natural ebb of a long relationship, and if he is sincere about making amends, they still have a chance. In any other century, they would have eloped or been pulled apart by now, but this isn't another century, and even if he offered to move to Dubai, he isn't sure she would accept. A coil of pain runs through his gut at the thought of driving these streets with no witness, no interlocutor, no toenails painted boudoir red on the dashboard. Looking at the malls and shop signs go past, Cyrus says, 'I'll miss her too.'

## *Rohit*

Alone in the studio, Rohit presses his tongue into the bruise on his cheek. Amanda left before he could stop laughing, and when she called later that night, you would think *she* was the injured one until he said he was done and she said she was done too. An excuse to end a serious relationship with someone else, that is all he was to her. Why else didn't she go for Naren, the older, more accomplished brother? And even as an excuse, he has failed. Andrei is still on the farm. She might have shown Rohit the door weeks ago if he wasn't also doubling up as her Indian bellboy and chauffeur. Is there anything inherently desirable about him? *A party boy with squat inside.* He is neither brilliant like Naren and Manasi, nor aflame with purpose like Ifra and Amanda, nor gifted like Omkar and Gyaan, nor sophisticated like Cy, or any of those who inspire love for nothing but themselves and whom he has always secured by playing an enabler. Can an enabler ever truly be loved? Or only used, and later, pitied or even despised? He shakes his head. Tells himself he is being ridiculous. What else would Gyaan do, given his situation? As for Cyrus, he could have brought up that his mother owns these premises, but he did not – and what is that but love? If only to prove that he, Rohit, is not the obnoxious brat that Amanda thinks, he will text his friends an apology. But when he checks his instant messenger, Ifra has blocked him. For an instant, he wants to smash his phone on the wall – that she should *block* him, like he were some sort of psychopath!

He is about to log into his social media accounts when the door squeaks. In keeping with a festive morning, Omkar is wearing a peach kurta and looks like he has taken three baths. By way of greeting, he says in Marathi, 'Best thing for that is curd mixed with turmeric. Just pat it on, like this.'

Rohit touches the bruise at its edges. 'You must have a lot of experience.'

'I've taken a hundred slaps, but never had the fortune of getting one from a girl.'

Rohit can't help but smile at his friend's small-town humour. Omkar sits in Gyaan's chair cautiously, as if he were afraid that it might break. 'I tried to reach you. Then your mother said you are here. She also said your cousin left before anyone woke up.'

'Just as well,' Rohit sighs. 'He's so extreme.'

Omkar says thoughtfully, 'These Marxists are anti-business for sure, but when he was talking, Agashe, that was the story of my village. I mean my father's village, Pachwadi. Twenty years back, there was a plan to build a dam on our river. Solid project, brought water to areas of drought, but our field was on the bank and it went under. Zero, it became zero. The contractors promised us jobs, then they got labour from other states. The politicians promised us land in another village, but when my uncle, Pargat's father, went to claim it, the villagers there finished him. Meaning, they cut him with sickles. So my father got scared and didn't go. He started drinking.'

Omkar pauses. Then, in a more objective tone, he goes on, 'In our Hindu culture, we don't regard businessmen as criminals. They are our engines of progress who work to feed their family and to give back to society. In the Vedic age, the temple economy was responsible for welfare, and the state is the modern temple economy. But what I am saying is, the people building this dam were corrupt…'

'Just so you know,' Rohit snaps, 'my father thought he was bringing progress to that village. If the miners buy a clearance or violate the limits, how am I responsible?'

Omkar twists his arms to let the energy out. 'I'm not saying it's your fault. I was thinking of my village, that's all.'

'You having a good time otherwise?' Rohit asks. 'Or were my friends too much?'

'Nothing like that. Just at times they need to be exposed, these so-called liberals.'

'Omkya,' Rohit says wearily. 'Look. They don't want to fund *Bappa*. I'll figure out the money, but whether it's Gyaan or any crew, we're here to get work done, so no more politics, please? It fires everyone up, then it kills the mood. They just walked out on me, and why do I feel you're angry with me too?'

Omkar's eyes grow large. 'It is not anger. I am not angry. I recognize Gyaan. He is another Jinx. You may assure him my film is not propaganda. When I am shooting, I have no thought that I am an Omkar, a Khaire, a class or caste Hindu. I am the camera! A person can be murdered and I will not turn off the camera. The footage will keep growing, and if there is a story, it will manifest, and if there is no story, then life is pointless, that is the story. The film will show how the world was when Khaire's camera turned on, and it will reveal what I am in what I saw, all the history and geography that ends in Khaire, who is hiding nothing. If there is a subconscious, you can guess at it as much as I can.'

Rohit lights a cigarette. Pointing to his heart, Omkar says, 'I'll be honest, Agashe. No movie that ever shook me here was political. The important thing is to pay attention. A film like *Gulaal*, it is about student politics but it doesn't take sides, it only shows how people are. Many of the characters are disgusting, but the director is looking hard.'

Rohit breathes the nicotine in deep. 'I want to look hard too.'

'Then let's go.'

'To the Bandra idol?'

Omkar sucks his teeth dismissively. 'The Bandra *Raja*.'

By the time they reach, there is already a queue with a clutch of BSL volunteers waving. The pandal is a replica of some famous temple that Rohit has never heard of, which makes Omkar joke, 'And he calls himself a Brahmin.' Rohit would protest that he never does, but the volunteers are laughing and there is an edge in Omkar's voice that shuts him up. The topic shifts to the public Ganesha idols unveiled all over the city. The volunteers are obsessed with their costumes and weapons, and when Rohit asks where they get their information, Hanmant is shocked. 'This year's Rajas went viral on WhatsApp hours ago!' Viral, and not one reached his phone. For his friends, religion is a private affair unless you're talking politics. Looks like they are the ones out of sync with their times and not him. Personally, he hasn't posted on social media in a while. It's like he is allowed this one identity and it has to be cool, consistent and socially aware. Who is the Rohit Agashe between two online exposures, like the blanks between frames in an old projector film? That's why there is this inward movement now, this need to arrive at oneself in privacy. What have his friends seen of the world anyway? They are only in their twenties, regurgitating others' ideas and spitting them out with such conviction that it gets hard to even think something that won't get a hundred 'likes'. Besides, as the BSL volunteers befriend him online, he is starting to see a parallel universe of data, events, heroes and priorities, and the mode is so similar – this constant sharing of links and stats, any dissent only a matter of degree and not of kind – that it makes a joke of both Gyaan's and Omkar's newsfeeds. Increasingly, he trusts only his own experience.

When they step inside, the Bandra Raja is thirteen feet of alabaster draped in crimson silk, a mace on his knee, and an expression so benign that Rohit stands gaping as the BSL volunteers take selfies touching the idol's feet. Then the crowd begins to eddy, and a woman in sunglasses steps in, her head peaking over her escorts' hefty shoulders. A Bollywood star? Yes, it's Preksha Verma! The crowd parts at her advance, and she touches the idol's feet before raising her hands in a high namaste. Cameras flash, and as Verma floats to the exit, her eyes run over Rohit from behind her tinted shades and her face relaxes in an almost-smile. 'She noticed you!' Omkar says in awe as her sedan rolls out, the paparazzi swarming it like locusts. 'Must be thinking what happened to his face,' Rohit says, but his mood lightens.

They step into the sunny courtyard. Under a festooned tree is the actor who played Krishna on TV right through the nineties, and his face looks like he drinks but some women start touching his feet like he really is god, and Rohit starts laughing. In fact, everyone who is anyone is here: skippers from the Indian cricket team, an industrial tycoon, a godman, and a local don who apparently regulates the rents in Bandra's slums; and everyone who is no one is here as well: schoolboys in brown uniform, businessmen in safari suits, aunties in flowery saris, villagers in Gandhi caps, children dressed as freedom fighters, a photographer with a mad beard, and even two Muslim men, one in a red Turkish fez and another with an orange beard and white eyebrows. Again he feels the expansiveness induced by those pre-filming recces. His wounds and his doubts feel inconsequential before this great confluence, and here, appearing like the boat that will carry him in, is Vikram Singh.

To justify his apolitical presence under saffron flags with lotus symbols, Vikram spreads his arms and says, 'On occasions like this, all sections of society come together.' Omkar replies in Hindi, 'We are not here for filming either. We only came for Raja's blessings.' Vikram puts an approving hand on Omkar's shoulder though his eyes remain on Rohit. 'What happened, bhai?' 'Don't ask,' Rohit says, touching the bruise. Vikram laughs. 'All right, tell me another time. Now come, I want you to meet someone,' and he takes the name twice before Omkar, embarrassed by Rohit's ignorance, explains that Advocate Kadam is the Bharat Party candidate from Bandra for the upcoming state assembly election. According to Vikram, Kadam grew up in a Lalbaug chawl, and instead of making trouble, he got a law degree and joined the BSL. He held Vikram's post a decade ago. At thirty-eight, he is tipped to become the next chief minister. He is also the chairman of the Bandra Raja Mandal. They walk over to where Kadam is standing in a circle of fawning BSL boys. He has a brow you could plough a field with, but he is wearing a tailored white shirt and jeans. When Vikram makes their introductions, Kadam's voice is so soft it gives him an air of mystery. He seems to notice everything sideways, like that god with eyes all over his body though the ones in his face are looking straight, and fixing these on Rohit, Kadam lisps in Marathi, 'Films, I have an interest in that. Follow me on Twitter to see all the Bollywood celebrities who visit our Raja. If we had met sooner, I would have introduced you to Preksha-ji.' Now, Rohit may have a studio in Juhu, but he doesn't have connections in Bollywood's A-list, and as Kadam lists the cinematic greats who visit the Bandra Raja, he starts to get giddy. Then Kadam says, 'Stop by our media cell sometime, Agashe. Tell us what you think of our campaign video. It was shot by a young film-maker like yourself.'

Rohit says he will, and that's it, but something in their interaction must be a sign to Vikram because he leads him away by the elbow and starts introducing him to all these 'worthies' from different Brotherhood outfits. Most are cement blocks with virile moustaches, gold frames, pastel kurtas and jackets, red or saffron tilaks, and a slight attention to dress that affirms politics is theatre. Most speak with Kadam's enigmatic smile and decibel as if you are in on a conspiracy even if you're only saying hello. Gradually, Rohit is learning that the Indian right wing is not one fanatical block, but a seshanaga, a many-headed snake. The Bharat Brotherhood is the big ideological head at the centre, the head to its left is the executive wing or the Bharat Party, the head to its right, the religious wing or the Bharat Hindu Forum that Omkar scorns as regressive, and the dozens of little heads fanning out on either side are the Brotherhood's endless outfits, its platforms for women, students, tribes, Dalits and Muslims, its unions for farmers and labourers, its publishing houses and associations for every profession. 'What funds all of this?' Rohit asks. Vikram says like it were obvious, 'Donations. Our branches have days when the members leave an unmarked envelope beside the flagpost with whatever they can afford. The Bharat Brotherhood is the world's largest NGO.' Who knows what the actual answer is, but Rohit asks, 'What is it all for?' 'To preserve our culture,' Vikram says, but when Rohit looks sceptical, he smiles like an indulgent teacher. 'Think of it like this, Agashe. The day society reflects the supreme Hindu ideology, there will be no need for the Brotherhood. The Brotherhood will be society.' Rohit decides to read and make up his own mind about their ideology. But first, where is Khaire? Since last night, the boy has been acting funny. The last he saw him was during the introductions to Kadam, trying to get credit for bringing Rohit there, which Vikram took.

# *Kedar*

Six hours down the coast, an expressionless officer photocopies Kedar's FIA request. The original sheet is folded into an envelope, a photocopy punched into a cardboard file, and another slipped back under the mottled window. The officer reports that the appeal will reach the mining ministry via registered post in five days. Kedar hauls his backpack to his shoulder. Naren has given him a crucial lead, but walking out of the government post office, he feels no triumph, only vitiation. Riding all night to a series of imagined comebacks, he is angry with the part of him that shrinks in homes like Imperial Heights and desires what his cousins have if only to spit in their eye for looking down on him and his father. And what was the result? His arguments turned personal, as if he was no less a hypocrite. He is dusting the leaves off his motorbike when his phone buzzes. A thick village tongue asks if he is Kedar Agashe. 'Heard you are coming for the public hearing today. Not a good idea, we think. If you must do these things, do them elsewhere. Not here in Talne.' Kedar listens, then says, 'You do what you want. I'll do what I want.' The voice becomes a shout, but he cuts the call. That he has done something worthy of a threat is invigorating. His work, he decides, will validate him.

At the next trucker's stop, he breaks for tea. His latest tweet on capitalists who dress up greed as national good has attracted the usual trolls, reposts and new followers. His inbox is quieter. He calls his editor at *Nayibhumi*. Prakash says they can't run his mining story and suggests another on the ecological damage caused by the Ganesha immersions in Mumbai. When Kedar asks what is wrong with his story, Prakash says, 'It's too angry. People are in a positive frame of mind. We're not asking for a feel-good piece, but at least be objective.' Kedar asks him which lines were too angry. 'It's the whole tone,' Prakash says. 'Rashi called me in yesterday. She had your Twitter open on her screen.' Kedar knows where this is going. 'What I do on social media is my thing,' he says. 'Yaar,' Prakash says, 'you can't always get away saying you work here, then adding *all views are my own*. I see what you're doing. You're building your cred through your byline with us, then you use these online platforms for your anti-national rants. But some of that voice is spilling over. Look, son, you can't fight every cause. You have to focus.' Kedar drains his tea. 'Prakash Dada, my compass is the constitution. Hindu supremacy violates the right to equality, and land grabbing violates the right to life and liberty, so I don't see how these causes are so different…' But already, he senses resistance. Prakash says, 'Make a pickle of your constitution and eat it. Ninety-nine per cent of Indians don't give a shit. I'll tell you what's common to all these causes, Agashe. It's your keeda. Whatever beat we put you on, even if we put you on Mars, the worm in your arse will start wriggling to set off some fireworks. I was like you, son. I get it, fourth pillar et cetera, but if we aren't practical … You know they're coming after small publications? They're shutting us down. What use is your keeda then? Will Twitter put food on your plate?'

Kedar sticks a note under his empty glass. He tells Prakash to find a flaw in his story and he will make the change. Prakash exhales like Kedar is incorrigible. He says he will give it another look, but Kedar knows he won't. For all *Nayibhumi*'s progressive stand, it runs one story out of every five he sends, and he gets that he is young and this is a life of rejection, but it is good honest work! He pushes his motorbike's starter hard. To disappoint his parents as he gets fired from publication after publication for being too hot to handle is the toughest part. He resists calling home. They don't know about his work at Talne, and he doesn't want to lie about his whereabouts. For years their Chitpavan pride saw them stand by their principles, but with the statement made and Aaji dead, they want peace. He suffers his mother glowing after Rohit's visit, how she went on about what a nice young man he has become, and how his father kept talking of his own 'roots tour'. As a teenager, Kedar thought these hills a wilderness full of echoes and adventure too. There were signs of trauma everywhere – bald slopes where forests had been burned, animal corridors broken by highways, the waters dammed, every inch of earth contested – but trekking to Shivaji's forts with his friends, his head was full of ancient battles. He never asked whose feet pressed down the rough paths. He slept in villages too poor for electricity and marvelled at the brightness of the stars. He recalls the time Naren joined them and his distress (to Kedar's delight) at the earth staining his new sneakers 'like betel spit'. His cousins didn't live in Imperial Heights then, but Naren was born for civilization. Ajoba once called him 'the little gentleman' for his habit of pulling out chairs for old ladies as a boy. Even today, Naren is that guy on the bus who would act if someone harassed a girl. But what's the use? Men like him don't take the bus.

An hour south, a green hillside reveals a gaping hole. The cashew trees on either side of the road have been ruined since the leopards disappeared and the monkey population got out of hand. The tired houses pick up, their thatch roofs hazy with red dust and courtyards stacked with plastic drums to hold tanker water, hot and contaminated. The river must have changed course since the miners broke its spring and sandbagged the drain off. The air is stinking from the fumes of a hundred ore-filled trucks, but the village is so still that a calf is scared off the road at Kedar's bike. When he reaches the public hearing, though, he smiles. The notice went out two days ago yet the turnout is three times that of the first. There are police and press vans, guys from Conflict Watch. To accommodate the crowd, the venue has been shifted from the primary school to a red-and-white tent with horn speakers tied to bamboo poles. In its tinted shade, villagers of all ages are sitting before a stage and two scratchy mics on which Salim is leading a protest song inspired by a verse by Balli Singh:

*Le mashalein chal pade hain, log mere gaon ke*
*Ab andhera jeet lenge, log mere gaon ke –*
*Arey bol re bandhu – zindabad! Mazdoor, kisanon – zindabad!*
*Yeh jal aur jangal – zindabad! Zameen hamari – zindabad!*
*Talne bachao – zindabad! Talne bachao –*

Kedar is revived by the singers' earthy faces, their dusty white shirts, the eloquence of their rough voices, the youngest beating a drum, the oldest slapping a pair of cymbals as if this were a prayer, and the crowd from old women to toddlers chanting *zindabad*. Salim's partner, Bidisha, is the only woman on the stage, and she is petite and bespectacled, but she has a leader's decibel when she announces that this is a public hearing organized by the Talne Bachao Samiti to discuss the renewal of the mining lease to Brahma Mines. Testimonies follow. Some are speakers from the last time: the temple priest, the school principal who attests that asthma has increased among his students. There are new faces too, like the tribals from the other side of the hill, and though the state government is absent, given the upcoming election, the district collector has been sent to acknowledge the show. 'Who is for the mine?' he shouts. Crickets. 'Who is opposed to the mine?' All hands go up. 'Does *anyone* support the mine?' Two truckers stand. 'We don't, but if the mine shuts down, give us some alternative to feed our children.' The villagers shout assurances. The last person to take the mic is a

Brahma Mines representative in a collared tee with a blue logo. He says drily, 'We have all the clearances from government agencies, and we will ensure that the issues raised are taken care of.' Angry shouts follow. Bidisha yells, 'Show us the papers!'

When the singing starts again, this time without a leader, Salim and Bidisha join Kedar on a parapet for kulhad chai. Salim reports on how the mining mafia crushed Talne's protest for jobs. Two villagers were killed and thirty put in jail because a policeman got hurt. He and Bidisha had to speak with the authorities to arrange for bail. 'Sometimes I think, what's the point?' he says. 'Even if the farmers stop working at the mine and get their land back, nothing can grow there. They will just sit around drinking and beat their wives.'

To distract his friend from his despondency, Kedar tells him about the threat he received this morning.

Salim grips his shoulder. 'Are you serious?'

'You remember Pinto, my colleague,' Kedar says. 'He's not on this beat any more. We were getting pictures of the mine when a jeep started following our bike. I sped up, but another jeep came from the front and blocked the road. Six thugs got out. They smashed our camera.'

'You didn't tell us,' Salim says, his eyes large with admiration.

Scratching a cross in the sand with a stick, Bidisha is more solemn. 'Heard about Dilip Baiga? The reporter, yes. He was on more than one hit list. The mining mafia was after him for exposing things, and a local politician was unhappy with his anti-national stand, and the two were in cahoots. One night, he was biking to some village when they pushed him off the road and beat him with sticks. Then they ran a car over him. The whole thing was framed as an accident.'

'Always a bike accident,' Salim says. 'You think they would get more creative.'

Bidisha tosses her stick. 'Be careful is all I'm saying.'

Kedar thinks what he always does at such moments: Let's see what happens. If the source of this confidence isn't courage but indemnity on account of his privilege, who else should expose this tale? Those farmers would be sleeping in the river if they tried. Still, on the off chance … the weight of a rugged wheel on his skull, the crack. To reassure his friends as much as himself, he says, 'I'm not the only journo on a bike here.'

'But you're the culprit,' Salim says proudly. 'Everyone knows *your* article brought the ecosystem down on Talne. Getting the story out with different opinions from farmers, activists, officials, that's the basics of good journalism. But you went deeper and filed an FIA appeal. That's how everyone sat up.'

Kedar laughs nervously. 'Can you believe it, the harami *Investor's Post* is here.'

'Not like we didn't call them the first time,' Bidisha says. 'We had fifty names on our media list. All were like, who else is coming? Only you showed up.'

'Maybe it's best they are coming now, after the protest,' Kedar says. 'The turnout today isn't just because of me. That's all your work with the villagers.'

Bidisha smiles and Salim blushes. Just when Kedar doubts himself, friends like these give him hope for what love and having an impact can look like. He updates them on the status of his FIA request to the forest ministry to corroborate the tribal testimonies on illegal mining on the hill's eastern slope. But the one that will make a real difference is the FIA appeal he has filed with the mining ministry to investigate whether a state minister's son secured the clearance that started it all. 'That story I will write in English for a national paper,' he says. 'My goal is to get an Aruna or Nikhil here by the next hearing.'

Bidisha's eyebrows rise. 'With activists like that, it won't be just a public hearing.'

Salim shouts, 'It will be a full-on movement!'

Bidisha tousles Kedar's hair and Salim laughs at the red dust rising off it. Watching them walk back to the tent, Kedar whispers to Dilip Baiga's ghost, though he knew the reporter only through his writing, 'Lal salaam, Dada.' His spirit feels cleansed, his heart in communion with his heroes, those comrades across ages and nations whose healthy arrogance was nothing but moral clarity. Screw Bandra people and their talk. That was the last time he'd go to Imperial Heights to please his mother.

# *Amanda*

When Chagan enters the office, Rosy gives Amanda a furtive smile. Since his promotion to Nadiya's role, Chagan has dyed his greys orange. Tehsin says he is the kind of man you put in charge of winding things up, others believe he was promoted on account of his 'connections'. In either case, there is resentment. With the title of education director on his résumé, Chagan may quit for another NGO once the department shuts, but he won't go back to being a field officer, and unlike Bhagwat, who was loved, Chagan is viewed with suspicion. Rosy refers to him as a 'social worker', a word which, if Amanda understands Deonar-speak, has unsavoury connotations that don't always relate to philanthropy. Chagan looks over the reports on their desk as if this were an inspection. Pointing at the numbers, he says, 'So many times I am telling Ifra Ma'am that you are taking thirty years to build one centre, so how in one year you can build four new centres? Mitti ka ghar hai. But who is thinking about the future? You show to the board that you are making big targets. Then bye bye and you go to World Bank.'

Amanda asks bluntly, 'You don't think the department is being shut down because of Bhagwat?' Chagan raps his metal bracelet on the desk. 'Our sub-inspector is little mad. If you came to me, I would tell that, Amanda-ji, let us go for tea to the house of our operator. We go with Humera's father and Bhagwat, and he is solving the issue with no noise. After everything is becoming news, this is not possible. Look, I have our operator's number on my phone. He is a very helpful person. But this is a Muslim area, so he has to be careful to whom he is showing support.' Amanda remains silent. Chagan says something in Hindi that Rosy translates. 'You are worried about Sheela, so Chagan Sir is helping her to get some money from the widow pension scheme.' Between what feels like censure and an unasked-for favour, Amanda isn't sure what to make of Chagan. She doesn't thank him, but when he invites her to the pensioners' event later that afternoon, she accepts.

After lunch, she and Rosy walk down to the municipal hospital grounds. There is a new and unfamiliar energy in the streets. Roadside trash has been cleared, the shabby walls are covered with posters, and festooned platforms have sprung up on every inch of open ground. India's national, state and local elections run on different calendars, and now, six months after the nation, it is time for the state. India also has countless minor political parties, and Rosy points out the green flags of the Muslim Unity Party, the navy blue flags of the Bhim Republic Party, and the red flags of the Socialist Party from the large northern states that supply Deonar's migrant labour. At the pensioners' event, the orange flags on the bamboo stage bear the symbol of a tiger. Rosy says that the Bharat Party does not contest elections directly in Deonar, but it gets the seats it needs through its local ally, the Marathi Bana. Recalling their role in the riots, Amanda gasps, 'What are they doing in a Muslim slum?' Rosy looks impressed. 'Many families are moving to Deonar after the riots because they are feeling safe here. But now they are needing toilets, schools, hospitals. They are needing someone who can get things done.'

As the stage gets peopled, Rosy points out the municipal councillor, whom she calls the 'corporator' (not 'operator' as Chagan seemed to say), the Marathi Bana Party candidate, and an elder from the local 'mandal'. This community organization, of which Chagan is a member, has promised the Bana candidate Ward M's votes in return for welfare benefits like ensuring fifty local widows receive their government pensions. 'So this event is to take credit for what the government should do anyway?' Amanda asks. Rosy laughs. 'From where the money will come to make everyone happy, Amanda-ji? If the person our mandal is supporting wins, Ward M will get a new drain. If he loses, some other ward will get it.' Meanwhile, the Bana candidate comes forward. He is wearing an embroidered skullcap and a grey jacket on his white kurta. Gripping the mic with both hands, he says (according to Rosy) that he could not deliver on his promises in his last term because he was with the Conclave Party. The dynasty has lost its connection with people, he rails. The party is a tree hollowed by termites and sat on by vultures. That is why he is with the Bana now. He has plans for converting waste into energy, for public health, for sanitation and a dozen other things long due to the hard-working, upright citizens of Deonar. He concludes with a religious salutation to allay any doubts about his loyalty to 'his people', and the salutation gets more clapping than his manifesto. Then Chagan invites the chief guest to give the widows their pensions. Amanda's breath stops as the sub-inspector who had Bhagwat beaten ascends the stage. The widows queue up on the other side. Sheela's head is covered in a sari down to her nose, so the sub-inspector puts the pension in her son's tiny hands and the crowd sighs.

To leave abruptly would raise questions, so Amanda sits in the audience until Chagan presents each dignitary with a bouquet of roses and a shawl, and they all smile for a photograph. On the way back to the Ashray centre, passers-by commend Chagan on his good work, but Amanda can barely meet his eyes. Did he invite her from spite, or to impress her, or because her presence was strategically useful in god knows what scheme? She chews a piece of gum to hold her stomach down. *A man is dead because of you.* She doesn't know whom she hates more: Rohit for his cruelty, or herself for that slap. She was surprised by her force, his tan turning crimson and lip starting to swell where the inside of her ring struck him. For all that he had provoked her, in the instant after, he looked as hurt and shocked as a puppy. Then came that hysterical laugh, either from discomfort at his humiliation or delight in hers, her violence debasing her more than him. Well, whatever the case, she is relieved to be done.

Back at the Ashray centre, the news that Ifra is joining the World Bank in Dubai has got around. Khala says, 'Allah ta'ala, she will still be serving the qaum.' *Qaum*, an Arabic word for a nation with no physical boundaries, or at its most protean, any form of solidarity. Whatever Ifra's shortcomings, her presence as an influential Muslim woman who is profiled in magazines for leadership was a source of security and hope to Deonar. To Amanda's frustration (or is it envy?), the children show her a scrapbook they are making as a farewell gift for Ifra. The opening pages are covered in drawings inspired by henna designs, eulogies, and photographs that employ the skills they have learnt in her camera class. This is the potential that Ashray is abandoning by shutting its education centres. She thinks of Omkar's Brotherhood branch, its reach and effectiveness. She googles the atrocities that Amal and Sainoo found too painful to elaborate: the burning homes, the foetuses ripped out with swords, the pins and needles inserted in private parts, a boy forced to drink petrol and then swallow a match. But despite that incident in the car, she can't imagine Omkar engaged in such brutality. Then again, Ashray has revealed how even decent folk can generate a synergy that ruins lives. Her stomach turns cold. She assures herself there is no comparison.

At dusk, she comes downstairs to find the new India Impact fellow sitting by Khala's feet as Rosy translates her laments. To them, Kayla Smith is an extension of her, fellows like variations on a theme, a fact of Ashray's life to everyone except the fellow, who emerges in this tenement world, staring like the first blue eyes making contact with brown across the bush of a new continent. *Fellow.* The word has turned absurd; it makes Amanda want to add 'just a regular' before it, but regular to whom? Initially, she distanced herself from her cohort for a deeper immersion in this world. Since Bhagwat's death, she avoids them more from shame. But there is no avoiding Kayla, who insists on travelling back to the western suburbs together. In the rickshaw to the station, Kayla says, 'The thing is, I'm used to the train coming at a certain time and finding a seat, and here it doesn't work that way…' She is clearly less interested in Ashray's goings-on than her own experience of India, but Amanda feels no judgement; in fact, it is an unexpected relief to trade insights about the city, and to complain about the things one can't around Indians, like the fatigue of contextualizing everything in reference to what you know, or of locals who launch into the one aspect of your country they are familiar with and feel let down that it is on the penumbra of your life, or of all the energy expended on cooking food your gut can stand and a dozen other self-care routines rather than what you really want to accomplish. Kayla agrees that the culture shock is huge, yet her textbook responses are a reminder of what this experience is intended to be.

The train rocks towards Santacruz and another evening alone. She has no intention of reaching out to Rohit or his friends, even Manasi, who texted a timid *hi* this afternoon. Worse still is the thought of calling home and telling Andrei how things ended with Rohit. Kayla promptly agrees to dinner at the Yogi Café. She loves the printed tiles and chai tea. Amanda confesses her initial discomfort with such exoticizing cafés, but how little things like silence and white furniture can become central to sanity. 'I still feel guilty about it,' she says. 'One minute I'm in a slum where I can count the ribs on the kids. The next I'm in a café pouring cream on waffles.' Kayla brightly replies, 'It's like they say on airplanes: you have to put your own mask on before you help others.' And suddenly Amanda wants to tell this kind, pragmatic stranger everything. It could lead to gossip, but she is done being silent. She tells Kayla about Bhagwat and Humera, and of her haste and culpability. She says, 'Do you ever feel like, when a sentiment becomes so powerful, you're more mesmerized by it than what it is focused on?' Kayla looks unfazed. 'If there's a riot and I'm on the street, I'd be afraid, but if I'm safe behind a window, I'd … watch. Fear would become something else. Awe.' Irritation sparks up in Amanda. 'Doesn't that trouble you? I've asked myself if there's evil in me, and I know it's in this blankness.' Kayla says, 'Most people are like that. Are they all evil?' Amanda exhales, 'I'm only saying empathy requires *attention*. Kayla, don't you get it? I was so mesmerized by my ideals that I made a man's world intolerable to the point he killed himself.'

Kayla says gently, 'Do something to atone then.'

Atonement. A word so Christian, it hits her like a blast of cold air in this wild, burning world. 'Maybe help his wife or son?' Kayla suggests. 'Or get a master's in development and help a hundred Humeras and Bhagwats. Then be done. Forgive yourself.'

Were it that simple. And yet, she feels calmer.

## *Omkar*

Lalbaug smells of sugar and sandalwood even through the reek. Girija waves from the chawl's rotting balcony, and Jyoti Mami smiles, a plate of clay lamps in her hand. Three noisy floors up, Ramesh Mama's home is barely the size of an Imperial Heights bathroom, but every piece of furniture has been rearranged to honour Bappa. Against a curtain strung with fairy lights, His small form sits surrounded by abnormally large fruits and cheerful flowers, but the mood is sombre: Uttam has lost his job at the chemical factory. As maternal cousins, the elders of the family have always intended for Girija and him to marry, and to proceed now feels as precarious as to call things off. Girija looks understandably sullen, but when Jyoti Mami sends her and Omkar to the market to buy cotton wicks, she confesses that the source of her upset isn't Uttam but that her brother has not taken her to meet his fancy friends. 'You worry they will say what kind of nonentity is this Khaire, his sister can't speak English.' Paying the vendor, Omkar says, 'I brought Rohit home, didn't I?' 'Did you?' she sulks. 'I thought he heard of your sister's beauty and invited himself.' Omkar laughs. He promises to take her along for the Ganesha immersions. Walking back, she wonders aloud which of her three kurtis to wear. 'Nothing too bright,' Omkar says, and his tomboy sister, who always has a snarky reply to every proposal and neither a yes nor a no for even her uncle's son, smiles, shy and grateful for the tip. What mental block kept him from seeing it sooner? Bargya, you ass.

When they return, Uttam is shelling peanuts on the cot. He is wearing a moth-eaten vest on shorts, and hasn't bothered to shave even for the festival. Without a sideways glance at him, Girija walks to the kitchen corner to help her aunt roll the dough. Suddenly forgiving of his cousin, Omkar tells Uttam not to worry, this situation is temporary, the new government will fix things. 'When? After I'm dead?' Uttam asks. 'I am campaigning for the Marathi Bana this time.'

'You party workers have no loyalty,' Omkar teases.

'Are you social workers any better? Half our young men in this street are sitting on their doorsteps, tossing stones. If the Bana comes to power, there will be a strike outside the factory. Maharashtra for the Marathi man, we will shout. That is loyalty.'

'The Bana is a party of the Maratha caste, not all Marathi-speaking men…'

'Who is for us Kunbis then, your Bharat Party? Oh I know, everyone calls everyone brother at your branch, and your prime minister claims he is backward caste because this is a democracy and the Party can't ignore that we are fifty per cent of the country. But just look at the rest of your leaders, all upper caste. And tell me the day you see one of us heading the great Brotherhood.'

'You tell me the day you see anyone but the old chief's lineage heading the Marathi Bana. The Bharat Party is the only major party in this country that is not about one dynasty.'

Uttam mutters to his peanuts, 'It is all a numbers game, saala. The Maratha caste is politically dominant in our state, so the Bharat Party will unite everyone else against them: the Brahmins on top, and the Kunbis and Mahars at the bottom. Then they will tie up with the Bana and get the Maratha vote too. That's how they make their Hindu majority. And now they have power in Delhi so they are showing us this big brother attitude. Know how many seats they are asking for in the state election? I tell you, the Bana should break away. The saffron tiger should take on the lion and show how to keep this city clean.'

Fanning himself on the doorstep, Ramesh Mama says, 'They didn't give your job to someone else, son. The whole factory shut down. It was in financial trouble.'

'The owner is a Hindi-speaking seth,' Uttam says. 'I hear the Bharat Party is giving him land for a new factory near Kandivali where he can hire filthy migrants for pennies. At least with the Bana, we are Marathi people fighting among ourselves on how to run our state. Not a bunch of Northerners and their local bootlickers.'

Omkar could ask where his cousin gets such information from, but he lets the snub pass. Uttam's insecurity is manifesting as anger, and he is trying to put Omkar on the back foot for something that isn't his fault. Omkar stays through the evening prayers, then takes the bus to Lalbaug station, and from there the train to Bandra, and from the terminus, the bus to Pali Hill, though he has to walk up the slope since there are no rickshaws, only sedans gleaming past the high walls topped with lights and bamboo. At the Imperial Heights gate, a watchman looks him over and phones the Agashes before letting him in. A sleepy maid gets the door, then retreats to her room behind the stairs. Either the senior Agashes are out for the evening or everyone is already in bed. Even Bappa seems asleep, His splendour corked in the prayer room, the rest of the place startling in its lack of sound and scent. Omkar places his palm on a white couch, its quiet energy grounding. He has seen larger bungalows and farmhouses, predictably showy, the old maharaja-style pomp and heft, but he has never been intimate with an apartment this high and coldly classy, its abundance manifest as a mysterious sparseness. There is no cabinet of old toys, no heap of shoes or papers, no plastic bag stuffed with bags, all hinting, so subtly, that those who live here routinely discard old stuff, and in one of the densest cities in the world, they have space to waste. Of course Rohit was well off, yet when he said he stayed with his parents, who would have assumed such a plush private apartment? How naïvely Omkar had laid out his wares: his dowdy home, his desperate dreams, every provincial joke he cracked on the assumption that Rohit's laughter was with and not at him. Here Rohit is demonstrating his extent, and though Omkar doesn't lust for any of it, though he honestly believes in a simple, virtuous life, had he seen this home earlier, he would have let Rohit in more cautiously.

A creak around the corner. Omkar turns sharply – there's no one there, yet his reaction undermines him. He makes for the stairs with a forced casualness. This is the home of a friend! But the word 'mitr', once as wholesome as milk, has soured. They may have met only recently but their dynamic has been addictive, their texts incessant, their connection already famous in Omkar's circles, and after all that, Rohit's insinuation that if he is difficult, the Box won't fund *Bappa*, Rohit's request that he keep politics out of it and dance like an ape for his friends! Half his headspace these days goes in imaginary conversations with Rohit, how he will position this, justify that, and if only this were about the contacts or the money – isn't the real trouble how much he wants this mad Agashe for a friend? Meaning, just as he has transcended the snares of his rural background, he saw Rohit reaching past the corruptions of wealth and Western influence towards the same ideal, a brotherhood that unites all Hindus as inheritors of the same ancient civilization, guardians of the same new nation. Well, what sort of brothers are they if, at the first sign Omkar shows of being his own person, Rohit lays a hand on the money tap?

As the door swings open, Rohit looks up from a beanbag with bloodshot eyes. The room reeks of alcohol. Rohit tries to stand, wavers, then sits back down carefully. In his childlike Marathi, he says, 'Arey, stop looking at me like that. Come, sit here. What's on your mind? You've been acting strange. Are you worried about the film? Something at home, then? It's about a girl, isn't it? Or a boy? Kidding. But yaar, tell me one thing. Where are all your BSL ladies? I hardly see them.'

Omkar sits at the edge of the sofa, then, because he feels odd sitting a foot higher than Rohit, he shifts to the floor. He quotes Vikram, 'If there are more boys than girls, it is a reflection of society, because more boys go to college. We are trying to change that.'

'Yaar, save the official spiel. I mean why are there only boys on our recces, in the Dadar office, in the hostel?'

'The girls have their own hostel. We meet them at public events. We consider them as our sisters because they tie us rakhis on Raksha Bandhan.'

Rohit starts laughing. 'What happens if you fall for a sister?'

Hotly, Omkar says, 'We are joining the BSL to serve our country. Mixing romance and alcohol with service, that is for Marxist frauds. Meaning, it is not encouraged ... but what to say, it can happen. Our honourable education minister did meet his wife that way.'

'So have you met your wife?'

'My mother has the same question. First she was worried I will marry inter-caste, now she is worried I won't marry. Last time I was at home, I told her I'm married to the nation.'

Rohit looks grave. 'Hmm. Your thinkers are celibates. Your prime minister never touched his wife. A servant of the people remaining a bachelor – Aai would approve. And you know, it's funny, but around you kunwaras, it's like ... my masculinity feels restored. Wait, are you a virgin? Thank god, but yaar, don't tell me once is enough. Kidding! You take everything so seriously.'

Omkar forces a smile. He would rather swallow acid than admit he is a virgin. He doesn't have time for girls, the ones at the BSL are sisters, the ones in film, the less said the better, and as for an arranged match in Wai, he knows he is bigger than its stunted ambition, the claustrophobia of ritual and gossip, the limitations of rank and caste; he knows his worth is with men like Rohit, but he will always be second class here. What made him assume otherwise? Whatever it is, surely Rohit is complicit. He never projects himself, so you project what you want on him until you see his set-up and recognize he is a city brat who revels in the filthy habits our culture scorns. And having talked up Rohit hosting him, with what face to return to his relatives in Lalbaug?

'Actually, forget girls,' Rohit says in English, his arm heavy on Omkar's neck, his sweet-stale breath in his face. 'Girls are trouble. Honestly, I couldn't be happier Amanda is out of my life. That night we broke up, she threw me a phrase only an American can. She's like, you fall in love with people and they're so flattered, they give you everything, but once you chew them up, you spit them out like a piece of gum. *A piece of gum*. When she's the one with a boyfriend on each continent. I guess I did what I'd do for anyone, driving her around and buying her drinks because her fellowship stipend goes only so far, but sure, she's the lionheart, she's magnanimous as long as she's queen.'

Looks like they have properly split up: a satisfying thought. Amanda was overly friendly at first, but how quickly she went cold on him, as if she sensed past their cultural chasm that he is a nobody. She is perfectly happy to let Cyrus wrap himself around her (even if Cyrus is *like that*, he is still a man) but if his own leg so much as grazes hers – that incident in the car – how the disgust in her eyes startled him, the accusation he was getting fresh, *he*, Omkar Khaire, who was raised by his mother and would draw blood for his sister, and whose respect for women runs so deep, they overwhelm him. Besides, he doesn't have the white-skin fetish of these English-speaking boys, and even if he did, he wouldn't care for loose women like Amanda. And no, he doesn't approve of Rohit's philandering either, but boys will be boys. Without leaders or a good woman's influence, their natures are base. Or is that what he wants to believe?

Telepathically, Rohit asks, 'Where is Girija? Why haven't you brought her here?'

'She is in Lalbaug.' Omkar says, then adds, 'With her fiancée.'

'She's engaged!' Rohit exclaims, making no effort to hide his disappointment. 'You never told me.'

Omkar would relish his protective feelings towards Girija if it wasn't obvious that the attraction is greater on her side. He could never imagine Rohit marrying her, but the real sting comes from his doubt that his friend might not think her worth even an affair. Already, Rohit is joking about attending Girija's wedding. Then the bell rings, and he doesn't stop Omkar from getting the door. The delivery boy has messed up the order, but when they start to argue, Rohit says, 'How's it his fault, yaar? He is only delivering.' Omkar closes the door softly but firmly. It is easy to be generous when the blood is warm with vodka and the belly with kebabs. Sniffing the boxes, Rohit says in English, 'I ordered paneer just for you, my sacred herbivore.' Omkar hasn't eaten since lunch, and the paneer is fresh, the mint and pepper sharp, but it is hard to swallow. Flashes of Pachwadi: the sun-baked earth, trees the colour of dust, the cattle and children all ribs, his baba's breath going rancid, Aai hearing drills in her sleep. The sofa under him starts to hum as if there were little drills in it, so he moves to the window ledge, but the veins in the marble floor have turned crimson. *Blood money.* A term he learnt from Kedar, and how it brings everything together. He shakes his head. A practical man doesn't judge a son for his father's crimes, and what have the Agashes done to him anyway? Their land was on the other side of the state … and yet, they are the type that keep his country in chains, and where are his principles if he reforests a hill one day, and uses mining money to fund his film on the next? Separating art and politics doesn't mean he will turn into a hypocritical liberal. He has a sudden, sharp impulse to punish Rohit – yet he won't stand up and leave. O Bappa, he thinks, his grip tightening on the window frame, Bappa, I believe every word I speak, but there are nights when I have no religion and no politics, I have only desires.

# *Naren*

The investment banks have been lukewarm about endorsing Magnus Inc.'s IPO, but Ankush Jain is in town to meet his uncle, and Naren assures his subordinates that something will work out with the great Jain's influence. Janki and Shivam look relieved, and Jay should contest him, but the subtle twist of his mouth makes Naren wonder if his silence isn't contempt. Cyrus left before the showdown with Kedar, yet the memory of his cousin's words makes Naren's nape tingle: *Even if it is legal, it isn't ethical.* As his team exits his cubicle, he gives himself the answer he intended to give Jay: No Indian company would be perfectly clean under a microscope. And besides, the numbers are so modest. A deal like Magnus Pipes may blow Janki's mind, but the entire New Cities budget is less than the marketing spends of some of his erstwhile Wall Street clients. Then again, he could never play a Wall Street board the way he played the Magnus Jains, and a handful of such clients is all he needs to pivot into India's uber elite. He imagines Ankush telling R.K. Jain about him. If the government passes the new mining bill, he has a pitch in mind for Brahma Mines. Waiting for an Uber, he surveys his cubicle, the whiteboard marked and corkboard pinned, but the walls still bare. He hasn't had time to think of art, just like he hasn't had the time to connect with old friends unless there's scope for business. He is done with the past. He is done with even the present. He is all about the future.

He packs his laptop bag and heads downstairs. Here is another step towards that future: Indrani Dey's request that he accompany her team in presenting a report to the state ministry of urban development. Dey's team has compared the sanitation systems in ten cities globally to arrive at potential solutions for Mumbai, and given how late this is in the sanitation minister's tenure, the report is clearly motivated by what can become a talking point on a manifesto for the state assembly election. Things have got hotter since the Conclave Party's local partner, the Janata Conclave, severed their alliance over a seat-sharing row. That is why this report has been so hasty and informal, with no proposal requests to other consultancies, with nothing beyond a call to Dey, who shares a close connection with the minister, and a request to do the work pro bono on Landsworth's social responsibility budget. But riding over with Dey's team, no one mentions any of this. Dey only says that Sanjay Vaze is more like a Bharat Party minister than an old Conclave Party hand in that he is 'consultant friendly', by which she means 'his ego isn't so big that he won't seek professional help'.

The meeting is not in the Old Secretariat with its gothic tower and flowering gardens, but in the newer, modern building at Churchgate, and Naren likes what he sees: apart from the cupboards full of papers that give off a government vibe, the conference room may well be a corporate boardroom with its modern table and ample light. The crew is setting up their laptops when Vaze walks in with his posse. He must be in his fifties though his hair is dyed black, his grey suit and blue tie are in keeping with his reputation as a technocrat, and he speaks English in the way Baba does, with a Marathi inflection. You wouldn't guess from his demeanour that he has a master's degree from Ann Arbor, and has held several influential portfolios. Dey introduces everyone. Her junior partner goes next with their findings, before Naren, as an associate with a client in this industry, presents a section. And indeed, Vaze keeps an impressively low profile, but as the meeting proceeds, his reserve seems increasingly like passivity. It is his principal secretary, a young man with rolled-up sleeves and a brisk moustache, who gets down to brass tacks and inspires the room with questions like whether Barcelona is a fair model for Mumbai. Vaze comes in only at the end, his questions centred on how the findings might be positioned for the public.

When the meeting is over, Dey stays behind to chat with Vaze, while the underlings on both sides leave. Exiting the secretariat, Naren feels a quiet satisfaction at being right about the impotent Conclave Party, yet he suffers none of Kedar's rage. The person who truly moved him was Vaze's principal secretary – there was a man taking the long view regardless of who was in power – and the person he would most like to grow into is Indrani Dey, whose connections span the entire political spectrum. *Don't talk about institutions, talk about people, that is how you get things done.* Of course, unlike Omkar, he won't flatter himself that he is here for anything but mutual benefit. The Landsworth name lends Vaze's manifesto credibility, and working with the government brings Landsworth industry cachet; as for himself, this has been the perfect opportunity to impress Indrani Dey. And impressed she was, even the inscrutable Vaze took notes during his presentation. And who knows if it is this brief success or just a residue of the energy in those halls of power, but the morning's doubts have given way to a clear-eyed vigour. Kedar and Amanda won't believe it, but he does well enough by this world: he lives within the law, pays his taxes, and even believes in charity. As for ordinary vices, history is proof of their persistence; anyone who tried to vanquish all evil engendered more evil still. For the rest, he'd rather be an efficient man than a good one, this obsession with good and evil a relic of the Christian West with its schizophrenic division of an ideal and a practical moral code. And walking into the Kala Ghoda Café, he feels apathetic towards all kinds of change except the organic unfolding of the universe. At best, he is curious how it all pans out: the rise of the East, the fall of the West, and the chaos in the middle, his gambles and the gambles of friends and enemies (though he feels detached from all outcomes, but then, this detachment doesn't compromise his desire to play).

Rohit looks up from his beer on the mirrored bar. The bruise near his mouth is going inky. Naren orders a pint and asks where things have landed with Amanda. Rohit says they haven't spoken since that night, and he doesn't intend to call her. He is done.

Naren says, 'That's not a nice note to end on.'

'Tell her that. I'm the one with the bruise.'

Naren pauses. 'You know, back in the States, I never asked Cathy why she called things off. I thought I knew, but I had no idea. I was the one with the bruise, you might say, and I had too much pride to ask for another conversation. Then I spent years wondering about her reasons, and the longer the time ran, the harder it got to reach out.'

Rohit says to his beer, 'Would asking have got you an honest answer? Would you have spent less time thinking about it if you knew?'

Naren isn't sure, but that it doesn't trouble him reaffirms his confidence that India – or is it Manasi? – has healed him. 'Good point,' he says. 'To be honest, I don't know. What I do know is that I wish the end hadn't been so … graceless. When you're young you think it doesn't matter, there will be many others. Then you get older, and you can count on one hand the people with whom you've known that intensity.'

'I'm not you, and Amanda isn't Cathy.'

The line carries an unexpected sting. So much for healing. Enough vulnerability, he thinks. Coldly, he says, 'No, she isn't.'

So, they have hurt each other. Rohit's tone turns apologetic. 'I meant … what you shared was special. This was just a fling. An infatuation.'

'You don't call a fling to your parents' place for a festival. You don't use family connections when she's sick and tell all your friends about her.'

'Just a friend then. We had a situation. It's over. If she wasn't your friend before mine, she might never have met Aai…'

'That didn't sound like friends fighting the other night. Or friends who have known each other only five months.'

Rohit takes a sullen sip of his beer. A waitress sets a plate of fish croquettes between them. Once she leaves, he redirects the conversation to the reason for their meeting: his business partner has quit midway through a production, and he needs financial advice. Naren tells him not to worry. He is happy to fund *Bappa*. He has no problem with Omkar. 'He has that hunger to prove himself. I'd hire him over any of your other friends.'

'If I have any left,' Rohit says.

'The problem with your friends is that they deny basic human tendencies. Like the common man's desire for efficiency. Or the common Hindu's need for revenge.'

Rohit flinches. 'When I drove into the countryside, I thought it was too desperate to vote for anyone who doesn't make daily life more tolerable. Now I don't know. Shivaji and the Peshwas ruled Maharashtra almost until the British. There is no Partition trauma in Wai. Omkar didn't experience the Bombay riots. Why should he care for revenge?'

Naren layers a croquette with tartare sauce. 'The party will become more moderate as it becomes secure, but don't expect the Hindu unifying project to vanish overnight. Whether or not your family suffered directly, you can't wish away the humiliation of a people not ruling themselves for half a millennium. You can't wash away his desire for an identity that pre-dates colonial India. Kedar can get all righteous calling it the revenge of the plebs when he is a pleb himself and gets his ego boost from ranting against the elite.'

Or was it Gyaan's phrase? In either case, Rohit smiles. 'This tartare sauce is really good. But yes, Kedar and Omkar. Weirdly similar, aren't they?'

'A reformer and a radical should have less in common,' Naren muses, 'but both are men of extremes. And after the other night, I think, fair enough, one man can't be all things. Kedar's power is his critical energy and Omkar's is his constructive force, and men in the middle, men like you and me, we keep things stable. Brahma creates, Vishnu preserves, and Shiva destroys so that creation can begin again.'

Rohit's eyes brighten. He tells Naren about a Bharat Party leader, one Advocate Kadam, who has invited him to his media cell. 'They're warming up for the state election, and Black Box has everything we need to make a stellar scheme or campaign video. With Gyaan out, I could hire Omkar. He gets the country's pulse. And Kadam knows Bollywood's entire A-list. Did I mention he's tipped to become the next chief minister?'

'You didn't,' Naren says, excited by his brothers' new connections. Unlike in America, he is not alone in building a life here. 'You know, since you were a kid, you've always had a way with people. You get the mood, you get along with all types, but you also get things done. I'd say you'd be a perfect fit for politics. Don't laugh. I'm not saying take the stage. Just that you'd be useful to anyone on it, so don't underestimate yourself. Need contacts, money, ask me. My client Ankush Jain donated to their campaign. My senior partner Indrani Dey is superbly connected…'

## *Rohit*

Revving the Audi, he feels like he has finally found the magnet that will bring his scattered filings together. He has spent the past hour discussing career paths with his brother, and all his traits, even the seemingly useless ones, suddenly make sense – and what do his friends or Amanda matter when he has Naren's validation? Naren's words have reinforced a feeling that he has had around the BSL boys all month: it's like they are responding to some *potential* in him. When Vikram isn't around, they turn to him like he is their natural leader, and when the meeting with Advocate Kadam ended in a photograph, even volunteers he had never met pushed him up front. Doubtless, he doesn't see himself in training camps and crummy hostels, but enough of Tinseltown has run for office; all he has to do is stay at the hub of this great wheel until his chance comes. And as the ghostly cables of the Sea Link bend past, Rohit feels touched by a sense of destiny. There was a moment at the Bandra Raja pandal when the homage, the photos and networking were all done, yet no one left. Policemen looked up from their transceivers. Officials looked past their cronies. The press did not blink. The BSL volunteers were all alert and vigilant as if they were on the lip of momentousness: the right time and place for the Big Event. We are the largest Indian generation in history, he thinks, and if no event presents itself, *we* will be the event.

Turning into Bandra, he phones Omkar to tell him he has figured out the money. Turns out Omkar isn't with his relatives in Lalbaug but with the BSL. Vikram promised a volunteer that *Bappa* would feature his neighbourhood idol, and since Omkar did not want to pressure Rohit about the film, he borrowed a friend's camera. Then Vikram grabs the phone, and by the time the street lights come on, Rohit is getting out of his car at a bus stop in godforsaken Kandivali. There is a new face in the crew, one Brijesh Nishad, who is all of four feet ten and wears a googly smile, yet he is the first volunteer whom Rohit can imagine pointing a gun. Brijesh leads them into a network of badly lit alleys. The peeling walls shift past like curtains, and suddenly, they are on the inside: an open square amid the tenements with goats and cycles roaming wild, and at its centre, six men sitting on plastic chairs beside a large, closed tent. Brijesh introduces the men as the mandal committee that he has pulled together to make Ganeshotsav a public event in the slum.

The committee welcomes them warmly, but there is still an hour to go for the evening prayers, so Brijesh takes Vikram and the crew to his home. A shanty piled on a shanty with a metal ladder for stairs. The door is a hole in the floor, the room ends before it begins. Brijesh's mother, her sari pulled over the head, welcomes them to sit on mats stinking of kerosene. Vikram introduces the film, but Omkar refrains from interviewing the family. The expectation that he will speak leaves Brijesh's face. His mother says in Hindi, 'It is a small place, I know.' To cover up the snub, Vikram says, 'Ma-ji, a lot of people have big houses in the village, but they come to the city because they value other things, like a good education for their children.' Ma-ji brightens. 'Yes, our house in the village is bigger. We had plans to rent a better room here as well, but my elder daughter got married and the groom took seven lakh rupees in dowry.' Vikram nods sympathetically, but then he asks if Ma-ji will take a dowry for Brijesh, and she replies sheepishly, 'If the girl is nice, not much.' Rohit notices the reformer in Omkar go stiff as

Vikram patiently explains that the BSL encourages volunteers to save money for their sister's weddings, but it disapproves of taking dowry for their own. The whole time, Brijesh's sister has been refilling their tea so silently, her voice is a surprise: 'I don't want anyone paying dowry for me,' she says. 'By paying, you keep the custom going.' She looks prepubescent though she finishes school next year. She intends to apply to some unheard-of college (but Vikram has heard of it, like he has been to their unheard-of village), and he says, 'You look like a smart girl. Why not try for Mumbai University? The BSL will guide you.'

The girl shoots her mother a million-watt smile. Vikram gives her Sarita Holar's number. The volunteers beam, and even Omkar brightens. Climbing down, Rohit sniffs hooch under the ladder. It is good to think that wide-eyed girl will go to university and have friends like Sarita. How he wants to tell Amanda that this is what change looks like, to both impress and to humble her. But when he asks Omkar why he didn't interview the Nishads for *Bappa*, Omkar gives him a look that says, isn't it obvious? Honestly, it isn't, and Rohit is tired of his friend's sullenness. He talks with Vikram the rest of the way. With his usual positivity, Vikram says that camps, rallies and functions are all fine, but what he likes most is talking to people about their lives and solving their problems. He is what they call a 'full-timer'. That means he has no career or family beyond the Bharat Brotherhood and has attended their training camps. When Rohit asks what they do there, Vikram says, 'Back in the day, it was military drills to build our muscle so that we are never colonized again. These days, we still do some physical training but the focus is on ideas.'

Before Rohit can ask what ideas, they are back at the tent, the mandal president holding the canvas flap open. Inside, the darkness smells of synthetic incense. Faces spawn: gaunt yellow-eyed men, women with covered heads, barefoot children half in shadow. Before them, a six-foot-tall, blue-and-orange Ganesha idol is glowing, its backlit ears lined with cheap crystals. There is no priest, only an enthusiastic local who leads the aarti by striking a steel plate with a spoon, the lyrics a mash of Hindi and Sanskrit, the lack of melody made up for by gusto. In Rohit's turn to proffer the fire, he raises the oil lamps with the élan of an actor who knows the truth in the act and the act in the truth. The ritual unites him with the unfathomable mass of his people, an expansion near-religious, and for the first time in years, he says an earnest prayer: 'May it all work out.' Then he opens his wallet and sticks a pink note in the donation box. Brijesh gives him a wide smile as the ceremony ends in four raucous chants:

*BHARAT Mata ki JAI!*
*GAU Mata ki JAI!*
*RAM Janmabhoomi ki JAI!*
*KRISHNA Janmabhoomi ki JAI!*

Rohit has never stood in a crowd shouting slogans that affirm the motherland and the Hindu holy land are one. Ifra would say, This is how they create the atmosphere. Brijesh's face is shining with a crusader's ecstasy. *Foot soldier*, Gyaan would call him, foot soldiers deriving motivation from this 'well-wishing visit', foot soldiers whipping the jingoism before a state election. Even the children are shouting 'ki jai'. Naren would say, They will get more moderate. And as the crowd empties, the mandal committee rushes up, and everything that follows has a theatrical quality: the courtesies, the garlanding, this holding sweet boxes from either side for a photograph. 'Sir-ji has not said anything,' an old man croaks, and Rohit takes a second to realize he is the 'Sir-ji'. The speaker is the mandal president, a bent man thrice his age, his wrinkled eyes expectant. 'I am still in a trance,' Rohit hears himself say, and everyone smiles approvingly. On the way back to the bus stop, Vikram asks if Omkar got good shots. Omkar shrugs. Vikram says, 'Our Khaire is a man of the soil. He still has to learn that his soil doesn't mean only Maharashtra but the soil of the whole nation.'

Omkar retorts, 'Nothing like that. One of my friends is Telugu. You won't believe it, but he speaks better Marathi than our Agashe. I have Gujarati friends. Bengali friends. They come here for work, they live, they contribute. But the big states in the north – see the police records anywhere in the country, the maximum criminals are from there.'

'So, like your Marathi Bana Party, we should abuse and throw out Brijesh? This is your idea of Hindu unity?'

The air gets tense. The headlines this morning announced that the Bharat Party and Marathi Bana have broken off their long alliance, and each will contest the election independently. 'Vikram-ji,' Omkar says, equal parts defiance and supplication, 'I consider any Hindu as my brother. You know what I think of the Bana. I am only saying that our honourable prime minister contested from Varanasi, so he should spend his first year in office fixing the big states up north. That people have no jobs there is nothing to be proud of. And if other states pick up the burden, you have to give them the money.'

Vikram waves a hand to cut him off. 'Mumbai will see development. Don't heat your head about that. Do your job and trust your leaders.'

The hierarchy is clear. Vikram diffuses the tension by addressing the group. 'The Brotherhood is like a joint family. The parent organization, the political party, the religious wing, our allies – many times we contradict each other, but in front of the public, we are united. Our critics will say this is our hypocrisy, our schizophrenia. But society is complex. At least we are not pretending there is no contradiction between ideology and practical politics, or religious and welfare agendas. The problem of our liberals and lefties is that they have no model for working together. To put yourself first is not a Hindu value. Personal hero-giri is not what the nation needs. It needs people who put the nation first.'

When they cram into the Audi, Vikram, up front and still the only one talking, changes the subject. 'Agashe, now is that a Chitpavan name?' he asks cordially. Rohit is taken aback; telling castes by surnames is the sort of knowledge he associates with his grandparents. Vikram explains, 'It crossed my mind because our senior leader is an Agashe and he has the light eyes of your people.' Like Omkar, his tone is half teasing and half stating the facts. A volunteer in the back seat says, 'Four out of five presidents in the Brotherhood's history are Chitpavans.' 'And the fifth was a Rajput,' says the other, and the way he says it suggests Vikram is a Rajput. Everyone laughs except Omkar, and Vikram pulls a dismissive yet indulgent smile that delights and hushes his volunteers. After leaving them at the metro station, Rohit drives home with Omkar. He doesn't approve of Vikram's casual casteism or the jingoism in that tent, but what is the alternative? The Bharat Brotherhood is no longer history's backstage player, but a century-long kindling that has finally caught fire. Its independent branches alone reach every district in the country, and with separate timings for kids, students, householders and retirees. No political party, not even the Bharat Party, has a reach so wide. Mostly, parties have youth wings that wait until a boy like Omkar is in college to make contact, but then parties are about politics, and the Brotherhood's vision is wider.

Omkar turns the stereo off irately, which brings Rohit back to the car. 'So you and Vikram have a real brotherhood going.'

'Why not, yaar?' Rohit asks. 'What's with you this evening anyway?'

'Yaar,' Omkar says in a tone that suggests Rohit is missing the obvious again, 'what am I saying? Do what you want to get by in life, but don't mess with Bappa. These people from the north, wherever they come, crime increases. They don't know respect for women. They only know politics. Politics is their shadow and you can't avoid your shadow. Unlike other migrants, jobs are not enough for them. They form a community and prop their own candidate, and for some political gains from the Bharat Party they have installed Bappa. There was a time mandal committees were set up by eminent persons to preserve our Marathi culture. Today, every corporator has one, and the members play carrom and collect donations and make a nuisance in the name of connecting with voters. Vikram is a North Indian, for him all this is fine; the organization knows that migrants here influence their families back home, and if they win the Hindi-speaking heartland, they win the nation. But you are an Agashe, you have grown up with Bappa in your house, so you understand. Want to see the real Ganeshotsav? Come to a Marathi neighbourhood like our Lalbaug. Hear the beauty of the aartis. Simple, working-class women get so tearful when Bappa is leaving, their friends have to force them out of their homes to throw flowers. That is real devotion!'

The headlights of a passing truck blind Rohit. When Omkar talks like this, referring to Ganesha as Bappa – father – he doubts how much he understands his friend. If Vikram hadn't spent a decade among the nationalists, Rohit could see him in a corporate job, but would Omkar be different had another party given him the books? Just when Rohit thinks it's all about ambition and networks, Omkar will say something so outlandishly earnest, it makes him feel tender and mildly nervous. Then Omkar says, 'You remember when we were in Wai, you asked me what comes after my ten-year plan? I'll answer in one word. Politics.'

Rohit smiles. 'I thought the BSL was about welfare.'

'It is, it is,' Omkar says. 'The Bharat Student League is the Brotherhood's baby, which is why the volunteers are always showing that their pure ideological hearts can't be corrupted. For training in politics, I will transfer to the Bharat Party Youth Wing.'

'Aren't you afraid?'

'Why, what do I have to worry about?'

'Your life?'

Omkar laughs. 'The trick is not to make it public yet. You have to arrive in the company of the big boys, that's how people know they can't mess with you. Until then, you make films or do some social work that shows the public your face.'

'Who are these big boys?'

Omkar says, 'Our tourism minister, he is like a father to me. Once, at his farmhouse, his son put his personal revolver in my hand. That is the level of trust. So when I'm ready, I just tell them.'

The back of Rohit's neck prickles. Omkar doesn't seem violent, though he is always twisting his wrist to let his metal bracelet fall back and emphasize his forearm. Noticing the kada has been noticed, Omkar says, 'These days a kada is in fashion, but to me it is a timeless symbol of our bravery and culture. From Guru Gobind to Shivaji, every Hindu mahapurush has worn it. Meaning, Guru Gobind was a Sikh, but Sikhs are also Hindus if you look closely, right? In any case, it is also useful. Slap a man like this and he'll be stunned, but pull your kada over your knuckles and the same slap will split his face.'

Cautiously, Rohit asks, 'Have you ever been in a fight?'

Omkar tugs the kada affectionately. 'Just scuffles with boys in school.'

By the time they reach Imperial Heights, Omkar has recovered his humour. Relieved, Rohit takes a long shower. Smoking on the balcony afterwards, he feels fresh yet languorous, moist but clean, the benediction of water soothing away the day's stress, and every inch of skin calm and breathing. He paces the moonlit tiles, stroking his triceps, the health in them igniting a desire that not an iota of this youth be wasted. Gradually, the tingling focuses on his groin, his longing like the light trapped in a firefly. He comes inside. Flashes of a girl, and as he strokes himself, he considers what face to give her. He is high on the volunteers' energy and smitten by their earthiness, but he can't think of Girija naked without shame, so he imagines Amanda. Past his anger at her, he sees parts of her body without the face – breasts, hips, jaw – until he is the vitality of a crowd meeting her angles, and aware only of his own swelling pecs, the mammalian curve of his back, and his smooth, sharp thrusts. A current surges through him, peaks in a rough moan. Expended, he lies on the sheets, the shower's freshness replaced by a musky damp. He wipes himself with his tee and throws it at the hamper. *Friends don't fight like that*: a gratifying thought. He likes that he could get that slap out of her. Nothing like a little drama to cut through the inessentials and bring the blood to a boil, to know you can reach that height of feeling with a woman even if the pleasure is retrospective.

## *Amanda*

There is constant talk of the election at the centre, and unlike at the Agashes', the subject is rarely the nation, but always individuals: corporators, candidates, gangsters, social and party workers, and who knows whom and can get what done in the vast shadow state that helps Deonar press an overburdened bureaucracy for basic life support. A day after the widow's pension event, Rosy reports, Chagan accepted an offer to join the Bhim Republic Party. Named after an iconic Dalit leader, this party is the only one in Deonar whose candidate is not a Muslim but a Mahar. With the Bharat Party and the Marathi Bana calling off their alliance, the former has made the Bhim Republic its chief ally, which has given its candidate more prominence. And this very person has recruited Chagan, saying he should call him instead of the corporator, who is Muslim, with any 'local problems' faced by 'our people'. As Rosy is speaking, Amanda looks at the street below where Chagan's 'visitors' are waiting. This morning, an old woman in a threadbare sari broke down. Her husband had pneumonia, and she needed help securing a bed in a public hospital. And as Chagan reassured her of his influence, Amanda noticed the disgust on Khala's face. She is starting to suspect that his unpopularity has less to do with his temperament than his political ambitions. According to Rosy, Bhagwat's death has become a rallying cry for the Dalits of Deonar and Chagan intends to become its face.

When Rosy leaves for her other duties, Amanda returns to files she is digitizing for Ashray. She has not complained to the management about Chagan's use of the office for political work. She doesn't see the point, only the irony that people with such despair in common should stand so divided. *Isn't it possible to elevate the agenda?* Ifra asked. But how? She recalls Nadiya talking about Deonar's excitement for what she called the 'Indian dream': *Vote-bank politics has given Ward M a new bus depot and latrines, the price of recyclables is going up.* Bhagwat and Humera were the face of this confidence. Here at the end of each pencilled entry is Bhagwat's careful signature, in English, which she shuts the file on too quickly. She tells herself that breaking down and building into a new configuration is the fate of all civilization, even if, in Deonar, there is no zenith before the crumbling, any velocity is felt only at the outset of efforts, optimism is the luxury of a young CEO, department head or fellow. For old hands like Khala, latching the office windows and smiling her toothless goodbye, there is only the loop of an exhausting pattern, a long-stretched heartbeat that will neither race nor halt.

Faint from the lunging motion of the train, Amanda leans dangerously against the open door. A trinket seller flashes a ring of baubles in her face. His eyes remind her of Rohit. She doesn't respond; he doesn't persist. Her chapter in India is coming to a close: this winter, she will apply for a master's in social development. When the train clanks to a halt, she follows the crowd down the dripping exits. The clouds shift and the day turns preternaturally bright, the wet station roof glistens, and pedestrians look up and smile. A strange numbness swells her chest, as if a spirit were passing, and like a sonic boom, it hits her: she is homesick. India will always be the genesis of her calling, but it will be good, for a while, to rest and gather strength in the familiar. She boards a bus, waits out its wheezing lurch above the crowds, walks up the grimy stairs to her room where she puts some tea to boil and her cell phone to charge. Three emails, all from home. *Please call, it is urgent … Why won't you pick up your phone? Trying to reach you … Nana is gone.* Gone? Everything in her collapses at the sight of that word, and in the vacuum left, the shock and inevitability rises: O Nana! O Nan, Nan, Nan!

Day is breaking in Jaffrey. No one has slept. Ghosts of familiar faces move in and out of her screen. 'She was eighty-four,' they repeat to soothe themselves. But apart from minor blood pressure, Nana wasn't ailing, and the abruptness of her death – no slowly thickening dusk in a hospital room, but a stroke, simple as the long hand of a clock falling as she forked peas – shows in the fear and confusion on their faces. 'Her father lived till over ninety,' Dad says. 'Just last week, she called herself a spring chicken,' Mom sighs, 'she spent the day gardening.' Pale blue Crocs, dirt in the holes, practical hands snapping beans at the stem. For years, Nana's skin had been so frail, the tiniest bug or nettle caused the blood to blotch. She was breaking, but they never thought of it like that, she wouldn't let them, not while she went about in a shirt and straw hat, a crate of bulbs at her arm. O gardener – but already the face is frozen, and a vision from the back door flares: her shoulders hunched over the loam, tending her square of earth in defiance of the field growing wild and the trees closing in.

Then her parents step aside and Andrei takes the screen like a man standing trial, says his solemn hey. He looks resigned as he waits for her to ask why he is still there, playing the surrogate son, calling the ambulance and taking charge for those too paralysed by grief, even though his reason for hanging on is continents away and his chief supporter dead. Having embraced the farm of his adult will, he is the only one other than Nana to love it without conflict. Her face contorts despite her effort to hold back tears. 'I'm so sorry, Andrei.' He looks at the floor. 'When my opa was dying, he said, Don't grieve me, I've lived a full life. Nana lived a full life, Mandy. She wouldn't want you to cry.' Tears. Deep springs press through the mountain, bits of rock break until she is flowing, and the mountain crumbles. Mom is in the screen again, awkwardly comforting her across her distance, her artist's soul that sees things too closely yet at some perverse remove, her numbness to the immediate confused by her sensitivity to the abstract, death as unreal and magnified as in a nightmare; while Dad stands behind, breathing heavily, his intellect convincing his ego like a parent convinces a terrified child that this is what all things come to, so we are humbled, nature runs its course – be still, heart. Accept.

They discuss the funeral logistics. Amanda will fly home for a week, but Nana would want her to finish her work in India afterwards. Then they return to memories, confessions and long silences until, sick with sleep and wakefulness, Amanda clicks the laptop shut. A stroke. She imagines it in Dad's scramble of medical terms, a slideshow of memories, a tunnel to white light, the opening of a star, but all she can conjure is a blotting. The arteries narrow, the blood thickens, and one by one, like houses down the line of a power outage, the neurons go dark, the complex map of a mind goes out. How must it feel? A wave of nausea, some final thought, or is there no time to think as the scene freezes; you are no longer witness to memory or sensation, the I watching the I gone, and no revelation in its passing but a simple childlike confusion no living hand can soothe and which must be faced alone with that preparation which is no preparation: the physical frailty and psychic stripping of old age. By the time they got to the hospital, Nana was dead. Is there consciousness in hands, in organs, in the spine, is there a screaming in them as it comes, the final signal or lack of? When does the last cell turn opaque, on the gurney, at the morgue, in the tomb? If Amanda was there, she wouldn't let them cover her, she'd gather Nana's body and rock the final corpuscles to sleep, pushing the force of her comfort into the tissues collapsing to deadweight, so that some of her will might still reach the undead in her Nana and breathe into what is passing: solace, solace, solace.

A rickshaw goes by below, a thick sputter through the rain. These floral curtains, these damp sheets – why? Her kurtas with absurd prints of kites and elephants, the water drop at the lip of the tap, the moth beating against the light – to what end? Her hands, bloodless on her knees, are too weak to check her phone for the profound and silly news people encounter, their opinions, vanities and insecurities piled over in the bowels of the web: all of it futile and incredible when juxtaposed against the simple beat of her heart. She smiles ironically. Here, disaster has struck from the back door as she stared out the front, and most stupefying is how ordinary death is, how easily construed in the context of others. *You can't know hunger by sitting next to it*. This is the first death she has experienced so intimately, and Bhagwat was as irreplaceable as Nana, a cosmos of sentience no scales can balance. There is no way to atone.

Midnight. Amanda splashes water on her aching face. In the mirror, the drops run from her brow to her chin. She has Nana's strong jaw, but the rest is softer. They were talking India over dinner, and she teased, 'Hey Nan, how do you think you'd feel at the other end of the world?' Nana said, 'I'd feel at home.' Helpfully, Andrei added, 'You've been to Cuba so you know what to expect?' Nana said, 'I always know what to expect.' Mom and Dad looked up. Nana shrugged. 'Wherever I go, people are people.' Unimpressed, Mom and Dad returned to their steaks. For them, to be a world citizen, you had to have that Asian friend or Spanish lover, the unforgettable journey South or East, yet speak for no one but yourself. But Nana judged all people by the same attributes. She'd say of a great-granddaughter, four and barely visible in the clutter of a Harris reunion, 'Squirt's got brains, she asks questions,' or of a farmhand met on the Peace Corps decades ago, 'He didn't have an education, but he worked at it, and boy, did he have a green thumb.' Cultural difference went as deep as the style of your clothes or the taste of your spices, a barely visible gauze on a person's burning and self-evident humanity. And if circumstances had nothing to do with the credit Nana gave them, it did not absolve their failings. She had no tolerance for stupidity, violence or laziness. Dad often said in a mix of reproach and affection, 'Doesn't matter where you come from; everyone's a good or bad egg to Nan.' Good and bad eggs. At times, Nana railed about terrorists strapping bombs to babies, or the liberal president running the country to the ground, and Mom and Dad exchanged a glance to confirm that this was just the problem with old conservatives. Secretly, Amanda felt superior too. And for all that, here in India, she was the first to cast the stone, to decide Bhagwat was a bad egg no matter what his context. Nana, she suspects, would have fared better. She wouldn't wear a kurta or learn one Hindi word, yet her sharp old eye would have recognized all of them: Bhagwat, Humera, Nadiya and Ifra. Isn't that why Jaffrey loved her, including the people who felt uneasy around her parents, like the unschooled painter, the Mexican farmhand, the poor immigrants who benefited from the church fair proceeds? Andrei worshipped Nana. She surprised him, though he was no surprise to her. Once she established that he would support the farm, he was a good egg, and since she had never put it past him to be one, she accepted this as plainly as the morning light.

Amanda presses her palms on the cold enamel. How did Nana do it? Nana didn't care for the lofty and the theoretical, she was humble about her intellect and perhaps all intellect, yet it wasn't only common sense that made her as effective, it was – Amanda recalls the word from their talk about Bhagwat – *prudence*. Nana took her time in assessing people and situations, and once she made a choice, she stood by it; like when she married an outsider, a working-class boy whose only mystery came from the fact that he was English. Nana was her own compass; whatever dismay her actions brought her supporters or pleasure her detractors, she acted in the light. She was free of that vein which Amanda, for all her good intentions, suspects is a little rotten in her. Rohit, on the other hand, has something of Nana. When Amanda's Deonar experience is complete, she will abandon its people as she talks for them over wine in living rooms far away, but Rohit has brought Omkar Khaire home, and has thrown his lot in with him. Was Bhagwat ever as real to her? To face his death, the ethical response was enough, a theory enough, her resolve to balance the karmic scales adequate. His death did not make her world meaningless. If anything, in fortifying her purpose, it was an occasion for her development, and surely, even before Nana died, some part of Amanda knew how perverse this notion was – when Rohit exposed her, she slapped him not from anger but panic that her core was under attack.

Was there more to Nana's core than prudence and resolve? Once Gramp died and the family moved into the old house, the drama of Nana's life was past; she was already an elegy to herself. But Amanda can recall an older memory: a glimmer rushing past the trees, Gramp at the wheel as he droned on with a story for her (zoned out in the back seat), and only when Nana responded did she realize that, despite hearing Gramp's story countless times, Nana was actively listening because it was impolite not to. That's how they were: when they disagreed, they never let silence harden into contempt but kept repeating their stand on something as silly as whether it was safe for a buzzard to build a nest on an electric pole, and even as a girl, Amanda could tell that it was in the responsive nature of their arguing that she saw love, marked by a quality so obvious then, but that has proved the hardest to emulate: *decency*. She writes Andrei a long email. She thanks him for everything, makes it clear that there is no point in him waiting, and requests that he should leave the farm. Of course she can't send it tonight, but her head feels clearer for composing it. She weighs her phone in her hands, then texts Rohit an apology, a sincere one, not to get back so much as to end things as Nana would. She expects a slow reply, but her screen lights up instantly. His voice is gentle, free of ego or cruelty. Within minutes, her resolve is broken, and when he comes over, it feels good to collapse into him at the door, to have his sympathy and his beauty – the handsome head, the bird-bone ridges – to comfort her.

## *Manasi*

Resting her neck on the cool, curved stone of a bench in Joggers' Park, she looks up at a night pregnant with artificial light, and like a giant embryo at its starless centre, a saffron moon waxing. The long commute has done little to silence the scatter in her head from too much data, too many emails and texts, and the agitation past which she has pushed herself all week to convince retailers on monsoon promotions for cola. Meanwhile, her gang has been cleaved, their chat group is as silent as a tomb, and unlike Rohit, who has disappeared into the city with others, these are the only friends she has. The day after Gyaan and Cyrus quit the Box, she texted Ifra, who made it clear that it was either her or the Agashes. Manasi is still to reply. Her forefathers did not have the luxury of voting for anyone unable to offer immediate aid. For her parents, politics was learnt at the university and through an inter-caste marriage. For her friends, she is starting to recognize, no matter what they learn online or out in the field, the blood enters their arguments only when those they take for granted surprise them with their fire. The scatter starts to rise again until she sees Amanda running over in shorts and a neon vest. Manasi apologizes for being late. Amanda smiles. 'The track is too wet to walk in heels anyway.' Sitting on the bench, she pushes off her sneakers with her toes. Usually Amanda leads the conversation, but she is silent, her chest gently heaving.

For the sake of saying something, Manasi says, 'Worked my arse off today.'

'I was wondering why you were in office on a Sunday. Some deadline?'

'A personal deadline. The city will shut for the immersion parades tomorrow, then I have a conference in Bangalore, and I want to get this analysis done before that.'

'Why?' Amanda asks. Her tone is flat.

'I'll be in a different headspace there. It's good to align what you're working on with where you are.'

'Why?' Amanda asks again.

Manasi looks at her. 'What, why? Why do we do anything?'

In the silence, sounds nearer the bench become audible, like the moths beating against the street lamp. Manasi wants to say she knows the deadline doesn't matter, nothing matters when someone in the family has died, but the heat of their bodies is fading and she is tired of talk. The whole point of suggesting this run by the sea was to get the endorphins going in other ways. Manasi tries again. 'Booked your tickets?'

'For Tuesday, yeah. The weekend was expensive, and I … I'm helping Rohit with his film. We made up, and he needs someone for the B-roll shots. I've called things off with Andrei … he's packing his stuff and will leave my parents' place after the funeral.'

Given how things ended with Rohit, it is fair enough that Amanda is embarrassed about getting back together. Even so, Manasi's irritation rises. She has cancelled dinner with a client on the assumption that she is Amanda's only comfort. Suddenly, she resents coming all this way to a place convenient to her friend, even if the present crisis is Amanda's, because when is the crisis not? First it was Humera, then Bhagwat, then her sickness, then the education department, then the breakup with Rohit, now her nana's death.

Though Manasi hasn't asked, Amanda feels the need to say, 'It's not like I haven't thought of Ifra. I feel she's making the same mistake with Omkar that I made with Bhagwat.'

Manasi holds her silence. Amanda is projecting her motives on to Rohit. For her, this is about wanting to be good, and for that reason, she will never see Omkar clearly, just as, Manasi suspects, Amanda does not see her. She recalls Amanda bringing up the incident with Omkar, and her surprise that Manasi got similar attention. As if reading her thoughts, Amanda says, 'Omkar has been super respectful since that episode in the car. I almost think he is afraid of me. You know, Nana didn't care much about humanity, but she cared about human beings. I believe she'd give Omkar a chance. You should come for the filming. Naren is funding it.'

Amanda started out defensively, but she must have read a different sort of judgement into Manasi's silence, for there is a challenge in that final note. Rohit knows enough people for the B-roll; if Amanda is doing it, she is more in love with him than she lets on, and she needs Omkar to be justified. Manasi says, 'Omkar doesn't seem all that fanatical to me. He's just trying to make the most of his opportunities. I can relate to that.'

'So you have an opinion! But you're always silent when everyone is arguing.'

The sullen one now, Manasi says, 'I was listening.'

Brightly, Amanda says, 'Listening is good! But sometimes you have to speak, or no one will know you were listening and there is no point in your listening.'

Does Amanda know how close Rohit is getting to the Brotherhood? When Naren mentioned it, he was wildly excited, talking of all the places his brother and the country will go. They were on a rooftop lounge, and the skyline gave his words a touch of prophecy. He had ordered edamame in truffle oil, oysters on ice, pork sliders, and a white wine that was as good on her nerves as his mature laughter. It was one of those moments when she felt on a tightrope from where she was coming to where she wants to go, this decade of her twenties pivotal, her choices now definitive, and the last thing she is going to do is jeopardize her luck, like Gyaan, over stakes so vague. Here are her family's faces when she told them about Naren – Mummi's doubt, 'Chitpavans can be snobs'; Pappa's confidence, 'I'm telling you, young people don't care about these things, the boy has lived in the States, they are both MBAs'; Aaji's worry, 'But the parents…'; and her own pleas that they were jumping the gun until Lata Aunty texted her an invitation for the visarjan puja. 'It's happening so fast,' her sister cried and hugged her … and there now is Ifra, a friend of a friend, she thinks, putting distance between them, and who else? Back in school, she took for granted her visits to friends and neighbours for Ramzan, but it has been years since she was invited to an iftar party. Where had they all gone? Other buildings, other streets, other countries? Her skin goes cold as the cymbals of an evening aarti clash over the din.

Meanwhile, Amanda marches on, 'That's what a woman should want, right? To be little Miss Watchful. All my life, I've been told I'm difficult. At twenty-seven, I'm starting to ask, what does it mean, *difficult*? Difficult for what? Difficult for whom? There is an Anne Carson line I love. It goes: *I want to be unbearable.* We must be unbearable, Manasi.'

Manasi sighs. 'Some part of me is tired of anger.'

'My dear, the world needs you to be angry.'

From the patronizing tone, Manasi can tell that Amanda has recovered. She feels the urge to push back, to prevent her friend from reviving at her expense. And everything she has suppressed around her friends for weeks (or is it months, or years) froths up, and she asks, 'Why? Because I have a Mahar surname? I know, I've never brought it up. I'm the third generation in my father's family to get an education, even if I'm the first to go to a private school. No one talked about caste in that school, or I was too innocent to notice, and my parents didn't raise us thinking about it either. Our housing society wasn't fancy, but we had as much as anyone and everything was about the children: that they should look forward, that they should get on with life. So why should I see myself as a victim?'

Amanda is listening with a strange expression, as if it were inconceivable to her that Manasi is what she is and who she is at the same time. She could bring up her MBA professor or her aaji's worry that the Agashes are less progressive than they appear, but she can't stand the thought of Amanda airing it at a dinner party – my Indian friend Manasi, a Dalit – to show off her own experience. Amanda says, 'We talked so much about Bhagwat and you never mentioned…'

'Is it relevant? Does it make my point of view matter less or more? In fact, I'm only half Mahar. My mother is Maratha. She and my father met in college and fell in love. There was some resistance from her family, but it's all in the past. I mean, it's not like there's anything to hide, but unless it comes up naturally, it's not like there's anything to confess.'

Amanda looks out of her depth. Breathing to keep her tone even, Manasi says, 'My point is, what if I don't want to be what the world wants me to be? I've got the dream job I worked my arse off for when all my friends were partying, and yes, sometimes I look around and see my boss and his boss all the way to the top, and I don't want to be any of them. Then I wonder why I'm typing a spreadsheet at one a.m. My father has a regular job. It's not like he needs my money. But he dreamed the dream with me, and my mother is a housewife and didn't ask my sister or me to help in the kitchen so that we could study. And all they want is that I excel. Excel. Some days I have no idea what that means. I only know I'm building a foundation that isn't in place yet, and I have crises too, but I don't have the luxury of spending six months in another country to find out what I'd rather be doing.'

When Manasi stops, the intensity between them is palpable. Amanda challenges her by showing her there are ways to be that weren't in the deck she was raised with, and she worries that she has upset their equilibrium. To make her point more subtly, Manasi says, 'Now that we're at it, here's another story about me. I went to an all-girls convent school. There was a girl in my class, Anya Mehta. When we were all picking zits, her skin had an unreal glow. Our class teacher said she looked like a Japanese doll, and the name stuck. We took the words dreamily, like the name of a famous painting. Anya was never first in class but always in the top five. And while our topper was a nerd, Anya was an ace at drama and swimming, and everyone thought her amazing for not being a snob. None of us ever said: Anya is rich. Anya is upper-caste. Anya has pedigree. The uniforms helped, though I think the girls who were in love with her sniffed it out. They responded without knowing what they were responding to. I once led the senior march with Anya, and for some time after that, I thought we shared a bond, like of recognition or mutual respect. We would look at each other in class, and I'd blush like she was a boy. I hated that I blushed. I wanted to be good too, and not just for the praise.'

'I can see that,' Amanda says sympathetically.

Manasi goes on, 'I never saw Anya after school. She went to college in Boston. Years later, our class reconnected online, and I saw her photos and said, of course. Anya was like those glossy horses at the racecourse. You could spot one without a harness in the wild. I may have gone to a top school and got the top job on my campus, but I stink of my sweat. No one showed me how to write a CV or give an interview. Then I stalked Anya online. She did a *Boston World* internship to see if she liked journalism. Now she's an associate with McKnight. I don't have that luxury to hop around, to cruise on precociousness, to think through whether my every action is ambitious and moral and sexy at once, and just like you're asking yourself what it means to be difficult, I'm asking myself what it means to be good. First you don't speak up because you want to be good, then you're told that being good means to speak up even if it is at a cost. Tell me, my friend, have you ever felt so angry that you don't care to be good, and if being good means being angry, you don't care to be angry?'

Sensing the unfair comparison with Anya, Amanda snaps, 'Congratulations. You and Naren are perfect for each other. You ever bring this up with him?'

Manasi says, 'You mean my caste? I have. He finds my family's journey inspiring. He said it makes him optimistic for India.'

'I mean what you were just saying to me. You were angry at rich people. Now you've found someone privileged to date. Your politics won't help you, so you abandon your politics...' But the exhaustion returns to her voice. 'I'm sorry.'

'That's fine, you're right,' Manasi says bitterly. 'I don't date casually, and Naren is in a serious place too, so I'd be an idiot to mess this up, but I don't see why I should apologize. The Agashe boys grew up middle class, so Naren knows what hard work is, even if his people were always better off than mine. I guess what I'm asking is ... what about me makes prioritizing my happiness so appalling to you?'

Amanda doesn't answer. She picks up one of her sneakers and beats it on the bench. As the mud flakes off, she asks, 'What's in it for Naren?'

Manasi flinches. Pain camouflages itself as confusion. 'You should know. You call yourself my friend.'

It's Amanda's turn to flinch. She makes a girlish face, her charming face. 'Aw, I'm sorry. I didn't mean it like that. You're lovely. I just ... It wasn't easy breaking up with Andrei.'

Lovely. Not beautiful or brilliant or any of the adjectives that Manasi would use to describe Amanda (or Cathy, whom she has looked up more than once online). She could tell her that Naren can't get enough of her big eyes and hair, or that he admires how she's acing her job. She could say, That's a shoddy cover-up, my friend. But Amanda is back to confessing vulnerability, and Manasi accepts the truce. 'Honestly, I don't know,' she says, pulling the strap of her laptop bag up her shoulder. 'Take my new iPhone. I love the little gadget though I've no idea what goes into it, what the little gears or chips do under the screen. When something is working well, I don't see the point in overanalysing why. I just press play.'

Is Amanda's laughter ironic? As they walk to the gate, she asks again if Manasi will come along to film the parades. 'It will feel safe to have another girl there.' Her tone is unsteady, and in the passing headlights, her pupils are enlarged, the clear ring around them glittering. Manasi says yes, though a part of her never wants to see Amanda again.

## *Naren*

The room is dark, the sky outside pale. The tide is receding under south-west thunderheads, and he can feel its suck on the top floor of Silver Palms. He leans across his quilted bed and checks his phone. For four days, Kedar has been unreachable. The only update on the family chat group is Rohit saying that this isn't the first time their cousin has disappeared. Naren couldn't care less for Kedar's theatrics. He checks the rest of his inbox. No word from Ankush either. For a few moments, barely awake, he couldn't care less about anything. The tide becomes audible again, its roar so much wider than the river in Waverly, a reminder of the mad and unthinking cosmos. Then, through the void, Manasi's warm foot shifts drowsily on to his, an umbilical cord – to what? Life. Meaning. They have been together for barely two months, but the years Rohit has known her have accelerated their intimacy, and he can already imagine marrying her. The foot withdraws. 'You awake?' he whispers. She shakes her head, no. Over dinner, he did not persist in asking why she was quieter than usual. A Landsworth pitch needed reviewing, and he felt guilty only when he came to the bedroom and found her asleep. This is the first time she has stayed over that they have not made out. He pulls her close, asks what's keeping her up. She doesn't turn, but she doesn't resist him either.

'Amanda,' she says. 'I like that she is honest. Makes her addictive. Then sometimes it gets too much and I pull away until I need her voice in my life again. I said to her, why shouldn't I be happy? Is that the same as asking why I shouldn't be selfish?'

He slips a hand under her hair and presses her nape. The muscles are stiff. He tells her what he told Rohit about people acting according to their make-up and the inevitable cycle of creation and destruction. She says, 'So you don't care at all about saving the planet.'

Cautiously, he asks, 'Why should I?'

'To save ourselves?'

'Why?'

'To save yourself?'

Naren frowns without emotion. 'If the planet blows up tomorrow, I know my last thought. It will be: So this is how it goes.'

A sceptical silence, like she suspects he enjoys his fatalism, its manliness. He can't see her eyes, only the grey light on her lashes. She says, 'If there's no purpose to life, no meaning, why not end it?'

'Because I like little things,' he says. 'The weight of a good whisky glass, white sheets in a five-star, airplane sunsets. Between the huge void behind and the huge void ahead, there's this bright little spark: our life. Think of how absurd that is, and it is incredible how good some things feel.'

He nuzzles her neck suggestively. She moves her head away though their hips remain spooned. 'I like little things too. Often, I think I don't need all this stress. I'm fine away from the action. All I want is a small balcony and books. But these simple joys don't add up to everything life puts us through, all the loss and sickness and death. Life is unbearable, and the only thing that makes it bearable is a purpose that justifies all the suffering.'

'Sure. *Purpose* sounds weirdly lofty, but when I think of the people I'm responsible to – my boss, my subordinates, my clients –

I want them to succeed. In the end, the men who matter to me are the men I can see, and if I do well by them, that's enough for my conscience.'

Manasi presses her ear to his chest as if listening for his heartbeat. The pale folds run off the bed into the shadows. Why doesn't she say what is on her mind? Ifra, Kedar, Omkar, the mines, whatever else she wants to judge him on? He looks over to check if her eyes are shut. They aren't. She says, 'You don't believe all things are interconnected?'

'Not in any oceanic, Freudian way.'

At the contempt in his voice, hers grows harder. 'Right. You don't believe in God either. If you're so convinced there's nothing out there, how are you different from someone who's convinced there is?'

'I'm not sure there's *nothing* out there,' he says. 'As far as I'm concerned, it's pointless speculation. I may have another life and there may be a god, but I'll never know anything about it. What I'm sure of is that I'm here and want to maximize the trip. That doesn't include just the taste of Scotch. It includes the big pleasures, like playing all the roles. If I'm backing Rohit's film, it's because it makes me happy to be a good brother. I like responsibility. I like milestones. That's why I want to marry. I want the wedding to be grand and to put pictures online. I'm aware this has no meaning in some grand cosmic order, but baby, no amount of convincing me it's irrational makes me not want it. Because this is what life is, this irrational persistence. Try examining too hard what it's all about and you'll get sick. Most people would.'

Naren savours his phrases – pointless speculation, irrational persistence – and he feels his edge return, the person he is in the office, the boardroom, the Sofitel. He is about to stroke her head when she props her chin on his chest. 'So you never feel despair … just for how things are? Amanda says this blindness is the closest ordinary people come to evil.'

'How dramatic!' Naren says, pressing his brow. 'Your friend has to live a little to see we're all wired a certain way, and the less you resist it, the less you despair. Want my advice? If charity is in your wiring, do what you can, and for the rest, enjoy your privilege and be grateful. To think of it, apart from family, my other irrational hang-up is status. However stupid it is, I feel like shit if a classmate overtakes my City in a Merc. I used to think I'm above competition because that's how a person should be. Then I got to a point where I felt really marginal, and no amount of convincing myself that it's all maya made me feel better. That's when I started to act in a way which gratifies my instincts, and my mind became healthy again.'

With a child's indignation, Manasi asks, 'What if everyone thought like you? What if everyone made the same choices?'

'They don't.'

'If they did?'

'Pointless speculation.'

Manasi sits up, her face puffy with sleep. She is wearing his undershirt down to her thighs. He doesn't care for kittenish charm, revolting in statelier girls, but even the tiny ones are never so alluring as when they sit still, drawing the weight of a room towards them; like Aai, who didn't smile for her wedding photographs, but at other times did so privately, it threw open every window of the heart. 'Narry,' Manasi says, 'I don't believe God is an old man with three heads either, but a philosophy is valid only if everyone can live by it.'

He moves a strand of hair off her face. 'The trouble with philosophers is that they had to think about whether their dictums could hold across a society. But I'm not a philosopher who has to share my thesis with anyone, and I'm not a psychopath either. I'm just a regular guy who's found a comfy nook in the system.'

'Then why share all this with me?'

'There was a time when thinking like this helped me out of a nasty place. You couldn't sleep, and I figured there's enough room in my comfy nook for one more person.'

She smiles guiltily at this invitation. 'Sometimes I wonder if … when we're all caught up in the trivial, something tectonic isn't shifting…'

'Where do you get these phrases? You should be a writer. I want to see that poetry.'

'*Narry*,' she says, falling on him in a hug, and they lie silent and entwined.

So much for their first disagreement. Any tension between them feels released, and their ability to align their values without undue strain reinforces what they share. When they first met, he assumed she was wearing the blinkers that he did through his twenties, but her ambition is not an end in itself; it is already corrupted by her desire to make good on the opportunities denied to her forefathers, to avenge her housewife mother, to outdo the unborn son. Sometimes she speaks under Amanda's influence, lured by a youthful sentimentality she has not had the privilege to cultivate, but on most days, she is sharper about the world than he was at her age, like the time she told him about her uncle, an immigrant who found his fortune in Uganda. 'He is worse than born conservatives,' she said. 'The bone ossifies hardest where it was broken.' It is this eye, so unclouded by gentility or idealism it is almost crass, that makes him cautious. He knows that blind love gives way to blind contempt. He loved the West, then hated it, loved Cathy and Eric, then hated their type. Then again, is looking too hard precisely the trouble? Was it not what he wanted most in America: to be recognized as containing multitudes? Let him never limit Manasi by saying, *I know you.* And stretching against his mirrored bedframe, he has never felt more aristocratic than in this lack of exactitude, this extreme openness. He puts a protective arm around her. Returning to sleep, he thinks, who knows why we talk so much, talking like talk were a national obsession, global even, certainly generational; if anyone asks years later what we remember best about our time, we will say that we talked and talked and talked…

# ATMOSPHERE

# *Mumbai from the Heights*

Twilight.

Day fourteen of the lunar fortnight.

Hour of amrit, for which the gods and demons have churned the ocean of time –

*Jai Deva, Jai Deva!*

In a cosy fug of camphor, seven illuminated faces hover before Ganesha.

Tonight, there is no priest. The Agashes are confident in their moves –

*Jai Mangal Murti!*

Lata Agashe ties a coconut stuffed with jaggery to His hand, food for His journey back to heaven. As she bows to touch His feet, she says a silent prayer for Naren. She is grateful her son has found a partner she can relate to, and not some snooty woman in New York. Then she proffers the fire with élan before handing the lamps to Manasi, an act full of the graciousness she feels at inviting a girl of her humble background (but many fine qualities) into their fold.

Lifting the idol for a final tour of the home, Naren feels a near-superstitious gratitude to the fates. Since Ankush Jain met his uncle, an investment bank has approached Magnus Pipes. The deal is the talk of the office … and here is Manasi, watching him adoringly. When he told his parents they are dating, Aai texted her an invitation for tonight despite his protest that it was premature.

Then again, his family has known her since she was a teen, and their endorsement bolsters his confidence that she might be the one.

When the tour ends on the balcony, Manasi crouches to help Naren remove Bappa's crown. Without a priest, the cosmopolitan Agashes know little more than the most basic rituals, and it is easy to display what she has learnt from her mother, an advantage with which Amanda can't compete. Looking on, Naren's parents are alight with approval. Tonight, she is the legitimate daughter of Imperial Heights. Enjoying her triumph, she thinks, Let Amanda know what he sees in me.

Rohit breaks the ceremonial coconut with a smash on the threshold. Pleased by his impact, he looks at Omkar, but it is Amanda who gasps. She has broken up with Andrei. Or then her nana's death has released something in her, because she is more potently alive and open than she has ever been with him, and yet, without domination or pride. She no longer averts her eyes in bed or holds back tears. She is flooding into him with a tenderness that makes him think: *Be careful.*

Amanda clicks a handsome shot of Rohit for the B-roll, but her sentiments muddy when he asks Manasi to join the rituals instead of her. He values Manasi, and even if it isn't sexual, it stings. Why does his validation matter? By now, she knows the answer. Rohit has something of Nana, which makes even minor slights burn. She tells herself not to look for redemption in the wrong places, to do a master's and help a hundred Bhagwats and Humeras instead, but since Nana's death, that plan has lost its power.

Omkar turns off his camcorder, and though there is no breeze, the hair on his forearms lifts. The rest of the crew is already at Lalbaug, that working-class locality which truly loves Bappa. Here, the dry-eyed Brahmin rituals recall when Rohit jovially confessed the dubious origins of his people. Imagine that from a

Chitpavan's mouth. Of course, Omkar isn't saying a priest *must* stay poor, but Bappa hang him if he doesn't condemn those who feign lofty thoughts while swindling his motherland.

To conclude the ceremony, Raghu Agashe immerses the Lord of Wisdom in a brass bucket near the anthuriums. He does so with a manly mechanicalness, his discourse with God too personal for display. As the water inches up his arms, he requests Ganapati to keep his nephew safe. Activists in Talne have confirmed that Kedar was with them until yesterday. His phone got smashed, they said, like there was no other way for him to call his mother. Damn the boy, does he know what he puts his parents through? Bappa, take care of him. Bappa, show him sense.

So, the Agashes' idol dissolves, its watery grave reflecting the last red streaks in the sky.

And all over the city, Ganeshas of varying size move hypnotically towards tanks or lakes or the sea, each saturated with ten febrile days of worship, the incense of endless sticks, the pollen of endless flowers, and the frantic adoration of eyes and eyes.

The processions spill out of every quarter and street: personal idols on heads, family idols in cars, street idols on wooden carts, the idols of the rich and famous on trucks, and the largest, those of the public, on floats with volunteers waving flags and hurling flowers:

*Ganapati Bappa – Morya!*

In Versova, the drumming brings Ankush Jain to the Magnus guest house balcony. Wearing only a Turkish towel and an Om pendant, his hairy chest expands at the sight of this new market rising faster than the tide. Here comes the Raja of Santacruz, His skin as ruddy as His silk. Since the suburb has expanded, His audience includes not just factory labourers, but the starlets and yuppies who throng its glitzy malls. As He advances, Ankush holds his Om to his lips for luck.

Further south, in a JVPD living room styled to match its focal point – a Husain goddess straddling beige and ochre horses – Indrani Dey says over a crystal tumbler of Chivas Regal, 'Nothing will come of nothing unless we get financial inclusion right.' And her husband, a venture capitalist with lush grey hair, replies over his Talisker Storm, 'More than two-thirds of the people on that street don't even have a bank account. You can't go wrong with that kind of baseline meeting political will.'

In an art gallery at the five-star Marriott, Tariq Abbas shakes his head despondently. This is the first Indian modernist retrospective of this scale, and the most enigmatic oil in the catalogue is not on display. Tariq did not think the curator would buckle, but Husain's *Ganesha* has been removed for offending Hindu sentiments. 'Even in death, they come after you,' he whispers to his mentor's ghost as the Raja of Santacruz floats past him to the sea.

At the Palm Grove Hotel on Juhu beach, tourists leave the pool to photograph the crowd below the deck. The crowd below photographs the tourists above. Kayla Smith, in a bikini and shorts, points to a man selling glow-in-the-dark ornaments. 'He's wearing devil's horns on a Gandhi cap,' she laughs, and her expat lover replies, 'Adorable idiots, they think it's something new and Western.' Kayla buys a pair of neon horns. Silver stud in his dark ear, white pinstripe pants, spit quivering on his lip, snot quivering on his nose, the barefoot vendor puts a hand in his pocket, draws out a damp wad of notes, and peels one off like a gold leaf. When Kayla asks him to smile for a photograph, he spits violently on the sand.

In Seven Bungalows, a neighbourhood of princely families and erstwhile traders of brocade, the Bandra Raja's drummers bring the chatter to a halt. The Raja may have a cavalcade of film stars, but he isn't Meher Bulsara's idea of royalty. Perched on a chesterfield in the last surviving titular mansion (lamentably rented for shoots these days), she says, 'All the rats in the city's bowels have surfaced,' and her host replies, 'Wonder where all those heads and arms are stacked for the rest of the year, just waiting to erupt.'

Within earshot on the veranda, Cyrus watches young men the colour of the night sea splashing in the tide. One is face down, chortling as his friends slap and knead him with mud. Long before the Pride marches, Rohit never cut him off from this kind of love, and for months Cyrus assumed that he had befriended Omkar from this same openness. But he has seen past his need to project an innocent image on his friend. The person he is missing is the old Rohit or the Rohit he wants to believe in but does not exist.

Across the Sea Link, the Marathi Bana Party chief waves at his followers from a balcony overlooking Shivaji Park. Reporters ask if his receiving them at home instead of the celebrity pavilion on the beach has anything to do with his recent split from the Bharat Party. Others ask if he expects 'trouble' tonight. The chief gives both the same reply: 'Why spoil the mood with such questions? We are here for Bappa, and He will take care of everything.'

Indoors, his wife laments about how empty the home feels without Bappa. Her dinner table is covered in silver trays heaped with sweets, fruits and flowers, and her visitors are still coming thick and fast, but the home's festivity has seeped out with Him, and she would follow Him to the sea if she wasn't afraid of what is surging through the streets.

In a sooty Wadala high-rise overlooking the salt pans, Gyaan scrolls past drone footage of the seething millions. Since he cannot call Ifra, he calls his mother. 'Look at the cops, the barricades, the bloody army. This is a contained act of aggression, a valve on a pressure cooker to let off steam.' His mother tells him to ask for Ganesha's blessings anyway. 'He is the God of writers,' she says. After the call, Gyaan deletes his long-laboured screenplay. Then he takes his only printout, a cacophony of edits on every page, and rips the stack in batches down the middle.

Separated from Gyaan by the euphoria at Lalbaug, Ifra stands on the stucco terrace from where her mother once saw a man being set on fire. The branded stores have rolled down their shutters. The only light is from a billboard sporting the architect of the Bombay riots. *Let Us Fulfil His Dream. Make Maharashtra Great.* Since the Marathi Bana severed their alliance with the Bharat Party, both have sharpened their rhetoric as they compete for the state's Hindu hearts. And if the union and the state turn saffron, she thinks, should violence erupt, who will keep the police from looking away?

Moving south, the towers of Delta Corporate Park rise so high, associate partner Esha Pai can only see the bright arteries of light inching towards the dark heart of the sea. Yohan Joseph, also working overtime, looks out of the bay windows and teases, 'I'll give you Hindus one thing. Your gods are really cool. Take Ganesha only. He disapproves of austerity. He eats so many modaks, his stomach bursts, so he just wraps a snake around his belly.'

Higher still, on a helipad above Billionaire Row, R.K. Jain clasps his hands in brief but sincere piety. God of businessmen, he thinks, and since he has nothing more to ask for than auspicious times, God of progress and prosperity. Then he climbs into his chopper for a meeting on a new mining bill, and as the rotor blades start whirring, he tweets: *Ganesha gives us divine strength to look at opportunities in odds. He reminds us of our duty to be optimistic.*

Thirty private floors below, his wife smiles over a diamond and emerald choker for the Entertainment Press. 'My husband is Jain, but we celebrate Ganesha,' she says. 'Brahma Industries has provided the Lalbaug mandal with free electricity.' In the background, her lavish puja is being attended by politicians, cricketers, the who's who of show business, and from the staff to the decorators, everyone has performed outstandingly.

Over at Malabar Hill, in an art deco building of genteel height but panoramic views, Anu Sehgal sighs at the saffron flood along Back Bay. To acknowledge that this is a class war would turn the whole sodden onus on the city's liberals. Easier to condemn the flags in an English editorial. She returns to her study and signs her last Ashray check. When the cling-clang-clong gets too loud, she thinks, I've given enough, and she pulls the soundproof windows shut.

At the Orient Club, the retired mayor of Mumbai leans over the carved railings to watch the processions coalesce on Chowpatty beach. The festival is always huge in an election year, and this is a year of two elections, the centre and the state, but he has never seen such gusto. This is how he imagines the mood during the freedom struggle when Tilak, the fiery Chitpavan, the Father of Indian Unrest, led the Ganesha processions in the face of the British.

Well, the city no longer needs Tilak.

The city resounds with its celebratory mourning, its worship of the end, yet its conception of time is cyclical, for the final note requests Lord Ganesha to return –

*Pudhchya varshi lavkar ya!*

The idol may dissolve, but its journey will be retraced in essence, if not in its particulars. A year later, a pandal will rise again in the empty square, a tribute to whatever temple or architect or flower is in vogue; and an avatar reflecting the economy, political will and public sentiment of the times will be crowned Raja of X locality; and in the swirling incense, the ancient chiming of bells and the adoration of hazy devotees, its tusked face will blend into the one from this year and all the years past and each of the hundred thousand idols across the city's complex and luminous geography.

## *Mumbai Central*

'Aala re aala!' a child shouts as the Lalbaug Raja appears atop a cataract of revellers.

The crowd on the flyover tips buckets of rose petals over the rails.

The procession on the street below hollers.

Women raise lamps from open corridors in every soot-stained chawl, and throw fistfuls of dry rice and gulaal in the air.

Boys cram on the narrow tarp above shop signs, their cell phones flashing.

And amidst the waving flags on the twenty-foot Raja's float, an old priest wearing only a dhoti and a caste-mark thinks: People of Bappa, colour me red.

In the eddy of heads below, an office boy knows he will lose his slippers tonight. Last year, he was out until dawn and his kurta got ripped, that's how many devotees there were and so emotional! Crazed by the squeal of tutari horns, he leaves his slippers on a divider piled with deserted footwear. What do his feet care if they walk on sewage or roses?

Looking past the priest, a Koli fisherwoman fills her ancient eyes with Bappa: His velvet seat, His sapphire crown, His pearly ears rising from a garland of banknotes, His mysterious expression, His mighty tusk, His silk crimson in some lights and saffron in others, and His four arms spiralling: one palm curled in blessing, one cradling the modak of the mind, one casting a lasso on desire, and the last wielding the vengeful axe of Parshurama.

The sound of the throng is the sound of a roaring furnace.

Hunched on a footbridge, a small film crew adjusts their lenses at the Raja's advance.

Rohit says to Paul Pinto, a cameraman hired for the establishing shots, 'What a crowd! Zoom out.'

This isn't a *crowd*, Omkar thinks, this is a montage of intimate moments. Even when Pinto isolates a face, he doesn't pause long enough to complete the dramatic arc. For that, you must know what the people are thinking and what they will do next. On Omkar's instructions, Paul refocuses on a priest throwing sweets for which the devotees fight –

'Like animals,' Amanda whispers with awe, the benevolent idol hardly distracting from their primal thrust.

Omkar's blood turns to quicksand. 'Where are you going?' Rohit asks. 'To Bappa,' he says, waving his camcorder. 'Is this the best place to catch the idol?' Rohit asks. 'He goes where He goes,' Omkar says. 'We only meet him in His path.'

As the boys discuss meeting at the Parsi statue after Paul is done, Amanda looks over the railing. Like a river in spate, the masses surge below. 'Looks crazy,' she says. 'Doesn't anyone get hurt?'

Omkar replies in Marathi, 'If you don't have faith, then no one can give you faith.' With that, he takes the stairs, the energy of the streets pulling him towards Bappa. Come Amanda-ji, he thinks, say what you like, but say anything against my country, and I will sweep you aside. And when he says his country, he means this old Koli woman in her thin green sari, her earlobes stretched, the jasmine limp in her hair, her triumphant smile opening on long teeth as she nabs a garland flung from Bappa's float – she will keep that garland for years.

At the Byculla fire station, the alarms blaze high and shrill in the Raja's honour.

A reveller hurls a crushed plastic cup into the air.

Another pulls his polyester scarf off his neck, bites it wildly, and starts to dance.

A little girl pulls down a toddler's shorts with matronly force so he can take a piss.

Walking past superhero balloons and fruit punch vendors, Vikram nods at the faithful's ardour, the political banners on bus stops, and the sidewalks bursting with commerce. When a phenomenon gets this big, he thinks, it draws in all aspects of life. To his BSL volunteers, he says, 'See, I am not a karamkandi. That is because I am a public servant, and rituals are prescribed for householders. But Ganesha is a way for society to come together, and we are the party of the masses, so it is important to connect.'

Volunteer Brijesh Nishad is hardly listening. To him, a night like this is fascinating because the thann-thann-thann of the gong goes off in a million brains in the same instant. Whether you are on the top floor listening or smashing the metal yourself, he thinks, the soul of the sound is the same in every ear.

Stuck in a parallel lane for diverted traffic, Paul Pinto pays the taxi driver a twenty over the meter and leaves for the metro with his tripod on his back. Traffic police are funnelling pedestrians into the only open lane. One waves his hands zombie-like at the sight of his camera.

The taxi driver inhales the sting of onions frying. It could be hours before he gets a bite. We poor people believe Ganesha understands our plight, he thinks. But He is the son of Shiva and Parvati, His ornaments are gold, His tooth is sweet, two wives sit on His lap, he has a serpent on His belly and a fawning rat at His feet.

On a parallel street, Rohit can see the ebony Parsi statue rising above the mayhem. Who knows how Omkar holds on to his camera in this madness, but that is Omkar's genius: he barely composes his shots; they happen automatically because he is true. Why isn't he picking up his phone? He didn't bring Girija either, and it isn't Girija that Rohit cares about, it's that Omkar doesn't trust him. His phone buzzes – it's Vikram. He's here, right across this street, and suddenly, Rohit is glad Omkar isn't around to claim him.

Deonar has taught Amanda that there is safety in numbers, and Rohit's protectiveness – her chest stuck to his back and her hand in his as they press into the crowd – is reassuring. Then a gap tears open between two women shouting and slapping each other on head and breast until they are pushed on. The onlookers swap smiles to demonstrate their own courteousness. She would judge them if she wasn't sick of her own pedantry. She presses her head to Rohit's shoulder. Isn't that the reason why Manasi has rejected her too?

A traffic signal away, buxom women in saris, sweat glinting on their chubby backs, bangles clashing green and gold, are offering permanent tattoos on the sidewalk.

Revellers crouch on a plastic sheet to get their biceps inked with knifed hearts, winged daggers, and serpents swallowing their tails.

The audience stares, lips paused on ice-cream cones as a cripple opens his mouth in a noiseless scream, his eyes riveted where the needle pricks his dark forearm.

Omkar ignores the spectacle. Hugging his camera to his chest, he wades into the grinding thrust of those with nothing but Bappa in their eyes. Their heels are on his toes and elbows in his ribs, but what is the body for if not this weathering? The Raja advances, now visible, now hidden by His devotees, when Omkar is lifted by the crush and brought before Him. Silver foot of Bappa: he touches it, expecting the rapture to infect him. He reconjures the throaty pleasure he felt at Bappa's beauty last year; he struggles to revive his camaraderie with the God of artists; he whispers, 'I adore You with every emotion Saint Namdev describes' – but the metal stays cold under his fingertips.

Nagpada. Hour of Maghrib.

The Raja halts before the ivory domes of the Hindustani Masjid, and the drummers pause in a show of deference.

A bearded man in a fez appears under the masjid's arches. The crowd cheers at the garland in his hands.

Women cry as he approaches the Raja, and when the garland lands, the sky turns vibrant with a rainbow of sparks.

All this goodwill notwithstanding, a hush soon comes over the revellers. Either the tenements here are darker, or their windows deliberately shut.

A scrap salesman in the crowd whispers to his wife, 'This is a sensitive area. With Ramzan before Ganeshotsav, there's been tension here.'

The reek of sewage and cooked meat intensifies the wife's anxiety. The salesman reassures her the right arrests have been made. 'Our new police chief is a hero,' he says, 'a real hero.'

Burning eyes of lamp posts flicker over the tentative hordes. Then, slowly, pockets in the crowd get louder, and the energy returns more potent than before.

Looking on, a mullah rests his weight on the marble railing of his deep green mosque. The Al-Qaeda leader has announced an Indian chapter to respond to this rabid new face of Hindu nationalism, but here at home, their own brothers won't stand with him. That the Hindustani Masjid trustees meet the Lalbaug Raja Mandal to ensure their procession doesn't clash with the evening prayers is one thing, but garlanding an idol? The mullah's establishment may be smaller, yet it is purer of faith.

Across the street, a sub-inspector paces his watchtower with a transceiver at his lips. The bomb detection squads and sniffer dogs have made their checks, and BSL volunteers in hazard jackets are helping to man the crowd. But standing here, he can see only two of the hundred watchtowers and one of the two hundred CCTV cameras in central Mumbai. How can we be everywhere, he thinks, his adrenaline quickening as a street light goes out in a side alley.

From a window in the alley, Rafia and Zaeem watch a ragtag procession pass by. It's only a dozen overgrown boys with saffron headbands, Nashik drums, and a melon-sized Ganesha on a decorated fruit cart – but one is whipping a gong so manically, he could kill a man in that trance.

The drummer's rip intensifies as they pass the Sufi shrine. A reveller holds up a slipper. 'They threw it from the dargah, sisterfuckers,' he shouts.

'Who are you calling sisterfucker, motherfucker?' someone shouts. An empty alcohol bottle catches a flare as it flies down and shatters. Stones fly up, hitting tarp and glass.

A knife gleams just as the police push their way into the scuffle.

Rafia's nani gathers the children in. She should have moved to Deonar with her son.

The night turns warm with the smell of butter.

A baker watches the navy blue vans, the commandos in khaki, and the plainclothes police hauling men by their collars through the crush. Handing his son a tray of hot puffs, he thinks: when men have bread, they thirst less for blood.

The boy pulls a long face. 'Heard about the slipper?'

The baker tells him not to believe everything he hears. He is grateful that his son has no memory of blood mixing with flour.

The boy takes the puffs to a UNITED INDIA stall, where a woman adds them to the table of free refreshments. Beside her, a community relations activist in a black fez is saying into a mic, 'Ganapati Bappa Morya. Brothers, in this heat, drink cool water.'

Walking past, the BSL volunteers decline the water cups though they admit the puffs smell sweet.

Gavade mumbles, 'At least some aren't terrorists.'

Brijesh replies, 'All this meekness is only when their numbers are in check.'

Hanmant adds, 'Saw the woman at the stand? So young and three babies already.'

And Omkar would participate if his thoughts weren't a step ahead with Vikram and Rohit, walking so close that their shoulders are touching. Why does he feel betrayed at the sight of their camaraderie? Shouldn't it be obvious, the alliance between a powerful Rajput and a wealthy Brahmin while the others trail in their dust?

Vikram points to a Conclave Party election poster, 'Look at that. Eid Mubarak on a Kamathipura sign.' He laughs at their lack of taste in placing a festive greeting over a name board for a red-light area. 'All their time in office, they did nothing for the people, so now they will mobilize the Muslim vote. They will make Nagpada a mini-Pakistan.'

Rahim concurs with Vikram. 'Riots would not happen if the Conclave Party didn't appease minorities. It is only in the press now because the press is liberal.'

Rohit is more interested in the setting. The notorious tenements bring to mind iconic gangster movies. That alley, for instance, would be the perfect location to film a soda-bottle fight (before bottles gave way to swords and swords to guns).

Now that Amanda knows this is a red-light area, the shadows look longer. There are no suspicious windows or bars, only two women in garish saris sprinting over the puddles, but just as she wonders, she notices a man with them, and over his shoulder, a girl in pigtails waving a mace. The child's delight in the toy shames her. In Deonar too, she thinks, she has seen only the ugly, listened selectively for tragedy, and mistaken this violation for compassion.

Watching the commotion die down from the slats of a shop window, a tailor flips a razor blade on his tongue. Such venality sanctified by tossing rice, such bloodlust held on the cusp by tinkling prayer bells! He mutters, 'They aren't burning our shops or slitting our throats, but does that mean they can insult us as they like?'

His teenage daughter snips a bit of lace and says nothing.

The cell phone on the bed starts ringing, and the tailor grabs it. 'Heard about the slipper?' the caller asks. 'Hindus in Lalbaug are preparing to attack. Keep your women inside. We will do what we can.'

A corner away, Zaeem crosses the littered procession route, his uber-reflective glasses on his head. People have come to their doorsteps to watch what will happen. 'Was it your cousin the police took?' someone asks. Zaeem does not respond. He walks to the madrasa's steps, where his friends are waiting.

Near the steps, a prominent social worker shouts, 'Taps and toilets, they promised. A man can live without water, but it is getting hard to breathe. We don't cook meat when their processions pass. We lose business at every Hindu festival. Is it the same in reverse? I ask you, we who have lived here a thousand years, how have we been quashed this way? Who let it happen?'

Meanwhile, muezzins clear their throats, and the azan swells from a dozen minarets.

A relieved sub-inspector stops pacing his watchtower and calls the control room. The Raja of Lalbaug has passed through Nagpada without incident.

Since cousin Omkar is strutting about with his BSL secretary, Uttam arrives in the company of Tejas Tambe, a Marathi Bana organizer with a plucky moustache. To Uttam's relief, Vikram greets Tejas warmly despite the recent split between the Bharat Party and the Marathi Bana. In turn, Tejas invites them aboard a mandal truck sponsored by his uncles. 'We can take you to the beach. The Lalbaug Raja won't reach there until dawn.'

Everyone agrees including Omkar, who likes the idea of a new vantage, and they follow Tejas into Girgaum's labyrinth.

Shops belch pools of light on alleys clogged with minor processions.

One cart follows the next, some pulled by bullocks with painted horns, others by cars gummed with cut-outs of swans and buxom nymphs.

Most of the idols are large enough to command a throne or a parasol lined with gold tassels, and each is accompanied by a band and outsized speakers, the asphalt in between a wild dance floor with laser beams cutting through a fog of fireworks.

Walking through the smoke, a local thug called Battery tells his carrom partner about a gangster whose career took off after the Bombay riots: 'When he showed that he could fire people up and was not afraid to kill, a corporator gave him his number. He used the new connection to solve his basti's problems. That's how his reputation grew from a thief to a bhai to a local leader. Then he joined a Hindu religious outfit. Politicians started calling him to offer him support. Three years later, he was running on a ticket.'

The carrom partner laments, 'Bhai, today it is not as simple as stab one of theirs and they retaliate by shooting two of ours and the cops watch the fun. The new chief is overactive. I wouldn't do anything unless a corporator calls me and says, do it, we will handle the law.'

Sita has never seen anything like the parades in her tribal village in Jharkhand. She has taken an evening off from work at the Agashes, and the clacking of her heels, the sequinned hem of her sari, and the sugar in her candyfloss make her feel free and full of potential. Her eyes flicker briefly over Battery's ample chest before she notices his diminished legs and looks away.

Mukta, who grew up in these wadis, pretends not to notice as she tells Sita stories about the local ghosts. Here is a tiled shrine to a female Dalit spirit who protects Shenwadi's families and has a taste for sacrificed chickens. Sita fingers the cross dangling from her rosary. 'Even ghosts have castes in this city?' she asks in a tone that surprises Mukta enough for her to notice that the girl has started threading her brow.

An alley away, an activist from a Hindu religious outfit has called a meeting to discuss the rumours. Standing on a chair in the shadow of his chawl, he shouts, 'My contact in Nagpada saw women taking swords out of their burqas. Tell me, should I distribute glass bangles here? Is that the kind of men we are? Why do we tolerate persecution from those who live in our country at our expense?'

Walking past, a Koli fisherwoman cradling Bappa's garland says to her friend, 'Last time, my husband convinced the youths in our chawl not to listen, and these thugs beat him up.'

The friend nods, but says nothing. The activist is from her caste and the first to offer help when she needs a gas cylinder, or when her son, who has a violent nature, lands in trouble. The fisherwoman's man may have a lot of opinions, but when it really counts, he is useless.

Grant Road. The narrow alleys give out to a bright thoroughfare, and riding down its centre is a line of decorated trucks, the idols smaller than the Raja of Lalbaug but grander than those in Girgaum's wadis.

On either side, the elegant theatres, stone banks and quaint Parsi houses shrink in the dark, as horns of every size blare defiantly – and Uttam smiles at his cousin triumphantly, but Omkar looks pale and preoccupied.

Rohit laughs at the loudspeakers of three processions overlapping in a racket of Western trance, religious chants and a sexy Bollywood tune. Past the noise, painted faces holler from a truck, but it isn't for their cameras. This is Tejas Tambe's ride! The crew is hoisted up and given flowers for Ganesha's feet. The idol is the size of a wardrobe, its skin violently red, and it has been named for the middle-class locality where it stood rather than its chief sponsor, the Marathi Bana Party.

Vikram makes a humble namaste when Tejas introduces his uncles. Both are wearing white shirts, jeans and tikas, but the mandal president sports a radium watch, and the municipal corporator, a gold chain. Perhaps in reference to the recent split with the Bharat Party, the corporator says to Vikram, 'Behold the proof of Bappa's omniscience. Even the God of the wealthy Brahma Jains waits on the same route as us. Even Muslims or Christians who receive Him are blessed. Whatever your position, all are united under Him.'

At the mention of Muslims, the talk turns to the slipper in Nagpada, and the mandal president says, 'There will always be troublemakers.'

Vikram says, 'The point is not who is a nuisance to whom. When I say *Jai Ganesha*, I'm saying there is a god called Ganesha and I salute him. I'm not saying he is the *only* god. Five times a day, you can't keep shouting from loudspeakers that your god is the only god. And these people talk about secularism.'

Tejas concurs, 'That is why they can't adjust in any country. Their first loyalty is to their faith.'

Uttam adds, 'But when they want a country, they snatch it.'

Tympanic rip. A procession of girl drummers, their hair flying, their chests out under saffron stoles, their kettledrums struck with masculine vigour:

*Jai Shivaji, Jai Bhavani!*

Rohit thinks, Look at those heart-shaped faces.

And Vikram: these are our women – proud, traditional, powerful.

And Omkar, noticing the lechers stomping and catcalling from the sidewalk: who are these wretches, naked waist-up, feeding off the ecstasy? Sheh.

As the lechers get more aggressive, the mandal volunteers help the girls on to the truck.

Amanda puts her hand in Rohit's, but now that they are safe, he feels less chivalrous. This is not the kind of crowd or occasion where you hold hands in this country. Besides, it is not his job to take care of her. Breaking up with Andrei doesn't mean she is his: it has simply clarified the thing in her blue eyes that is free of all men and that will always look through him at some far horizon. Soon, she will apply for a master's abroad. She will reinvent herself again, and who wants to be a highway stop on to something better? He leaves her hand.

Watching Rohit talk with the drummer girls, Amanda's skin goes cold. She is starting to recognize the beauty of brown women: their large eyes and tiny, curvy bodies. She feels like a giant, clunky and lumbering, not only in her thinking but her form. She touches her jaw, Nana's jaw, which remains strong and beautiful. Nana, she thinks, guide me. What will end this breathlessness and the pain behind my eyes? Your last impression of me was the mess I'd made in Deonar, and I'm better than that, I promise.

Getting off the metro line a street away, Chagan Ingole checks his smartphone. A list of the contact numbers of Mahars celebrating Ganeshotsav has got around on WhatsApp. Since he changed his profile picture to a blue Ganapati, he has received threats from not only the upper castes but also Buddhists who believe he has betrayed Ambedkar's vows by worshipping Hindu gods. This endless hate and strife and division, he thinks, when will it erupt and destroy them all and return the earth to silence?

Near Opera House, a Bharat Brotherhood organizer, a Bharat Party politician and two BSL volunteers watch the spectacle contentedly from under the awning of a masala rice stand. They smile when Vikram Singh climbs down from a truck. 'Namaste.' 'Namaste.' They offer him and his handsome friend boxes of lychee juice. When they learn about Rohit's film, they appreciate his interest in 'our culture'. Vikram says proudly, 'He is also interested in Advocate Kadam's media cell.'

The Bharat Party politician invites Rohit to the celebrity pavilion after he is done shooting his film. 'Advocate Kadam will be there.' Rohit confirms the plan excitedly. Watching him return to the truck, the politician notices a familiar face. He asks Vikram, who has stayed behind, 'Is that Omkar Khaire? I knew him when I was heading the BSL in Pune. That boys like him are with us shows how far the Marathi Bana has lost its hold on its voter base.'

Vikram says, 'I've seen a lot of young Marathi men obsessed with Shivaji. Slowly, the Brotherhood widens their horizons.' In places like Pune and Wai, he thinks, they are taught about the nation, but the crowd is so local that the learning remains in theory. Perhaps he should get Omkar to Mumbai. If Agashe has invested in him, he must have talent. Here at the headquarters, you quickly find a friend closer than family regardless of his state or caste. That is when you understand real brotherhood. Wasn't it the same with him, Vikram Singh, once a young and hot-blooded Rajput boy?

On the truck, Tejas asks the driver to halt so that Omkar can get a steady shot. But Omkar's hand is shaking. An excuse for politics and commerce, that's what they have made of the festival! Bet the volunteers on this truck beat up those of another mandal down the same street because their idol was an inch taller. The mandal president will get a ticket to the corporation next year. As for Rohit, he is here for Vikram, and even if their chemistry is personal, how unique is the Bharat Party if outsiders can bypass the ranks on charm? And who am I, he thinks, but a poor boy of the black earth of Wai, yet what I am is up front, and I can stand anything, but I can't stand fake people.

As the truck crosses the intersection that leads to the floodlit beach, the chant of *Ganapati Bappa Morya* changes to *Har Har Mahadev*. So we invoke not the remover of obstacles, Uttam thinks, but Shiva, the lord of destruction.

## *Chowpatty Beach*

The beach is so packed there is no telling man from man, just a blur of heads and cell phones flashing. Still, the sea is a release from the claustrophobic interiors, and as the procession routes coalesce, the crowd is effulgent.

Coming through on a truck, Tejas's heart lifts at the sight of Bappa's many splendid avatars, the largest suspended by construction cranes. There is the Raja of Tejukaya, seated in the lap of a seven-headed snake; there is the Chandanwadi Ganesha riding a sabretooth tiger; there, the Khambata Ganapati on his own sturdy thighs; here, a Vishwacha Raja perched on a model of the globe – and so many others crafted by Khatu-ji, that beloved idol maker of Mumbai.

Amanda photographs a saffron flag cleft like a forked tongue, so unwieldy that two men can barely control it against the monsoon wind. Beyond the flag, Ganesha statues brandish axes, spears, swords and tridents. The procession is galling in its display of might, the rabid hordes celebrating a spirit terrifying to her world and values – but who is she to judge, based on their coarse features and fearsome gods, that they mean harm? Rohit looks at ease, Omkar transcendent.

Rohit takes in all the meanings of the gold-trimmed flags waving over light and darkness. Ancient hue of wisdom, the masses, their redemption, their politics, even their perversity. When you love a man, he thinks, you love all his shades, and these are the shades of his blood tonight: neon blue, pewter grey, the brownish-purple of thick lips, the metallic red of a woman's hairline, and a saffron flag like a fiery bird above the thrashing foliage. Beside him, Amanda's disdain for the crowds feels like a judgement of him. To hell with anyone, he thinks, who cannot see the beauty of my shades.

Omkar's throat tightens as a second saffron flag rises to meet the first, both unfurling like unchecked flames as they celebrate the spirit of his country, his religion and his king. O Shivaji, he thinks, what has become of your armies? Janata Raja, would you approve of Bargya from Wai? He wants to punish Rohit, but one look at his friend's handsome face shames him. Rohit is princely. Like Arjuna, he will smile when his guru cuts Ekalavya's thumb because the savage has got too good at the bow, yet we forgive him because he is Arjuna, and we are in love with him and loathe ourselves.

On a raised bamboo pavilion for celebrities and international guests, the Conclave Party's Sanjay Vaze, minister of sanitation, looks over the hordes, and his chest tingles at the sight of a marvellous beast waking. At any minute, he thinks, it could break its chains and hurl a manic hoof at his pedestal.

Beside him, his chief secretary mumbles, 'See how fast the waves are rising, Sir. They will come up to this wall. The city will get flooded if we don't fix the gutters.'

A tier below on the same pavilion, the Bharat Party's Advocate Kadam walks over to a leader from the Janata Conclave Party. 'You hardly smile when you see me these days,' Kadam says. 'Do old friends forget each other like this?'

The leader holds Kadam's arm and laughs. He says nothing of his party falling out with the Conclave. He merely points to the Khetwadi Raja with his free hand. Suspended by a crane, the giant saffron and navy blue idol is inching over the masses to the water. 'Keep looking,' he says. 'It will fall any minute.'

Watching them, the Bhim Republic Party president wonders if the Janata Conclave will ever join hands with the Bharat Party. Unthinkable … then again, did he ever imagine that he would? Many believe he has betrayed Ambedkar by contesting with the Brahmins, but what is the alternative? For decades, the Conclave used his people for votes while keeping them passive players in the state's power circles. His alliance with the saffron side could mean a new era of Dalit politics.

Meanwhile, the King of Bollywood, Murad Khan, ascends the pavilion's stairs, and the paparazzi on either side go wild. The actor, who claims to have a 'special attachment' to Ganesha, is telling an industrialist who runs an art gallery in Delta Corporate Park that he will sponsor the Lalbaug Raja's pandal next year. 'It will look like a Mughal palace,' he explains, 'complete with arches and filigree.'

The only person not intent on the Bollywood King is a secretary with the Muslim Unity Party. His black kurta is creased and his face pale. When he locates his erstwhile boss, a corporator with the Socialist Party, he leans in and whispers, 'There is trouble in Lalbaug.'

The Khetwadi Raja lands with a splash in the terrible broth of the sea. The wave hitting it is so large that it heaves, and its crown catches a final shaft of light and sparkles.

The crowd, mesmerized until the fall, roars. Then they return to speculating on what famous idol will appear next on the carpeted avenue that carries the trucks to the sea.

Coming through, Rohit scans the press box. Chitra Kaki mentioned that Kedar might be here, but his cousin would never be on a story this easy. If Kedar is in the city, he is at some dingy pub knocking back a rum and Coke. Rohit's ribs swell at the thought of his new vantage compared to his cousin's. Here he is at the beating heart of his country, his networks spinning outward, his gaze neither high nor low but on a level with the vast public idols riding the crowds. This is the range of my access, he thinks; from the towers to the streets, the bridges and drones, I am everywhere.

Tejas says he will manage things on the truck, so his uncles, the corporator and the mandal president, climb down and walk over to the pavilion. Uttam and Omkar jump off as well. 'Send some corn back with your cousin,' Tejas tells Uttam as they make for the colourful bulbs and posters of the food court.

Her slippers in her hand, Girija can't stop looking at the stars on the pavilion. Her uncle says with a wink, 'Maybe we will see our Bargya there some day.' An exciting thought, but her mood sours when Uttam says he is taking his parents home and Omkar insists she leave with them. 'It won't be safe near the sea.' He buys her an ice gola with rose syrup to make up, but she hands it to her aunt and keeps silent.

At a juice and lassi stall, Chagan runs into a friend from Deonar, a healthcare worker who shouts *Jai Bhim* at every opportunity. Both look sheepish to find the other here. His friend says, 'My children wanted to witness the tamasha, so I said okay, let's go this one time. They are well protected from the Gauri–Ganapati epidemic. I have already given them the Babasaheb vaccine.'

Chagan says, 'I had some work, that's all,' and the healthcare worker needs no explanation. 'Is that your party chief?' he asks. 'I hear the Bharat Party has promised him a berth for our votes. The Dalit movement used to be a force in this state. Now we are all divided. Some of our leaders are with the Conclave, some with the Bharat Party, others with the Marathi Bana. They give us some seats, but it is a short-term dose for a disease needing long-term treatment…'

Chagan is well aware of the accusations against the Bhim Republic Party. People say that the movement has become an exclusive Mahar club, or that the Bharat Party will always care for Dalits like the Mangs, who remain Hindu because they are too weak or lazy to convert. Besides, the threats on his phone have given him pause. If he is in this for the long term, he needs a face, someone more sympathetic. He texts Nadiya: *Has Sheela Bai come?*

To one side of the trucking avenue, in a brightly lit area reserved for women, Nadiya sits on the mats with her girlfriends. She has received a new position as the Mumbai head of a Brahma Industries non-profit, and is in a celebratory mood. Biting into a hot samosa, she says, 'I am coming here every year for five years. Ganesha is lucky for me.' Her Hindu friend, a manager at a skill development programme for women, replies, 'I have always wanted to visit Haji Ali, but life is so busy, I just can't find the time,' and Nadiya laughs awkwardly.

Sheela looks at the edge of the carpeting where families relax. A man wipes the sand from his toddler's mouth and bites its cheek lovingly. Her own son, her Babu, thinks his father is in the village. At times she believes he is there too. For weeks, all she has known is darkness and confusion: a blind longing for his return; a blind fear of the empty plate and unpaid rent; a blind rage at him for abandoning them, at herself for going home, at those he trusted, and every face in their street, and all this world and its empty gods. Now she looks past the crowd at the spotlights searching the sky. Nadiya's friend has offered her a chance to train for a regular job. She will learn. She will persist. She will raise her son to be a lion.

Babu is dancing with a little girl from the group. His father is in the village. His mother is not crying. Everything is beautiful: the shiny feel of his shirt, the delicious smells, the girl's dress as thin as an insect's wings, the glittering laughter of the crowd, the red balloon he has been promised before they go home. Then his favourite song comes on, and he starts dancing with such vigorous joy that the girl stops and simply watches him, but he doesn't care; the music is an electric current in his limbs –

*Aata majhi satakli, mala raag yetoyyyy!*

The avenue ends in the sand.

The trucks halt at the traffic barricades; only those carrying the idols may proceed.

By now, the families have fallen behind, and the crowd, mostly men, turns mad and frightening, like a giant nerve centre with no brain.

Those on the trucks can see the sea, the tide high, the wind fast, a wave dark, dark, dark, until it clefts white and the foam expands in both directions.

Strobes illuminate the vapour rising off the foam. Haloed in mist, a giant Ganesha hoisted by a crane topples prematurely, and the men under it scurry.

On the cab of the red idol's truck, Tejas thinks: How many drunks will die here tonight, trapped between a wave and a falling idol; in what glory, confusion or terror will they choke on the sewer of the sea?

The mandal volunteers pay some labourers to carry Bappa to the water. The men look exhausted, their vests torn or stained, still they bring their ropes and lower the red idol on to a soggy wooden cart.

'Will you come?' Tejas asks a drumming girl. She laughs and looks over the barricades. The crowd is less suffocating, and some of the larger processions have women but no children. 'Maybe halfway,' she says, feeling the thrill of his warm, wet hand help her down.

Squeezing in with their troupe, an unemployed youth who has dodged the police all the way from Nagpada thinks, All this tension, where to shove it? I'm buzzing like a wasp. I'm rubbing my legs like a cricket. Booze gives you energy to do something stupid, then it takes all your energy, but at least your body feels as wretched as your mood.

Behind them, the police slam the barricades shut.

Intent on the horizon, the red idol inches forward in its small procession of labourers, mandal boys, drumming girls, and what's left of a film crew. The troupe is singing and clapping or focused on their cameras, when the drumming of a parallel procession whips up. Ghoulish in the floodlight, men with brutal faces dance as in the face of death, one ripping his vest open to the song –

*Yeh jeena bhi na jeena bhi, jo hua voh tumse hua*

– though it isn't a girl he holds his hand out to but a fresh-faced young man with red gulaal on his cheeks.

Rohit steps forward, high on his intimacy with the public, confident that he can ride this beast, contemptuous of anyone who doesn't find it as redolent, as pulsing and joyously uncontrolled. Black face gazes into brown, and the drumming grips his heart, swirls it around, throws it up, and injects his spine with movement. The band turns up its decibel to obliterate all thought, and dancing, he gets it, the Hindu obsession with noise; the noise is transcendence, and this is the sound of his heart: a fusillade of kettledrums, the clang of a metal gong, and the dhol's eternal rumble:

*Dhantanana dhantanana dhan dhan dhan dhan!*

Watching Rohit, a rill of raw sewage passes through Omkar's blood. This is what Rohit has been doing with him, locking shoulders in some perverse dance. Rohit may love him, but his love is fascination, a child's fixation on a new toy. Look at the fire in his eyes as he thrusts with that drunk, no mandal volunteer but some filthy tagger-on. O Bappa, he thinks, tell me where to take my hot, lonely anger. Won't the sound of the gong release me? Won't You thresh it out with lezim cymbals? I am tired of the tumour it is in my mind, the cramp it is in my liver. I beat against my attachment to my anger, yet I am afraid to break free. What will propel me if I lose it, and slip into that wide-eyed, fawning servitude?

Watching Rohit, Amanda's skin lifts and the briny air seeps into her bones where it whistles. Against this wild backdrop, his expression is banal, and any desire for either his validation or to judge him gives way to an impossible fatigue. Her body has developed a will of its own, but what it wants to say with its tantrums remains opaque; if there was an instinct connecting her thoughts with her gut, India has undone it.

Omkar wants to fling his footage into the boiling sea. If he is replaceable, let Rohit find him in that dancing idiot. But he can't bring himself to throw the camera, glossy and steadier than the one last year. Casting for an idol to show him a path, he thinks, Vighnaharta, why do I stand in my own way? My vehicle is imperfect, my mind scurries like a rat. Bring Your mace down on my anger, Your axe on my desires, lasso my ego – and as if on cue, a thirty-foot God draped in banknotes advances against the saffron-black sky, an army in His wake, their features coarse, though you can hardly tell the faces behind eyes that glint like dying fish, eyes shifting between servitude and aggression, eyes flush with drink and mad with noise. Distracted from his feverish prayer, Omkar thinks, Stains on the Hindu name, how dare they shove us! In an instant, he can see the chaos coming: the mandal volunteers and drummer girls backing off, the float advancing on to the rascals Rohit is dancing with, the tussle starting up between the dancing circle and the aggressive group coming in. He must warn them.

Amanda feels a hand on her shoulder. Omkar! The world comes into focus again; repulsed, she shakes free, but this time, his expression matches hers in disgust.

Die, Omkar thinks, die, both of you. And he turns and walks away, one head coming up between them, and then another and another.

Amanda is calling Rohit when a strobe hits her eyes with epileptic force. A mountain of an idol is bifurcating the crowd, and Rohit disappears on the other side. The massive silhouette advances, a crazed rush of faces below; if the idol falls, it will crush her. Panicked, she elbows her way out of its path when, from the sour hold of the crowd, a wrench on her breast makes her scream. She scans the mob for a saffron headband or a drumming girl, but the faces closing in are strange and grotesque, their foreheads slick, their jaws agape. A rough clamp seizes her groin. She strikes the arch of a ribcage, strikes past her half-sense of their euphoria, sadism, ferocity – though none of these maps on to words. The clamp loosens, yet the hands keep coming, hands on her hips, her stole, her hair. Trapped, she strikes in every direction with a wild, instinctive charge. A man half her height gets hit on the temple so hard, he recoils. He covers his face with his palm, the tattoo of a serpent swallowing its tail magnifies. His friends roar with laughter. When he looks up, she sees hatred in his eyes as she has never seen. Then the world is a sharp crack and pain, pain, as she falls back into the darkness in her skull and her body sinks forward on the arm at her waist. The final sound is that of drums, swearing and drunken laughter.

# *Mumbai from the Depths*

The static on the wireless crackles.

The control room team asks a mobile van, 'What's the issue?'

The tone is trouble. The police commissioner grabs his phone.

There has been a fracas at Bharat Mata Junction near Lalbaug Temple. Onlookers claim that a Muslim biker riding from the Takia Mosque to Nagpada collided with a Hindu woman; others say he assaulted a traffic policeman who pulled him over for riding three men to a bike. Hindu revellers-turned-vigilantes used bamboo sticks from a construction site to reprimand the bikers. Yes, there were rumours. Something about a slipper thrown from a shrine.

'What's the status *now*?' the commissioner snaps.

The traffic police have let the bikers off. But the vigilantes, enraged, are hurling stones and smashing windscreens with iron rods.

The commissioner doesn't blink. Shabby balconies of Hindu and Muslim ghettos face each other across that junction.

Local squads, reserve forces, rapid action and riot control teams are deployed. The traffic division diverts vehicles and installs blockades to stem the influx of new rioters. From Dharavi to Parel, shops swallow the light as mouth after metal mouth rattles shut.

Despite these measures, when the commissioner steps out of his jeep at Bharat Mata Junction, metal barricades along the temple side of the street can barely hold back the Hindu mob jeering at the Muslims on the side of the mosque. A fallen motorbike is flaming on the asphalt in between, the stench of burning rubber charging the air.

The officers on duty are emboldened by the sight of their chief. He is wearing a pale blue helmet and armed with only his baton, but his guards are carrying machine guns, and his gait exudes confidence. The officers request the Hindus shouting over the barricades to leave. Someone shouts, 'Them first.' So they convince the Muslims to retreat on the promise their women and children will be safe.

Neither crowd has a leader. On the police chief's advice – a deft mix of cajoling, assurances and threats – they slowly unknot and thin down the dripping alleys.

But the sites of trouble have multiplied.

Images of dead and bleeding people, some in saffron headbands, others in fez caps, are going viral through the city.

Moonshine bottles are breaking on sidewalks in six suburbs; more than a handful of liquor stores have received large orders.

In a migrant slum in Kandivali, a mandal president asks a self-styled protector of the faith if the men are drunk. Yes, and they have been paid in cash, given knives, petrol bombs and two pistols. Their families have been assured the police will not be a problem.

Lush with energy, the men climb into a covered lorry. As the headlights move south, they chant *Bharat Mata ki Jai!*

In Byculla, a pack of young men advances with drainage rods and bamboo poles. Most have covered their faces, but not Battery. He wants the eyes in the windows to recognize his pistol, his kada, and the muscled chest that compensates for his height. And in the public's gaze, he is a god of many metal arms, a god of profound spectacle, a jaw-breaking cyclonic force. Tonight, they will witness his capabilities; tomorrow, schoolboys in these chawls will take his name with awe.

An unemployed teenager looks down from his window. The leader is vaguely familiar as the bhai they call Battery. The rest are automatons, their helmets gleaming in the light of a blazing car as Battery shouts, 'Be like lions, my brothers! Shoot the traitors! Smoke out the termites!' The teen has returned from a street meeting that the police broke up, and these words land like fresh water on the stagnant trough of his thoughts. He pulls on his jeans and ties a bandana across his face. Then he straps a cleaver to a hockey stick.

At a petrol pump, Battery's gang spots a bearded man running towards the mosque. Battery fires his cheap pistol, but it sparks and burns his hand. 'Daughterfucker,' he shouts, falling behind.

When the man is cornered, the rods come down, but the teen stands frozen until Battery catches up and wrests his makeshift weapon. The blade slices the bearded cheek, and the man hunches, transfixed by his blood. Battery goes for his stomach, but the knife sinks into the man's thigh, and when it can't go further, he twists it. Blood sprays the teen's face with the force of a water gun, and its metallic fragrance, his adventure is complete.

A bylane in Nagpada flickers and goes dark.

'They've cut the line,' the baker whispers to Hindu neighbours hiding on his terrace.

On the roof across, women pour acid into plastic bottles, and the liquid fumes in the moonlight. A child is heard crying and is hushed.

In the darkness below, a tailor's wife grabs his arm. 'They will kill us. They know our homes.'

'We'll show them first,' the tailor says, pulling his father's sword from under their wedding mattress and kissing the blade.

The mullah says a prayer for the young men walking past with knives. Bless them, they will guard the entrance to these alleys. Then he wraps the sacred texts in silk and places them in a pit that he covers with broken tiles.

A block away, his heart thudding in his ears, Omkar tells himself not to run. Any minute, acid could melt the bones of his face, or a butcher's knife rip out his guts … Walk. And walking, he is neither a Kunbi nor a Maratha nor a Brahmin, neither a Hindi nor a Marathi speaker, neither a Southerner nor a Northerner, neither a poor son of the black earth nor a wealthy miner … Walk. And walking, his nakedness grows; he is neither Omkar nor Bargya nor Khaire, he is neither film-maker nor friend nor brother nor son, he is not even human if they find him, he will be only one thing when they kill him: *a Hindu, a Hindu, a Hindu.*

By midnight, a thin acid rain starts to fall.

Three telecom providers have suspended their services.

On other networks, a cybercrime cell is cracking down on rumours.

Near Parel, a covered lorry is stopped at the barricades. The drunks inside are rounded up, and their weapons seized. The police officer in charge gets a call from a corporator in Kandivali. 'Sorry, Sahib,' the officer says. 'There's a new chief. We won't file a report, but we will keep the men locked up until the curfew ends.'

Frustrated, the corporator tries an electoral candidate with the Marathi Bana, but the minister has orders from above not to let things escalate tonight.

With his black fez in his pocket, a community relations activist texts his mohalla committee a report from a hospital: twelve people have been injured, including a mandal volunteer caught under an idol … an American tourist, a woman, was assaulted on the beach … of those brought in on account of the riots, almost all have been discharged … the viral image of a bloody teen on a gurney is from another night…

The activist's colleague uses these facts as she goes from door to door in Nagpada, pleading with young men not to rush to Lalbaug in revenge. 'A Muslim man was taken to the hospital by Hindu friends,' she tells them. The news that his leg will be amputated can wait.

Across the city, politicians' second cell phones are ringing without pause.

Still in his tussar kurta from a Ganesha party on Billionaire Row, Sanjay Vaze tries both numbers of a contact at the All India Muslim Council. Then he calls a minister with the Conclave's erstwhile ally, the Bhim Republic Party, who is popular among the Dalit youth.

Soon after, a Bharat Party corporator gets a note from a municipal colleague in the Socialist Party. In response, he consults Advocate Kadam.

Through Kadam's connections, the Lalbaug mandal committee, the leader of the Janata Conclave, and office bearers across central Mumbai are approached.

Soon, Hindu and Muslim religious leaders, corporators from every outfit and multiple state ministers join the police in placating those on the streets.

By two a.m., over a hundred detentions have been made in sensitive areas across the city.

Armed escorts are taking families in hiding back home.

In a volunteer's living room in Lalbaug, Vikram is making calls to ensure that his cadres are accounted for and their families safe, when the doorframe crowds. Hanmant and Brijesh stand on either side of Omkar, his face as colourless as ice. Is he all right? 'Just shaken,' Brijesh says. 'Where is your cousin?' Vikram asks. 'Where are your friends? Do they need help?' Omkar doesn't reply. When Vikram touches his shoulder, he sinks to the floor and sobs on his leader's knees.

At Bharat Mata Junction, an uneasy silence prevails where the mobs have been stuffed back into their chawls, and a police force deployed to keep them there.

The wet asphalt is littered with bricks and glass shards that flare in the street light.

The traffic police have towed away the bike's charred skeleton, but in other streets, cars with smashed windshields gape, and in a back alley, a fruit cart lies on its side, the upturned wheel slowly circling.

A stray with bitten ears is sniffing a smashed orange when it notices a human pack. One is crouched low and clicking his tongue. The stray whimpers and wags its tail between its legs as the man grabs it and strokes its head. 'The man got away, so you take it out on a dog?' 'Shut up.' A plastic bottle appears; the stray's jaw is opened to a pungent whiff. The spray fumes in the moonlight. The stray's mouth prickles, its howl chokes in its burning throat.

The man throws the dog down expecting it to dance or bolt, but it only shudders and falls on its side.

A watchman says to the pack, 'Party over? Get lost then, go home.'

By five a.m., press reporters gather outside Conclave minister Sanjay Vaze's home. A text urging Muslims to take legal action for damaged cars that provides his number has been tracked. Vaze denies any involvement. 'I have asked our police chief to investigate who sent it. He has saved the city from full-blown riots. Please congratulate him.'

On another news channel, the chairman of the All India Muslim Council affirms that such alacrity on the part of the police is rare. They will be sending a delegation to thank the new commissioner.

Meanwhile, a former secretary of the Lalbaug mandal committee smiles when asked why right-wing leaders, not known for restraint, helped to control the mobs rather than spur them on this time. 'We are running the country today,' he says. 'For the sake of one state, we can't afford a bad name. The Bombay riots took us back ten years. I was young and caught up in the fever of those days. Now I have children.'

Tejas Tambe, a Marathi Bana organizer, tells a reporter that bikers waving green flags and shouting slogans against Shivaji had been zipping over the Lalbaug flyover in the afternoon. 'Our Raja passed through their area, and they welcomed Him,' he says. 'They are good people except for a few. Many are willing to die for the country. I'm starting to think our political rivals planned this.'

The Bharat Party's Advocate Kadam concedes even less. 'What happened in Lalbaug was a local issue. No point giving it a Hindu–Muslim angle. It could have happened anywhere.'

But a baker in Nagpada tells an independent news website that a similar ruckus transpired on Eid last year. 'Even the story was the same. A Hindu hurt when a Muslim biker hit him. If it can happen anywhere, why does it always happen in our area and on days that celebrate the Prophet or Ganesha?'

At Chowpatty, the Raja of Lalbaug makes his way over the sand.

Other titans bob on the water, their backs flat, unpainted and ghostly against the sky.

The beach is deserted except for the blinking red-and-blue lights on patrol cars and shadowy figures of commandos on the pavilion.

Exhausted from over twenty hours of activity, a mandal volunteer who has not abandoned the Raja thinks, Bappa has danced His way through us, He is focused on the infinite, and until He comes again, our hearts are desolate. The receding tide leaves a frill of rotting garlands, cigarette butts and the broken limb of an idol at his feet.

By the bruised light of daybreak, the Raja of Lalbaug is lowered in the sea, and the city has been pacified.

# VIGIL

## *Rohit*

Prabhat House. The living room is crammed with women in pastel saris and men in white kurtas. A priest murmurs over a table arrayed with three mounds of rice, incense in a silver holder, and a photograph of Kedar, sandalwood daubed on the glass and jasmine strung across the frame. On the priest's instruction, Ravi Kaka places a red hibiscus and a pinch of sesame seeds on each mound. Rohit's eldest cousin, down from Brisbane, is nursing her newborn on the four-poster bed in Aaji's room, and each time the baby cries, Chitra Kaki's chest heaves. He gets up to let someone else take their turn at observing the rituals. While the mourners in the living room are earnest and restrained, those in the vestibule are livelier. Near the main door, Asha Atya, also down from Brisbane, whispers, 'What is the use if you die for the cause? You have to live for the cause,' and no one responds. So Kedar Agashe, who made people uncomfortable during his life, continues to do so in death. Rohit ignores his aunt's opening to join the company. He is being difficult, like Kedar, as he walks past her group in a way that must intensify whatever discomfort their conversation was struggling to release.

In the garden, the caterers are warming lunch. The scent of fresh spices mixes with that of the wet grass and lotus pond, but Prabhat House has lost its enchantment. The bungalow looks small and ordinary, a place where people live and die, and the living wake to the ticking of clocks, unheard footsteps and the sighs of antiquated furniture. This is the weight that Aai and Baba escaped by moving to Mumbai, and their escape allowed Rohit to go in search of only those aspects of the past that caused neither shame nor guilt. For months after Kedar's death, Ravi Kaka and Chitra Kaki's silence was complete, and Asha Atya was not invited to the funeral either, a snub that had Baba rage, 'Ravi's acting like we killed his son!' Aai reassured him it was on account of the bizarre nature of the death, a shock that called for an immediate and private cremation: Kedar's body was found by a railway track north of Talne; an autopsy determined from the marks on his neck and the depth of the charred alveoli that he had been strangled, then taken for dead and burnt while still alive. Since the Special Investigation Team got involved, they have reason to suspect the mining mafia, and Ravi Kaka had no option but to accept his siblings' help with the legal fees. A year later, this shraadh ceremony is the official truce.

The lawn crowds with mourners. The priest steps into the winter light holding a brass plate. Keeping with the ritual, the first offering of food is made to crows. None come. Since the guests are restless, the meal is served, but Chitra Kaki refuses to eat before the crows and is taken back inside by her sister. Traditional and elaborate, the lunch reminds everyone of their grandmother's kitchen. The conversation grows less cautious, laughter is hushed, a match for a cousin arranged, and the caterer's card requested. An obese woman pinches Rohit's cheek. 'Didn't recognize me? I'm Suniti Kaki, your father's second cousin. Mahesh, see how Raghu's son has grown!' Her husband comes over, asks with a wink if that girl there is Naren's fiancée and if he can expect an invitation to the wedding now that the mourning period for Kedar has elapsed. Suniti Kaki enquires about Manasi's full name and when Rohit tells her, she says quizzically, 'Bansod … I don't think I have heard this surname?' Rohit knows what this is an invitation to gossip about. Manasi's background has not gone unnoticed by the Pune clan, and while Aai and Baba may indulge or ignore them as old-fashioned, Rohit can't conceal his irritation. 'Now you have,' he says, and walks away. Would Kedar have gone further? The next time, Rohit will too.

Naren and Manasi aren't formally engaged yet, but talking over their plates, they look like a much-married couple. Ironically, Naren, like Asha Atya, thinks of Kedar's death as impotent martyrdom. Gyaan would think the opposite, that Kedar's death was not punishment for his ways but proof that he was brave and on the right side. Cyrus believes that Kedar wasn't fully aware of the consequences, of the fragility of life and the finality of death, but that is what it is to be young. Were they in touch, Omkar would note that Kedar was lost to the age-old corruption that the Hindu nationalists are trying to fight. Ifra would suggest it might well be the nationalists who killed him, given the rise in intellectuals branded as anti-national and shot. Manasi only sighs like this is the world, the status quo that Amanda would never accept. For himself, Rohit has been blank. Kedar did not involve him in his furtive world, and until this afternoon, his death, like his life, felt abstract. A few vernacular papers carried news of a 'journalist found dead'. He did not even make a headline in the English dailies. Amanda fared better. 'American tourist assaulted', the *Mumbai Now* read the day after the immersions, but for the most part, the papers were dominated by images of the vast public idols going out to the sea. Some carried a second story about communal flare-ups near Lalbaug and Nagpada, and that several cases of arson and unlawful assembly had been registered. Those arrested claimed to be locals with no political affiliation. Activists on social media insisted this was a lie and there were paid mobs and instigators. But how much worse if the rioters were just ordinary people? Thirty men and an American tourist were reported 'injured'. The tourist, a white woman, was assaulted in 'an isolated event'. The police chief who saved the city from mass riots has since been transferred to a role with more pomp and less power.

And for these drops of poison, where was the amrit of that grand churning? The historic election has thrown up neither a golden economic age nor a genocide, only another cycle of Little Events, but here in Prabhat House, one more loss becomes concrete: a son, a brother, a nephew, a cousin, a boy with buck teeth pointing a finger-gun over a Singer sewing machine, his head full of stars. Rohit sees Aai gesturing at him to have lunch. They will be leaving soon. He isn't hungry, so he exits the garden, leans against the stone compound wall, and lights a match with shaking hands. Manasi comes around the gate. 'Rohit?' He shudders. 'It's not your fault,' she says. He drops the match. 'Then why do I feel guilty?' She takes a cheap lighter from her tote and holds up a flame. He sucks the nicotine in deep. As the smoke steadies his blood, he feels grateful for her. It is unlike him to have a female friend this long and not get curious, but maybe he intuited all along that she would make an ideal sister. He offers her a drag. She makes big eyes that say, Not here. When they go back inside, Ravi Kaka hugs Baba and cries, but Chitra Kaki refuses to come out of her bedroom. Driving back to Bandra, everyone is silent.

That night, unseasonal thunderstorms rattle the windows, and the lightning flashes white on Rohit's eyelids. His head jerks up from his pillow. He imagines the impulse in the man who thought, She's strong, hit her hard; the impact of the weapon, blunt and clean, since there was no blood; the assaulters turning on themselves and taking flight as the mandal volunteers rushed in to help her. By then, her brain was shifting against her skull, the connecting fibres sheared. Timely medical care could have arrested the swelling, but the city was in chaos, the ambulances diverted. People on the beach had started running. The mandal volunteers promised to send help, then disappeared. He remembers cursing his phone for the network to revive, then crouching over Amanda, *Please, you have to walk*, his arm around her waist as they struggled to stand. At the edge of the beach, she was still conscious. The hospital was five hundred metres away, but he could not carry her, his twin in height and weight, over the footbridge, and the taxis sped past his raised hand: *There's tension on that side of the metro line, bhai.* He recalls his terror at every minute lost as they hobbled to a police car by the celebrity pavilion, her weight collapsing against his.

The crack again. Pain imploding. He has imagined it to the point he wants to smash his skull against the wall. How he wishes Amanda's father had balled his hand into a fist and socked him, but he only stood to his full height, his face under the hospital lights like the cadaver of a once handsome man saying, 'William, Mandy's father,' and he extended his hand in a gesture of devastating decency. Hours later, Amanda came to a confused waking, her frozen face contorted at the sight of Rohit, breaking like a rock under immense pressure, and as she pressed against her father's neck, her pupils widened from panic as if Rohit were a beast rising out of the grass. Who knows what her father knew or did not about them, but he was not wrong in requesting Rohit to keep away. Any help he needed from there on, he took from Amanda's fellowship director, and after the Harris Martins returned to the States, their silence was complete, as if, like Ravi Kaka and Chitra Kaki in the year of Kedar's death, they thought it best to stay away from the Bandra Agashes.

The next morning, Rohit wakes up nauseated. His mind has made a habit of expressing despair by ruminating about Amanda even if the trigger is unrelated, the trigger this time being Kedar's shraadh. But how unrelated were these losses … or any from that time? Indeed, Kedar did not disappear on the same night. He called home eventually, and Chitra Kaki had it out with him. For a while, he sent her daily texts on his whereabouts, before lapsing into his evasive ways. A month later, he was dead. Omkar did not leave Rohit's life on that night either. He showed up at the hospital the next day with Vikram, who offered help from neurosurgeons among the BSL's alumni. Ifra moved to Dubai over the winter, and Gyaan, heartbroken and broke, eventually returned to Delhi. And while each of these fates including Kedar's feels comprehensible, what happened to Amanda was like a door slamming in the dead of night, jolting Rohit awake from a frenzied dream. No one saw it coming, yet he can't accept that it was a freak occurrence, and whenever he recalls these events, they play out on that single night that exemplified the mood of the hour and held at its fulcrum all their tragedies.

Driving to Black Box Studio, Rohit notices a roadside poster – so faded and ripped you can barely tell the faces – for the last state election. The Bharat Party won that election, and while they could not form a majority without the help of their old ally, the Marathi Bana, their position as the dominant partner in the alliance, and by extension, in Maharashtra, is no longer in debate. The reconciliation with the Bana was brought about by the Bhim Republic Party chief, who received a ministerial berth. Advocate Kadam, whom Rohit met in Bandra and who was tipped to become the chief minister, became the new minister of urban affairs. The top post went to a Brahmin from Nagpur who, like Kadam, had held Vikram's post at the BSL in his twenties. The last time Rohit saw Vikram was at the annual BSL conference he attended as his guest. Two thousand young men and women from across the country had gathered under canvas tents on a public ground for a weekend of ideating and networking. Vikram introduced Rohit to Bharat Party politicians, the BSL's top brass, and other eminent alumni from all walks of life. And as these dignitaries took the stage, the tents resounded with slogans on the country's greatness and impassioned speeches on education, history and culture. Then, after dinner, all the high-ranking people, Vikram included, left for their homes and guest houses. Angry at being sidelined, Omkar had disappeared into the crowd. He must have assumed Rohit would leave with Vikram, but Rohit stuck around in the quad between the tents, and the crowd grew larger as student leaders took the stage. Dialogue gave way to rhetoric. The voices on the mics went from harsh to hoarse. Brijesh went up, then Sarita, and finally Omkar. The crowd roared with every call to show the infidels their place, to smoke the termites out, to defend Mother India, and at every chant of all that is sacred to Aryan blood, countless fists were raised into the night in a thunderous, synchronized salute, over eyes as hard and bright as diamonds.

Soon after, Rohit told Omkar they could no longer collaborate. There was only a week to go on post-production for *Bappa*, but Omkar did not protest. 'I was thinking the same,' he said, and hoisted his backpack. He wasn't bluffing. He had already deleted all the footage of *Bappa* at the Box. Whether or not he kept a copy, the film was never made. Rohit wonders at his own surprise. He held such confidence in their dynamic that he ignored the fault lines until there was so much pressure on them, the friendship came apart. Only afterwards did he have that dream in which they are in a hospital corridor and he is shouting, 'You knew what would happen and you deliberately left us in the madness … you knew, you knew,' and Omkar says, 'Bas, Rohit.' His hands are coiled in low fists, his kada glinting, and Rohit says, 'Khairya, I'm sorry,' and he holds Omkar's wrists down and presses his head to his friend's shoulder. Sometimes, Rohit still googles him. For all his contradictions, the Brotherhood has retained him. His public posts are of the videos he is making for Advocate Kadam's media cell. He has quit Jinx Studios and divides his time between Wai and Lalbaug, where he stays with

Uttam, now his brother-in-law. Although Omkar unfriended Rohit online, Vikram continues to like his posts as if to suggest the door is open. It has been months since Rohit responded. Strange that he ever imagined he might be fit for politics. He is neither as radical as Kedar, nor a career politician like Vikram. He was merely high on the country's euphoria and his proximity to power, and he read significance into everything from Kadam's nod to the volunteers' treating him like a leader. More likely, they were only responding to his privilege or the kind of voter they wanted to extend their base in, and no other potential or talent, or then, it was simply the Brotherhood's way to have a plan for everyone, and if you were on their right side, it was easy to believe that, with a little focus and dedication, who knows to what great mandate you might be called?

Rohit reaches the studio to find Gyaan on the steps. 'You could have texted,' he says, surprised but smiling, and Gyaan replies, 'Since when did we get so formal?' He has returned from Delhi. They have been receiving each other's news from Cyrus, still it feels good to have Gyaan back in his chair. Ifra is doing well, he reports. She worked in Dubai until the World Bank promoted her to a position in London. She is living with her brother there, and she and Gyaan still talk, but it's clear there is no getting back together. She is dating again. Gyaan admits he took their break-up harder. A psychiatrist put him on antidepressants; he gained ten kilos and developed high cholesterol. Finally on the other side, he is eating lightly and working out, and has completed a script for a bilingual TV miniseries set in Mumbai. In describing the plot, which is centred on an interfaith gay couple, Gyaan uses no jargon or arcane references. His words are simple and true. In his turn to listen, his eyes show genuine empathy not just for Amanda but for Rohit too. When Rohit says, 'I was high on the crowd and it felt good not to give a fuck. I didn't think...' Gyaan says, 'No one can be safe or alert enough in a moment like that. You can't go on hating yourself.' He confesses how, for a long time, he believed it was his fault that Ifra left the country and not because she might have anyway. Every mention of Ifra increases Rohit's nausea. Cyrus was the first to return, now Gyaan, but Iffy never replied to his apology and still has him blocked online. Gyaan offers advice on insomnia, exercise and self-compassion.

'Self-compassion?' Rohit says so bitterly that Gyaan leans in.

'You didn't *do* anything,' he says. 'You were just sympathetic, ambitious … young. When you saw what you had to see, you pulled back.'

Rohit looks at his hands. 'On whose time? At whose cost?'

And for the first time in their friendship, Gyaan has no reply.

In the weeks after, Rohit considers it an achievement when he gets so busy he forgets Amanda, yet to acknowledge this is to think of her again, and to admit that she was there all along, the pressure against which he compelled himself to work with more zest than the task required. Of course there are rare unadulterated moments, like when the Box receives funding for its first production (Gyaan's miniseries starring Cyrus in a lead role), but just when Rohit is at the height of the experience, he becomes aware of his respite and darkness heaves over his soul, a routine so incessant that to concentrate too fully on anything has become exhausting, and he has to pause between tasks for the relief of lapsing into rumination. As for those demanding spells when a deadline swallows his day to the point he blacks out from fatigue as soon as his ear touches the pillow, there she is in a dream all the more vivid, and unlike in his waking, he has no defence as she advances, not merely the flash of her face as they kissed, but her entire person – her wrists, the pitch of her laughter, even things he has no word for, like the style of her sandals or how her hair swirled into a knot fixed with a single pin – and defeated by the precision with which she persists in some recess of his mind, he wakes up worse than on those nights when he has not slept at all.

What did he want from Amanda? Whatever it was, he thinks (still in bed on one such morning), he had wanted it on a leash, that leash being Andrei, the length of her visa, their gap in age. The moment she was free, he cowered. He was so intent on her submission that he never thought what he would do once he had it, and it threw him off balance. Where he first dodged her like you would a tornado, he then dodged her like you would an abyss. That instant on the red idol's truck when he shook off her hand – what was he so afraid of? Of losing himself; of being hollowed out like his brilliant brother by the West. Would it have been less threatening if he wasn't afraid that she would treat him like she had Andrei? Or is this only a way to convince himself of his innocence: that she was the one rejecting him and not the other way around, that he was selfish and holding out for a wider range of experiences than she offered? Naren once said you meet only a few people in your life with whom you feel that level of intensity. Of course it was never love, if love is what Naren and Manasi share, where you can see your whole lives together, your children, and your photographs side by side after death – but what other name do you give the desire to consume a woman like that, to digest her into your blood, and to secure the worlds she has opened up in you to the point of such agitation that you can barely speak even as you lie naked in her arms?

There were times when (let him admit this too) her missteps and illness brought him pleasure. What inside him was pleased, what felt flattered by his relative vitality? An ego whose subterranea he cannot guess at, but that Naren's return awakened, that amplified around the BSL boys, and reached its peak amidst the crowds on visarjan night. Would things have been different if he'd had the courage to say to her or even to himself: *I am insecure about my worth. Teach me how to be full. Teach me how to dissolve into something great without vanity or malice.* But was Amanda really full or was that just his fantasy? He has looked her up online compulsively to little avail. He has written emails and a letter to Jaffrey to which her father never replied. He is behaving like a man in love – but whom or what is he in love with? At the outset, there was the image he projected on her; by the end, he always saw himself through her eyes, even in bed, and not her. And yet, Amanda's mythology keeps growing. She seems near perfect, neither Andrei nor him deserving. He has lost all perspective on his worth and hers; whatever they shared has been irredeemably distorted by how it ended, but whether the loss he feels is for her or a fantasy of her, what torments him now is that, for no reason other than that she was human, he might have been more compassionate. *A man is dead because of you.* How he regrets that charge. When she apologized for slapping him, he said he was sorry too, though he might have come across as merely polite since he did not say for what, and how little it would have taken to assure her even once in all those weeks she suffered Bhagwat's fate: *You meant well. I understand.*

Over and over he rephrases these lines that he will say to her even though he knows the meeting will never come. For the first time, he is in a situation that he, the enabler, cannot fix. By the end of the winter, he has put in more hours at the studio than Gyaan and at the gym than Cyrus. Sets and sets until his instructor reminds him to maintain proper form so the effort isn't shifted to muscles that can't handle the weight. But as his body gets stronger, his mind only feels like a madman crashing against the cement walls of a lockup. Aai often looks his way tenderly, as if she loves him but fears that his time and experience is of a different variety and full of new emotions that she cannot comprehend. Baba's silence suggests he would rather not interfere with what he sees as a rite of passage, the cultivation of an adult capacity to go on despite regret. But as the months pass, the wound opens out instead of closing up. Rohit stops going to the gym because the mirrors feel oppressive. His friends' enthusiasm for their TV miniseries exhausts him. He takes hours to fall asleep and hours to get out of bed, and he worries that those five months, so swift and impelled by such reckless insecurity and pride, will carousel in his head even as, years later, he slips into perennial sleep. He tries Gyaan's guided meditation apps, but he is too worn to muscle his mind into anything new. Even sitting still makes him nervous, regret so alien to his temper, it is like a monster taking on a life of its own, rising out of his chest and overpowering him at will, and though prayer isn't a habit of his, at times he is so relentlessly assailed that he has to stop what he is doing and say out loud to no one: *Please.*

## *Naren*

Jaipur airport is small but pristine. At the exit, a man in a white livery and a peaked cap is waiting with a placard reading AGASHE. For thirty kilometres, they drive past arid tracts of ker trees and scrub, and Naren is grateful that the chauffeur, sleepy himself, keeps silent. When The Regal comes into view, his first impression of the erstwhile Rajput palace is that the renovation is unfinished: the high walls and arches have been plastered in unpainted, grey cement; the gardens, which must have housed a wide variety of plants, have been replaced by manicured lawns and young frangipani trees; and along the gravel driveway, where torches once burned, electric lamps shaped like flames ascend. A few metres ahead, Gerald Scott, the new American CEO, and his wife are about to clear the entrance when, from a perch above the gateway, men in turbans blow the buffalo horns that once announced the arrival of kings. The doormen and the trumpeters stifle a laugh, and Indrani Dey, who has just stepped out of her sedan, smiles at Naren. Only Gerald and his wife, whose happy confusion at this royal welcome lacks irony, wave like shy celebrities as a cough of marigold petals flutters down on their heads. At the entrance to the hotel, Dey introduces Naren, and of course Gerald knows him, the year's top performer!

From within, The Regal's opulence is bolder. The lobby boasts an enormous silk divan on which a musician is striking a sitar. The reception hall is a cornucopia of exotic flowers, and mirrors multiply the endless satin couches and marble tabletops. Relieved of his luggage, Naren follows the bellboy on a circuitous route to the elevators along which he is informed about the antique and jewellery stores, and the library fitted with a bar because The Regal is a Canadian brand and Canadians, who finish work by five p.m., spend their evenings sipping Scotch and reading books bound in leather. And Canadian it may be, he thinks, looking at the buffalo head protruding from the wall, but The Regal's décor lacks cohesion. Except for the granite pillars, everything else, like the wallpaper and bouquets, seems held by glue and tack, ready to be dismantled should the fashions change. In the elevator, Naren flips open the hotel's brochure and finds a term for The Regal's cocktail of Rajput and Mughal royalty and some generic notion of Western aristocracy: Indo-Saracenic. Soon, he imagines, there will be a new name encompassing the modern touches for its corporate clientele. His suite overlooks sandy desert hills, and in the foreground, the marble vaults of a temple that is now a spa with a jewel-blue pool, its fountains faintly audible. And taking in the rich stillness of the palace (even if it is a hotel now with a name as bourgeois as The Regal), Naren recalls a notion he picked up from Ankush Jain of Magnus Inc.: that questions of authenticity have always been pointless for self-made kings.

Shortly after, the twenty senior, junior and associate partners who have made it to the Winners Circle gather with their spouses in the Mirror Hall. The human resource team starts on a presentation titled *What We Do and Why,* ostensibly for the information of the spouses, but also for any Winners having doubts whether the lamb cooked in clay all night or the sparkling sangrias are worth their labour. They are still to digest lunch when teatime is announced. On long tables along an inner courtyard, cakes and spiced cookies have been laid on decorated trays amid fruit sculpted in the shape of wild birds. Naren has barely finished his coffee when a lousy but enthusiastic compère summons the party to the lawns. From their expressions, everyone would rather enjoy their suites than pick team names and leaders, yet they go along, and soon they are running about refreshed, their competitive natures stoked as they dash for the finish line or close a human chain, shout hurrahs and team slogans, and enjoy the back slaps and chest thumps of the winners and the well-played-well-played of the losers. Naren isn't on the winning team, but in the group photograph he looks sweat-free and relaxed. Returning to the elevators, Gerald, whom he let win but not without a fight, gives him a toothy grin. Finally, at sunset, the group returns downstairs, all pomaded and dressed in smart casuals. The Maharaja Durbar is draped in velvet, its circular tables decked in satin and its chairs with rose-gold ribbons tied in large bows. The waiters go about serving an unknown brand of champagne in flute glasses. And the Winners Circle Award ceremony begins.

On a platform stage, a 'live artist' unveils a whiteboard and inaugurates the evening by sketching a 'live painting' of a bunch of grey suits waving a Landsworth banner (everyone cheers) and a splotchy portrait of the American CEO (everyone laughs). The senior partners give short speeches about Landsworth India's achievements, followed by Gerald, who pauses on his way to the podium to look at his portrait incredulously (everyone laughs again). Gerald congratulates the crowd on increasing the parent company's revenue and market share, though his talk concludes on a note of caution. 'India is still one of the fastest-growing economies globally, but we can't expect a sprint,' he says. 'The new government's promises got concretized in the budget last year. For all the big business talk, the prime minister is veering towards socialism and spending heavily on defence. And while we all expected a market correction, the extent has come as a surprise. The coming financial year will no doubt be harder, a year where real performance will count more than optimism … but I have no doubt the tigers in this room will deliver!' Everyone claps. Naren hoots. The market nosedive last year hit Magnus hard. This winter, he handheld Ankush Jain in shutting down two factories, but Naren's other babies, a logistics company and, unexpectedly, a dairy, have defied trends to become market darlings for strained investors and manna for college graduates, and his pitch for Brahma Industries' foray into telecom is coming along splendidly. Then Gerald felicitates each of the year's top performers with a ceremonial plaque and a handshake. The clapping is emphatic as Naren ascends the stairs to praise for his 'passion for growth' and 'appetite for risk'. The plaque is too glossy, yet it pleases him to run a finger over his name engraved below the words *Winners Circle*.

After a Mughlai dinner with Italian salads and French desserts, a partition within the Maharaja Durbar is removed to reveal a dance floor. Disco lights speckle the hall and the compère announces a 'Rewind to the Seventies' party. Everyone is too heavy with food to dance, but the booze and karaoke loosen them up, and soon the winners are posing in cardboard cut-outs of hippies and Rastafaris, the men thrusting their shoulders and hips at other men, and the women their breasts at other women, except when they all form a circle and dance something sexless like a kick-chain. Watching them from the bar, Naren is about to tell senior partner Pavan Bisht about a new hedge fund, when Bisht asks, 'Agashe, are you married?' Surprised, Naren says no. Bisht says, 'You remind me of myself at your age, so listen carefully, because I'm going to give you some advice. Get married. Get a membership in at least one club. Make a list of people you would like to better your acquaintance with. Get your wife to meet their wives, your kids to meet their kids. Where do you live? Worli? Good. Even as a young man, I never lived north of Juhu. At thirty, I began calling four promising people home every week. My apartment is now big enough to entertain fifty at a time. That is how you build a network.' Bisht looks meaningfully at Naren when Esha elbows her way into the conversation. And as the subject turns general, Naren savours the pleasure of floating above the chatter. If he is bold tonight, charming senior partners or flirting with Esha, it is on account of not just his success but also Manasi who, should he make a fool of himself here, would judge his company.

Naren heads out to the lawns to phone her. 'I know it's all a bit silly,' he says about Gerald's praise and the plaque. Manasi says, 'It isn't silly, Narry. They are telling you they value you. They have to show you that you are among the employees they intend to promote, and this is the ritual.' He tells her about Pavan Bisht – 'He knows everyone, he is on a hi-hello basis with the finance minister' – and Bisht's advice about networking. Like it is the most natural thing, Manasi says, 'You can't entertain anyone in your apartment yet. The sofas and curtains are good, but we need some art to bring it all together. And a longer dining table if you're thinking dinners. Oh, and a bar. You can't serve Scotch off a kitchen counter.'

Naren smiles. 'You can't,' he says, thinking of what diamonds cost and the best place to propose – certainly not here, over the phone. He asks about her day.

'The usual,' she says, but her tone shifts, and he can sense that her enthusiasm for his talk has been a patient waiting out. 'They've closed the investigation on Amanda's case. Lack of evidence. It was a CCTV blind spot. No one will bear witness.'

Naren isn't sure what Manasi expected. 'Sweetheart, it is sad but not surprising. A women's protection group caught over thirty molesters on tape during the parades this year. There was so much violence in the streets that night. These festivals are polarized, there's always the risk of a riot. Still hundreds of journalists and film-makers go every year, and it was a fucked-up coincidence it happened when Rohit and Amanda…'

'A coincidence? It was a year of two elections. One brought you home. Isn't that where it all started?'

'It started long before us, Manasi. It will go on long after us.'

Manasi exhales sharply. 'That's right. Brahma creates, Vishnu preserves, Shiva destroys. The problem is out in the streets, the slums, the villages, it has nothing to do with us. They keep calling it an assault, Narry. Not rape. Like it had nothing to do with being a woman … They didn't just *assault* her. Think of what it means, the loss of a mind, all that potential. I thought she knew what she was doing. She had spent months in Deonar. Or that was my excuse. I didn't want to upset things between her and Rohit. I told her I could relate to Omkar. Then she made me guilty about my choices, so I shut her out. Your parents liked me and we were happy. A city is going nuts and we shut the windows and lie in bed discussing a new car. Remember, I asked you what if everyone makes choices like us? You said they don't. Well, they do, they do…'

Hunched on a cold stone bench, Naren's head is starting to hurt. The music from the party is coming over the lawns and the playlist has moved to Bollywood songs. Rohit and Amanda should have known better – the beach had women-safe areas – but Rohit refuses to accept that the consequences were in excess of anything either of them deserved, and Manasi is starting to internalize his guilt. She believes they are all culpable, that their motives and actions, inconsequential in themselves, but magnified and intersected by those of others, created an atmosphere in which what happened, happened. He listens as she telescopes into her little cosmos of regret. Man would rather suffer further believing he has some hand in his suffering than accept that he has no control. He resists his impulse to close the call and return to the party. He asks if there is anything else on her mind. There is. She has spent the evening with Rohit. 'He's really gone down since Kedar's shraadh. Things are going so well at the Box but I can't remember the last time I saw him smile. When I asked, he said he couldn't see the point in anything. I'm worried. Have you ever felt that depressed?'

Naren makes a note to himself to speak with Rohit. He recalls that winter night in Waverly when he walked out in his slippers. Slowly, he says, 'There was a time in my life when … I didn't think I could go on. The thing is, for years I couldn't imagine any future other than Wall Street or being any person other than the one I left in New York. And I could have gone back. The market was recovering. I'd got my green card, and paid off my student loans at a time when people had lost their homes and life savings. But sometimes it isn't the material repercussions of an event that throw you, it is the values the event upsets. Once my faith in the American dream broke down, even if I achieved something, it felt pointless. Then I saw all the talk around the election, everything about India leading this century, and I finally thought, okay, here's an alternative.'

'And that healed you?' Manasi asks.

Naren pauses. 'When I caught the flight to India, I was acting on instinct. I thought it might help to be rooted in my culture, or closer to family, or that working for my country would take the focus off myself. I thought, when there is no goal to occupy us, our hands go to our throats. But I didn't need just any goal. I needed new values, because values give the goal weight. Not like I ever believed I was on Wall Street for anything other than to maximize my utility, but after the financial crisis and the Occupy protests, that ideal lost its gloss. Personally too, I believed in meritocracy. I believed in the land of the free, and my experience at KMC upset that. I didn't think that my class and caste in India were the reason I never doubted such ideals. We didn't have much money growing up, but if you ask me the difference between an oppressed and a privileged mind, it is that the privileged mind has no doubt that if he plays his cards right, he will be the protagonist. Anyhow. Now I have new values, and in them, I accept the world for what it is and that I must situate myself in a place where the system works for me … Hello?'

'I'm here. I'm listening.'

He wants to see her. The lawns are dark, so he goes up to his suite and they reconnect over a video call. She is in bed in his apartment, the lamps soft in the mirrored bedframe, her eyes low. He asks her what she is thinking. She says, 'Just, in what country would I be the protagonist?'

'You?' he begins, then catches himself. He cringes to think that there is an Eric lurking in him, an alpha whose default assumption is that everyone is the tinsel while he is the tree. Perhaps it is true that what we most despise in others is what we secretly can't stand about ourselves. Indeed, *some* ego is required; without it, one has no fire to resist the aggression of the world. But at what point does a healthy egotism slip into entitlement – the thought, not that I deserve to compete as an equal, but that I deserve to win? It is a question he might ask of himself, but not Manasi. He has no doubt it is essential that she cultivate such an ego and assert it against all Erics including the one in him.

'Actually,' Manasi says, 'I'm not sure I want to be a protagonist.'

'Why not? You should want it, you must–'

'What if I don't? Some days I don't want any of this. This job. This appraisal. This protagonist's life.'

'You want to quit your job?'

'Maybe.'

'What will you do, write poetry?'

He is being ironic, but Manasi frowns like Aai does at a knot in her needlework. A flicker crosses her face, a clarity so fleeting that to interrogate it feels like a violation. She may be eight years younger than him, yet she has that dark vector in her that will not be bent. If Catherine was the queen of hearts, Manasi is the queen of spades. And Naren is happy to recognize that, for the first time in years, he wants someone to have what they want more than anything he wants for himself. 'Whatever it is,' he says, 'I'm on your team.'

'We should sleep,' she says, her grateful smile in contrast with the slight alarm in her eyes. Naren wishes she were here in this bed. Nothing holds the walls of his heart as wide apart, as ample and leonine, as her head on his chest.

He changes into his pyjamas. The ensuite bathroom is as meditative as a cave, the glass basin and bathtub as eloquent as art, and brushing his teeth, he recalls another bathroom, that sublet in Philly … Amanda. He didn't think of her as American then, or not in the way he did when she visited Imperial Heights. Did he find her beautiful? He has always taken pride in rising above a superficiality he associates with the West, and that, if he has ever admired a woman, it wasn't only for her looks. Even so, an all-boys school followed by an engineering degree left little room to be platonic. He felt something, still feels it, and it is neither lust nor love but a strange tenderness. Amanda was the first woman he shared a home with (excluding Aai of course, though from his entire childhood he had no memory of seeing a woman's undergarments in the laundry, or hearing the hiss of urination behind a door; in short, he had no proof his mother was not a dream but a pulsing living thing). And then there was that evening when, as he was replacing his shaving blade, he noticed a neat packet in the bin, and near it, a small drop. It seemed so fragile, so unlike anything that might come from Amanda's robust body. On the cheap white tile, it was a translucent cherry red, and he wondered if even his blood was darker. When she came home, he was suddenly aware of her as full of all those intricate and mysterious mechanisms that make a woman. There was nothing to be shy about; with new confidence, he took the grocery bags from her arms, and later, walked her to the launderette. She didn't make things awkward by asking after his courtesy. She only smiled her sweet elusive smile as if it were reward enough, and he instinctively understood what was expected of him as a man sharing an apartment with a woman.

Lying face down on the bed, Naren breathes in the linen's scent. When he thinks of Amanda as a student or Kedar as a boy, and of himself at the age he knew them best, a cold blade presses on his liver. The suite's opulence induces the bodily sensation that Kedar's presence did: one of defensiveness, like a child who knows from his mother's tone that he has messed up, though he isn't entirely sure of his crime. But unlike when Kedar was alive, Naren has neither indignation nor sanctimony to keep the blade from pressing harder. The old Waverly emotions surface, images of the bridge, a cold foot in his hand, and then, smoke spreading into the lungs … *Stop*. He breathes into the heaviness, the agitation clouding a voice saying *Dada* that he can't bear to recall, that he must not recall. And as his breathing steadies, the tincture of his regret is there but contained, and he is grateful for his new mental strength. Slowly, his mind starts to flicker, and when his eyes open again, it is morning. The brass lamps and mahogany furniture appear with a direct and quiet clarity. He calls for coffee and spends an hour attending to emails before he showers, stretches into a polo shirt, buckles his khakis and a new field watch, and each of these little routines slowly restores his sense of well-being.

In the Royal Tent, the winners are treated to a lavish breakfast – eggs to order, smoked salmon with chives and sour cream, bacon and beans on toast, unless you go for the even longer Indian buffet – before safari jeeps carry them to a colonial hunting lodge for a morning of 'cultural entertainment'. An oasis after miles of desert track, the lodge has a sage green roof, a colonnaded patio with striped sofas, and three waiters to every guest. Elephant and camel rides chart slow circles on the sun-soaked lawns. Along the periphery, flowering trees shade bamboo stalls selling crafts made from brass and lacquer, while in a far corner, folk musicians twang a tune and women in mirrored skirts dance with decorative pots on their heads. The show reminds Naren of childhood outings to clubs, where his friends' parents made a big deal of the terrible service and over-boiled tea for no reason other than prestige. But the tea here is good, strong but not bitter, flatly sweet and aromatic. 'The corporates are the new maharajas,' Gerald says, watching Esha fire a rifle at the range. And his wife, who despite her turquoise kurta is in every way, as Indrani Dey put it, *such a Patty*, throws her bleached bob back and laughs. After tea, Gerald and Patty go over to the range. The ambient music changes from Hindustani to Western classical. Naren can't identify the composer, but he has an impulse, after ages, to listen to Bach, those chords whose geometry belongs to all men because they were reaped right off the cosmos. The sunlight on the patio is growing stronger, and his blood reaches towards it, pulls back in the shadow of a passing cloud, reaches out again. He smiles at the thought of Manasi saying *yes*, but unlike the happiness he knew driving into NYC on a day when all of life lay ahead, this happiness is not potential; it is gratitude. He refreshes his market app, but the network is down, so he slips his phone into his pocket, puts on his aviators, and walks out to where the lawn is greenest.

# *Amanda*

Since his mother's death and his daughter's accident, William Harris Martin has been living on the surface of things, evaluating his life as if it belonged to someone else. Here he is, manning the little 1800s schoolhouse, its flag hoisted and door open to Jaffrey's 99th Congregational Church Fair. There on the hill is the old brick church, the pews inside lined with paintings and books, and on the patio, the Sunday Bible group has organized a bake sale. Across the lawn, in the white clapboard meeting house, long rough-hewn tables have been laid with antiques, jewellery and china, all overseen by the women, and on the steps, the electronics and outdoor equipment are being handled by the men. Everything on sale is from donations brought in boxes and trash bags by locals, and the oldies of the town have spent three laborious days unpacking, sorting and pricing the goods. *Wasn't much lifting, but it was enough to put your back out.* Between the meeting house and the graveyard that hosts Willa Cather, the carriage stalls of once-prominent families – Worster, Spaulding, Gilmore, Harris – have been renovated into cupcake and tattoo shops for children, and for the ladies, stalls for furniture, gardening and handicrafts. *Millie's out selling scraps for quilts at unreasonable prices.* And here on the central turf, under a sunny blue sky, is the hotdog stand, Dan fumbling with napkins as he apologizes for the slow grilling though the hotdogs are perfect – juicy beef sausages in toasted rolls, the homemade relish thick with gherkins, the way Mandy would love it. Behind the grill, Robbie, sporting a straw hat with a black ribbon, is a one-man band playing a banjo, a bass drum and a harmonica to the boisterous shouts of camp girls, all denim shorts and tank tops, riding the antique Model T down the gravel path.

Happy sounds, William thinks, listening to the tinny tune, the woo-hoos and oh-nos at the whump of a sledgehammer, the splash when someone is dunked, the sputter of the old motor, and the clanging of the bells that marks the drop to half price at one p.m. and to fifty cents a bag an hour later – *Isn't that nice?* Isn't it. Meanwhile, two inquisitive visitors have stepped in. The young man is frowning and the woman smiles politely as she thumbs an illustrated book by Eric Sloan on just such a schoolhouse. The locals are more interested in the sales; these are summer people for whom this annual fair is an occasion to indulge their parents or children or their own nostalgia even as they cringe at how hokey the whole show is, and he, William, feels the sting of humiliation. Nana might have thought this the biggest event of the year, but he knows there is only so much to see before you exhaust all that the afternoon promised; not all of their phlegmy voices saying 'what a gorgeous day' can absolve the crude art, so much of it old junk, nor does their talk of trips abroad or the Asians and Indians their families have married into hide the fact that there is only one brown man and one maybe-Hawaiian girl on the lawns. When the couple leaves, William notices on the open page the subjects of composition for children back in the day: faith, charity, decency, honesty, patience, humility. Nana would have wanted this, his helping her friends in an initiative whose proceeds go to charity. Despite their lack of sophistication, how kind and genuine they all were, how eager to be useful and to espouse all these values, yet it is just old Republicans like them who have voted a power-hungry thug through their primary.

His wife thinks it is a failure of the liberal project; his friends, just racism. How does a single well-intentioned life or community unfold into the violence so far away from this sunny afternoon? Was his Mandy simply a victim, or was she too culpable in her fate? Claire said, 'Don't give me that be-the-bigger-person bullshit.' Of course his wife is right. Nothing can condone what those animals did to their daughter. But vast democracies, capitalism, the internet and what have you put so much distance between an action and its consequence that it is beyond the imagination of an ordinary man how evil gets amplified. You are insignificant and expanded at once. You are responsible and acted on at once. The questions are too big, the links too foggy, and in the confusion, it seems enough to do well by you and yours, and to let the rest take care of itself ... and yet, something had not taken care. When he walks out, people are hauling unsold items back into their cars. Such a surplus, he thinks, putting the Ford in gear, and imagine the place Mandy was in, where you couldn't plant a tree or a trashcan without it being hacked and stolen. On her birthday, he sent Ashray a cheque without telling Claire. Weeks later, he received an email from one Chagan Ingole asking for money to support Sheela Kamble's run for a municipal corporation seat. When he looked them up online, there was no mention of either, at least in English, beyond Chagan's name on the Ashray webpage. Besides, the tone of the letter put him off. He spent a few days after convincing himself that he did not owe them anything.

But in the time since, either from curiosity or boredom, he has taken to reading about the civic elections in Deonar. Locals talk off the record about the nexus between elected representatives, civic officials and a mafia that maintains the appalling status quo because it keeps them in power. A report mentioned women being used as a political front for male actors, and he wondered if this was the case with Sheela Kamble. Then last week, from being non-existent online, she suddenly appeared in an English article about contestants from the city's poorest wards. Sheela was a trained staffer at a public childcare centre, it read, and she had helped to push the authorities for better midday meals for the children. Though she was unavailable for comment, a female voter from Deonar said, 'Sheela Tai has been through a lot in her life. We can share our problems freely with her because she is not a man.' The journalist, a young woman herself, was confident that whether or not Sheela wins the election, she has a promising future. The piece was accompanied by an image of Sheela in a sunflower yellow sari, talking to a group of women across a metal desk. She looked curiously young yet old, her skin tight and shining but her hair greyish, and her eyes inscrutable in a way that both shamed William and inspired his respect.

It is past five when he parks the Ford under the maple. Claire comes out in a cocktail dress for an evening at the Russells'. 'Mandy's on the porch,' she says. He raises a grateful hand. Should he tell his wife that she looks beautiful, or let their silence mourn that taking turns at sitting Mandy means he can't get in the car with her? The moment passes. Their marriage has survived the loss, the losses if you count Nana in her grave, Beau put to sleep, and Andrei taking off for California. William looks out of the back door: there she is, his daughter, her face turned to the last field still under the Harris name, the field he hoped she would return to tend. He pulls a stool to the kitchen counter, and inspects his hand, the thumb yellow and pinched. Got it baling hay, the fungus, who knows how long back. He applies his antifungal iodide with careful strokes, the applicator shaped like a nail-paint brush. His old man would find it feminine, his old man who never visited the church fair because he thought it full of 'uppity-ups', by which he meant summer people and the country retirees who gathered at the town's centre after selling their old lands. Who knows if Dad harped on his ordinariness because he believed it or felt inferior to his wife's family, or if it was a ploy to keep one of his sons humble enough for haying? He recalls Dad's favourite anecdote at family gatherings – 'We were loading the barn one morning when the time came for school, and Willy said, Dad, I have to change my clothes. I said, what's wrong with the ones yer wearing? He said, there's hay on 'em. I said, what's wrong with hay on yer clothes? He said, I don't want everyone at school to think I'm a farmer. I said, well if yer bailin' hay, yer a farmer, so what if yer six years old?' – and the laughter from his siblings, mostly at Dad cracking up at his own joke, but also from pity for him, their Willy.

How plausible that he should always have been too vain for the farm and that it was his father's job to put him in his place. And yet, what was his 'vanity'? As a boy, he loved this life with a heart as open as a hay field to the summer sky. He recalls the mud ploughed dark by his brothers' steps, the rough sound of the baler's engine, the dull thud of a bale as it lands, and how he would roll them into piles for his brothers to hoist. As the youngest, he was barely noticed until he was ten and could hold two at once, and it felt good to make the family news, *one bale in each hand, would you believe it*, to be admitted into the fold of working men, and promoted from the cab to the wagon top for the ride home to his mother's cooking in a time he still called her Ma, not Nana. And right until his teens, even once his brothers had left, he felt the romance in this labour: going out for the last cutting, his chest caved against the damp until work got the blood warm enough to take off his sweater; how he'd think a dozen thoughts while at it, then run out of thoughts, and finally have nothing on his mind but the steady heft and motion of hoisting, the strength rising from his young hips to his back, the veins roped blue in his forearms, and the burn where the twine scratched his knuckles raw; and he liked it in all seasons, but especially on days like this, cloudy days when the air was heavy, the grass a dark ochre, the daises glowing; and most of all, he liked the hayloft in the old red barn: the winter's economy secure, the sensual smell of the bales, the single window, so spare and full of light against dark walls that, looking back, he has an impulse to kneel and pray.

Iodide on his fingers, the incurable fungus. By high school, he knew the experiment of farming in New England was doomed, and to renounce it was less vain than to persist, yet here he is at sixty-one, spending his days driving bales to the local stables with nothing but the radio for company. In the back door's shadow, behind the coat rack, hang his certificates. He might have been a professor at Dartmouth like his Grandpa Harris (though they had caretakers for the crop back then), he might have been a man of ideas … or action, had he retained the spirit of the young man in a headband shouting, *Hey hey LBJ*. When did he grow into this person who changed his name to accommodate the Harris, even if Harris is no Bradford? For all that the town still refers to his mother as Edie Harris, *she* never cared. Edith Martin was how she introduced herself, and she might have gone by any name or none – she was Nana, immaculate, who ran her farm. When she died, he recalls the sting as Mandy cried, 'She was so good, so good,' as if bemoaning the last great Americans, and his half-desire to say, They were just regular people. Still, there was something to his parents, a solidity he once attributed to living deep in the rhythm of this life, but having lived the same rhythm for decades, there remains a difference between them and him, and it is this: they kept the farm going not from humility or pride, but because they believed in its virtue. Does he believe in its virtue, he who was born last to ageing parents and wanted this life just when everyone needed him to? And now he has spent his life loving yet resenting his siblings for finding fortunes in Boston while pressing him to keep the farm so that their impressively impertinent children could go berry-picking in the summer or overcome their fear of swimming in lakes, and which is the basis of their wistful talk of acquiring a country home that he, their Willy, would oversee.

This is the hour Nana would have turned on the kitchen lights for supper. Oh bright image: beans baking in meat sauce as the sun slants over the brick barn where the chickens roost and the metal barn where the wagons sleep and the maple shed falling on itself among the trees still united by empty tapping tubes: oh preservation, preservation, preservation. How long will he hold on to his property? A failed experiment – and why not be the one to see it out? He will send Sheela Kamble the money. Mandy would want him to. He looks past the door to where her back is still turned to him. Even now, that part of her feels intact, the part that has looked down the other side of the hill and wants to be free. He recalls the sturdy voice in which she told him that she would fly back to India after Nana's funeral to finish her task. For the first time, she sounded less like a child straining at her tether than an adult, not Mandy, but Amanda. 'Nana'd appreciate that,' he said. He should have added, I'd appreciate it too. He knows what she was on to; what she must be released for. When she has recovered, as the doctors say she should, he will remind her.

#

*Look closely at the salt-and-pepper road and it breaks up and moves. Leaves of grass shiver, a gold beetle lifts a leg, bits of shell flash like diamonds. She picks a shell so small it reflects only the sun or the tint of her skin.*

*Bands of light, the field in planes. Smell of the salt road. Smell of light on packed dirt. A single stalk rises from the shadows, the thistle and an inch of green luminous. At the edge of the field, the bowers sway lower at her approach. Come, the spruce says. Come, the pine says. Don't go there, Mandy, you won't remember. Come. You will get lost, poor dear. Come.*

*Dip of sun and shade, like warm and cold water from a tap on her hands. The sun walks along behind a screen of pine, its branches held upward like soup spoons. From below, the needles glitter as they trap the sun in their web. But just as they close in on its light, it overwhelms them and appears whole: rainbow petals emanating from its white-hot flower head with such force that she sees only its circle shrinking and expanding.*

*A blue branch nearly trips her. Silver legs of birch askance, basal scars, blasted stumps grown into unnatural shapes, their naked whorls axed repeatedly. Terror of the human path. Startled deer tracks. Site of a tussle, of mutilations and carnage, the doggedness of the men who cleared this land, the trees their enemies, worthy nemeses, for they were men like trees.*

*She walks faster through the green light and changing densities of shade: golden shade, blue shade of the underbrush. Sinking weight of foot and peat. The path wet as a riverbed. Slush slide, a neat fudge on the outer edge. Ferned rock cool under her thighs, a light chill on her skin where the forest breeze meets blood warm from walking. Her face trapped in the brown glass of a beaver pond. Insects skate the surface. Between the rocks and rotting wood, tadpoles dart: life already.*

*The mud slips from her foot, pale as a foetus, the water swirls around it and moves on down. Light speckles the pool, but a coin of light stays suspended in the leaves. The wind moves these speckling, shifting coins of light. A frog patterned in bark and mud browns appears on a rock before it jumps back into camouflage. She stands again. Walks on. A trickle sparkles through the rocks and trees like a thought; follow it, follow it until it disappears into the dark.*

*The westerly slope gets only partial sun. Brown leaves drift through the air before vanishing against the earth. The air turns red. The forest floor is covered in bark and pine leaves more olive brown than green. Somewhere over the canopy, a cloud passes. The sun gleams on the forest, orange light, golden light, an oven without the heat. And at its centre, past the hooting of owls, the rustle of glossy leaves on trees and dry leaves falling and crisping over, she hears the clean, low note of an unknown bird.*

*The path gets steeper. The trees shorter as she rises past their tops. 'On a clear day, you can see as far as Boston.' She clutches the mementos for*

*Nana's grave in her pocket: a snakeskin, a fishhook, a wishbone. A heavy wind blusters through the passes, wind rushing like a charging train over rocks, wind a fist through the trees. She climbs the peak. Sits wedged by the granite boulders, her thin white tee flat on her breasts and slapping frantically like wings off her shoulder blades.*

*A drone roars overhead. A small silver jet is making its way towards the setting sun. She doesn't wave. Behind her, the wind picks up again, wind rising through the forest like a wave, the forest rising like a wave on the wind. The wind comes to such a roar, she almost turns but doesn't, and it rushes past, shudders and dies in the forest down ahead.*

*The low note anew. And then a second, like someone were playing a flute, a high tooo, a low hooo. In the distance, the dull thud of wood being chopped. In the distance, the hum of a motor, an anxious honk, Dad's faint shout: 'Mandyyy.' And his voice again, this time from many years ago: 'Even little waves roar when you shut your eyes.'*

*Pockets of chaos and terror in her brain. Half thoughts like lights in a prairie at dusk. Then a thought comes whole, sharp as the sun when it overwhelmed the pine: You will go back. You will remember. It will come, slowly, wholly.*

*The wind comes up again. But like the granite, and even wee things – lichen, blueberry leaves, white flowers in crags, a ladybird, its wings quivering – she holds.*

*Holds like a tree. Leaves rough on one side and smooth on the other.*

*Holds like a town, the woods closing in on its pastureland…*

*The sun flickers. Her leaves fall. Her town empties. The sun streams through.*

*Amanda. A man. Ada. Damien. Adam. Dame. Am. Da. I. Am.*

*I.*

*i.*

.

# RELEASE

?

The season, of course, was winter. The vapour in the air stung like dry ice and smelled of camphor. Slowly, Varanasi appeared through the mist, its faint ramparts and shikharas the colour of dirty bone. I had arrived in the city at dawn, and warmed by little more than a steaming cup of milk and a prickly sweater, I stood on the terrace of Sita Guesthouse surveying the Ganga. Nine months after my father died, I learned of his request to have his ashes scattered here. It seemed quaint, to say the least, from a man whose ancestors had lived for generations on the south-western coast of the country, who was born in Pune, studied in the States, raised a family and a small business in Mumbai, and for whom faith was such a private affair that when I asked at the age of seven if god existed, he told me to find out for myself. I knew from the small but cherished library in his bedroom that, as a young man, he had read several religious texts including the Bible, the Gita, the Quran and some works of Zen Buddhism, but he had also read Darwin, the Russian novelists and existentialist thinkers in vogue during his student days, and a prolific range of histories. And while I hadn't forgotten the quiet relish with which he would remind us that the idea of swaraj and the man who wrote our constitution were both born in our state, he was as quick to distance himself from Marathi people he considered 'extreme', like the Maratha sons of the soil or staunch Chitpavans, as opposed to his own privileged subcaste that he never mentioned except with some embarrassment when asked outright. A year before he died, once politics was no longer beyond the purview of dinner-table talk, he clarified his position as an 'unapologetic liberal'.

In sum, my father's yearning, as he died, for a city that he had never visited in his life went beyond what might easily be ascribed to his genetics, education or temperament. Were it to do with divinity alone, he might have requested us to dispatch his ashes exactly as my brother and I did, which was to drive an hour north of Pune and immerse them in the Indrayani river at the thirteenth-century temple town of Alandi. While Hindus believe that releasing the ashes of the dead in Varanasi leads to freedom from the cycle of rebirth, Alandi has a local reputation for achieving the same. Varanasi, however, is mentioned in the oldest epics of Hindu literature and Alandi is not. Any yearning that reached past Alandi to the fount of Hinduism itself was more than religious; it was civilizational.

Now, before the reference to civilization sets up lofty expectations, let me clarify that this is not an epilogue. In any long-steeped fiction, the premise evolves, fissions or becomes irrelevant as the story grows; new answers give rise to newer and subtler questions. This chapter, then, is simply the next movement in a long and diffused meditation. As to the relationship of the Marathi man to Varanasi, and of all people to their Varanasis by whatever name they call them, it is one of several nebulous and recurring anxieties in the work, foregrounded here for no reason other than my own reaction to my father's request. I was visiting my mother on what would have been their fortieth wedding anniversary. Touching the thin gold chain that had replaced her mangalsutra, she told me that she had barely registered his wish in the terror of his final days, and later, splintered by grief and the chaos of a Hindu funeral, it slipped her mind entirely as the family elders decided on Alandi. She then contradicted herself, saying that she had in fact remembered, but could not imagine the logistics of carting his ashes to a faraway northern city where we didn't know a soul, and did not want to burden those who were already being so helpful with a demand they would find hard to ignore. When I assured her that my father would have understood, she sighed, 'But Kashi ...' and in her discarding the city's textbook name for its ancient Hindu one, I could see that she was berating herself for more than failing his request. The ghats at Alandi, like those in Wai, are built in the image of Varanasi, and she regretted that the soul she loved most had been released at a place short of the real deal. And for all the irony implicit in that phrase, 'the real deal' – how different was I? I had spent years working on a novel set almost entirely in Maharashtra. Several of my characters spoke Marathi, but given the times, even those who did not were forced to contend with the question of why Hindu nationalism was taking hold of this vast state so far away from the Hindi-speaking heartland. And though Varanasi was hardly on my mind as I wrote, the project suddenly seemed incomplete without visiting the prototype of the ghats in Wai, and by extension, inappropriate to conclude in Jaffrey, Jaipur, Pune or even Mumbai.

By the time I finished my milk, the mist had risen. On either side of the roof, Varanasi stretched out in an arc, its sandstone walls catching the light until they shone a rich sepia gold. The Ganga was a luminous scroll on the city's lap, and in the distance, a dull cacophony of bells filled the silences between the screech of gulls and the slap of oars as the dinghies left the ghats. I recalled a line from a Ghalib poem: *In Kashi, every grain of sand glows like a sun.* I shut my eyes and opened them slowly, trying to take in the ancient capital like all those pilgrims who walk thousands of miles for darshan, which is to say, not as Varanasi but as Kashi. And how easy it would be to describe the undertow in my chest for that sombre pageant of a many-thousand-year-old heritage, unified and transcendent in the morning light, but I had never felt more detached from my writing or the goings-on in the country; to say I was in Varanasi from creative integrity was only a little less dubious than saying I was there from familial duty. I was in grief, and since my parent's untimely death, I too was yearning for something that holds beyond the pain and terror of the moment. In the weeks before my trip, I told no one besides my mother of my plans. And while I rarely give up the chance to jest or philosophize with a fellow traveller, getting in on the overnight train from Mumbai, I did not encourage conversation with the family across the aisle. Varanasi was the closest I had come to any kind of motivation in months, and it felt dangerous to analyse why; my only journal entry from that time is a single line: *I am going to the place where seekers go, even when they do not know what they are seeking.*

February in Varanasi means it is impossible to go anywhere without getting your foot caught in a kite string. I walked down the narrow alleys, kicking bits of hay and string off my shoes. With the panorama of the ghats behind me, Varanasi did not look very different from Alandi or Wai. The main market, for instance, was the typical bricolage of shutters rolled up on every utility from incense to soap to rubber pipes, cows nosing through rot, and men cycling amid the bustle with bottoms so small as to fit in a palm. On mats spread over the sidewalks, or at times, right down the centre of a street, women were selling ugly vegetables – brinjals swollen like melons, white carrots – while the men hawking idols and copper bells called out with the same word they use in Mumbai for the promise of a special rate on the day's first deal: Boni, boni, boni. There were also the ever-present flags and posters of a state assembly election. Now, as a writer, I should have asked the man selling plastic masks of the prime minister's face how business was going. I might have gone further and reached out to student leaders at the Banaras Hindu University and poets at the Kabir Chaura, or sought inspiration in the musical quarter where Hindustani classical tunes spill from every window or in the designs coming off the textile looms that have struggled since Partition, or sat under the fairy lights at Dashashwamedh Ghat to record the famous Ganga aarti at dusk. At the very least, I could have made notes of everything I passed until a pattern emerged. But the thought of chasing patterns exhausted me. A fiction laboured on long enough is shaped by life more than intention, and life is not tidy. The novel, much like the night at its climax, was merely the eye of a needle through which many threads had come rushing, only to run on, opening ever outwards.

Besides, I had a two full weeks ahead of me. On that first morning it was enough to visit the Shiva temple where my mother, whose asthma kept her from coming along, had asked me to pray for my father and buy a red thread for her wrist. And as I walked, I was interrupted by a distinct, feminine pitch: 'Donation, Madam?' I turned to see a young man in an apricot sweater pointing at a shrine carved into a tree, its canopy bare and bark painted frost blue. The man had kohl-lined eyes and didn't look like a priest or a beggar. 'Okay, don't give,' he said coquettishly in Hindi. 'Where were you going anyway?' When I asked about the temple, he offered to walk me there. The map on my phone had proved useless, and I could tell from a long-honed instinct that this stranger was safe. I followed him into a maze of alleys, one of which was flanked by an increasing number of log piles. There were many deaths in my novel – Bhagwat, Nana, Kedar – and yet, being a woman, I had never seen what happens to the body after it is swaddled in white cloth and carted away. My father's last rites had been performed by his only son. Sensing my curiosity, the man offered to show me the burning ghats. Clearly, I had been summed up as a tourist instead of a seeker, but I didn't mind. 'In the winter,' my guide started on what was probably his usual script, 'the body shrinks and takes three hours to burn. The ash and bits of bone are given to the family to be immersed in the Ganga, but first the Doms search the remains for the gold and silver jewellery the body was burned with...'

By now, the alley was barely two feet wide, and the log piles were the height of the homes. A figure with a towel wrapped around the face looked at us from a hole in a broken wall, then looked away. An impossible number of crows were cawing. The air was so charred we might have been walking through a giant pyre. Stepping over a half-burnt stump, my guide continued in a hush, 'This is a Dom gully. People believe they were cursed by Shiva when one from their community stole an earring of the goddess Parvati. To atone, they accepted the job of...' but I'd had enough of his spiel. The riverine sounds of washing and bathing were audible again, and I told him I would find my way. 'Best not to go alone,' he said. I asked if there was any danger. 'Not of that kind, not to someone like you anyway,' he said, using the respectful 'aap'. My face flushed at my privilege. 'I just meant,' he went on, 'at times, the aurat jaati can't bear to see such things.' I assured him I wouldn't faint. He looked offended. He refused my money but offered me a card and told me to call him when I really needed his services. He said he was born in Banaras and could arrange for anything, his intimacy with the city evident in his use of its popular name. I watched his apricot sweater disappear down the tunnel of logs, a hint of wounded bravado in his gait. Then the brick walls fell away and the ghats opened up, and between me and the Ganga stood the pyres.

Noon at Manikarnika Ghat. Twelve columns of smoke met in the draft coming over the river. I pulled my scarf over my nose, the ash blowing thick in my face. Everything was grey – the river, the earth, the sky – except for the marigolds in the slush. A group of mourners walked past with a corpse on a pallet. *Ram naam satya hai*. One negotiated a rate with an undertaker, who removed the shroud to inspect a mangled face. As I walked down the steps, the deliberate laughter of a club or yoga class came over the river. At the base, feet sticking out of a pyre blistered yellow. On another, the flames were dying, the body almost ash. A young man sobbed as the mourners held his shaking hands in breaking his parent's skull with a pole. At an unattended pyre, an undertaker prodded the ash with sticks until a skull surfaced, the top golden yellow and the rest charred black. He picked it out of the logs with a stick – it still had a neck and shoulder bones, like a hanger divested of its coat – and flung it into a metal pan. I tried not to think of my father. Beside me was a small bundled body splattered with mud: a head, and under the limp, white sheet, twin knobs of tiny knees. A man carting a log stared at me. There were no other women on the ghat. 'Is this a child?' I asked him, talking to calm myself. The man smirked. There was ash on his teeth. 'This is an old woman, could be a hundred years old,' he said. 'Children aren't cremated here because a child's soul is yet to see the world. We don't burn pregnant women either, nor holy men because they have already achieved moksha, nor lepers because they are not worthy of it. Their corpses are tied in a sack with a stone and dropped in the river.'

As he turned away, a whiff of the poison he numbed himself with came through my scarf. I became aware of my breathing, and now I caught a second smell, that of the foulest gutters, rising up from that little corpse. And once I caught it I could smell it everywhere, the stench of offal rising from the whole carrion earth. I hurried back up the stairs to the grey temples above, their ashen walls and empty windows like a trinity of skulls. My lashes were singed, my nose clogged with ash, and I could not tell if it was the heat of the pyres on my skin or if I was running a fever. I stumbled into a thin alley with walls the colour of parchment, a bitch warming her teats on a heap of burnt refuse, scattered bits of dung, and beside a latticed door, a bubbling vat of kheer. Taking the vessel off the coals, the vendor offered that I warm my hands. 'Banaras is dirty today,' he said, handing me a clay cup. 'The sweepers come at the end of the week, so it is the worst on Fridays.' A customer added, 'A little dirt in such an old city is all right,' but the vendor asked why. 'It isn't the tourists who dirty the place. This is our own garbage. Who will keep your home clean if you don't?' 'The prime minister, who else?' said another customer. 'He does the cleaning he has to,' said the first. Their Hindi accent and metaphorical way of talking politics reminded me of the young men I had interviewed to arrive at some of the BSL volunteers. In the years since I first reached out to them, many had become, as they proudly said in English, more 'radical'. Among those who breathed into Vikram Singh, one was deployed in Varanasi to strategize the prime minister's election campaign. The vendor said to me, 'It's not only for the numbers that we say whoever wins our state wins the country. This is the birthplace of Rama, the home of Krishna. Even today, if a politician from Gujarat wants to win the nation, he contests from Kashi as the son of Ganga.' The hot cream and sugar had calmed me, but I was out of words. The vendor asked if I was going to the golden temple. When I said yes, he gave me an insider's smile and pointed me down the alley. I offered to pay for the kheer, but he laughed kindly and refused my money.

Further on, the alley thrummed with barefoot men and women, souvenir shops, and guards slung with assault rifles. Plastic awnings kept the temple out of view. A tout told me to take off my shoes, then handed me a basket with marigolds, incense, milk and a spool of red thread. The cement floor was cold and the marble floor of the temple colder, and on it there were wet whorls of mud, but I didn't mind my soles getting dirty. Like Omkar in the parades, I felt no concern for my body's autonomy, my basket held aloft as the crush ground me in. Bells clanged, cymbals clashed, and there in the barred enclosure was the Shiva linga, its glossy black head poking out of the garlands, and like everyone I emptied my cup of milk on the flowers and threw my garland, though I could not see where it landed before I was jostled on. In the courtyard, the tout rushed up, and feverish, I let myself be guided into an inner chamber with an ornamental stone roof, and under it, dozens of lingas in different sizes. Sitting beside them was a priest who asked about my family, offered me some leaves and had me walk three rounds of the chamber. When I was done, he murmured in Hindi, 'Each man meets his fate in accordance with his karma. Each man carries his karma with him.' All I had to do to aid my father's salvation was to feed the Brahmins, the minimum donation a thousand rupees. The tout gave me a nervous smile. The priest's hairy fingers were pressed on a linga, other men's notes in between. He said I could pay him after the prayer, that God only wanted what I offered with my heart. Then he started on a Sanskrit verse, and as I turned and walked out, the verse morphed into an expression of surprise and then outrage.

At the exit to the compound, an urchin Shiva with a trident said he was hungry, so I gave him some notes, and more to the tout, who was not much older than the urchin, and when the tout said it was too little, I doubled it, and on retrieving my shoes, I gave some to the woman who had watched them, an amount that disappointed her but I had no cash left. I staggered out, the basket surrendered and the red thread in my pocket. That was when I finally looked back and saw the whole edifice: the stone walls carved with magnificent birds and foliage, the pyramidal spire that the tout claimed was made from a hundred kilos of pure gold. The sight induced a kind of vertigo. I made my way back to the river, which I could not look at now without thinking of all the bits of skull and spine and red rags in it, and at its watery bottom, rising up from their weights, the bloated forms of pregnant women, children, lepers and saints in varying stages of decay. The sugary high of the kheer had pulled away leaving a dull headache, and by the time I reached the guest house, my neck was hot and breath heavy. The bellboy asked if I was all right. I nodded and went straight to my room where I collapsed on the hard mattress.

In the narrow, living arteries of Banaras, there is no civilization, only the clamour, the flux and the detritus of everyday life. This in itself was no surprise. We go to holy places and ancient capitals knowing that the city will not live up to the one in our minds, that the vistas will invoke both pride and shame, the fine temple architecture will be riddled with outdated rites and superstition, the poetry resplendent until it sanctions slavery, the people genial and violent, the holy river majestically curdled with ash. Still we go, hoping that *something* in the place will transcend what we encounter. We arrive ready to look past the decrepitude that in our home cities would appal us, we walk about in a dreamlike state, a detachment easily mistaken for spiritual depth. The death of a loved one has a similar effect. The sublimity of grief, after the initial shock, invites you to accept the world for what it is, and in a city where the cremation fires never go out, the feeling only amplifies. So I was twice removed from this world, and my fever added to my estrangement. I slept with my socks and half the clothes in my suitcase on, but the pale blue walls seemed to radiate cold, and the crimson blanket, some polyester blend, did little to trap the warmth of my passing fevers.

And yet, illness was what I needed. My sinuses fattened my face in a way that was mercifully numbing. I slept the long, drugged sleep that had evaded me for months. Though I placed no orders, the staff sent up soup and hot ginger water, and in what felt like an act of supreme kindness, a small space heater that was of no use in warming the room but did a fine job when snuck inside the blanket. In its comfort, I thought of my childhood. The joy of running a fever because it meant skipping school. I thought of my father's hand, cool and smooth, resting on my burning scalp. Since I had been too distracted at the temple, I now said a prayer that took the shape of a single word: the name by which I called him. And every cell of my skin reached towards his invisible touch before my stomach turned cold and returned me to the room. The pyres had shown me what I was too afraid to imagine, but having confronted it, I recognized my attachment to my grief. The vertigo I felt outside the temple was not from disillusionment, but from the tension between the demands of everything I was looking at and a desire to retain my almost romantic state of abandon. And though at first unbearable to contemplate because it felt like a betrayal of the dead, lying in that blue room, I found a new freedom. There were times in the past when, just as Naren once took upon himself the shame of all that his ancestors had suffered, I had taken upon myself the guilt for all the suffering my ancestors had caused and of which I was a beneficiary. But with my father gone, this sentiment felt as trite and pointless as Kedar feared, if not dangerous. I recalled a line from the Arendt that Ifra gifted Gyaan: *When all are guilty, no one is.* And yet, nothing marks the end of one's quarterlife like the death of a parent, nothing announces as strongly that the world is left in your care. To give up guilt does not mean giving up responsibility. I thought of Amanda, how she never spoke of herself as Christian yet believed in the power of service as instinctively as any Hindu in that of meditating under a tree. Were these paths irreconcilable?

I did not know the answer, but I found myself thinking about my novel. Fresh out of university, I had started with a literary scheme that foregrounds shifts in perspective from one character to the next. The scheme was well established, and writers had varied motivations for its use. For me, at least initially, it was a way to explore a loosely related set of anxieties. And as my exploration transformed me, much like my characters, I grew aware of an increasingly complex and simmering milieu, as well as my potential (or was it duty?) to represent an ever-wider variety of irreconcilable yet interdependent perspectives, each a responsible part of a whole. So, the scheme became a way to not only survey but also embody an evolving political consciousness. But my characters were not mere segments of one mind. Each drew into itself so many conversations, sites, faces and texts that I often felt the tale was telling itself. And if indeed this is the case, if the voices of others come through the work unbidden, and the scheme self-selects which ones it will amplify or erase, and the headlines every morning form a composite plot that reaches a climax over which the writer has as little control as the characters – with whom does responsibility for the outcome lie? I thought of Manasi, who quit her job to write fiction after marrying Naren. Throughout the writing, it was my intention that she would be revealed as the author in the end, but as identities, ideals and choices other than mine fed into her, she walked away, as she should, determined to tell her own story. Why else was I in Varanasi as myself?

On the third morning, after a breakfast of cardamom tea and hot puris that I was now strong enough to eat without gagging, I put down my first notes towards this chapter. There was little to be gained from revising the novel further. The old castle had fallen and the new one was yet to rise, and as I scoured my imagination for the shape of its turrets, I had a sense of all the work only beginning. My grief for my father was still clear and present, but where it had been all-encompassing for months, for the first time it felt integrated into a wider conception of my journey and my times, just as my birth and our relationship was in his. A folksy tune drew me to the window. A flute seller was standing on the ghats with his peacock's fan of flutes and a checked towel around his neck. I had seen little beyond Varanasi's surface with the result that what I saw told me more about myself than the city, yet I wanted to step away for a few hours, to escape the claustrophobia of my room and the narrow lanes behind the guest house. I looked over the Ganga, not a ripple on its surface for all that goes on in its depths, while the far bank, glinting silver where it shone pale pink minutes before, was so clear and sandy it seemed near-mythic, as did the single dinghy leaving such a small trail in that vast expanse as the boatman made his way across. I extricated the guide's card from my unwashed jeans. *Shrihari R.* I phoned the number under the name, and a woman picked up and said, 'Asghar isn't home.' I said I was calling for Shrihari. I heard muffled sounds, then an urgent, 'It's me, Shrihari.' Could it be Asghar, a young Muslim, talking of the castes and their mythology?

It was late afternoon. The first kites were going up. My guide stood at the demarcated spot in his apricot sweater. He looked tentative, but the moment I said 'Shrihari?' he ignored the question in my tone and beamed. I asked if the boatman was here. 'I am the boatman,' he said. We walked up to a cluster of wooden dinghies, and he pulled in one with a small, faded flag. When it bumped against the wharf, he climbed aboard and extended his hand, cold and a little sticky but not calloused. And drawing at the oars with no apparent effort, Shrihari gave me a tourists' history of Varanasi. The legend goes, he reported, that the city was founded five thousand years ago by Shiva. Through the glorious eras of Magadh, the Mauryas and the Guptas, Kashi grew famous for its trades and art, yet it retained its position as a centre for religion and philosophy. The last Jain tirthankara graced these steps, and the Buddha passed by en route to his first sermon, before Adi Shankara arrived to unify the orthodox Hindu schools with these new currents, only to restate that Kashi still belonged to Shiva. Then came the Musalmans,

Shrihari said with such spite that I doubted he was an Asghar after all. The city first kneeled to Qutbuddin Aibak, and Feroz Shah razed the temples that the Turk did not … but there was a Mughal emperor who cared! Akbar's reign saw new temples built to Shiva and Vishnu, and the mystics and poets continued to seek inspiration here throughout that era: from Kabir, a Muslim orphan raised by Hindus, and Ravidas, a Dalit saint whom Brahmins revered, to Guru Nanak, who visited the city on a trip seminal to Sikhism, and Ghalib, who called Banaras the Kaaba of Hindustan…

Here, Shrihari scanned my face as if to check where my sympathies lay. I wondered about his too. His loyalty seemed foremost to his city, the sweetness in that 'ras' when he took the name, and this was clarified when he started talking about the British, whom he praised for laying roads and decried for building prisons where freedom fighters were flogged and tortured. It made me curious about his take on the present regime, but before I could speak, Shrihari asked where I was from. Maharashtra! He was impressed. Shivaji, he said, sought refuge in Banaras after escaping from Aurangzeb's prison, and he swore to rebuild the city that his captor had destroyed. For centuries after, Maratha rulers and aristocrats from Nagpur, Indore, Gwalior and Pune poured money into Banaras to restore the old ghats and temples and to construct new ones. The most iconic sights in the city, from Manikarnika and Dashashwamedh Ghat to the golden temple were all shaped by them. Here now was a Peshwa palace floating past on Bajirao Ghat. I looked over the long sandstone steps, which I had taken to be as ancient as Kashi. For the rest, I had anticipated a montage of Hindu, Mughal and British traces – neither the church of St Thomas in the market, nor the white domes and minarets beside the golden temple had surprised me – but I had not known the extent to which Marathi hands had created the city. Was Wai built in the image of Banaras then, or Banaras in the image of Wai?

As Shrihari spoke, the city walls caught the slanting light, and Varanasi was subsumed in a deep saffron wash. The Ganga, teal at the hour and steady as a river of stone, offered the city no reflection save the pale flickers under its pyres. But unlike that first morning on the terrace when the vista felt outside me, I could now see an entry point: here, in the space between the city's mutable and variegated fragments, was the scope for an intervention. After all, to write is not only to meditate but also to act. And if I am creating Varanasi even as it creates me, on what image of the city should my shifting impressions coalesce? I thought of Kolatkar, who went to the temple town of Jejuri to write of its dubious priests and fallen pillars, but still he went, and clarified by his irreverence, Jejuri rises stronger and subtler. I looked to the other side of the river. The far bank was the same frail blue as the water and sky, and I strained my eyes to see it. Shrihari asked if I would like to go there. We could even fly a kite. He had one in the hold. I confessed I had never flown one. Astonished, he asked my age. Thirty-two? He was the same age, he exclaimed, as if it were enough to make us kindred. As the dinghy turned, a plastic sheet wrapped itself around one of the oars, and Shrihari reached out to dislodge it.

We fell into a companionable silence. I could not speak to Shrihari's romantic preferences, but he had something of Cyrus's flair, and I could imagine him charming men and women, a trait reminiscent of Rohit. I wondered what I would call a character based on my guide. Ideally, a name with multiple meanings that might provide me with a referent as I arrived at the person on the page. 'Cyrus', for instance, implied the sun, a worthy heir, and one who humiliates the enemy. And 'Rohit' meant red, both blood and saffron, and the first light of dawn. But is that who they were? To say no would be as presumptuous as to say yes. I revisited my notes from the morning: *While each character holds the potential for a truth that rivals the narrator's, each is a world impossible to fully realize in her written voice. The forest grows in ways that surprises the soil* … I looked at Shrihari over my journal, or should I say 'I look'? Here he sits on a boat made of many boats, the faces of many guides blending into his, and behind him is a city that flickers and shifts even as I nail the frame. And here is a river so dense with ash that when I gaze into it, I see a reflection that is less a mirror image than a glittering shadow, and I realize that I too am a composite, a mercurial dream of a 'writer' who is neither absent nor encompasses the work. In other words, to betray the narrator's vantage may be one way to take responsibility for the limits of a tale, but my presence neither reconciles nor subsumes the contradictions the characters present; if anything, they wrote me even as I wrote them, and is my writer any different? I look up and laugh. I tell the sky that I am writing the writer who is writing me now, and who I am and am not, and here into the space between us, I invite you with a tallow candle and a cheap sweatshop lighter.

It is dusk when Shrihari helps me off the boat. The sand is so clear, it reflects the changing colours of the sky. 'This was all under water once,' Shrihari says, pressing his heel on the ground as if to check that it will hold. In his hand is a kite made from old newspapers, the print collapsing across the spine. I wrap the string around my finger as he takes his place some feet away. Then he throws the kite up and gestures wildly until it starts to climb. 'Pull it this way to loop, that way to dip. How else will you cut down another kite?' he shouts, but I don't try very hard. It is enough to see the kite up there, a dot blinking in the sun as it flips back and comes straight again. I sense the hour has come to bind these pages, and yet I hesitate. To call this a novel or a book implies more closure than I wish to claim. Even 'a work' seems incorrect, though it perhaps runs nearer to what this is: an effort that another will carry forward, whether or not with any reference to this one. I call Shrihari over and hand him the string. Before us, the Ganga's lacquer briefly melts, and as the water turns reflective, Varanasi starts crumbling into the river. There isn't a single tree or house where I stand, but there are families picnicking on old saris, vendors sharing a smoke, and children laughing. And I know that I have taken these pages as far as I could, and while to hold on to them further would limit their potential, nothing is complete: I do not end here, nor does the work. We are merely released, yet again, into the world from which we were culled. There are people even on the far bank.

## *About the Author*

Devika Rege was born and raised in Pune. *Quarterlife* is her first novel.

# HarperCollins *Publishers* India

At HarperCollins India, we believe in telling the best stories and finding the widest readership for our books in every format possible. We started publishing in 1992; a great deal has changed since then, but what has remained constant is the passion with which our authors write their books, the love with which readers receive them, and the sheer joy and excitement that we as publishers feel in being a part of the publishing process.

Over the years, we've had the pleasure of publishing some of the finest writing from the subcontinent and around the world, including several award-winning titles and some of the biggest bestsellers in India's publishing history. But nothing has meant more to us than the fact that millions of people have read the books we published, and that somewhere, a book of ours might have made a difference.

As we look to the future, we go back to that one word—a word which has been a driving force for us all these years.

Read.

Harper Collins · 4th · HARPER FICTION · HARPER NON-FICTION · HARPER BUSINESS · HarperCollins *Children'sBooks*

HARPER DESIGN · Harper Sport · HARPER PERENNIAL · HARPER VANTAGE · हार्पर हिन्दी